Colin Everard is a Civil Aviation and a Civil Aviation Consultant, and a Fellow of the Royal Aeronautical Society. He worked in the field with countries of the developing world for forty years. Over a period of 20 years he lived in various African countries, working as a technical co-operation practitioner. He then moved to Canada, from where he continued his work to support developing countries (especially those in Asia) specializing in civil aviation development. He now lives in Vienna, Austria.

To

Dr. Joseph Spence
The Master of
Dulwich College.

With my best
wishes!

Vienna   Colin Everard.
2021

BY THE SAME AUTHOR

The Guardian Angel

Colin Everard

Safe Skies

Troubador Publishing
9 De Montfort Mews,
Leicester LE1 7FW, UK
Tel: (+44) 116 2555 9311
Email: books@troubador.co.uk
Web: www.troubador.co.uk

*This is not a true story; it is fiction. No character is intended to depict any
real person, living or dead; nor is any situation described factual.
Where historical facts have been mentioned or described, the inclusion
of these is intended only to enhance the plausibility of the story as a whole.*

ISBN 1 904744 55 9

Typesetting: Troubador Publishing Ltd, Leicester, UK

t² is an imprint of Troubador Publishing Ltd

Safe Skies is for all those who board an aircraft

Contents

Author's Note

The aviation industry is highly demanding in the sense that our lives literally depend on the technology employed and the judgement of those responsible for applying the technology in so many sophisticated ways. One of the main purposes of this book is to recognize all those who work in the aviation industry, in whatever capacity.

In particular, this recognition extends to those who work in the developing world. Often, in comparison with their counterparts in the developed world, the lot of these workers leaves much to be desired, whether this might involve remuneration levels, working conditions or the need to ensure that outdated equipment functions properly; in my experience these men and women selflessly and tirelessly work in the interest of maintaining aviation safety.

It is these workers, and the contribution they make to aviation safety on a day-to-day basis, who inspired me to write this story.

I would like to express heartfelt thanks to all those who showed interest in the writing of this book. Whenever I needed information to help examine some aspect of my subject, without hesitation my friends gave me guidance as to where to find data and explanatory material. I am very grateful for their assistance.

I also appreciate the time and effort which friends unstintingly gave in reading the text and offering their ideas for improvement. In particular I would like to single out, first, the efforts of Mr. Geoffrey Thompson, aeronautical engineering specialist and, second, the comments made by Dr. Christian Schickelgruber, Curator for Himalayan Cultures, Museum of Ethnology, Vienna. Without their invaluable and detailed suggestions, I would not have considered offering this book for publication.

Chapter One

Tashi of Bhutan

The Himalayan dawn cast a faint pink light over the snows of the high mountains whose noble forms rose in majestic silhouettes against a clear, lightening backdrop. Tashi, who loved his native Kingdom of Bhutan, opened his eyes. Just for a moment he had to remind himself that he was awakening in unusual surroundings. His mother and his uncle Gyeltshen had suggested that he should visit a monastery for a week's retreat. Tashi had diligently followed the instructions of the Mahayana Buddhist lamas and monks. Now he was beginning his fourth day of instruction, prayers and meditation in the mountain retreat; the monastery had been built on a ridge in 1659 and was some 12,000 feet above sea level.

In a material, temporal sense, Tashi's cell was simple and poorly furnished; but spiritually, the atmosphere of the monastery was rich. He felt relaxed and at peace with the world. He would forever be grateful to the numerous Buddhist deities and saints for this inner feeling of contentment.

In 1969 Tashi had just reached the age of thirteen. Although a good student, he was not expected to have yet learned the particular qualities of the main Buddhist deities; after all, they were many. Tashi could not know how many times he had been reincarnated, nor in what forms. What he felt, though, was that in this particular life he had reached a new level of contentment, and this bode well for his striving towards Nirvana. As he matured, he was conscious of the primary need to avoid offending the gods. Along the way, he had already received one or two warnings in the form of signs. From now on he would always be good in thought and deed; this was the only way to avoid the vengeance of the gods – as long as he was good, they would protect him. He would always remain conscious of the deep belief that if he defied Buddhist teaching, in certain circumstances his community might also be affected.

Tashi's bed was made of wood and jute, and it creaked as he left it. As he began his prayers he looked out of the square window set in the thick monastery walls. The temperature was just above freezing point, and the pink of the sky was becoming deeper. He was mesmerized by the colours of the heavens, and he realized that sunrise was imminent. Tashi was seized by a great force; he had to rush outside and run in the wonderfully bracing mountain air.

Barefoot, he ran along a narrow track, legs brushing against the ferns. He'd previously noticed that the ridge was only about a mile long, at which point the slope of the mountain plunged into the jungle below. After five minutes he stopped and sat on a rock. When he looked north eastward, his whole being was over-whelmed by the power and majesty of the dawn. A ball of fire, the sun, had just risen on the horizon. Looking ahead, the Himalayan snows reflected various hues of pink; and when Tashi turned his head to the right, the distant snows were transformed into gold. In the centre of this incredible panorama rose the huge mountain of Jomolhari. He wondered about the great god who made his home there, in a cave just below the summit at some 23,500 feet above sea level.

When he looked downwards from the ridge, he was struck by the magnificent trees which reached up towards him, towering above the thick, lush vegetation. Many of the great boughs were strewn with wispy lichen; watching it gently sway back and forth reminded Tashi of prayer flags, sending their messages on the winds across the vastness. It was this thought which reminded Tashi that it was time he returned to the monastery; the monks would be waiting for him, eager for his instruction and meditation to continue.

As he rose he noticed a dense cloud of mist billowing up behind him; now it was obscuring the surrounding jungle. Yet on the other side of the ridge, the sun was still shining brightly and he took this to be a good omen. He began to return, the sun on his left and the wall of thickening cloud on his right. As he trotted along the path, he felt his footsteps sometimes being cushioned by spongy moss. It was then that he began to realise that he was not alone; apparently keeping pace with him, something caught his

2

attention out of the corner of his eye. He was not afraid to face what seemed to be a form. After all, in those surroundings anything was possible... and he was inquisitive. He stopped, turned to his right and clearly saw the form in dark outline against the light grey cloud. Was he looking at his shadow, or was this a mystical messenger? He fell to his knees, clasping his hands above his forehead. He closed his eyes and said in firm tones, 'I am your servant. Please tell me how I may be of service?' He heard a rumbling of thunder, which seemed to echo from the valley below. He opened his eyes. The form had disappeared.

Tashi soon reached the entrance to the monastery. Ahead, he could see the lamas, clad in saffron-coloured cassocks; they were sitting along the walls and before the main altar. Their low, prayer-chanting voices, mingling with the ringing sound of prayer mills, steadily grew louder as he neared. Tashi was not anxious about the form which had briefly accompanied him; if it was a sign, he hoped it was good. After all, there had been no indication of a warning and, as far as he was concerned, he had no evil feelings against anyone. His conscience was clear.

As he entered the monastery he admired the Guardians of the Four Quarters – the Four Great Kings, beautifully sculpted in slate, would ensure protection against attack from north, east, south and west. With such protection, it was to be expected that the monastery should survive any form of assault. Apart from natural disasters such as earthquakes and mudslides caused by torrential rains, the fortress monastery had been attacked by other armies, especially during the 17th century. It was also in the 17th century that the deity *Mahakala* had appeared in the form of a raven to Shabdrung Ngawang Namgyel, instructing him to unify the country. After much strife he had done this, and since the mid 17th century, life in the *dzong*, the religious and administrative centre, had become more peaceful. The same could also be said for the predominantly Drukpa people who inhabited the surrounding valley and beyond. It was these people who had given the country its name, *Druk Yul – Land of the Thunder Dragon*.

The retreat served to purify Tashi's spirit and, all too soon, it was time for him to bid grateful farewells; he would always remember his meeting with the abbot, the *Neten*, of the *dzong*, who had commended him for his assiduous religious attitude and had prophesied that Tashi would become a great servant of the Drukpa. The abbott had also explained that the monk population of Bhutan numbered about 4,000; this congregation of lamas was spread all over the country, most being attached to *dzongs*. The lamas of the monastery were under the overall jurisdiction and administration of the head, called the *Je Khempo*, who was prominent in the social affairs of the people. The abbott said that if Tashi had been born in the last century, he would almost certainly have become a lama. In those days, it was compulsory for each family to donate one of their children (usually the first-born) to a monastery, where the child would become a monk; the practice was called *Tsuenthrel*. During the twentieth century the custom had died out.

Although he recognized that the central monastic body had no legal right to keep Tashi in the monastery, the abbott hoped Tashi would continue to develop his Buddhist knowledge, and always strive to please the Lord Buddha. The abbott's final advice to Tashi was that provided Tashi observed the basic tenets of the Buddhist faith, he could feel confident that, whatever the challenge, he would always be safely looked after.

Now Tashi had to start the three-day walk which would bring him back to Thimphu, the Kingdom's capital. Because of the varying altitudes of his journey, he was treated to a breathtaking display of many types of flowers and trees. At the highest altitudes, and especially as he approached the narrow passes, he found himself crossing moorland. But as he descended through the tree-line, he would see juniper and high Himalayan fir trees, as well as several species of orchid. Near the bottom of the valleys he marvelled at the prolific display of rhododendrons. He followed the tracks he'd used on the outward journey, at night sleeping in villages. The villagers, whose main occupation was to find good grazing for their yak herds, were friendly and hospitable.

On the third day, as Tashi approached Thimphu, he decided to take a closer look at some major road construction; he had first noticed the dust and noise, about a quarter of a mile from the track, on his outward journey. From time to time he'd heard that roads were under construction; now he could see and touch the asphalt surface. After his long walk on forest tracks, he was at once intrigued and amazed to walk briefly on the hard, stable surface.

4

He was also saddened that the earth below the road should have been completely covered with such a hard layer of tar.

Before continuing, Tashi walked a few hundred yards in the direction of the gangs of men working on the road. He wondered where the labourers had come from. Compared with himself they seemed very dark, though he had to admit that his own skin was exceptionally light, even by Bhutanese standards. Perhaps they were Nepalis from the lowland border area, or they might be Indians from Assam? In any case, they looked ragged; and the nearby, dirty-looking flimsy shelters, which he took to be sleeping quarters, reinforced his impression that these were wretched, unfortunate people who had been specially imported to do the heavy road work.

At last he approached his house. He had lived his whole life there, and he felt a strong attachment not only to his home, but also to the many activities which revolved around his family. The house was spacious, and was built on two floors. Finely carved woodwork framed the windows, constructed in three adjacent sections; some of the carving's detail had been picked out in bright colours of red, white or green. The walls were white and the whole house was covered by a roof that generously extended well beyond the walls. As he neared the entrance he briefly looked yet again, as he had done so often, at the phallic paintings on each side of the front door; they were there not only to repel evil spirits, but to symbolize fertility. If only he had a father, Tashi thought, he would surely have brothers and sisters by now.

A feeling of excited anticipation took hold of Tashi; he knew he would get a warm welcome. His still young and beautiful mother ran to him in front of the house and embraced him. Inside, his uncle was delighted to see Tashi – when someone is loved, in a close-knit family a week or so can feel like a month.

While his uncle and mother listened intently, Tashi gave an account of what he had learned. They were pleased with what they heard. It was early evening, and the sun had already disappeared over the mountain. Now the air was fresh and the temperature would drop rapidly.

Tashi's mother put more logs of wood on to the fire. She had prepared a special dish to celebrate a safe home-coming. The three of them sat near the hearth and enjoyed not only the food, but one another. Tashi seemed to be maturing as a young man ahead of his time, and uncle Gyeltshen loved his questions; Tashi's intelligence seemed to dart out of his head like sparks from a young fire.

A little later, his uncle announced that there were important matters to be discussed. Tashi should sleep, and all would be settled the following morning. On his way to bed, Tashi visited the family shrine, permanently installed upstairs, as in most Bhutanese houses. He bowed and knelt before the altar, thanking the deities for looking after him. On his walk back through the jungle, he knew that wild animals had been watching him, but he had not once been threatened. The only animal he had seen was an inquisitive, but shy, red panda; the small bear, sitting on a stout branch, had peered at him through the leaves.

He promised to practice all the good things he had learned during the retreat. Kneeling in meditation before the altar, he well knew that he was not qualified to initiate any form of ritual; however, he noticed that small cakes made of dough, *torma*, had been placed on the altar. He was sure that on that very day his uncle and mother had asked a master of rituals to request purification of the household, as well as the protection of the deities against worldly evils. There lingered a faint smell of incense. He was mystified; there must have been good reason for the ritual having been held – but what great happening could be at hand?

Tashi was tired, and once he was lying comfortably under his Yak-hair blankets he knew he would soon be asleep. As he drifted off he thought how fortunate he was to have been born into a noble family, a family which traced its lineage back to the fourteenth century. He was proud of his noble heritage; he hoped he would live up to the high expectations of his uncle and reflect creditably on the family.

Before falling asleep a thought nagged at him. It was about his father. In answer to his questions from time to time, his mother had told Tashi that his father had been killed in a car accident in the mountains on a narrow track between Thimphu and Paro. Tashi felt uneasy about this, and was puzzled that there were no signs of his father in the house. When one day he had asked his mother if she could show him a picture of his father, his mother had been dismissive. As for his uncle Gyeltshen, he had treated

Tashi like a son from his birth, and took a great interest in everything he did.

His last thought before falling into a deep slumber was that he should be grateful for the affection showered on him. He was at peace with his family and surroundings, and he felt sure that in time he could attain perfect harmony, in keeping with Buddhist teaching. Dare he begin to think that in his future lives he might reach Nirvana?

Chapter Two

Great Happenings

When Tashi woke up, the sun's rays were streaming through his bedroom window. A shaft of intensely bright light dazzled him; instinctively he closed his eyes and turned on his shoulder to avoid the glare. He still felt sleepy and wondered what had awoken him; perhaps the bright sunlight had quickened his senses, or was it that it was well past the usual time when he should be up? In any case, it was nice of his mother to let him sleep for as long as he liked so that he would feel refreshed after his three-day walk. His school holidays had just begun, so there was no pressing reason to jump out of bed.

While he was musing, he heard a commotion downstairs; people were arguing. His uncle and his mother never argued, but nevertheless the voices seemed familiar. One of them now rose to a crescendo, unmistakably the voice of his uncle. Tashi sat up. Never in his life had he heard his uncle raise his voice in anger; and he could hear that his uncle was angry. Dismayed, Tashi sprang out of bed, opened the bedroom door a little and sat on the floor. Every few seconds, he could hear that his mother, Pema, was sobbing.

'I want an answer, Pema. Why should I always give money for the boy and yourself; at least you could buy your own clothes. Why don't you answer? I think you should train for a job. Since His Majesty decided we should not rely on barter, and that money should be used, it is not so difficult to earn some cash. Have you thought about that?'

Uncle Gyeltshen's voice was not only strong; he was almost shouting. Tashi was shocked and he began to feel frightened. There was a short pause before he heard his mother reply; she was whimpering, and her voice was weak, 'I am sorry.'

Tashi had no idea what might have happened; what he did

know was that his mother was involved in a very serious situation. Then he heard his uncle's voice again. It was still strong, but the shouting had subsided; the tone of voice was more controlled and measured:

'Pema, your problem has been the same for years – you loved everyone, especially men. The men always said they loved you. This was nonsense, Pema. They didn't love you; they loved your body. And now you have an illegitimate son! And I am the one who pays. All I'm saying is that it's high time you earned some money and contributed more than love. Do you still have contact with the father – he was from Morocco wasn't he?'

There was a long silence. Then Tashi heard his mother say, 'I had contact with Tashi's father. He wrote me letters; he always said he loved me as a person. His love was not only for my body.'

Tashi was incredulous. His lips began to tremble; he felt cold and suddenly he started to shiver. His whole body was shaking. He stood up and threw himself onto his bed. The sun had risen further and its rays no longer streamed into the room; tears ran over his cheeks. He heard his mother's voice again. Pulling a blanket over his shoulders, he returned to listen at the bedroom door. His mother seemed to be speaking more calmly:

'Do you remember when some years ago His Majesty decided to investigate whether our country could start its own airline? He was advised that Bhutan would need a civil aviation law. So His Majesty arranged for a legal specialist to visit Bhutan to advise the Government. The consultant was a Moroccan. I met him at a cocktail party. He was very handsome and courteous. I was just 19, and men seemed to like me. Then I met him at another party. When he told me he felt lonely, I invited him to tea. I was living with my parents, but when he came they were visiting some friends. The two of us just fell in love. After he left the Kingdom, he wrote me letters. They were beautiful; and he always wrote that he would marry me. I loved to get his letters; I could hear him talking to me. I loved him so much! To begin with, I used to get one or two letters a year. But then he stopped writing altogether. I kept his letters in a special box. He was an important man in his firm or wherever he worked; it was to do with aviation, and helping to make aviation safe. The head office was in the United States, in Chicago. Once he wrote that he would soon arrive and we would be married. But he never came. Then he wrote that he was delayed; I began to wonder if marrying a Bhutanese woman might be bad for his image and affect his social life. About ten or eleven years ago he wrote that he wanted to leave what he was doing; I never heard from him again. I suppose he left. I have no idea where he is now.'

'Has he ever sent you money? Does he know about Tashi?' Gyeltshen asked.

'No,' Tashi's mother replied. 'After we parted, at one stage because I did not hear from him regularly, I became deeply upset. Then when I heard from him at last, he wrote that he had written previously, but he had never received an answer. I wanted to believe him and I hoped he was being truthful. I know that the mail comes through Delhi and Calcutta; then it is sent to Thimphu by truck. I am sure a lot of mail does get lost. But I was not sure whether I should really believe him, so I decided to be careful and not tell him about Tashi; after all I was still not married. I was not sure what to do. But I was worried that if he came to know about Tashi, he might find a way to take him away from me. If that had happened, there would be no reason for me to go on living this life.' There was a pause. Tashi heard his uncle say, 'So much for love, Pema!'

Tashi sat at the door transfixed, a prisoner of his emotions. He was at once shocked, disappointed and, above all, confused. He wanted to do something, but he felt almost paralysed; when he wanted to stand up he felt a resistance in his limbs. His understanding could not possibly absorb the full meaning of what he had heard. The only thing of which he was certain was that he himself was helpless. As this feeling of helplessness took hold, powerful emotions swelled up within him. He could not avoid hearing his breathing, which now seemed to have changed into a noisy, uneven panting. He still wanted to do something; but what?

Tashi wrenched himself out of the cauldron of his still-rising emotions. He pulled on a gown and went to the bedroom door. He hesitated, wondering what might become of him. Then he walked slowly down the stairs and into the main room. He stood before his mother and uncle Gyeltshen, and noticed his uncle was in national dress. The patterned tunic, with deep turned-back white cuffs, looked new; he was wearing heavy woollen stockings and ornamented pointed shoes. Across his body he wore a wide sash of red silk, denoting his high rank of nobility. Tashi wondered why his uncle should be so immaculately dressed. Calmly, he turned his head and looked at his mother's beautiful face, a face saddened by the stress of the moment. Tashi said, 'I am your illegitimate son. Please don't stop loving me.' Then he cried, just for a few minutes, the tears streaming down his face.

His mother began to sob; her legs gave way and she sank to her knees on the royal blue woollen carpet, her head bowed. Tashi's uncle exclaimed:

'I pray for the forgiveness of the gods that I have been so indiscreet! May the saints bless Pema and Tashi.'

Now all was quiet; the silence was punctuated only by the weakening sobs of Tashi's mother. To Tashi, the quietude which ensued seemed endless; whatever might become of him, he thought, he would never forget this interminable silence. He was gradually beginning to control his emotions; what struck him was that the longer the silence persisted, the stronger he felt. Tashi looked at his mother and uncle, and thought they looked pathetic in their distress. They seemed to be incapable of speech.

After what to Tashi seemed an eternity, the near-silence was broken by uncle Gyeltshen's voice, 'Come here, Tashi.'

Tashi felt the reassuring hand of his uncle gently caressing his shoulder; now he was sitting on uncle Gyeltshen's lap, his head tilted against his shoulder. He could see his mother sitting in a chair, her head in her hands; although he could not see her face, he knew that she was still distraught and her body seemed weak, almost lifeless. Tashi began to cry again. His uncle asked him to try and be calm. Uncle Gyeltshen had important things to settle. There had been one main matter which he had wanted to explain; now there would be two.

Tashi felt stronger and managed a faint smile. He loved his uncle and he knew that his uncle loved him. He snuggled into his uncle's shoulder and smiled, just for a moment. Tashi was ready. Uncle Gyeltshen smiled also, and gave Tashi a hug; then he started.

'Now Tashi, first I want to tell you that your mother and I love you dearly. Whatever happens to you in this life, we will always love you. Your mother and I had intended telling you about your father when you are older, when you reach the age of 18 or 20. Now you know six years earlier. You are a clever boy, Tashi, and you can easily understand that your birth out of wedlock was nothing to do with you. In fact, in our country this is not something that anyone worries about at all; we accept that such things are natural and they happen. Of course, in a noble family such as ours we prefer that the family maintains noble blood as much as possible. And in our relationship with the royal family we are careful not to mention that there is this indiscretion within our family.

Something else we like to avoid is that we have children who have only one parent, especially when it comes to boys. They need both their mother and father, otherwise they are missing half of their parental care. For us, the family is very important and we should try and keep all the main parts of the family together. Both the parents and children have certain duties, and these help them to lead good lives. If part of the family is missing, then our way of life is changed, and this can lead to all sorts of problems. In your case I have tried to compensate for your absent father; I do my best, and I hope I do enough, but of course, I can never truly replace him. In the Kingdom we already have too many children who are born out of wedlock, Tashi, so your case is not so unusual. In fact, as far as you are concerned, there is nothing for you to worry about.

The only time you have to be on your guard is when you leave Bhutan. In many societies of the world, especially in Christian societies, it is not good if you have been born out of wedlock. Unfortunately, they will use it as an excuse to look down on you. They use moral arguments to blame those born out of wedlock.

As you know, until a few years ago our Kingdom was isolated from the world. Our rulers decided that the only way for us to survive was to prevent foreigners entering the Kingdom. But now things are changing, and we have to accept that in future we will have much stronger contact with the rest of the world.

Now, how shall we prepare you for the future? The main thing to understand is that we are not going to tell anyone, especially foreigners, that you were born out of wedlock. That is why we say that your father was killed in a road accident. Up until today, only your mother and I knew this, but now we are three. Do you understand what I am saying? Do you agree to keep the secret, Tashi?'

If Tashi were being lectured to by someone he didn't know so well, he might have felt under pressure. But he not only regarded his uncle in a fatherly light; he loved and trusted him. At the age of 13, Tashi did not expect to understand every detail of what his uncle had explained. But he certainly grasped the main thrust, especially the reason for keeping the circumstances of his birth secret.

In a thoughtful, deliberate way, he replied: 'Uncle Gyeltshen, I have heard what you told me and understand most of what you have said. For me, the most important thing is that you and my mother love me. I have tried to be a good student, and I have always obeyed your instructions. When I am older, I want to be a faithful servant of the people. Whatever you think is the best for me in the rest of this life, I will follow your guidance. If you think I should keep the secret about my birth, then I agree. But I think it is better not to share that secret with my father, that is, if we ever meet him again. Although my mother says he loves her, he does not show his love by helping to support our family. Uncle Gyeltshen, now that you have explained everything, I don't feel so unhappy any more. It's quite nice to have a secret!'

Tashi already felt better. He jumped off his uncle's lap and approached his mother. He wiped the tears from her cheeks and smiled at her. Then he embraced her. His mother squeezed his hand and said, 'Thank you, Tashi.'

Then he went back to his uncle and said, 'Uncle Gyeltshen, you told me there were two things to be settled; what else should I know?'

Tashi's uncle looked at him with a grave expression; Tashi could see that it was something important. It was clear his uncle was not entirely comfortable with what was now to be said. Tashi became apprehensive, and looked at his uncle's face for a sign of what was to come. His uncle wanted to smile, but instead his countenance reflected sadness, with a trace of anxiety.

'I want you to listen very carefully, Tashi. I want to talk a little about our country's history. But first, Tashi, at school you have studied geography; do you know where Switzerland is?'

Tashi thought hard. It was his nature that pushed him to know as much as possible about things in this world; he always wanted to be responsive. There was an inner feeling of competitiveness which urged him to know more than others. His concentration focused on his geography lessons.

'Uncle Gyeltshen, Switzerland is situated in western Europe. It is a mountainous country and it has borders with France, Germany and Austria, as far as I know.'

'Well done, Tashi. You are quite right.' Tashi saw his uncle was becoming more relaxed; uncle Gyeltshen smiled and continued, 'The reason I asked you that is so you can make a comparison. Switzerland is a small country in Europe. Our country is also small; in fact, it is about the same size. Switzerland has many mountains, too, but ours are much higher. On the other hand, our population is much smaller; in the Kingdom we have only about 600,000 people, and in general our people die at a much earlier age than Europeans. If our hygiene improves and we have more medical care, then our population will increase over the years; one of these days it might reach a million. In any case, the main point is that the Kingdom is a small country, not highly populated.

Tashi, let me talk a little about our history because this will help you understand later. The Kingdom is really very isolated, and up to 15 or 20 years ago our government felt that this was the best way for it to survive. When the British ruled India, we sometimes used to quarrel, usually along the border. When they tried to punish us, we showed them we could fight. Yet, at the end of the 1800s we made peace with them. They promised to leave us alone, and even agreed to pay us some money every year! They did this for two reasons. First, they had pushed us out of parts of Assam and Bengal which we had taken over; because some of our noble families lost revenue as a result, the annual British payment helped as compensation. Second, the British needed our co-operation from time to time. For example, once they had some problems with Tibet, and they wanted to cross the Kingdom with their soldiers. Because the British had paid us money, we helped them.

In general, in return for our co-operation we asked them to protect us if we were attacked, and we entrusted our foreign policy to them. This all worked very well. But inside our country, we had many problems. The rulers of different areas often tried to

14

take over other parts of the country. This is one of the reasons why we have these *dzongs*; they are fortified monasteries, used not only for religious purposes, but to accommodate government administrations as well. This was where the rulers were usually based.

The fighting for power really came to an end in about 1885, and since then we have lived peacefully. Unfortunately, time and politics do not stand still. The British organized the partition of India in 1947 and prepared to leave. Our government discussed the new situation with the British and Indians, and the result was that from 1949 India took over from the British. In fact, the Indians give us even more money, and they returned a town near the border which we had lost when we fought the British. India also helps us with aid projects, and that is why we see their technical people working in the Kingdom sometimes.'

Tashi was beginning to feel perplexed. He loved to listen to his uncle, who always seemed to be able to explain things so clearly; but he wondered what this was leading to. He told himself to listen carefully, and be patient. His uncle went on.

'One of the reasons the Kingdom has been peaceful is that our country is unified under a king. About 65 years ago our nobles decided it would be better to agree on one family that would continuously rule the Kingdom, instead of the leading families in various districts fighting amongst themselves for the best position. Now we have our third king. Tashi, you are being very patient. I will soon come to the point. During the last 15 years or so, under the guidance of our king great changes have taken place. Our king realised that the Kingdom could not continue in isolation, because our neighbours have become very strong. In the north we have China. As you know, it was in 1965, just four years ago, that China took over Tibet. We were lucky that China did not also claim Bhutan! The Chinese always talk about 're-unification,' and any country with the remotest connection with China can become a target. In 1962, before the Chinese took over Tibet, they and India had been quarrelling about exactly where the border should be. The Chinese decided to teach the Indians a lesson, and they invaded the northern part of India. Just when we thought there would be a full-scale war, the Chinese withdrew their army. We were very worried in Bhutan at that time.

And then there is India, another big country. India is supposed to guide our foreign policy. It is quite amusing really that the Indian Government is always chanting 'territorial integrity, mutual respect, non-aggression, non-interference, peaceful co-existence,' and phrases like that. This is what we call political hypocrisy, Tashi. They have already taken over part of another Himalayan country, Ladakh; and since 1950 they have occupied Sikkim, which they call a 'protectorate.' Perhaps we shall be next. At the moment, we think India prefers to support our sovereignty and treat our country as a sort of wedge between India and China.

That is why all these roads are under construction. The Indians are constructing them; and they pay for them. If we are invaded by China I am sure India will send troops and supplies to our Kingdom, so that they can fight the Chinese on our soil. That is why they are building the highway from their border; it will run from Phuntsholing, the main town on our southern border, for 120 miles up to Paro and Thimphu. It is a huge project.

His Majesty is very well aware of the present situation. He consulted the nobility, and reached the conclusion that if the Kingdom participates in international affairs, there is a good chance that the Kingdom can survive as a nation. His Majesty wants to maintain strong links with India, but at the same time, he is trying to establish relations with other countries, and with the United Nations. Bhutan already receives some benefits from the Colombo Plan. And within the Kingdom, there has already been a lot of progress. When slavery was abolished in 1956, that was a big step forward!

Early this morning, Tashi, I was granted an audience with His Majesty. I even bought new, traditional clothes for the occasion. I have been on very good terms with His Majesty, even before he ascended the throne in 1952. As you know, Tashi, I am already a member of our parliament, the *shogdu*; this morning His Majesty told me that he was considering my appointment to the Royal Advisory Council, the *Lodoi Tsokde*. This would be very prestigious for our family. In any case, I wanted His Majesty's advice regarding how he saw the future for young nobles such as yourself. How can you best be prepared for the future of our country? His Majesty repeated the same word three times: 'education... education... education!'

With all this explanation, Tashi, you have to prepare yourself for what I am going to say now; are you ready?'

In one sense, Tashi was ready. In another he was not. His uncle's explanation had been clear, but at the age of 13, Tashi could not accept that his uncle had actually consulted His Majesty about his own future; surely there were more important things to discuss? He hoped his uncle would now come to the point, because the monologue was beginning to disturb him. Now it was Tashi's turn to look anxious, but he nodded.

Uncle Gyeltshen immediately came to the point. 'Tashi, in one month you will be leaving for a boarding school in England; the school is called Dulwich College. So far, you have been educated in our national language, Hindi and English; at home we always speak English, so you won't have a problem with the language. I have sent some of your school work to the college, and they are impressed. Thank goodness you are so clever, Tashi! We thought of Darjeeling, which is where I was educated. And then we thought of Lawrence College in the Murree Hills near the Swat Valley. But I have decided that the best place for you will be Dulwich. The school was established in 1619, and has a wonderful record. It has produced many excellent students who later became famous; and it is strong in sports. You will work hard there, and in the end you will be well prepared to return to the Kingdom to serve the people. Are you happy?'

Tashi was silent. How could he know whether he was happy; what should he think? He felt tears forming in his eyes. He thought of his house and the beautiful mountain scenery framing the Paro Valley. He thought of the love he received from his mother and uncle. At his new school would anyone love him? Was he happy; would he be happy? He could not know. Yet he did not wish to offend his uncle, so through the blur of tears he muttered as bravely as he could, 'I hope so'.

Fortunately for Tashi, uncle Gyeltshen was a sensitive man and he could not only see, but understand, Tashi's emotions. He said, 'This has been a very difficult day for you, Tashi. You need time to digest so many things. Why don't we have some tea and then practice our archery. If you like, we can have a match.'

Pema brought some tea, which warmed Tashi. But the atmosphere in the room seemed icy. His uncle did not talk to Pema, and for her part she was silent. After tea, uncle and nephew stood up, both ready for their archery, the Kingdom's national sport. It was only then that Tashi noticed his mother had stood up, near her chair. Her eyes were fixed on his uncle, and she looked unhappy. Tashi heard his mother speak, but her voice seemed strange – sounded distant and cold.

'Gyeltshen, you have arranged to send my Treasure to a distant land. Darjeeling might have been bearable. But now Tashi will be very far from us, well out of reach. You never consulted me! I am his mother.'

Gyeltshen looked at Pema and his eyes narrowed slightly; Tashi had the impression his uncle was trying to control his irritation. Surely there would be no further angry outbursts? Gyeltshen gave Pema a hard look; in a firm, controlled voice, he said,

'In the house, Pema, you are an important person and the decisions you take for the house have to be respected; and they are. You even have ownership of the house and the land around it. As you know, once we leave the house we conduct ourselves at a higher level, which means that when Tashi leaves the house, your opinion has no value. I have made the arrangements, and it is I who will pay all the bills. That is the beginning and end of the matter; do you understand?'

Pema's response was short; with a tone of resignation she said, 'Yes, I have to accept the situation.'

Gyeltshen took hold of two bows and some arrows. He strode through the front door and into the sunlight, closely followed by Tashi.

Pema slowly sank into her chair again. She was not simply alone; she felt lonely. In spite of her pensive, somewhat sad countenance, anyone watching her at that moment would have admired her. She was still a very beautiful woman and she looked much younger than her 30 years of age. It was easy to see she was not merely an attractive person; her beauty had great depth. Equally, one could understand that her high cheekbones, widely-spaced deep brown eyes, and her beautifully formed, firm, full breasts, enhanced by a slim waist, cast a spell over men. They not only admired her beauty, but they loved her nature, which matched her generous lips and warm expression. She laughed easily and this put her admirers at ease. Today, clothed in a long, cornflower blue silk dress, set off as it was with a deep-blue sash at the waist, she looked especially striking. She would never know that even her brother Gyeltshen, who tended to treat her as a lesser being, secretly considered her to be the most beautiful example of womanhood he had encountered in his entire life.

Glancing out of the window, Pema noticed the bushes moving ever so gently in the breeze. Her thoughts went back over the tumultuous events of the day. As she mused, her thoughts touched on the man called Duale (a name which she had soon learned to pronounce as 'Doo-ah-li'), who had come to write Bhutan's civil aviation law; and there her thoughts lingered. Pema was slowly drifting into a reverie.

It was twelve years ago that she had invited Duale to tea. She learned that Duale had first seen the light of the world in Marrakesh, a city in the foothills of the Atlas mountains. Born of the union of a Moroccan mother and French father, he was tall, good-looking and the epitome of courtesy. His father, who had been the 'black sheep' of a well-known family in France, had been a member of the French Foreign Legion. The family stemmed from the aristocracy; however, they had had the misfortune to be Huguenots. In the sixteenth century, some members of the family had been persecuted; others had fled to England during the seventeenth century and had settled in East Anglia, not far from Norwich. From the time of Napoleon, however, the ancestors of Duale who still lived in France had again come to the fore, this time in the academic world, as well as in political circles. When he had reached the age of twelve, Duale had been sent to England to learn English. Because he liked England, and especially Norwich which during its long history had developed strong connections with France, his father had agreed that he could stay there. He had been brought up as a Protestant. Since his early childhood in Morocco he had always been called 'Duale'; although this was not a Christian name, he had decided to keep it. A Moroccan friend had once explained to him that the name 'Duale' was hardly used in Morocco, but this made no difference to him. He liked being called 'Duale,' and that was the end of it.

He was about seven years older than Pema. She had been enraptured by his charm and the breadth of his knowledge. Duale had been educated in Arabic, French and English. He had finished his formal education by studying law in London, followed by a doctorate at Oxford in aviation law.

Pema found Duale not only amusing; he was someone who seemed to have a real understanding of many subjects. The more they conversed, the greater attraction she felt towards him. She could not explain why this was so; it was simply that she could not take her eyes off him. Perhaps one of the important reasons why Pema enjoyed talking to him so much was that he seemed to treat her as an equal. In the Kingdom, although men warmed to her easily, she knew that she was not regarded as of equal standing. On two occasions she had been reminded that there was only one way in which she could become equal to a man; she would need to be re-incarnated ten times!

In his loneliness, Duale had been very grateful that Pema had invited him to tea. She was not only a beautiful woman but also well educated and knowledgeable. After tea, cakes and much animated conversation, he had smiled at her and looked into her eyes. As he slowly approached her, her whole body began to tingle. He was taking the initiative, but at the same time he was not in the slightest aggressive. When he kissed her hand, she could not help herself; she raised her head – and he softly kissed her lips. Gently, he had opened her dress; he kissed her neck and then her back. His hand caressed one of her full, firm breasts. He told her that she was utterly beautiful and he wanted to love her. She knew she was totally out of control. With Duale, everything seemed so natural. He loved her and her body. She respected and adored everything about him. And when he made love with her, she was helplessly ecstatic. She belonged to him.

When Pema was about twenty, her parents gave her a house to live in; now she would live on her own. However, shortly after, her brother had moved in to live with her. His wife had recently died after losing her still-born baby. During his grief, Gyeltshen had become ill and suffered from a lingering disease of the stomach, a disease caused through drinking unclean water. On the one hand, Pema had the company of her brother; on the other, Gyeltshen was steadily nursed back to good health by Pema.

Choosing his times carefully and with discretion, Duale sometimes visited Pema. It was only when Duale was with her that she felt fulfilled and her life was really worth living.

After a few months, Duale had presented his legal report to His Majesty and the government. He had drafted a civil aviation law for the Kingdom, as well as the regulations which defined the meaning of the main sections of the law. The presentation had lasted two days, and many questions had been discussed. Now his work was finished, and three days later he was to leave the Kingdom.

The day before he departed, Duale had called on Pema to say goodbye. He knew they would both cry, so he wanted the farewell to be as brief as possible. He had kissed her gently. Although he was greatly tempted to stay with her, he had embraced her for the last time. Before leaving, he had said he would always love her and he was sure that one day they would be married. Pema had told him she would always belong to him.

He had smiled and said, 'How wonderful! Yes, we will be married – and we will make so much love! We will soon make a baby. What a beautiful child it will be!'

Then he was gone.

After Duale's departure, Pema had expected her life to have become lonely and empty. As it was, unknown to Duale his wish became reality sooner than he could ever have imagined. Once Pema realized she was pregnant, her baby had become her purpose for living. She called her baby 'Tashi'; like many first names in Bhutan, 'Tashi' could be used as a name for a boy or a girl. In the case of Pema's 'Tashi,' from the beginning there was never the slightest doubt that Tashi was a male. Pema regarded Tashi as her Treasure. Now with Gyeltshen's announcement that day, Tashi too would soon leave her. So her life would be empty after all.

Pema's reverie was brought to a sudden end by the return of Gyeltshen and Tashi. Both were in good spirits, and Gyeltshen was especially happy because Tashi had won the archery match. Their arrival cheered up Pema, although she realised this would be short-lived.

After a meal, Gyeltshen turned to Tashi, 'Tashi, what we have discussed today will affect your life forever, and I am sure in the end everything will work out very well. I want to apologise to both of you for my bad temper this morning; I was very hard on your mother. Our religion tells us that under no circumstances are we permitted to lose control of our calm and good behaviour. I want to say that I am sorry. I think I should also pray to Lord Buddha and beg forgiveness. Because I was anticipating great happenings, yesterday I arranged for the master of rituals to purify our house. No evil spirits are near us; only goodness surrounds our house. I think the three of us should pray now and thank the deities for having led us on the right path.'

Tashi and his mother followed Gyeltshen upstairs. They quietly entered the little room which was a chapel, and they prayed. Uncle Gyeltshen led the chanting. While Tashi was praying, his eyes strayed from the altar to the adjacent wall and he meditated on a *thangka* with its religious scenes. He saw how men travelled on their way to Nirvana; soon, he thought, it would be his turn to start his travels. Tashi was now rapidly regaining his composure. He thought the archery practice and his match with his uncle had helped him; fresh air always did him good. Now he was beginning to feel happy again.

After prayers, Tashi slipped into bed. He knew he would soon be asleep. There was no point in going over the great happenings of the day; in any case, he was already mentally over-burdened. He only had two thoughts. The first was that as long as the secret about the accident of his birth remained a secret, his life would remain unaffected. His second thought was more in the nature of a question. What would it be like at Dulwich College?

Chapter Three

Back to School

As a thirteen year-old, Tashi had grown used to the 'back to school' routine. On this occasion, however, he realized his return to school would be very different. He would be travelling to a foreign land several thousands of miles away, and he had no real knowledge of the school which he would be attending. As a matter of course, he normally accepted arrangements made by his mother and uncle; and he experienced little difficulty in adapting to new arrangements. He did as he was told. But this time, things were different. He was about to step into another world, a new world which was unknown to him.

As Tashi left Thimphu with his uncle Gyeltshen, he turned and looked at the small town. The houses, built in traditional style, stood out with their picturesque large roofs and high, slender windows; most of them had been built on slopes, on the edge of the town. His view also included the extensive *dzong*, the seat of government and the base from which the Buddhist faith was administered in Bhutan; by any standard, this was an impressive complex. As for the rest, the houses seemed to have been built in clusters without any discernible order; which was in fact the case. Since the country had no sizeable towns, it was simply that the government lacked experience in town planning. Now, however, as development was slowly taking hold, Thimphu was expanding; and increasingly people from the villages were coming to settle in the capital.

As the rugged four-wheel drive vehicle travelled along the road which hugged the mountainous landscape, Tashi thought back over the previous three weeks. His uncle had studied all the information he'd received from Dulwich College. Tashi had been told that he should prepare to start the journey to England in mid August. Uncle Gyeltshen had originally wished to transit East

Pakistan, a country which had been created when the British had left India in 1947; East Pakistan had formerly been part of eastern Bengal and the Sylhet district of Assam. His Indian contacts in Thimphu, however, had advised Gyeltshen against this. There was increasing tension between the governments of India and Pakistan, and much unrest in East Pakistan, as the people there felt like underdogs in their relationship with their government in West Pakistan. Already there had been demonstrations in Dhaka against the government in Islamabad, which seemed uncaring and aloof.

Gyeltshen decided the best route would be the road running southwards from Darjeeling and Siliguri to Calcutta, a distance of about 450 miles. By following this route, a border crossing into East Pakistan would be avoided. Visas were soon obtained from the helpful local Indian representative – when Gyeltshen collected them, he mentioned that he found it extraordinary that a large country like Pakistan should have been established in two parts, with a part of India (itself a large country) situated in-between. The Indian representative had agreed, responding with a smile, 'You are quite right; it is unrealistic. We are working on it! Things should become normal quite soon.'

One matter which had not come up for discussion between the Indian representative and Gyeltshen was the Indian government's policy towards granting visas to those who wished to visit Bhutan. When the government of Bhutan invited visitors for one reason or another, in the absence of an airport in Bhutan the normal travel route was to fly to Dhaka in East Pakistan and drive northwards, crossing the Bhutanese border at Phuntsholing. However, between the borders of East Pakistan and Bhutan there was a strip of land about 50 miles wide, which was Indian territory; this was a remnant of the British Raj, which the Indians exploited to maximum effect. Travellers had to apply to the Indian government for a visa to cross the narrow strip. In the case of professional consultants who were needed by the Bhutanese government, the Indian Government perceived these visitors as a potentially competitive threat, and usually refused visa requests. This was one of several methods devised by the Indian government to maintain a degree of control over the affairs of the Kingdom.

Uncle Gyeltshen had arranged to hire the vehicle in which Tashi was sitting. The driver was an Indian, and Gyeltshen sat in the back with Tashi. The first part of the journey would take them to Paro, a small town about 5000 feet above sea level, some 2000 feet lower than Thimphu. Towards the end of August, some of the mountainous landscape was just beginning to look autumnal. A cold wind swirled in the valleys, and this seemed to accentuate the occasional alpine patches of brown which Tashi could see here and there. At the bottom of the valley, the river was a rushing torrent of frothing water, as it crashed against rocks and large stones. He noticed a woman, burdened with heavy pieces of firewood, negotiating a narrow swinging bridge which had been suspended over the river. Her form seemed to make slow, somewhat erratic, progress over the raging river. One of her hands grasped the cable which served as a rail, while the other helped to steady the heavy load on her bowed back. The waters of several of these rivers would eventually join the mighty Brahmaputra as it flowed through the Assam valley.

Tashi seemed lost in thought. 'You were turning round, Tashi. What were you thinking about?' his uncle asked.

'I was thinking about my mother and the way she always looked after me. When I said goodbye, uncle Gyeltshen, my mother smiled through her tears; she was trying to be brave, but I hope she will be all right.'

'Don't worry,' Gyeltshen responded. 'I have had a long talk with your mother. She will be busy looking after me and the house. Also, she has decided to train for a job; she is going to take a course in typing and shorthand.'

'Then there is something else, uncle,' Tashi said. 'Before we left we prayed together to *Mahakala*, and I am sure he will protect us. But as we will be moving through different towns, even countries, how can we keep the deities of these places, the *Yulha*, happy? I know I must be brave, but we must not irritate the *Yulha*.

'Tashi, I am looking after you, and when I made all the arrangements I was very careful to ask *Mahakala* to make sure that you will reach your destination without any interference. There is nothing to worry about. You are beginning a great adventure. Just follow my instructions and you will enjoy yourself. Be happy, Tashi; and don't worry!'

The driver was careful on the mountain road, and only rarely managed to reach a speed that would allow him to change into third gear. The partly-completed construction of the tarred road made the driving easier. Already, however, parts of the road had been damaged by falling rocks and mud which had spilled over the protective barriers built above the road.

After about three hours, the small town of Paro came into view; soon Tashi could see the magnificent *dzong*. His impression was that it had great authority. His uncle directed the driver to the house where they would stay for the night. On the way, Tashi saw a huge construction project in progress, which his uncle explained was an airport, which would be ready in about three years. This would be the only Bhutanese airport in the mountains. His Majesty had negotiated the whole project with India, and all the planning and construction was being handled by the Indian Government.

Like most of his countrymen, Tashi had never seen an airport. Although neither understood the rudiments of airport construction, in fact he and his uncle were looking at the base course of part of the runway, the foundations of the passenger terminal building and the initial construction stages of the air traffic control tower. In a corner, trucks were delivering loads of rock; and machinery was noisily at work producing coarse gravel. Huge clouds of dust drifted across the valley and slowly dispersed over the nearby wooded slopes, parts of which had already taken on a greyish hue. In the construction area itself, several digging machines were removing vast amounts of earth in preparation for the concrete. Tashi could also see huge rollers at work as they crushed and compressed loads of stone deposited by enormous trucks. Tashi's uncle then described how in a few years' time, aircraft would bring passengers to Paro from Calcutta.

Tashi found it impossible to take in the scene, mainly because he had never before witnessed such large-scale tearing apart of the landscape; and his country was not yet participating in an activity which most other countries took for granted: aviation development.

The following morning, after a hot drink and a cake, they were again on the move. Although the air was fresh, Tashi knew they would gradually descend and it would become warmer. At midday, Phuntsholing came into view. Now they were in the lowland area. Although Tashi did not mention it, he was already beginning to feel like a fish out of water. The high mountains were behind them, the climate was hot and humid. As they drove through the town of Phuntsholing, he noticed people did not look typically Bhutanese, at least as far as his perception of 'Bhutanese' was concerned. Gyeltshen wound the windows down, hoping that this might encourage any breath of air. From time to time, the vehicle slowed and Tashi could hear the babble of conversation emanating from groups of pedestrians. Their language bore no resemblance to Bhutanese, and Tashi recognized a type of Hindi intonation. Again, he looked questioningly at his uncle. Yes, these people were indeed different – they were called *Lhotshampas* by the Bhutanese of the north. One regarded them as of Nepali descent, although their racial origins could be traced to both Nepal and various districts of northern India. The government had become alarmed at the high rate of immigration of people who were 'foreign,' and had tried to control their entry into Bhutan. Gyeltshen explained that this was leading to friction. No one could tell what might happen; the important thing was to try and prevent outside interference in the situation.

After some food, Tashi and his uncle crossed the border. The Indians were friendly and gave the driver a map to follow so that he did not take the route to the East Pakistan border by mistake. Although the road was pot-holed and rough, by nightfall they had reached Siliguri. By starting the next day at dawn and driving in great heat for the following two days, Tashi and Gyeltshen reached the vast, steaming city of Calcutta. During their journey Tashi had seen few people, and this had surprised him. On reflection, however, he realised that with the scorching heat it would have been impossible for people to work in the open, however hardy they might be.

It was already dark. As they drove through the city, Tashi could see silhouettes of huge buildings. But his senses had become dulled by the stifling heat; the air was humid, heavy and without a trace of a breeze. He was exhausted. On arrival at an imposing house, he just managed to summon up sufficient energy to struggle up some stairs, where he was shown a small room. He explored an alcove set in one side of the room and discovered a large basin of water. Having splashed water over his arms and face, seconds later he was lying on a wooden bed, instantly asleep.

Shortly after dawn the next morning, Tashi was woken by his uncle. 'Tashi, I know you're tired, but we must start early. We are first going to the tailor. Have a wash and come down as soon as you can. My friend who is putting us up has a little car, and his servant will show us the way to the tailor's.'

An hour later Tashi was trying to achieve something that no visitor to Calcutta had ever managed to do. His senses wanted to take in and digest the ever-changing scenes of the vast city. Although he felt refreshed after his sleep, and even though he had the capacity to persevere, his first daylight experience of the great city soon proved overpowering. In contrast to Bhutan's 600,000 people, Calcutta's metropolitan area of 500 square miles already housed a population of 10 million. Tashi soon found that the word 'housed' was used in a loose sense. In fact, many were homeless, living on the streets, jealously guarding their stretch of pavement as they clung to their few belongings. When Tashi looked at the faces of these wretched people, their frightened, staring eyes seemed to follow him; even when the car had passed them, the images of these faces would stay in his mind's eye. Although the memory of what he had seen would pale in time, the expressions of despair on those faces would haunt him for years.

On either side of the road, the large, imposing buildings built by the British in the Victorian age seemed incongruously irrelevant in the chaos of noise and gasoline fumes which pervaded the dusty, pot-holed road. Stooped pedestrians carrying heavy bundles and labourers pushing carts of jute mingled with the cars and trucks, seemingly oblivious to the danger of being injured. The driver's hand pressed the weak horn almost continuously. At one point the driver and servant pointed to a huge complex of buildings, and Gyeltshen explained to Tashi that Calcutta University was one of the largest in the world.

Although impressed visually by what he was being shown, Tashi was conscious of a more compelling impression: noise. In contrast to the serene silence of the mountains he had left behind, his ears were assailed by a veritable cacophony. It seemed that most of the people on the street were shouting; sometimes there were screams. As drivers jockeyed for position to make best progress down the overloaded road, the roar of car engines (often punctuated by the blare of horns) repeatedly startled him.

As they slowly turned into a narrow street, Tashi realised the car had entered a sea of jostling humanity. The heat beat down mercilessly and the humid, almost saturated atmosphere inexorably sapped the energy of the visitors, especially since they were used to the thin, bracing mountain air. Tashi began to count the shops passing by; he stopped when he reached three hundred, convinced that there were thousands to come. With infinite patience the driver edged his way along the crowded street. The operation was repeated along another street; and the next.

Eventually, the driver stopped. The servant motioned with his finger, 'Tailor.' Gyeltshen and Tashi entered the shop, and the tailor greeted them with a smile; he had received a message and had been waiting for them.

'So you want two black barathea jackets, dark grey trousers and an overcoat for the youngster? Let me measure him. I will come this evening at 7 o'clock and he can have a fitting. I will be working all night; I am used to it. By this time tomorrow everything will be ready, and I will deliver the clothes by noon. Is that all right?'

True to his word, everything was indeed all right. The clothes fitted perfectly and Gyeltshen could hardly hold back his tears of pride and joy when he watched Tashi walk around the living room in his school uniform. He was sure Tashi would be an excellent student at Dulwich. And he was so handsome!

Gyeltshen's host had arranged for his cook to prepare a fine evening meal. Tashi ate quietly and listened to the wide-ranging conversation, which covered the main political issues of the day, especially the increasing influence of the USSR in India and the future of East Pakistan. He understood very little of what was being discussed, although he was surprised to hear his Indian host comment that, 'We will make sure that East Pakistan ceases to exist – it is just a question of time!'

Although after the first course he no longer felt hungry, in keeping with his instruction at home, he politely took small portions of all the food offered to him. Toward the end of the meal, his thoughts began to wander; the heat was also taking its toll. Tashi thought of his mother; although he was only four days' driving from her, she seemed a world away. And tomorrow he would be flying thousands of miles to England; he would be quite alone. He suddenly felt tears trickling down his cheeks; and he began to cry.

'I think you are very tired and it is time for a good sleep.' Gyeltshen looked embarrassed as he thanked his host for a wonderful meal, at the same time taking Tashi's arm. Tashi tried to stop sobbing and was relieved to reach his bedroom. His uncle would wake him early the next morning, just after dawn.

'Well, Tashi, this is your big day. We have to be at Dum Dum airport at 11 o'clock, in five hours' time. The flight stops at Delhi for about two hours and then you will probably land in the Persian Gulf to refuel. When you reach London, there will be a tall, clean-shaven man holding a sign with 'Tashi' written on it in big letters. The man is about 45 years old and his name is Mr. Rana Shah. I knew him many years ago, when he was in the government service in Thimphu. Then he became a businessman and went to Uganda, where I believe he became quite rich. Unfortunately, life has become unpleasant for most Asians in East Africa; although many Asians helped to develop business in East Africa, a man called Idi Amin put an end to all that. So now Mr. Shah has moved to England. He already has a son at Dulwich College. Mr. Shah will look after you, and I have sent him money so he can help you buy things you will need. He will take you along to the college and make sure the college people look after you. I am sure everything will be perfect, Tashi.'

Tashi would never forget the parting from his uncle Gyeltshen. His uncle had been quiet on the way to the airport, and he had been very calm as they had approached the check-in counter. Now Tashi was ready to pass through the immigration. He stopped. He let go of his uncle's hand and looked up at the face which had become part of his life, a face that had almost never shown impatience, nor anger. All Tashi could recall was wisdom, patient explanation and twinkling, humorous eyes. His uncle was smiling in his benevolent way, but this time there were tears which his uncle could not hold back. Gyeltshen hugged Tashi and said as firmly as he could,

'We are very proud of you, Tashi. You have a chance to become one of the great men of the Kingdom. If you need anything, send a message through Mr. Shah. We love you. Go through now. We love you!'

As Tashi walked into the departure area, he turned and smiled. Uncle Gyeltshen raised his hand and waved. Tashi disappeared from sight. Gyeltshen thought how alone he felt. On the other side of the immigration barrier, Tashi thought precisely the same.

Soon Tashi was sitting in the aircraft and a friendly flight attendant closed his safety strap. He heard the roar of the engines. Feeling nervous he looked around; there was no visible reaction from the passengers, so he said a quiet prayer to *Mahakala* and hoped for the best. Tashi had the feeling that a huge bird was carrying him away; and he wondered where all this might end. The captain rotated and the bird rose steeply into the sky. As the aircraft rapidly gained height, Tashi felt that he was being carried up to the heavens.

At Delhi more passengers entered the cabin, and soon Tashi's aircraft was again climbing, in a westerly direction. Once the captain had reached his cruising altitude, the noise of the engines changed and became more even. It was then that the friendly flight attendant walked up the aisle and stopped at Tashi's row. 'Tashi, the captain would like to meet you. Take my hand and we can go together to the cockpit.'

Tashi got up and took the friendly hand. Guided by the flight attendant, he walked through the bulkhead door and reached the flight deck. The first officer smiled at Tashi and gestured that he should sit in the jump seat behind the captain. Looking ahead, Tashi could see the sun, a ball of fire almost resting on the horizon. Flying in a westerly direction, the horizon would continue to be brightened by the setting sun for some time to come, as the aircraft seemed to chase the sunset. The captain turned around and shook Tashi's hand. In the darkened flight deck the captain's face was barely visible; one side of the face reflected some of the dim light of the instruments, and Tashi was impressed by the look of confident concentration. In a relaxed manner, the captain said, 'We are very pleased to have you on board, Tashi. I don't remember having a passenger from Bhutan. I understand you are going to England for your education? The first officer is looking after the aircraft at the moment. Down there it's mainly desert, but if we had flown northwards from Delhi, we would have soon seen the Himalayas and the glaciers shining in the sunlight. It will be some time before you see the high Himalayas again, I think.

If you follow my finger I will show you some of the instruments. This is the altimeter. You can see we are flying at an altitude of 31,000 feet above sea level; that's higher than the Himalayan mountains. This instrument shows our speed; we have quite a strong headwind and we can only manage 478 miles per hour, but later I hope we can increase our speed to 550. And this is our heading; soon we will pick up a radio navigational aid signal which is quite close to Karachi. There is not too much traffic on our route today. We can hear the Karachi area control centre talking to a few other aircraft. We are flying on the main east/west route and sometimes it can be quite busy. It's like flying on a big, wide road; we call it an airway.'

'Have you had this job for a long time?,' Tashi asked. 'I hope we won't crash into another bird. You must be very careful, otherwise we might all fall down!'

Turning slightly, the captain said, 'I have been flying for nearly twenty years. We call the bird an aircraft or aeroplane. In fact, I have over 15,000 hours of flying experience. Don't worry, we will not hit another aircraft. All the aircraft in the sky are separated by many miles and we also fly at different altitudes. There are people on the ground who are in radio contact with us; most of the time they can also see us on their radar. I say most of the time because sometimes there are problems in the poor countries; either they don't have radar or it doesn't work properly. But don't worry, we are flying safely all the way to London. Now we have to start descending towards Dubai because we shall need some more fuel. You can go back to your seat, Tashi; it was nice meeting you.'

Tashi felt a hand gently touch his shoulder, and the flight attendant led him back to his seat. He felt tired. Over the last week he had taken in so much. Although he could not attempt to define his feelings, in fact he was in an unknown world. Nothing was 'normal.' Would it end; and when he reached the limit of the unknown, where and how would things end?

After the departure from Dubai, Tashi was offered some curried chicken; at least his meal bore a faint resemblance to food with which he was familiar. The friendly flight attendant asked him if he would like a blanket; within minutes he relaxed, almost embryonic under the warm blanket. And he slept.

On arrival in London, he awoke to a steady shaking of his arm.

Smilingly, the attendant explained he had reached his destination. She accompanied him off the aircraft, through the customs, past the immigration desks and into the arrival hall. Immediately, he saw 'Tashi' held high on a board above the welcoming crowd.

'Welcome to London, Tashi. I am Rana Shah – you can call me uncle Rana. I may not be as good as your uncle Gyeltshen, but I will do my level best to look after you. From this moment we are going to be good friends. You can ask me as many questions as you like, and I will always give you a proper answer. You and I can trust each other, and we will get along very well! My son is at home. Soon it will be back to school for him, and on the first day I will come with you to make sure that everything goes along as it should at Dulwich. My car is very close; we can drive to my house.'

Tashi felt refreshed after his sleep, and he was happy to have received the reassuring welcome from the new 'uncle.' After his Calcutta experience, the drive of an hour to Hounslow was for him almost routine. He had grown used to the endless passing scene of houses and factories; his world had seemingly been transformed into an eternal city of noisily congested roads and buildings. As the journey progressed, uncle Rana described various points of interest. Although Tashi was amazed to see thousands of cars, he no longer found such an experience tiring; he was accustomed to the continuing unknown.

'Here we are, Tashi. This is your new home for now.' Rana led the way to the entrance of a neat, semi-detached house, one of about a hundred lining the street. Tashi was happy, and before going to bed ate supper that Rana's wife had prepared. Rana's son, Shastri, was encouraged by his father to tell Tashi about life in England. Rana suggested that after the tiring journey, Tashi should rest. The following morning was the first day of term.

Before he drifted off, Tashi wondered where he would pray; he was anxious to give thanks to the deities for having brought him safely to England. He felt confident all would be well at Dulwich. Uncle Gyeltshen had been quite right, everything was going according to plan. He loved and respected uncle Gyeltshen. But now his uncle had been left behind in another world.

✽   ✽   ✽

Tashi attended Dulwich College from 1969 until 1975. He was a member of a school that had been founded by Edward Alleyn, the Shakespearean actor, who laid the school's foundation stone in 1619, three years after the death of William Shakespeare. When founded, the school had been intended for a few poor scholars. By the time Tashi was admitted, it had grown into a large and well-organized educational complex, with over a thousand students; all were made aware of the strong traditions of the College. The school had an enviable academic record, and many of its students progressed to university, notably Oxford and Cambridge.

During the terms, Tashi was a boarder in Blew House. The housemaster had asked the matron to pay special attention to Tashi so that he would feel secure and happy. The matron was an efficiently firm person, and her charges never challenged her quiet authority. Tashi was glad that she also had a human side to her personality. In the evenings she would pass his cubicle and ask him how his 'prep' was going. Sometimes she would visit him at 'lights out,' and make sure he was fine. Once she gave him a little kiss and said, 'We want you to be happy here, Tashi. You can only have a healthy body if you have a healthy mind. If ever you want to talk to me about anything or you need something, just tell me.'

Tashi actively participated in many sports including cricket, tennis, squash and rugby. His forte was archery, and during his last two years at Dulwich he formed an archery section; as captain, he led the team successfully against various archery teams throughout the United Kingdom.

He also learned to ski when he was 17; during visits to Switzerland and Austria, for the first time he could not avoid noticing that girls of his age enjoyed being in his company. Sometimes the feelings of friendship extended to brief spells of infatuation, yet another new experience. Especially when he danced during 'après ski,' he felt a stirring in his body as a girl sometimes gently pressed herself against him; and when their eyes met he felt a dryness in his throat, not to mention a feeling of help-lessness. Although he tried to suppress his feelings, sometimes he found this to be impossible; he simply could not ignore the occa-sional surge in his loins. He did not feel confident when trying to manage his feelings toward girls, mainly because he sometimes felt on the verge of losing his self-control.

He also became fascinated with the languages spoken in Austria and the French-speaking part of Switzerland. He bought phrase books and learned many phrases by heart. Whether on the slopes or in après-ski cafes, his newly found friends praised him for his good pronunciation. Before going to sleep each night, he would learn more phrases. He pursued his language studies, as an extra-curricula activity, on a more structured basis in England. By the time he left school, he could converse in and understand French and German quite well.

When Tashi was first admitted to Dulwich, he was so busy trying to cope with his new surroundings that the lack of regular dedication to his religion did not cause him anxiety. However, once he felt reasonably settled, he progressively found that he was nagged by the situation; he was used to regular meditation and prayers. Saying his prayers in bed each evening before falling asleep was not an adequate substitute for what he had been used to since his birth, so he shared his anxiety with the matron.

The very next day, the matron told Tashi that she had found the address of a Tibetan Buddhist Centre in London. The matron and he could visit the centre at the weekend. Tashi was happy to discover that the ritual and prayers offered at the centre's temple were similar to the familiar Mahayana sect of his religion, although the priests and lamas insisted there were important differences. During his long stay in England, he was able to visit the centre two or three times each month. He became a familiar figure to the lamas, and they offered him guidance, especially concerning how he might reconcile the teachings of the Lord Buddha with the values of the materialistic society in which he was living. At all costs, he had to try and develop a way of life that would be as harmonious as possible; he recognized that in his present circumstances this would be extremely difficult, perhaps impossible.

A fundamental problem centred on the fact that he lived in a different world, which paid great attention to such factors as gross domestic product. In the world he had left behind, little value was placed on GDP statistics; what was regarded as of much greater importance was Gross Domestic Happiness. Nevertheless, he always strove for a degree of contentment; although he tried his best, his feelings of happiness and harmony never matched what he had known in the Kingdom.

Tashi's academic development took longer than he had anticipated. In the competitive environment of Dulwich, in contrast to the situation in his former Bhutanese school, he discovered that he was not as clever as he had been told by his Bhutanese teachers and his uncle Gyeltshen. However, in time his dedication and perseverance brought him the reward he deserved. With the encouragement of his masters he became a good student, especially in mathematics and physics; it seemed the longer he stayed at Dulwich, the better his performance. When he sat for his Advanced Level examinations he seemed to have reached the peak of his performance. He not only passed, but was awarded an open scholarship to study physics at Cambridge University.

When Tashi left Dulwich for Cambridge, he was conscious of the strong attachment he felt for the College. He had been educated in the widest sense of the word, learning not only how to study properly, but how to think. The Master of the College had excellent academic credentials, and was also a man of humanity. When they might briefly meet, perhaps in the cloisters, the Master always recognized Tashi and had a kind, cheery word for him.

Then there were Tashi's many friends. Uncle Rana's son, Shastri, was a boarder at Ivyholme, the house next to Blew House; Tashi and he became firm friends, and developed a bond of mutual support. Although the rivalry between the boarding houses could become intense, especially when it came to sports and Gordon Bowl competitions, this never interfered with the many friendships between the boys.

For his last year at Dulwich, Tashi was head of Blew House and a school prefect. He was often consulted by the master of the Blew House and other prefects. Sometimes he was surprised by the value placed on his judgement, and the views he expressed concerning the situation under consideration. Once he thought to himself, 'I must be growing up; soon I will be a man.'

While Tashi was studying at Cambridge, the opportunity arose for him to learn to fly a small training aircraft. He had often watched kites, hawks and eagles in the Kingdom; the way in which they manoeuvred fascinated him. As a boy, he had envied their ability to fly and he wished he could fly too. His experience in the cockpit on his flight to England had deeply impressed him. Now he was being offered a trial; if he was found to be suitable, he would receive a bursary to support his training to the level of the private pilot's licence.

Tashi not only made a great success of the trial, he completed his training and was granted a private pilot's licence within a short period. In his written and oral examinations he gained record high marks; his result for the air navigation test was singled out for a special mention. His flying examiner could not fault him, and described him as a 'natural'; he flew the aircraft as though he was an integral part of it. Whether demonstrating his ability to recover from a stall or a spin, or whether bringing the aircraft down for an emergency landing on a precisely defined touch-down point, Tashi performed perfectly.

Tashi loved to fly. He confidently used the power of the engine to manoeuvre the aircraft as he wished. One of his instructors described his ability as 'bird-like'; he had the feel of the aircraft and the atmosphere in which he was flying. He seemed to have an uncanny sense of how to create an ideal equation between the power of the aircraft and the weather conditions in which he was operating the aircraft.

After the granting of his private pilot's licence, Tashi received a letter commending him for the standards achieved during his training. As a unique exception, he was granted an additional bursary to enable him to be trained for a commercial pilot's licence. Tashi was ecstatic; apart from the challenging written work, he would be able to log at least a further 250 flying hours. Some of these would be actual flying, while a part would be undertaken in a simulator. He was challenged by the need for him to comprehend the purpose of many precision instruments and how they were used; the emphasis on electronic instrumentation fascinated him. Because of his competing university degree workload, Tashi completed his training over a relatively protracted period. However, twenty months later he was awarded his licence. In his examinations, he had excelled throughout.

In 1978 Tashi was awarded an upper second class honours degree in physics at Cambridge. He was now not only a very well educated young man. Tashi was a tall, well-built, athletic person; he was also quietly self-confident. Although he retained his modest, dutiful disposition, at the same time he had developed a dry sense of humour; in keeping with his character, this never approached cynicism. He was well-liked and respected for his academic achievement.

Tashi felt ready to face any type of challenge which might lie ahead. He positively looked forward to his home-coming in the beautiful mountain Kingdom. He wanted to make his contribution to the Kingdom's well-being and, he hoped, its prosperity. He planned his return for January 1979.

*   *   *

Standing on the threshold of his professional career, Tashi was conscious of the fact that during his education he had learned a great deal. Unknown to him, however, there was an important detail which was not included in his store of knowledge. This was a pity, as he would eventually discover. If he had been aware of this detail, he almost certainly would have piloted his career differently and taken the necessary avoidance action. In any case, he could not have had the slightest inkling of what was happening in a city on the other side of the Atlantic Ocean, a city which could be reached from London in a mere ten hours.

We all seem to have a destiny; unfortunately, Tashi was no exception.

Chapter Four

The Trust for
Air Safety Support (TASS)

In 1956 Duale was 27 years old. As he leapt up the steps into the high-rise complex that housed the Trust For Air Safety Support, he considered how fortunate he was to live and work in Chicago. And anyone who happened to be watching him at that moment would have been struck not only by his agility, especially for a man who was tall, but also by his handsome figure; little imagination would have been needed to envisage the slim, lithe body which functioned so easily within his well-cut suit.

Duale had read a good deal about Chicago's phenomenal growth since it had been first recognized as a city in 1837, when its population was less than 5000. Now the post-war building boom was in full swing, and already there were a good number of skyscrapers which he could see from his office. Within the ensuing years the city skyline would often change as new building projects came to fruition. Soon, the John Hancock Center with its 100 stories, and the Sears Tower, a building rising almost 1500 feet in the general downtown area called the 'Loop,' would dominate the skyline.

Duale passed from the brilliant summer sunshine into the shadow of the impressive, marble-faced entrance to his office building. By Chicago standards, this July day was hot; he was reminded of the heat of Morocco. Duale had enjoyed his half-hour lunch break by sitting directly in the sun's rays as he munched his sandwich. With a light step, he strode towards the bank of elevators and pressed the button for floors 18 to 40; his office was on the 25th.

By the time he reached his chair, he was deep in thought about his work priorities for the afternoon. For at least a week he had been meaning to follow-up on his Bhutan assignment. Although his in-tray, which contained several thick files, reflected the need to deal with a great amount of work, he was determined that his first task had to be to summarise what he had done in Bhutan and incorporate this into a letter to the government; in basic terms, he wanted confirmation that the government would adopt the civil aviation law. At the end of his assignment to Bhutan he had made his presentation, and had understood that the government's reception had been positive. In spite of three letters on the subject, however, no response had been received from the government. To strengthen the authority of the letter, he would ask his director to sign it.

As he put final touches to the letter, Duale's secretary, a pretty young woman with blond hair called Anna, told him the director would like to see him. Duale's relations with his director, John Atkins, were excellent. Although Duale knew his aviation law, he recognized that the older John Atkins was far more experienced; Duale also appreciated his discretion and mature outlook.

'Come in, Duale. I've hardly seen you for the last three weeks. Maybe we've both been busy! I have just received a letter from Bhutan; they say they are not ready to bring in the aviation law because they have put off forming their airline. They probably have a money problem. In any case, they don't even have an airport yet, do they? There's not too much we can do about that. I think it would be a good idea if you could draft a letter for my signature; tell them they wanted advice and we responded. When they are ready to go, they should get in touch with us again so we can update the work you did. OK?'

Duale was trying not to show his exasperation, but he soon realised he was not succeeding. He blurted out, 'I get really fed up with these so-called developing countries. Why don't they know what they are doing? I mean, what was the point of me doing all that work when it won't be used? Maybe I am not suited to working with people who say they need something, and when we do it for them they turn round and just tell us they didn't really need it after all. It's ridiculous. I think I should resign and look for something more rewarding. I mean, exactly what does the great Trust for Air Safety Support think it's doing? Tell me, John, why do we need TASS? Convince me it's worthwhile and I'll stay; otherwise you can find someone else to play these games.'

John Atkins was a mature man, dedicated to the mission of TASS. Unlike Duale, John was not intemperate of language in venting his exasperation. He had learned to be patient and persevere. Those who were associated closely with him admired his capacity for work, and his ability to show results. His first reaction to Duale's outburst was to treat him like a spoilt child. His next was that if Duale intended his challenge to be taken seriously, then why waste time; why not accept Duale's resignation? On the other hand, Duale seemed to be a good man; he knew what work was all about, and the end product was invariably of high quality. Why not treat this as an irrational outburst? Yes, he would explain why the world needed TASS, and he would convince Duale that what TASS was doing was worthwhile.

But not today. First, with Duale's unbalanced outburst, one should not expect to have a rational discussion. Second, the convincing which John Atkins needed to embark on would need some time. He looked at Duale with a relaxed, almost smiling expression on his face. After a few seconds he said, 'Duale, I really admire you! You are so honest and you call a spade a spade. If you really want to leave, do it today. Personally, I think you would be making a mistake; but obviously it's your decision. You have been with us for three years and you are highly thought of, both within TASS and in the Third World. If you carry on as you are, I think you would be a strong candidate to become the director of this division when I retire. Ten years or so sounds a long time, but you know when you are busy, time passes very quickly! And there is always the chance that something will happen and my job might be up for grabs sooner than we think. In any case, you want to be convinced that TASS is a worthwhile organization. Would you be free at 10 o'clock tomorrow morning, so we can get together? Let's see if I can convince you. I hope so!'

Duale readily agreed. One thing he liked about his director was that he always took him seriously. Duale felt better; as he left the office he smiled, and said he was looking forward to the next day's discussion. On re-entering his own office, he turned to his secretary and smiled at her; she did not return the smile, but just looked at him with twinkling blue eyes.

Duale sat down, took hold of the Bhutan file with two hands, swivelled to his left and dropped the file on the floor. He decided

41

to leave it there for three days, by which time he hoped to be in a better frame of mind to deal with it. He then worked intensely for four hours. He would have gone on for four more if his secretary had not briefly come into his office to say, 'Have a good evening.' Duale looked up; then he glanced at his watch. He was looking into those blue eyes again – and he smiled.

He left the office and was soon in the elevator which, at a press of the button 'G,' plunged into the bowels of the building. A minute later he was in the garage and jumping into his sports car; with a brief roar as he touched the gas pedal, he drove up the ramp and was again in the sunshine. Two blocks from TASS he stopped at the lights. He immediately saw his secretary, Anna, who nimbly slid into his car; seconds later they were contentedly driving to Duale's apartment. When they had almost reached his building, this lovely girl put her arm round his neck and pressed herself against him. With his eyes on the road, he blew her a kiss; in return, she kissed him on the neck. Five minutes later, both were undressing in his bedroom and ready for love. As Anna was undressing, a thought flashed through Duale's mind; he simply never seemed able to truly decide whether he preferred to see Anna in her negligee (she always wore white lace mini-panties), or if he was happier with her completely naked. In any case, just as had been the case with Pema in Bhutan, this beautiful girl seemed to love him; when he made love with her, she simply became part of him. Whatever he loved to do with her body, she smiled and agreed. She caressed every part of him. From time to time, she would huskily say, 'Don't stop, Duale; don't stop!' He would reassuringly whisper in her ear, 'I love you so much, Anna!'

About an hour and a half later, after a shower, Duale said he felt hungry. Anna went into the small kitchen to prepare noodles with seafood, to help replenish their spent energy. Over dinner, however, she became pensive. Duale looked at her and said, 'Anna, you are the most beautiful creature anyone could meet. Where did your beauty come from?'

'Well,' Anna replied as she sipped a little white wine, 'my family came to Chicago from Europe nearly a hundred years ago, that would have been just after the Great Fire of Chicago in 1871. Germany had invaded France and my grandfather, who was from northern Germany, was afraid that the whole of Europe would go to war. In fact, that happened much later, in 1914. My mother was from Poland, and I think her forbears were from Scandinavia. Perhaps that's where my blond hair and blue eyes come from? I applied for a job at TASS because at home we spoke English, German and Polish, so I thought languages might be useful. Duale, I want to change the subject. I was just thinking, we have been together two-and-a-half years. Apart from love-making, don't you think we get on well together? You tell me that you love me. Well, have you ever thought we might get married? I mean it would be much more convenient, and we wouldn't always have to play hide and seek with other people. I am sure some of them in the office know about us. When you are invited to official functions, we could go together.'

There was a long silence. Now it was Duale's turn to become pensive. At last he said, 'Anna, I hear what you are saying. I think your attitude is quite sensible. The trouble is that I am not ready for marriage, and I don't know whether I will ever want to settle down with one woman. That's the way it is.'

Without hesitation, Anna got up and spoke in measured tones to Duale.

'I have just wasted two and a half years of my life.'

Then she was gone.

Duale did not move for forty five minutes or so. Every train of thought ended in him becoming more confused. He began to ask himself questions: Who was he – really? Did he have standards of conduct? What about his job – would he leave it tomorrow, just as Anna had left him? Where might he be in ten years' time? Was he a moral or immoral person? Perhaps he was amoral?

Try as he might, he could not answer one question. He slowly rose from the table and moved to his writing desk, where he wrote a letter to Pema. He wrote that he loved her and he hoped one day they would be married. He also told her he was becoming seriously disenchanted with his work and the mission of TASS. He would probably resign from TASS, though he had no idea what he would try next. He was not sure if his occasional letters were getting through; in any case, he addressed his letter to the Bhutanese Mission in Delhi, and asked them to forward it to Thimphu.

The next day Duale posted his letter on the way to the office.

At TASS, he saw Anna working at her desk. He said cheerily, 'Good morning, Anna.' She looked up, but her eyes did not twinkle and her expression was sad. Nodding gently, she carried on with her work, and said nothing.

At ten Duale was in the doorway of Atkins' office. 'Morning, John,' Duale said.

'Good morning, Duale,' John responded. 'Let's sit by the table over there, it's more comfortable. We're both busy, so if it's all right with you, here goes.'

Duale smiled politely and said, 'It's really nice of you to take time out for me, John. I mean I do appreciate it. I won't interrupt you. I was only thinking this morning how I like working for you; and that's important to me. Please, go ahead'.

'Well,' John said, 'to start at the beginning we have to go back to the last war; come to think of it, the war ended just over ten years ago. Just after the end of the war, a billion dollar trust fund was established to finance TASS, an air safety support set-up quite separate from any other body associated with aviation safety. TASS's responsibilities have absolutely nothing to do with promulgating international standards for civil aviation safety; in fact, we are expressly excluded from undertaking any work in that area – period. But once a standard is there, then we try and help aviation bodies meet those standards. We are a bit like a super maintenance set-up, Duale. Of course, we're not limited to equipment and the engineering which goes with it; if needed, we can give economic advice or, as you have done, we can help in the legal field.

So why was TASS created? The brains behind the establishment of the trust, who successfully maintained anonymity, were convinced that if a politically-controlled organization were established to support the safety of aviation operations, this could never wholly succeed technically; such organizations become too politicized. Once this happens, technical integrity is much more difficult to maintain. To be specific, if a chief executive of an international organization depends on the support of the political international community, he has to be very careful to play the right political game; and if, for example, this means taking technical staff from certain countries to ensure their support, then it's not difficult to see that he may be tempted to take technical staff who may not be the best in the world. Obviously, in a relative sense there are not many good technical people in the Third World; in any case, most of the time those countries will not release their best technical people. And they are quite right; they really need them. So, because of the political factor, you sometimes get a drop in personnel standards.

Another aspect which the donor foresaw with great clarity was that organizations which might be involved with setting standards do just that; and only that. Some would argue that is the easy part, but ultimately, the only thing which is of crucial importance is the degree of adherence to those standards. So things have to go much further than setting minimum standards; implementation, or enforcement one way or another, is what matters.

In writing the principles under which the trust would operate, the donor explicitly stated that a condition of providing funding support for TASS would always be that TASS would remain apolitical; so we have to keep it that way, Duale.

Incidentally, the donor also foresaw the reality of the present situation very clearly, which is that in the field of civil aviation the developed world is far ahead of the Third World. Things will stay like that for the indefinite future. Unfortunately, the gap will get wider as the years pass. So what do you do? The donor's answer was to create TASS as an international, independent, technical organization whose mission is to support, on a totally objective basis, safe civil aviation development. Because the big boys have the expertise and resources to look after themselves, inevitably we find that most of our work is in the so-called developing countries. Of course, the more backward and poorer they are, the more they need us.

As I explained, TASS is legally-speaking apolitical. It is intended to constitute what you might call a bank of technical, economic and legal knowledge which can be called on by any corporate body or airlines which operate some aspect of civil aviation. The donor's intention was that TASS would take the standards which have been agreed internationally and help those in need to implement them by giving them the highest quality advice and assistance which is available in the international marketplace. Of course, TASS has to liaise with international organizations, but never at the political level. We stand or fall by our technical quality, which is why we insist on standards of excellence. So far,

45

we have been quite successful. That's why we are kept busy.

You know, Duale, a few months ago our CEO took our advice and decided that in addition to the divisional directors, TASS should have a small Executive Committee, which should have an international composition; the committee has six members. We try to insist on high competence of the members in a recognized civil aviation field; in other words we don't want political appointees. It seems to be working.

Off the record, I would have thought we could have done a bit better with the Italian. And the American lawyer is not everyone's cup of tea. I really don't know how we managed to employ him; when you listen to him, he certainly is not an aviation lawyer. The fact that he has a private pilot's licence is hardly a plus; there are hundreds of thousands who have a PPL.

In any case, the idea is to give us more of an international image. We thought it would go down better with the countries we help; and I think it does help. But of course, the most important thing is to maintain our technical integrity, which is something the donor stipulated in the rules of the trust as essential. We do that.

Now let me say a few words about the developing countries. The first point is that you can't generalise about the Third World. Because we have horror stories coming out of Africa, for example, you can't write off the whole of the Third World. In any case, in aviation there is no point in writing off any country; the whole system depends on a safety chain and a weak link can lead to a disaster – it's as simple as that! So somehow we have to come to terms with the Third World and help them make things as safe as possible. This can be very difficult. If a country needs expensive up-to-date facilities and has no money to invest in them, what do you do? And even if the money is found, what about the human infrastructure? It's a huge job to train people; if you manage that, then what about the experience they need? It all sounds rather hopeless, doesn't it? But the bottom line, Duale, is that unless an organization like TASS perseveres and succeeds, then the world is in for a lot of accidents.

The current ratio of developed to developing countries is about 20% : 80%. That means that about four-fifths of the world's countries are likely to call on the technical assistance of TASS. As far as the Third World is concerned, at one end of the scale you find countries like Bhutan, Nepal and most of the Pacific Islands; at the other end, you have countries which are beginning to develop rather fast, like Brazil, Thailand or Singapore. I think the more developed a country is, the more satisfaction we get when we assist them. When they have the facilities and human infrastructure, they understand what to do with our advice or assistance. But with the really poor, backward countries, it's a different story! Duale, technically speaking these countries are groping in the dark. And when their people are trained to do something professionally, all they want to do is get a job in a developed country so they can earn more cash. Definitely, the poorer countries give us the greater challenge; to help them meaningfully and to make a real difference is something elusive, however hard we work. But slowly, we are making a real contribution; and that means we are fulfilling the mission of TASS. But it's often a thankless task and you need endless patience and perseverance; yes, it's tough!

And if we succeed, what is our reward? Well, we have professional satisfaction that we helped to make something positive happen. And the world becomes a safer place. But no one, Duale, will sing your praises. This is something we have to do without. Of course, it's possible that in a few years' time the contribution of TASS to aviation will be recognized; and if we have been part of the effort, then perhaps we can bask a bit in a little bit of glory – until the next problem!

That's the way it is, Duale. You need a bit of a missionary spirit to succeed in our business; if you feel that you are at least trying to make a real contribution, then it helps you to maintain your purpose. But if you don't care what happens, then the whole thing becomes very empty.

I think I should stop talking now and get a reaction from you. But let me say one more thing. There is a terrific amount of work going on to produce technical standards, guidance material and so on. Off the record, I have to say a lot of this effort is focused on the needs of the developed countries. As a basic approach, I think this is flawed. As I mentioned, the big boys can look after themselves. Of course, they need to work towards uniformity and no one can object to some international co-ordination; but they themselves have the knowledge and expertise to manage on their own and to make international agreements as they need them. In most cases, they don't need TASS, do they?

What is the point of spending a lot of money getting agreement on sophisticated international standards when you know that the majority of countries, in the Third World, have neither the human resources nor the finance to implement them properly; it's rather like laying down the law from an ivory tower. In this case, even if the countries listen, they don't have the necessary technical resources to do what they are being told to do. What I am saying is that I think the priorities are ridiculously mixed up. I doubt that this attitude will change. As a result, I believe the role of TASS will become increasingly crucial, safety-wise. And the more political the international organizations will become as time passes, the more the integrity and credibility of TASS will be appreciated by Third World countries who really want proper cost-effective help.

So there we are, Duale. That's the way I see TASS. Personally, I think we are lucky to have you on board. But after listening to me so patiently, if you feel that TASS and its mission is not for you, I would be the last to dissuade you from leaving us. It would be difficult to find someone who could do your work as well as yourself. Incidentally, just of passing interest; by co-incidence, when you came to my office yesterday I was drafting a recommendation to the CEO that we should recognize your efforts and promote you to senior legal consultant. I know it's not a decisive issue in the context of our discussion today. But I thought you would like to know; of course, there would have been a nice rise in it for you. In any case, would you like to discuss any other points on the subject, Duale?' John Atkins looked at Duale with a serious, but good-natured, expression.

Duale looked down at the table in front of him and seemed lost in thought as he stared at a small vase of flowers. Atkins looked at him and consciously thought how he could 'hear' the silence. He could see that Duale was under stress. At last the silence was broken. Duale raised his head and a faint smile crossed his face. He spoke slowly, as though he was choosing his words carefully.

'John, I don't have any questions. I just want to say 'thank you' for talking to me. I have a lot of respect for you, and you have helped me identify with the mission of TASS. I am proud to work for you and, don't worry, I will never complain again. You are right, we all have a lot of good work to do; and it has to be done. If you agree, I will stay on board. Now I think I had better get stuck into some of those files!'

Atkins stood up, as did Duale, and shook his hand. Looking at John, Duale had the feeling that he was looking at a facial expression which was as solid as a rock; in fact, he was quite right. At the same time, Duale was inescapably conscious of his own inner inadequacy; he knew something was lacking in him, but he could not precisely identify why he should develop such a feeling. Both men smiled at one another and Duale returned to his office, his strength of purpose greatly renewed.

As he passed Anna, he glanced at her. He noticed her pale, delicate cheeks; he thought how withdrawn and lifeless she looked. She ignored him and made no gesture. When he reached his desk, as he sat down he noticed a neatly addressed white envelope lying in front of him; the letter was short and to the point:

Legal Consultant, TASS.

> *Having worked in your office for over two and a half years, I feel I need a change. I would therefore appreciate it if you would kindly arrange to have me transferred within one week to a division outside the legal division.*
> *In the event that the transfer cannot be arranged, this is to give TASS notice of my resignation, which will take effect in one week.*
> *Thank you for your co-operation.*
> *Anna*

Duale thought for a few moments; did he care about Anna, should he talk to her? Certainly, he had adored her body; but did he really care about her feelings? The short answer was, no! Within a minute he was talking to the personnel manager on the phone. 'Jack, my secretary Anna, she seems to be depressed or something; strange girl. Anyway, she wants a transfer to another division, or she'll leave in a week. What's that? No, I haven't the faintest idea what's behind it. Frankly, I'm too busy to get involved. She's a good worker; can you shift her quickly, please? I would say she's worth keeping. By tomorrow? Fantastic, thanks. Bye.'

When Duale left TASS at close of business, by habit he looked for Anna on the corner; feeling slightly foolish, he had to admit he missed seeing her. As he entered his apartment, he thought that it had been a long time since he had felt lonely.

Duale poured himself a whisky and thought about his day. He found himself focusing on John Atkins. John sounded totally genuine; but was he? Duale was not quite sure. He concluded that if John was not genuine, then he was certainly a superb manipulator. His balanced approach, the way he argued so articulately, and in such a gently persuasive way, had impressed Duale enormously. And then there was the carrot of some promotion.

Duale recognized John's easy and assured success. Then why not take him as a model? And there was the interesting reference to bringing some international flavour to the Executive Committee. No doubt, John maintained good relations with the American, the Italian and others; after all, he needed their support. The fact that John had reservations about their competence seemed to be of secondary importance. What was apparently of top priority was that John enjoyed good relationships. Now Duale saw John's technique clearly; the fact was that John absolutely never became involved in confrontation. And he was always assuredly calm. Duale had never considered such aspects. But now he was also beginning to understand the importance of good and supportive contacts.

Now the crystal ball in Duale's imagination was clearing. Yes, from now on he would adopt John's work approach as his model. He would cultivate useful contacts both within TASS and outside; and, for good or for ill, he would use them. The entire thrust of his progression within TASS would centre on his own interest and, he hoped, his continuing success. If others sometimes suffered through what would be, in effect, his selfish approach, so be it. He would have to learn how to remove obstructions and destroy, or at least neutralize, opposition. After all, that was the way of the world – was it not?

And what about the women in his life? There had been Pema and Anna, as well as one or two other short liaisons. He often had told these women that he had loved them. With the possible exception of Pema, he had never really loved anyone. Duale sometimes wondered whether he knew what it was truly like to love.

Yes, he loved the bodies of beautiful women; and he always physically enjoyed them. But in terms of his nature, he found love between two human beings as something exasperatingly elusive.

Sometimes he wondered whether his lack of feeling towards women reflected his early upbringing in Morocco; he tried to resist treating women almost as chattels, but his constant emphasis on physical possession of them reminded him how difficult it was to treat them as social equals. In any case, that evening he concluded that, essentially, he was a loner. If he felt attracted to women, and they reciprocated his advances, then he would sleep with them. But as far as he was concerned, that would be as far as things would go. In any case, he would need most of his available time to further his own interests.

The following morning, Duale found a stern, middle-aged woman sitting where his beautiful Anna had sat for the previous two and a half years. Duale gauged the woman's age as about fifty, and his immediate reaction on seeing her was that she should embark on a strict diet. She looked at him unsmilingly through her heavy, horn-rimmed glasses, and introduced herself as 'Dorothy'.

On reaching his chair, Duale opened a white envelope on his desk. The enclosed letter was from the CEO. Duale read that the volume and quality of his work was greatly appreciated within TASS; he was offered promotion to senior legal consultant, with a commensurate significant increase in his salary. He picked up the phone and thanked John for his support. Duale thought how typical it was that John should quietly thank Duale for his call, insisting that Duale was simply receiving overdue recognition, and that as far as John's role was concerned, this was really 'not important'.

From that day Duale put his game-plan into effect. He easily slipped into the role of John Atkins' right-hand man. Over the ensuing months and years, John found himself increasingly relying on the well-honed knowledge of Duale. For his part, Duale read everything that was published relating to his work; and he himself published a series of six professional articles on various aspects of aviation law.

Whether drafting TASS's contributions to meetings to consider the interpretation of certain legal instruments or agreements, or whether drafting background material on specialized legal subjects, Duale demonstrated a wealth of knowledge and a rare incisive, analytical talent. Sometimes, TASS was invited to attend internationally-convened gatherings, and Duale was asked to be the TASS representative. His interventions were invariably concisely articulate and refreshingly knowledgeable.

In 1968 John Atkins retired from TASS. His contribution as an air law specialist had been impressive. However, he would be remembered mainly as a superb manager. As a director within TASS he had never offended anyone. However, without exception he had always achieved what was best for his division and for TASS; not once had he been associated with failure. His thoroughly sound professional approach, linked with his clever, diplomatic style, had always won the day. Internationally, he was respected for his quiet, intellectual interventions which, so often, had thrown new light on complex aviation legal questions. And in the cauldron of half-truths and hypocrisy which pervaded international meetings, his maturity, incredible knowledge and honesty cut through the mass of falsehoods, like a knife through soft butter.

So who might be available to succeed a man of the calibre of John Atkins? There was really only one candidate who could aspire to the highest level of legal expertise. And that man had been doing his homework, not only on a purely professional basis but also in terms of his personal relationships, for several years. Duale was unquestionably TASS's legal star for the foreseeable future. When his candidature was discussed, the Executive Committee took little time in agreeing that Duale should be the new director of the Division.

Things were slightly held up in the Executive Committee when an Englishman asked John Atkins to tell the committee not about Duale's legal competence, on which there was unanimous positive agreement, but about Duale the man. John's response was typically honest. He could not tell the committee much about Duale's character, simply because his personal knowledge of Duale had been limited to sharing the odd lunch or dinner; or perhaps working with him for a few days at international meetings. All John could say was that in his working experience Duale had conducted himself in an exemplary way.

On the first day of 1969 Duale commenced his tenure as the director of the Legal Division of TASS. At the age of 38 he seemed to be at a peak. He was professionally very strong and he had an engagingly pleasant personality. At a small drinks party, the CEO congratulated Duale on his achievement. Duale knew everyone in the room, and slipped into the highest echelon of TASS with ease. When the CEO had finished his short speech, Duale responded with a suitably humble, dutiful and grateful statement.

Fortunately, at the gathering he gave not the slightest hint of his thoughts. In fact, he tried to suppress them; but they repeatedly re-surfaced. Looking around at the assembled members of the Executive Committee and his fellow directors, one overpoweringly strong thought constantly asserted itself. For some uncontrollable reason, each time this thought became stronger and clearer: 'I wonder what it would take for me to become CEO of TASS. Civil aviation needs a lot of hands-on support – so it needs me. And I need power!'

Chapter Five

Duale's Learning Curve

The mid-winter's day when Duale installed himself in the director's office was cold; but the sun's rays were streaming through the windows and, as he sat down behind his desk, he felt expansive and self-satisfied. He looked around his new office and took in the mahogany furniture, including the handsome floor-to-ceiling bookshelves which housed the first line of legal reference volumes; his immediate office reference material was supported by a vast array of legal literature which was available in TASS's main library on the floor below.

John Atkins' former secretary entered and somewhat formally introduced herself. She was looking forward to working with Duale and he should feel free to call upon her for assistance at any time of the day or night. She recognized that a TASS director had a 24-hour job and she had always identified with this fact.

Duale looked at his new secretary; he had noticed her from time to time but had never before really looked at her. She was tall, good-looking and, he thought, very quick; a silk white blouse set off her fitted black suit. Now that he was consciously looking at her, he immediately concluded that he liked what he saw, including her ski tan. He asked her to sit down and tell him about herself.

'My name is Mary Piggott; by all means call me Mary. I was educated in New York and later came top when I sat my secretarial exams. I believe John thought highly of me, and I always want to be the best. If at any time you think I can improve in some way, please tell me. I am totally discreet and you can always rely on me for that. I moved to Chicago when my husband was transferred here; we have two children. I am very happily married to the man of my dreams. Would you like to know anything in particular?'

Mary Piggott was smiling at Duale; she seemed to have poise and enormous self-assurance. She left no doubt that she was happily married. Was she letting Duale know from the outset that he should never suggest some extra marital activity? Probably.

Duale responded, 'Thank you, Mary. We have a lot of work ahead and I am looking forward to doing it with you. I'll regard you as my extension, if I may, and whenever I need some help the first person I will call on will be you. I am sure we will work well together.'

As a director of TASS, outwardly Duale epitomized self-assurance and confidence. In fact, the reality was quite different. Especially during his first year, he was constantly reminded of his less-than-adequate knowledge on various aviation subjects. When he attended meetings to participate in important discussions, he often found himself maintaining his silence or, when asked for an opinion, simply hedging. He soon realized that developing good contacts was not enough. He had a great deal to learn.

Within a few days of his appointment as a director, the CEO had called Duale for a chat. Al Willis was a man of fifty-four; although in his younger days he had been an athlete, his overweight form and flushed countenance betrayed a negligent attitude to his general well-being. His background had been in the aircraft manufacturing industry, first as a design engineer and later as an engineering trouble-shooter. He had a wonderful way with people and his ability to put anyone at ease, regardless of their level in the workplace, was the envy of his colleagues. In the boardroom, he could defuse a situation which seemed to be getting out of hand as members of the Executive Committee argued with total conviction their various points of view. During the war he had flown as a flight engineer and had been decorated for his courage in combat. He seemed always willing to talk on practically any subject; the only exception where he drew the line was the war. Since the war, he had travelled internationally a great deal and was generally well-known, and respected, within the aviation industry.

The 'message' that Al Willis had asked Duale to consider was that Duale should spend time in getting to really know and understand TASS. There were many facets to aviation; and many ramifications. Unfortunately, they were not only technical; as TASS had discovered, political influences sometimes intruded into straightforward situations. Under its mandate, it was essential that TASS steered clear of political aspects. But sometimes one might be drawn unsuspectingly into political turmoil. One needed to be sensitive, and to know how to keep out of embarrassingly delicate situations. The only foolproof answer was knowledge; and there was a great deal to learn about so many aspects of civil aviation.

Al Willis had acknowledged that Duale excelled in his specialist aviation legal work. But in his capacity as a director, Duale would need to contribute to many important decisions; to do this effectively, one would need to develop an understanding of at least the main branches of civil aviation. All of these interacted with one another. One would have to learn the why and how of various enmeshed fields of endeavour.

Although Duale functioned as the director of the legal division from the first day of his appointment, four long years elapsed before he began to feel confident that his knowledge was adequate to meet the challenge of what was expected of him in helping to direct the mission of TASS.

His first challenge was not only to acquire a good knowledge of the various divisions within TASS, but to gain an understanding of what these specialists were doing. TASS had 300 professional staff; as international civil aviation expanded, this number would increase to four hundred and fifty over the next few years. Duale's whole background had been in the aviation legal field. He had tended to think that civil aviation revolved around aviation law. From a narrow perspective, he was right. From the wider perspective, however, he was quite wrong. Although all civil aviation fields were interdependent, if one were asked to select one aspect which should be regarded as of over-riding importance, then the response would invariably be the same: air navigation safety. Flight safety was the primary aim of the aviation system. And without effective implementation of facilities and services to assure flight safety, there would be accidents and people would be killed. John Atkins had been quite right; the emphasis should be on implementation of flight safety measures. Thank goodness the world had TASS which, uniquely, was concerned with flight safety.

For those four years Duale, in addition to coping with his heavy workload, found himself on a steep learning curve; there were so many 'black holes' of knowledge that had to be illuminated. One of these holes centred on communications and air navigation systems. He had no background in electronics, nor in communications. But if, for example, he were to function properly during meetings to select specialist staff in electronics engineering, he would certainly need some basic knowledge of the field under consideration. He often heard technical terns bandied about. In time he became conversant with the strange language; but what did it really mean?

'Joe, it's Duale here.' Duale had dialled '34' and he was speaking to TASS's Head of Air Navigation Systems. 'Hello, Duale; what can I do for you?'

'Well, this might sound a little strange coming from a legal man. I've been doing some homework reading about Asian regional planning and air navigation ground facilities in Asia. I want someone to tell me what a VOR or a DME do; then there is the ILS – and yes, what about the AFTN? I have a general knowledge, but I would like to learn a bit more; would one of your people have a little time for me?'

Joe Wilkins was impressed. Here was the director of the legal division who wanted to learn more about air navigation systems. What an excellent outlook on the part of Duale. If only the CEO and the other directors had a similar outlook! Then people like Joe Wilkins would not have to spend so much time in meetings explaining things as though he was talking to a bunch of children.

Joe Wilkins was quick to respond, 'Duale, I'm impressed. May I have the privilege of dealing with this personally? Shall I come to you, or can you come down here?'

Two days later, Duale was sitting in Joe Wilkins' office. It was better that way because Joe had documentation and diagrams close at hand. Like most offices in TASS, there were bookshelves crammed with reference material; a few pictures of various types of navigational aids, commonly called 'NAVAIDS,' relieved the uniformity of the cream walls.

Joe was a thoroughly down-to-earth person who spent his entire working day on some aspect of aeronautical communications and navigational equipment; and if he had to meet the challenge of an especially complex problem, then he would spend nights too working at it until the right technical solution could be found. With thirty years' experience, he seemed incredibly conversant with the characteristics and capabilities of a vast array of aviation communications equipment. With his low-key, somewhat insipidly-patterned sports jacket, he struck Duale as the ultimate technical man, a man not at all interested in judgemental or people-related solutions; his only interest was in applying coldly precise technology to solve what he was employed to do – just that. Joe lost no time in getting on with his explanation.

'Duale, we can't cover everything so quickly. In any case, today we can talk a little about the VOR and the ILS. So let me start straightaway. VOR means "very high frequency omni directional range". It is a ground navigational aid which gives directional guidance; it was developed in the late 1940s. It's still in standard use throughout the world. In the US there are already several hundred of these VOR stations. The aeronautical charts indicate where VORs are installed. Now, provided the aircraft has a VOR receiver, then the pilot can use the VOR station for *en route* navigation or to reach a particular point, like an airport.

Each VOR station is identified by a two or three letter code, and this is shown on the map, called a chart. The VOR transmits a radio signal with navigational information in all, that's omni, directions. Once the pilot has made contact with the VOR, the pilot has the choice of flying on one of the 360 radials which are available, subject of course to any air traffic restrictions. Incidentally, in addition to transmitting its identifier, a VOR station often has voice facilities and at regular intervals the station may broadcast weather reports and other information.

As I mentioned, the pilot has a VOR receiver on board. When he plans the flight he identifies which VORs he will use. When the aircraft is within range of a VOR station, the pilot tunes the receiver to the frequency indicated on the chart and listens for the right morse code identifier. An indicator on his instrument panel will display the direction to the VOR, and the pilot can turn the aircraft on to the right heading; he also has a course deviation indicator, which tells him if he is straying from the selected radial. So this means he can take corrective action as necessary.

This is a straightforward explanation, Duale. The main thing for you, I would suggest, is that you understand the function of a VOR and how it is used. Are you with me so far?'

'Thank you, Joe. Yes, I think I understand. Perhaps sometime, with your advice, I should read some more. But thank you; now tell me something about the ILS'.

'Right, here goes,' Joe responded. Duale could see that Joe was encouraged and stimulated by Duale's interest; Joe's eyes were positively twinkling behind his glasses.

'ILS means "instrument landing system". Several hundred have already been installed in the States. There are supposed to be a whole lot in developing countries as well; the problem is that they are expensive, and you often have to spend a lot of money preparing the installation site. Maintenance is also a problem. In certain respects, there are some similarities between the VOR and the ILS, certainly as far as the aircraft equipment is concerned; in fact, both systems may be incorporated in the same airborne receiver.

Basically, to find out the aircraft's position, by tuning the aircraft's receiver into the ILS transmitter, just like with the VOR, you can position the aircraft so that you can follow the ILS guidance signal into an airport, that is down to the runway threshold.

The ILS consists of three separate elements. There is the localizer for horizontal guidance, the glide path for vertical guidance and marker beacons, of which there are usually two, for approximate indications of distance to the runway threshold. The localizer signal can usually be received about 30 miles from the airport. Now the glide path signal is radiated from an antenna beside the runway in the vicinity of the touch-down point. The angle of descent is usually three degrees. Finally, the marker beacons radiate a signal directly upwards and are installed on the approach to the runway. The outer and middle markers are located about four nautical miles and 3500 feet from the threshold. Don't worry about inner markers; they are rarely used.

The procedure for using the ILS is that the pilot first has to position the aircraft on the localizer approach to the runway, that is the localizer needle on his course deviation indicator has to be centralised. When the aircraft passes over the outer marker, a blue light flashes on the instrument panel; at this point he is four nautical miles to touchdown. This is where the glide path is intercepted. The pilot's job is to keep not only the localizer needle, but also the glide path needle centred. If he sees the glide path needle moving up from the centre, then the glide path is above the aircraft; if the needle is below, the glide path is below.

When the aircraft is over the middle marker, the amber light starts to flash; at this point, if the pilot is making a visual approach, he should have the runway in sight. The aircraft will be about 200 feet above the ground.

There are progressive categories of ILS capability. In each case, there is a minimum altitude by which time the pilot has to have the runway in sight so that he can land safely. If he does not see the runway by this altitude, then he can try again or simply divert to another airport. How are we doing, Duale?'

'Well, I hope! I have been so immersed in law for so many years, I don't think I have been paying attention properly. You work in another world, Joe. I suppose it's the same with the other fields. And somehow we all have to fit together – incredible! In any case, I think we have taken up enough time for one afternoon. Do you have any afterthoughts, Joe?'

Joe was quick to respond. 'Perhaps we can have a few more sessions. I'm going to need your support sometimes; the more you understand, the less time I have to take answering basic technical questions. So you see it's a two-way thing; it's in my interest too! We could talk about distance measuring equipment (DME), which is usually used in conjunction with the VOR. There is also the automatic direction finder (ADF), not to mention radar. Then we should talk a little about inertial navigation systems, which of course do not depend on NAVAIDS. Anyway, thank you for listening so patiently, Duale; I'll let you have a short list of readable books.'

Duale shook hands with Joe and smiled. Just as he reached the door, Duale heard Joe's crisp voice.

'Duale, it was so silly of me; I just forgot. Could you give me another five minutes? Just sit down; I want to quickly explain something that is very important.'

Duale dutifully returned to his seat. 'Of course, go ahead, Joe!'

'I am sorry, I forgot.' Joe looked irritated with himself. 'Duale, this is very important. NAVAIDS can experience all sorts of problems; so remember, *they must be regularly calibrated and checked that they are working within their tolerances*! They all have what you might call built-in accuracy problems; for example, even when it is perfectly maintained and calibrated, a VOR station may give an error of upto 2 degrees. Well, one can live with that (and in fact it is permitted). But if these equipments get seriously out of calibration, depending how long they are left they can become dangerously inaccurate, *even potential killers.* Imagine coming out of low cloud on the glide path of an ILS and you can't see the runway, or you are way off the approach! Equipment has to be regularly calibrated, Duale, and it needs good maintenance. There are too many ILS glide paths which are somehow not working properly. Part of the problem, Duale, is that a lot of developing countries don't have the right technical staff; and they can't afford the hard currency to pay for the cost of flight calibration. It comes quite expensive because you need a specially-equipped aircraft to flight test the installations. So you see, there are two sides to the coin. The NAVAIDS are an enormous help if you are looking for enhancement of flight safety; but if they are not calibrated or maintained properly, you can be very dangerously deceived. I am a realist, Duale. I want you to be part of the real world!'

And so these learning sessions progressed. By the beginning of 1973 Duale was altogether more knowledgeable across the spectrum of civil aviation, his confidence supported by what he had learned. He had followed up on his sessions with Joe Wilkins by following a similar approach with other divisions. Now he was conversant with air traffic control procedures, radar, airworthiness, flight safety operations, airport design and construction, licensing, search and rescue, as well as protection of aircraft against unlawful interference, a field which was rapidly increasing in importance as acts of aviation terrorism and sabotage became more frequent.

He would never pretend to be an expert in any of these fields; after all, Duale was an aviation lawyer. But now he could speak quite knowledgeably on many aviation subjects and in discussion he even impressed the specialists by his succinct, intelligent interventions.

Once the technical subjects had been covered, he turned his attention to air transport economics and statistics. He pored over graphs which showed growth trends and he was amazed how fast airline traffic was growing throughout the world, especially in the oil-rich countries and in Asia. He read various studies and wondered where it would all end. Would the system be able to cope with the huge expansion which was in progress?

Over the ensuing years, Duale's professional reputation steadily increased. He had excellent supportive contacts within TASS; members of the Executive Committee appreciated his clear, persuasive explanations. Outside, he represented TASS in an exemplary manner, gaining much respect through contributions of his detailed knowledge on a wide range of complex legal questions. In general terms, he had become the star director of TASS.

Towards the end of 1976, the CEO's secretary called him to enquire whether he might be free the following morning for a discussion with the CEO; naturally, Duale would be there at the appointed time. Such discussions were not uncommon. It was normal that the subject to be discussed would be mentioned beforehand, so that Duale could prepare for his meeting. Since on this occasion, however, he had no inkling of what would be discussed, Duale enquired whether he should prepare for any subject in particular. 'No,' was the quick response from the secretary, 'the CEO prefers to wait till tomorrow, when you meet.' As Duale replaced the receiver, he briefly thought that the secretarial voice had seemed familiar; within a second or two he had reverted to his work.

'Come in, Duale.' Al Willis was smiling as he shook Duale's hand. Duale thought how the CEO was aging. He looked more than his 62 years; and his complexion seemed even more ruddy than usual. Duale hoped that Al Willis was not experiencing heart problems; he was definitely overweight.

'Let's sit over at the table; would you like some coffee?' Al pressed a floor button, and within a minute a tray of coffee and biscuits, which the Americans called 'cookies,' was brought in by the secretary. Al Willis thanked his secretary. 'It's a pleasure, sir,' was the relaxed response. Duale looked up straight into the blue eyes of Anna; her eyes were twinkling and they seemed to open a little more widely as she calmly returned his surprised stare. He swallowed and consciously tried to collect himself; he began to feel physically uncomfortable. Then she was gone. Duale turned his head towards Al Willis, who seemed the personification of good humour and benevolence.

'Pretty woman, don't you think?'

'Definitely!,' Duale responded.

Al's expression suddenly became serious, almost grave; Duale looked at him expectantly. Al raised his head and he seemed to look down at Duale. Then he said, 'Duale, I know that when we talk from time to time, everything that we discuss is strictly confidential; I know that and so do you. I hope you won't mind me mentioning it, but I want you to be very careful that what we talk about today remains our secret.' Duale nodded, his facial expression reflecting the seriousness of the CEO.

'Now let me come to the point. First, I should explain that I want to use you as a sounding board; I feel lonely and I need to have a dialogue with someone I can trust. Unfortunately, I don't trust everyone on our Executive Committee. How we selected that fellow-American of mine I don't know; between us, all I know is that we made a mistake. Richard Spargel sounds so friendly and inoffensive; but I tell you, Duale, Richard Spargel is quite the opposite – as far as I am concerned, he is a pain in the neck! No offence, Duale,' Al Willis' mouth became less taut as he smiled briefly, 'but the man is a mid west lawyer with a smattering of American aviation knowledge; but really hopeless when we get into the international field. He has no concept of what is happening internationally. And all he does is give me a hard time. I think he has a line to the government; what he passes on, God knows. But I doubt that it's good.

I've been bringing myself upto date with some recent statistics. You know, Duale, aviation is going to burst at the seams. We keep telling the Third World to find some financing and get their aviation house in order. Well, it's not happening. Aviation can't rely on consultants reports. The world has to stop playing games. Something has to be done. And the big aircraft manufacturers are continuously planning new aircraft with more complex systems. I am very worried. We are totally stretched, but as you know it is not only a question of getting the right equipment in place; you need trained professional manpower. Even after a few years of training, the man is only trained; after that he needs experience.

Incidentally, I have got a consultancy firm looking at plans for a new building for TASS. We are also bursting! I am sure we'll need it in a year or two; but that's another matter.

To get back to the subject of safety. Have you any ideas, Duale? We can't expect much real help from the international organizations; they're quite good at rule-making, but what's the point if there is less-than-adequate implementation.'

There was a silence which lasted about a half-minute. Duale stared thoughtfully at the CEO's table. Then he spoke.

'First, please don't worry about this discussion getting any further; it won't! Second, I agree with your general assessment; safety can't be achieved on paper and there has to be implementation. If there is no financing for a developing country, there's not much anyone can do, unless we want to actually use our trust money in extenuating circumstances. I would advise against that; how do you judge and where will it end – possibly it would eventually mean the end of TASS, which would be self-defeating.

Perhaps we should set up a small working group within TASS and assess the progress of our projects. At the same time, we could survey each developing country and at least give them a blueprint showing what they need to do on a priority basis. Perhaps we should get into the financing business. Half the time, the developing countries don't seem to understand what a development bank needs in the way of documentation to support a loan.'

'Thank you, Duale. I'll consider what you have said; and if you get any more good ideas, feel free to share them with me. Now I want to move to a bit of detail.' Duale had thought that the discussion was over; but he was quite wrong. The CEO poured some more coffee and settled into his chair. After a few moments, he went on.

'During the last week, I received two similar letters. In fact, I thought it was a remarkable co-incidence. One is from Viet Nam and the other from North Korea, the so-called Democratic People's Republic of Korea. Both of the letters are asking for TASS's help.' Al Willis opened a folder on the table and glanced over the letters.

'Yes, as I was saying, Duale, these countries need help. As far as Viet Nam is concerned, the US pulled out about three years ago. As you know, this year the country was declared united under the communists. Now they have all sorts of plans. Apparently, one of their top priorities is to regain control of the airspace which they lost during the war; their airspace was distributed between other countries in south east Asia. And then they have the problem with those off-shore islands, the Spratly's. Last year they occupied six

64

of them; but it's only a matter of time before the Chinese will weigh in against the Vietnamese and try to displace them. Although we have nothing to do with politics, we can hardly ignore what is a very delicate situation.

When we come to North Korea, we have a quite different situation. Because of the division of Korea, everything is duplicated in the north and south. So there are two air traffic control systems, two airlines and so forth – everything is doubled. It becomes even more complicated when you realize that in the south they follow the American system, by and large, whereas in the north everything depends on the USSR systems-approach. It's all very complicated; and I must say again full of politics, especially when you look at the Chinese involvement.

Because of air traffic control problems between north and south, apparently, North Korea wants to bring its aviation system upto the international standard. Then they can bargain with the south, and with the Chinese and Japanese, so that their airspace will be used on direct flights. Of course, that will be a political settlement and TASS is not involved with that; in any case, it will be years before some type of agreement is reached. But for the North Koreans the first step is to get their civil aviation house in order; and I suppose that's why they have written to us.

Now Duale, how are we going to handle this? Normally, we would draft a summary paper for the Executive Committee and the committee would agree that we go ahead. But my own feeling is that this time round things are different. To be blunt, I am not sure how our American friend would react. I am afraid he is somehow political – with connections in Washington. The Viet Nam pull-out by the US is still very fresh in their memories. Remember the US lost nearly 50,000 men, with more than 300,000 wounded. Nobody knows precisely what the war cost, but estimates seem to indicate about $200 billion. I can imagine that at this point it might be anathema for an American to be involved with helping Viet Nam! I can also imagine a similar attitude towards North Korea; again it was the Americans who were mainly involved there.

I've been thinking pretty hard about how to handle this, Duale. My conclusion is that we should get on with it and tell the committee afterwards. We are responding within our mandate and we are apolitical. So why not get on with it; what do you think?'

Duale did not hesitate, 'I agree! When it will come to picking up the pieces with the committee, you will certainly have my support.'

'Good!' Al Willis looked relieved and more relaxed. 'Duale, I would like you to go to these countries and review with them what type of assistance they need from TASS. Since the main focus is bound to centre on an air traffic control centre and navigational aids, I think you should have the Head of Communications to help you; Joe Wilkins is a good man. Ensure he keeps quiet about the visits, but you don't need to tell him why. He must keep quiet. I will have a word later with his division director and give him a little background; you can approach Joe Wilkins directly.'

Duale was slightly taken aback. He had thought he was being consulted. Without having been asked, now he had been told that he would be the TASS man to go to these countries. What should he say; could he question the CEO's decision. And if everything went wrong down the line with the Executive Committee, who would be sacrificed? These thoughts flashed in succession through his quick brain. After a few seconds, Duale responded.

'My understanding is that you would like me to lead visits to Viet Nam and North Korea. These are very difficult countries! Right, I will make all the arrangements and we will do our best for TASS. Whatever the result, all we can do is our best.'

Al flushed a little, then smiled as he pushed a bell button. Anna was immediately standing over the two men. Duale could not resist looking at her. He had loved her physically when she was in her early twenties; now she was about 40. Duale was almost mesmerized by her perfectly formed body, enclosed as it was by a navy blue dress set off by a pretty white collar. His eyes briefly met hers; he would never forget those twinkling blue eyes.

Al broke the silence, 'Anna, Dr. Duale and Mr. Joe Wilkins will be travelling to Viet Nam and North Korea. When Dr. Duale has finalized the arrangements with the civil aviation people, he will ask you to organize the air tickets. In conjunction with the travel people would you personally make sure that the ticketing is done properly, please. We don't want any publicity; in fact, at this stage we would like the arrangements to be secret. I know I can rely on you, Anna.'

'I quite understand, sir. Dr. Duale, when you are ready please let me know what needs to be done. Thank you.' Before Duale could reply, Anna had left the office.

'Well, Duale, all I can say is good luck and thank you for supporting TASS without even raising a question. I shall look forward to discussing your report when you get back. Thank you for your time. Good-bye Duale.'

As Duale left the CEO's office he briefly turned and smiled. Again he was struck by that flushed countenance; he wished the CEO would have looked healthier.

Duale strode through the secretary's office and out into the corridor; he had expected his head to be full of thoughts on what he had just heard. But expectations do not always match the reality. Although there was no sign of Anna in the office, there was no escape in Duale's imagination. All he could see in his mind's eye was Anna – in her lace pants.

Chapter Six

Duale's Proving Ground

Duale was soon back in his office. He had never been a nervous man, as far as he knew. But now things seemed to be different. He felt a tingling in his body; he recognized that his thoughts should be focusing on his important trip to North Korea and Viet Nam. Instead, his head was filled with thoughts of Anna; he tried to erase her smiling face and twinkling blue eyes from his imagination. If anything, her image became stronger. Duale paced from one side of his office to the other, his excitement only briefly relieved by the beautiful colours of the Persian carpet in front of his desk. Then he stopped and looked out of the window across the city's skyscrapers; on that clear winter's day, some way away he could see the icy waters of Lake Michigan. He must return to normality; what should he do?

At this point his secretary, Mary Piggott, entered his office. 'You were a long time with the CEO; I am sure we are going to be busy. Just let me know when you need me, Dr. Duale.'

'Thank you, Mary. As usual you're quite right. We will be getting a couple of important letters away. But I have some thinking to do first.' Handing Mary copies of the letters which the CEO had received from North Korea and Viet Nam, he added, 'Could you open a couple of secret files with these, please, Mary. Be very careful the files are handled secretly. Probably tomorrow we can send responses and we'll see where we get to. Could you close the door, please. I have to think!'

Duale did not think for long. His priority was Anna. He called her number.

'Yes – er Anna. I'm not sure what to say. I just wanted to hear your voice. I feel very confused; I – er...'

Anna's voice was clear as a bell. Unlike Duale, she sounded totally composed and in control:

'It's good to hear your voice, Dr. Duale, and I'm happy you called. Surely, you're not ready with your itinerary yet, are you?'

'No, Anna. I just got back to my office. I felt I had to talk to you.' Then he blurted out, 'I was wondering if you might be free for dinner tomorrow evening. I discovered a very nice restaurant near the top of a skyscraper. There's a lovely view at night. Would you like to have dinner?'

There was a long pause; then Anna's voice crisply responded, 'I should love to.'

The following evening Anna and Duale met at the entrance to the Casablanca restaurant, high up on the 60th floor of a huge skyscraper. When Duale caught sight of Anna, his first reaction was to hug her and tell her that he worshipped her. As it was, he tried to rein in his impetuosity; he hesitated and just looked at her. As her coat slipped off her bare shoulders, he admired her beautiful form clothed in a gorgeous sand-coloured dress, which enhanced every contour of her perfect body. When she turned and smiled at him, he found himself glancing in admiration at her blond hair. His eyes suddenly made contact with Anna's blue eyes. They were twinkling.

As Anna smiled at him, in a relaxed way she said, 'It's quite like old times, don't you think Duale? I'm sure you have reserved a nice table with a lovely view. Shall we go in? You haven't changed much in twenty years. I suppose we have quite a lot to talk about.'

Over dinner Anna and Duale talked. Duale's appetite centred more on Anna than the sumptuous food which was offered by the restaurant. Did she know how he felt? He gently squeezed her hand. He received a glimpse of a smile in return. 'Anna,' he whispered, as though he might choke 'I can't eat. I feel like eating you! I can't help it.'

He looked at Anna adoringly and said quite firmly, 'Please come home with me. I'll never let you go again!'

Anna smiled gently and her eyes met Duale's. Then she said, 'I am afraid, Duale, that would not be appropriate. You see, twelve years ago I was married to the man of my dreams. I have two children, both of whom already go to school. My husband is adorable and the more we are together, the more we love each other. He's very handsome. He's about ten years younger than you. I always enjoyed younger men; usually they are much more virile! I would have brought him along this evening, but he happens to be away till tomorrow. You and I also had a great time together. But things move on. Now I am in a totally different situation.'

Duale looked out across the city night scene. A moment before, the view had seemed so romantic and he and Anna had, as far as he was concerned, been part of it. Now he felt ridiculous. The tingling had left him and he felt limp. At this stage, he was no longer confused. 'Thank you for spending time with me, Anna. I'll see you to a taxi.'

'Thank you for such a nice meal, Duale; I love seafood. I always liked talking to you. We sometimes hear that women can be unpredictable. Well, men are not always predictable either. There's only one thing that I find is predictable about men in general; that is they always want to sleep with a woman, as though they have a right to do it. It seems to be a sport. You're still at it! Before I leave you, may I say one thing?.'

'Well of course,' Duale responded.

'I want to say, Duale, that when you become CEO I hope I will be able to stay in my current job as your secretary. I love what I am doing. I have no hard feelings against you, Duale. I would love to work with you again. And I mean work, only work Duale!'

Duale looked confused again; this time, however, it was a quite different type of confusion. 'I don't understand,' he said, 'What makes you think I might become CEO. The question simply doesn't arise, Anna. Or do you have some secret information up your sleeve?'

As Anna got up from the table, she smiled again and looked straight at Duale. 'You have always been ambitious and you know you are very highly thought of. You're used to getting what you want. Have you ever heard of a woman's intuition? This evening, Duale, you have it! Don't ask me when, but be prepared.'

Soon Duale found himself alone in his apartment. 'Well,' he thought, 'I have made an unholy mess of that. I hope we do better with North Korea and Viet Nam!' But he soon realised that, in basic terms, his judgement had been right. He had put first things first. Certainly, he had made an idiot of himself and he hoped his stupidity would be known only to Anna and himself. In any case, now he could give all his attention to his secret mission, which he did.

In January of 1977, Duale made a visit to Anna's office to give her the itinerary, so that he and Joe Wilkins would arrive and depart in North Korea and Viet Nam on schedule. Because he wanted to consult an arbitration specialist in Geneva, he asked for ticketing on the return leg via Geneva. As Anna was finalising her notes the CEO appeared in the doorway.

'Progress, Duale? Everything arranged? When do you start?'

'We have been exchanging letters and telexes,' Duale replied. 'The visits will start in mid February. I have briefed Joe Wilkins and he has done an excellent job getting background information. We are quite confident. Let's keep our fingers crossed!'

Al Willis smiled and shook Duale's hand; then he spoke with a quiet, somehow distant, voice directly into Duale's ear, 'Good luck, Duale. I shall be thinking of you in mid February.' Then he was gone. Duale briefly thought how overweight Al Willis had become; and his face was much too flushed. He should definitely see a doctor.

It seemed that mid February was upon Duale and Joe Wilkins much too soon. As they flew on their first leg to Tokyo, both were immersed for most of the 12 hours' flight in bulky briefing files which each had pieced together. On arrival in Tokyo, they stayed overnight in the Prince Hotel at Narita.

Feeling rested the following morning, they were soon sitting in an aircraft of the Chinese People's Republic *en route* to Beijing. After they had embarked, Duale glanced through the Tokyo Times, an English-language daily newspaper which had been pushed under his door in the hotel. At the bottom of the front page was a small paragraph, which read:

TASS On The Move

A two-man team from the Trust For Air Safety Support (TASS), based in Chicago, is about to visit the Democratic People's Republic of Korea (North Korea) and the Socialist Republic of Viet Nam. Although the purpose of the mission has not been officially notified, it is understood that these countries intend to upgrade their civil aviation facilities and services. It is anticipated that TASS will assist them with planning and installation of new equipment; training will also be covered in any consultancy advice offered.

Sitting in the aircraft, as the captain set his heading for the first leg to Beijing, Duale felt bemused. He showed the newspaper to Joe Wilkins, commenting 'I love secret missions don't you, Joe? I wonder, I really wonder, where they got this from! For God's sake, don't tell the CEO about this; he'd have a fit, poor devil!'

Now the captain had the single runway of Beijing's Capital Airport in sight. Soon they would land. As they entered the passenger terminal, two well-dressed young Chinese stepped forward and greeted Duale and Joe Wilkins,

'Good morning, Dr. Duale. Welcome to the Chinese People's Republic. We understand you will stay in Beijing for two nights. Normally, we like to entertain our guests; in fact, we had wanted to take you tomorrow to see the Great Wall. However, we have been asked by our superiors to request that you attend meetings tomorrow, as our administration may wish to enter into a co-operation agreement with TASS at a later stage. Tonight you will stay at the Peace Hotel. We will take you there now and pick you up at nine tomorrow morning.'

Duale wanted to ask how his 'secret' mission had, apparently, become public knowledge. But he decided to keep quiet. It might be better to see how things worked out, he thought.

The following morning the car arrived at precisely nine o'clock and within fifteen minutes Duale and Joe Wilkins had reached the government building where the meetings would take place; standing on the steps were two officials, who welcomed the visitors. As on all occasions of this type, Duale was impressed by the punctuality and accomplished courtesy of the Chinese hosts. The relaxed atmosphere even extended to the meeting room. Contrary to normal routine, there was no long table across which the Chinese and their guests confronted one another. Instead, the visitors were asked to sit close to the chairman in comfortable easy chairs; the Chinese also sat around the room in armchairs. All of the Chinese were dressed in tunics which were buttoned to their stiff collars; most wore grey, although Duale noticed two men who were dressed in dark blue uniforms.

The meetings went well and served to provide each side with the opportunity to explain how the Chinese, on the one hand, saw the main challenges facing civil aviation development, and how TASS, on the other, was responding to requests from the Third

World for support in the civil aviation sector. Duale was struck by the openness of the Chinese, linked with a lively sense of humour. At one stage the chairman went into some detail on the subject of the acquisition of air transport passenger aircraft, explaining that the Chinese were in the process of buying some 500 passenger transport aircraft. Then he let out a bellow of a laugh, adding, 'You know, we are a developing country and we are hopeless when it comes to human infrastructure. We will never have enough professionally qualified people. But somehow we have to operate those aircraft; we always say in China that we are used to doing the impossible. I hope we can, otherwise we are going to have a lot of accidents! Then, as I am sure you know, we have the airspace problem. The military keeps most of it; so the passenger aircraft have to fly all over the place to avoid the areas reserved for the military. And we have to keep quiet! Nobody dares to ask the military to give us some more airspace.'

After several hours, the meetings ended and Duale returned to the hotel with Joe Wilkins. He had asked the chairman to write to TASS to confirm the discussions; if they wished, the Chinese could request some assistance from TASS.

The visitors had been told by the interpreter to relax in preparation for the flight to Pyongyang the following morning; they would be picked up at 7.30. Duale decided to take a taxi and drive around the centre of Beijing. The driver spoke only Chinese. The receptionist of the Peace hotel then wrote various names in Chinese on a scrap of paper, which was handed to the driver. The first stop was the bank.

'I need to change a hundred US dollars into yuan, please,' Duale asked the man behind the counter. 'That is very much money!' the man responded. 'You must be here for many days; it will take a long time to spend all that money,' he added.

'Well,' Duale answered, looking slightly mystified, 'in that case, let me start with fifty'.

After about five minutes, the man returned with the biggest heap of money Duale had ever seen; the man also placed a canvas bag on the counter. Duale looked at the enormous pile of paper with incredulity; then he said, 'There must be larger denominations; I can't possibly carry all that around.'

The man was unimpressed, 'These are your yuan and you must

remove them immediately; if necessary you can use this bag. If you find the amount inconvenient, when you get to your hotel leave the money on a table and take an amount as you need it each day. There is no problem.'

'And if it gets stolen?' Duale asked. The response was short and to the point, 'This is the People's Republic of China; we are communists! The money will never be stolen. There is nothing to worry about! Please take the money away!'

Resigned to the unexpected situation, Duale left and continued on his taxi journey. He briefly visited the Forbidden City, Tiananmen Square, the fifteenth century Temple of Heaven and other tourist attractions, before returning to the Peace hotel. As he left his taxi he offered the driver a tip; he was surprised to find himself on the receiving end of a growling rebuke, as the driver forcefully handed him minute receipts for the fare.

As he entered the hotel, Duale asked the receptionist whether it was safe to leave some money in his room, stacked on a table. 'And why not? This is the People's Republic of China!' was the mystified response.

Duale then noticed a European-looking man next to him. He looked ill, and was trying to support himself on the reception counter. His lips were quivering and his eyes stared vaguely in Duale's direction. Duale tried in vain to judge whether the man, who seemed to be on the point of fainting, was actually focusing on him. The man whispered weakly, 'Please help me. I think I am dying. Please get me to a hospital'.

With the assistance of the receptionist, Duale helped the man into a taxi and soon they were *en route* to a hospital.

Later that evening, Duale was sitting with Joe Wilkins in the hotel dining room. As they were picking at a grilled fish which was floating in a thick broth, they were joined by the man who a few hours earlier had announced that he was on the point of death. Duale looked at him and noticed his pink cheeks and lively eyes. 'So you survived after all? Congratulations! I didn't expect to see you again,' Duale said. The man smiled, 'I just want to thank you. I am German; my name is Hans Spitz and I have been trying to do some business here for three years. If you are doing the same, be careful! The Chinese are charming; they will get every piece of information out of you and then they will go their own way. You can invest a lot of money here; but in the end they will cut you out! I have even talked to them about it. They say they were used, corrupted and exploited for hundreds of years. Now it is their turn; yes, they told me that.

I heard you are aviation people. You probably know they are having accidents in this country. Did you hear they lost another 'plane last week? It was an internal flight. Everybody was killed. They always try to cover it up. It's a disgrace! I have met a few foreigners who refuse to fly; they prefer to take the train because they think it is safer.'

Duale's interest quickened; perhaps this was good advice. Then he said, 'How did you survive in the hospital, Hans?'

'Well,' Hans Spitz answered, 'I told them I had just left the train after a two days' journey from the north. I explained that the train people had switched off the heating. Somehow they got mixed up between February and April. Anyway, they turned off the heating two months early. All the passengers felt they would freeze. The train people said it was regulations; and the heating stayed off! When you got me to the hospital, they gave me acupuncture. And here I am!'

Duale listened to the story in amazement. On reaching his room he was even more astonished to find his pile of money totally intact. Certainly, a room attendant had closed his curtains, pulled down his bed covers and filled the thermos with boiling water; and his money was still there. His level of confidence in the honesty of his Chinese guests rose tremendously. The following morning, after paying his bill, he even considered leaving his unspent cash with the cashier for safe-keeping until he returned to Beijing a week later, when he would be in transit to Viet Nam. 'No problem,' was the instant response.

Sitting in the small departure lounge, Duale looked around the grubby room. He was left in no doubt that he had little in common with his fellow passengers; there were about 40 of them and they were all men. Most were thick set and they wore heavy overcoats; by their sides were their fur hats. They whispered or spoke in hushed tones, as they anxiously looked around to make sure that others would not hear what they were saying. To Duale watching their facial expressions, several looked sinister.

Soon the passengers were sitting in the turboprop which had

been designed and manufactured in the USSR. As the engines roared on the runway threshold, Duale briefly eyed a Chinese daily. At the bottom of the first page was a small report:

Aircraft Crashes In West Africa
A Russian-built turboprop aircraft exploded during take-off in West Africa two days ago. It is understood that maintenance procedures in this part of the world have been the subject of recent criticism.

Duale instantly decided that he should discontinue reading the daily.

Looking out of the aircraft's small window, Duale was reminded of a beautiful tapestry which he had seen the previous day. Below him, the vast, gently undulating, light green landscape was veiled by the early morning mist; its grandeur and serenity were beyond description.

The ultimate beauty of what he was looking at from his moving perch masked the reality of the human struggle being played out by the invisible inhabitants below. Did those people, armed with Mao's Little Red Book, know where they were heading? When they reached their goal, which their government seemed to treat as a moving target, would they be happier? Or would there be more strife, followed by the sacrifice of millions of lives? The thoughts passed through Duale's mind, but he knew he could only be an observer. And if he were a good TASS man, then he should always make sure his attitude was apolitical.

After crossing a part of Korea Bay, which was the northern section of the Yellow Sea, the little turboprop was soon on the approach to Pyongyang airport. After a steep descent, the wheels of the aircraft hit the runway hard and the pilot seemed to race to the apron where the passengers would disembark. 'He didn't exactly grease the aircraft on to the runway, did he?' Duale asked Joe Wilkins.

'No,' Joe replied, 'this is a sign of a military pilot. They often seem to be trained like this.'

As Duale and Joe Wilkins walked down the steps to the apron, a small group of well-dressed Koreans approached them; all were wearing black suits and, to their side, a photographer was pointing a movie camera directly at Duale and Joe Wilkins.

'Welcome to our country. You are Dr. Duale and this is Mr. Wilkins. I am Li Sok and I represent our government's foreign relations. Welcome; please follow me to the VIP lounge.'

Soon the group was sitting in easy chairs in the lounge. Close to each chair was a small table; a large red apple had been placed on each. 'Please relax and eat your apple; tea and biscuits will be served shortly. This is the programme. You will shortly be transported to the Pyongyang Hotel. At 6p.m. this evening we will have a formal meeting, after which we will entertain you and offer you dinner. Tomorrow you will be picked up at 8a.m. and we will show you our facilities. Please understand that all our communications and antenna equipment is for use to facilitate our work and interchange with Moscow. However, our Great Leader Kim Il Sung has decided that our perfect democracy should adjust to the current world, and that we should seek to exchange information and improve our communications with other countries. TASS is apolitical and we are non-aligned, so we should work well together. Now the cars are here to take you to the hotel.'

Duale and Joe Wilkins stepped outside and saw a waiting car. Mr. Li lowered his head to speak to the guests, 'Mr. Wilkins, please travel in the next car. Each of you will have an interpreter, who is also your guide; there is not sufficient room for all in one car.' Duale and Joe Wilkins soon learned that they would never travel together; it was the government's policy that the two visitors would be denied the opportunity to converse during their various journeys.

Although the journey to the hotel was uneventful, Duale was surprised that there was so little traffic to be seen. He also noticed that there were two white lines stretching down the centre of the road; looking towards the kerb, he could see another white line. He asked his interpreter, Mr. Guk, why the car seemed to travel between the crown of the road and the side line. 'Oh, this is quite simple. Well, let me say it is simple for us because we live in a perfect democracy. The centre lines are reserved for the Great Leader; the next lane is for our honoured guests, like yourself. Then the lane near the kerb is reserved for our own people. They are humble and they must travel near the side of the road.'

The hotel was a large, sombre building. Duale concluded that the plan was Russian. He followed Mr. Li and Mr. Guk up the sweeping staircase and along a wide corridor. When Duale's room was reached, Mr. Li smiled and looked up at a large red insignia over the door, 'Do you know what that means, Dr. Duale? I hope you do.' Before Duale could confess his ignorance, Mr. Li said, 'That sign shows that the Great Leader slept in this room. We have asked for this room so that your head will rest on the same pillow as the one used by the Great Leader! We want you to have inspirational thoughts. Imagine your thoughts on that pillow! You should go to lunch in 30 minutes. Mr. Wilkins is in room 114.'

Duale unpacked a few clothes and looked around his bedroom. He soon discovered that a sitting room adjoined the bedroom; he would have the use of a television and a telephone. He dialled 114 and hoped to hear the voice of Joe Wilkins. Instead, he was immediately confronted with his flustered interpreter, who had burst into his room.

'What are you doing; you are not allowed to use the phone without permission!' Mr. Guk was addressing Duale in very firm tones.

'I thought it was time for lunch, so I was trying to call my colleague; if you don't want me to, then I won't,' Duale responded. Mr. Guk left the room, saying nothing.

'How strange,' Duale thought, 'so this is democracy. Perhaps I should visit Joe instead of trying to call him.' Duale strode to the door and stepped into the corridor. Immediately, the door of the next room opened. Again Mr. Guk confronted Duale.

'Where are you going?' he said. Duale gained the impression that every nerve in Mr. Guk's body had been put to the utmost strain.

'I want to find Mr. Wilkins,' Duale said.

'That is not necessary.' was the curt reply. 'Please follow me downstairs to the dining room.' A few minutes later, Duale was sitting at a table with Joe Wilkins. The two interpreters explained that the visitors would always use the same table and they should not make any form of contact with others in the dining room. Although invited, the interpreters, whom Duale now perceived as permanent watchdogs, did not join Duale at the table, but sat a few yards away; apparently, their job was to watch the guests. Duale and Joe spoke little over lunch as they tried to accustom themselves to their situation. At one point, Duale quietly observed, 'So now we know what real democracy is all about; it really is something extraordinary.'

During the next six days, the visits to various sites used for aviation services went well, and these were followed by seemingly endless meetings. Duale and Joe sat on one side of a long table, while on the other eight heads of various divisions raised an unending stream of technical and legal questions. The Koreans were dressed in airforce uniform, and Duale found it intriguing that without exception, all kept their military caps on during the meetings. Each member of the Korean team remained unsmiling throughout; from time to time Duale thought that he would never forget this row of dark brown, chiselled faces. As he looked in turn at each countenance, he noticed the high cheekbones. When he looked at their eyes, they usually seemed to look straight ahead; but sometimes he was suddenly taken off guard as they fixed on him with a hard stare.

Duale and Joe Wilkins, always required to travel separately, were each treated to some aspect of North Korean propaganda. There were many references to the Great Leader, Kim Il Sung, and his wonderful exploits in ridding the country of the vile Japanese, who had plundered Korea over the centuries, and had colonised the country for 36 years in the twentieth century. No mention was ever made of the years spent by the Great Leader in the USSR, where he was trained in preparation for his take-over of the government of North Korea.

Sometimes the interpreters lectured the visitors on the significance of the oval, round or square badges bearing the face of the Great Leader, worn on the lapels of senior officials. Whenever the cars stopped, Duale could hear marching music or choirs singing victory songs relayed over loudspeakers; the martial music was aimed at exhorting the workers to greater efforts to reconstruct the mother country after the hideous attacks of the Americans. Pyongyang had been reduced to rubble, and would need to be almost completely rebuilt. With the help and foresight of the Great Leader, agriculture and industry would be revitalised. And so it went on.

After five days, Duale could not escape the feeling that these people were living in a make-believe fantasy land; since their birth they had been told about the Great Leader, and how their country had been liberated from dreadful aggressors. By the time they became adults, they had been thoroughly brainwashed; they lived in the promised land of equality and the application of democratic values. The people should feel grateful for the gift of the perfect life, a life which in time could only blossom in ultimate self-fulfilment. And all of this was made possible only through the efforts of the Great Leader!

At last, the interminable meetings were approaching their end. Duale had produced a draft agreement setting out the framework of assistance to be provided by TASS and the associated responsibilities of both the government and TASS. After some 15 hours of discussions, both sides acknowledged there were three points on which, apparently, a meeting of minds could not be reached.

At this point the chairman abruptly adjourned the meeting. He announced that at midnight the guests would be picked up by a black car and escorted to the railway station, where they would be put on a train. Eight hours later they would awake in the beautiful fir-tree covered mountains, and would be shown the Great Leader's personal museum. What they would see would reflect the love and respect of the international community for the Great Leader. Valuable presents had been offered to him from heads of state from all over the world, displayed over the vast area of the museum on two floors. Because the Great Leader was not only of humble disposition, but also generous, the entire museum collection had been given by him to the people. When they entered the huge, high gold-emblazoned doors, a broad crimson carpet would lead them to a 10-metre high bronze statue of the Great Leader, the almighty Kim Il Sung. This would be a sight never to be forgotten.

After two days of eating and living healthily in the wonderful mountain air, they would return to Pyongyang, refreshed in mind and body, and with new ideas. The agreement would then be finalised to everyone's satisfaction.

Duale felt nervous, but tried to remain calm. He had no wish to be 'lost' without trace in the mountains of North Korea. If he did not return, what could anyone do to find him?

'Mr. Chairman,' Duale responded, 'we are deeply grateful to you personally for proposing a privilege which I am sure is extended to only a few. We would love to make this interesting excursion to admire the museum of the Great Leader. Unfortunately, we have certain commitments and appointments in other countries.'

Cleverly, Duale then gave way on the main sticking point, proposing a compromise which he hoped the Koreans would accept, and which at the same time TASS could live with. If the Koreans would accept this gesture of goodwill on the part of TASS, then he hoped the Koreans would agree to TASS's position on the remaining lesser points. Within fifteen minutes the agreement was finalised for signature, which would take place the following morning at the airport, before the departure of the TASS team.

Duale woke at 6 o'clock the following morning, the day of departure for the TASS team. He felt claustrophobic and frustrated. For five days he had been escorted or shadowed by a guide, his movements controlled by others. Then there were the military; they seemed to control everything. He thought how shocked he had been in the meeting room when he had raised the subject of North Korea's civil aviation law. The chairman had simply replied, 'We do not know what you are referring to, Dr. Duale; we only have military regulations for aviation.'

What a relief it would be to re-enter a normal world. In comparison with North Korea, China was a paradise of freedom, he thought. He ruminated on the limitations imposed on his movements. For example, he had noticed a parapet from his window, and had been told that there was a beautiful river which passed close to the hotel. His request to see it had been denied. As he pondered in the darkness of his room, he first became restless and then obsessed with the idiocy of a system which professed freedom and practised exactly the opposite. Yes, before leaving Pyongyang Duale would see that river!

Duale quietly left his bed and pulled on some clothes in the darkness; there was no sign of dawn yet. He quietly opened his door and crept along the corridor – and stopped. Would Mr. Guk suddenly appear? There was no sign of him. Duale reached the stairs and lightly descended to the hotel's main doors; would they be open? He pushed and felt the fresh February air on his cheeks. He walked for a half minute to the side of the hotel. And he looked over the parapet.

His eyes rested on the gently flowing river for a few seconds; as he glanced at the far bank he could just make out some over-hanging branches of the trees. Yes, he thought, it is a normal type of river. But the main thing is that I have seen it – of my own voli-tion! Before returning to the hotel, he looked over the skyline of Pyongyang, a city rebuilt in the Russian mould. The heavy archi-tecture, sometimes relieved by pretty, sweeping upturned Korean roofs, was certainly imposing. Across the river he could see a giant monument which showed the Great Leader liberating the Koreans from the terrible Japanese. The Great Leader held a sword aloft which, illuminated, struck a shaft of deep red through the dark-ness, no doubt to depict blood.

Now he should return. If Mr. Guk should be waiting to confront him, what would he say? Yes, he would state the fact; he had been looking at the river. Would Mr. Guk believe him? Why did he feel so nervous, rather as though he was a schoolboy playing truant? In his case, however, he had a dreadful feeling that the consequences might be much more serious.

Relieved, Duale was soon back in his room. Then there was a knock on the door. 'Good morning, Dr. Duale,' Mr. Guk said. 'We have a nice morning. I hope you slept well. Soon it will be time to leave. Please have you breakfast as soon as possible.'

Duale was suddenly nervous; it was only after a few seconds that he realized that he had not been caught after all.

Breakfast was soon over and now it was time for him and Joe to pack their suitcases. Duale first made sure all his papers were properly filed and neatly arranged in his large briefcase. Suddenly he felt somewhat confused; his papers were not at all as he had left them in his room before breakfast. Yes, someone had been looking for something and they had almost advertised their search by leaving his files hopelessly mixed up; perhaps they had been surprised by him returning to his room so quickly. He hoped there was no secret information inadvertently included with his papers.

There was a faint knock on the door. Duale wondered what Mr. Guk wanted this time. He opened the door; before he could react a stranger had entered his room. The man whispered, 'Put the TV on loudly!' Duale was not quite sure what he should do; but he acquiesced. Then the man approached him.

'I am a Russian. I asked for the noise because all these rooms are wired and bugged. They listen to everything and they record everything. I am Russian and I am a CIA agent. Be careful! If you give them a chance, they will grab all the new aviation equipment and they will never pay. They think that's good business! Make sure they pay before you start. I have a copy of your agreement. You must make it clearer, otherwise you will waste a lot of money. Do you understand?'

Duale suddenly realised that he was again on a learning curve; he was dealing with the unknown. What was this man doing? Why should a Russian know what had been discussed? How could he work for the CIA? Was it some sort of trap? It took Duale precisely two seconds to decide what to do. He strode to the door and opened it; he gestured to the impostor to leave. He was preparing to call Mr. Guk. Fortunately, this was unnecessary; the man left.

Shortly afterwards Duale was conducted to the office of the air marshal who supervised North Korea's aviation; no one referred to civil aviation, and it was impossible to differentiate between the civil and military. Duale had gained the impression that all functions seemed to be supervised by the military. Air Marshal Hyok was a genial man and smiled easily. On meeting him, Duale briefly wondered what it might have taken for the air marshal to reach his present position. It was 9 o'clock in the morning and the aircraft would leave at 10 a.m. for Beijing.

After welcoming Duale, the air marshal said, 'Dr. Duale, as you may expect I am fully informed on the agreement. I think it is a good one. Would you like some ginseng? We should drink to success!'

'Thank you, air marshal,' Duale responded, 'certainly we can drink some ginseng, although it is a little early for alcohol, I suggest. Before we drink, I would like to add in my handwriting a short sentence because it is important that there is no possibility of any misunderstanding.' Duale extended his arm, dragged the agreement in front of him and added:

'This agreement shall come into force only when the government of the Democratic Republic of North Korea has deposited United States dollars three million with the Trust for Air Safety Support'.

The interpreter immediately translated the sentence into Korean and passed what he had written to Air Marshal Hyok. The air marshal's eyes twinkled as he looked Duale in the eye. 'Let us have our ginseng in any case, Dr. Duale; after all, we may not have an agreement to sign! Chin chin!'

Duale looked at his watch. His flight would leave in thirty minutes. He said, 'Air marshal, what I have added is not new. We believe it should make the agreement clearer. Who knows, you or I may not be available if there are questions; and the agreement should be crystal clear. I have signed it on behalf of TASS, I hope you will now sign. My flight leaves in 30 minutes. To our success, air marshal!'

Air Marshal Hyok smiled gently at Duale.

'Dr. Duale, since the agreement was already quite clear, I see no reason to add your sentence; I think it is unfortunate you have already done this! I am not used to signing documents unless every sentence has been analyzed by us. I cannot now sign.'

Duale thought for a moment; so the Russian had been right. Once the payment condition was clearly spelled out, the Koreans would back away. Without hesitation Duale got up, shook the air marshal's hand, explained that the flight was about to leave and bade adieu. Air Marshal Hyok appeared to be not in the slightest perturbed and shook hands with a quick smile.

Now Duale was striding over the red carpet in the direction of the departure lounge; he half trotted, conscious of the time. At last he could see the solitary figure of Joe Wilkins; the remaining passengers had already embarked. The two of them walked briskly out of the terminal building on the airside and soon reached the mobile stairs which were adjacent to the aircraft; just behind them followed an interpreter. At the foot of the stairs, they heard a voice, 'Stop!' The interpreter said, 'The air marshal wishes to see you. Please follow me'.

'I am sorry, it is too late; the aircraft is leaving,' Duale replied.

'The aircraft is not leaving, Dr. Duale. Please come with me!' Duale suddenly noticed two soldiers with submachine guns standing on either side of him. Then the interpreter said, 'It is better, Dr. Duale, if you come with me – immediately!'

Duale obeyed. Within ten minutes he had returned to the aircraft, this time with the signed agreement in his hand. 'We seem to be dealing with a bunch of Arabs, Joe. Perhaps if I had told them I am half Arab myself, they would have co-operated more easily and the flight would have left on time'.

After staying for one night at the Peace Hotel in Beijing, where the cashier handed Duale the money which had been held in safe-keeping, the TASS team flew south to Guangzhou, which used to be known as Canton. Unlike the more rigid attitude found in Beijing, there was a certain gaiety in the atmosphere of the large city, a city famed for its commercial achievements, especially in its dealings with Hong Kong. Unlike the drab, uniform-like boxy clothing of those who lived further north, the women wore attrac-tive, brightly coloured dresses; Duale was enchanted by their good looks and innocent countenances. What a pity he had to concen-trate on his work; surely a man was entitled to a bit of fun, he thought. After all, with his Korean exploits behind him, he deserved it.

But it was not to be. Within a day Duale and Joe were to fly from Guangzhou to Hanoi. Compared with the Antonov turbo-prop, the jet operated by the Civil Aviation Administration of China was smooth and quiet. Effortlessly, the jet leapt into the atmosphere and the captain set his heading for Hanoi. Looking down, Duale could see the lush countryside of the lowlands as they followed the coastline, which extended west and then south westwards into Viet Nam. The green of the gently undulating landscape became a vast quilt, as huge cloud shadows or patchy showers of rain relieved the sunlit panorama. After about one and a half hours, as the aircraft decended into dense cloud Duale realised they were approaching Hanoi. The approach seemed interminable. From time to time he peered at the amorphous mass outside; he tried to focus on the end of the wing and he felt a faint surge of anxiety as he saw the wing tip obscured by the dense cloud. He turned to Joe Wilkins.

'Do you think the NAVAIDS are operating properly, Joe?'

'I doubt it!,' was Joe's quick response. 'For one thing they almost certainly haven't been calibrated for a year or two. And then, who knows, they may not have the electrical power to operate them, poor devils. Let's hope we make it! Ah, we're coming out of the cloud. It's pouring with rain; maybe he'll have to divert,' Joe added. Suddenly, there was a bump; and they were down.

'Another military pilot, another military landing,' Joe said in a resigned way.

When Duale and Joe Wilkins disembarked, their welcome was very different from what had awaited them in North Korea. They soon realized the fact; there was no one at all to greet them on the apron. They became part of the crowd of passengers which moved in the steady rain towards the terminal building; the scene made a deep impression of unrelenting gloom.

The inside of the building was a dirty cream colour and huge cracks marked the walls. Apparently there was no power, which meant that no lights illuminated the semi darkness. They noticed that the passengers were filling in customs and immigration forms; they followed suit. They entered the jostling crowd; like their fellow passengers, they tried to gain the attention of a customs official. At last it was their turn.

'You have written here that you have 500 US dollars. Show them to me,' said a small customs man.

Duale withdrew travellers cheques from his wallet. He was about to return the wallet to his pocket, when it was aggressively snatched from his hand.

'There are more travellers cheques here,' the man commented angrily. 'Come here! Take your jacket off and empty your pockets,' he continued. 'You have lied to an official of the Socialist Republic of Viet Nam; this is a serious offence. I find you have 565 US dollars and some money from the People's Republic of China. Write everything on this form; hurry up! Next time you will be imprisoned. And when you leave, make sure you are honest. You must show all receipts for what you have changed or spent. All right, now you can go through'.

The next hurdle was the immigration office. Here, the visitors were treated more politely and their passports were duly stamped. At this point Duale, peering through a large, dirt-covered window, could see a crowd of Vietnamese; some of its members had their faces pressed against the glass, producing a blurred effect. One of the figures seemed to be waving in the direction of Duale and Joe Wilkins. As they entered the passenger hall, the waving man walked up to them.

'I think you should be Dr. Duale; and you are Mr. Wilkins? Yes? My name is Do Dong; you can call me Mr. Do. I am from

Foreign Relations. We are pleased to see you and there is a lot of work to be done. We could not meet you outside because the military never let us through. They do not treat us well. I hope you have not been offended, Dr. Duale. We need TASS's help. There is no power at the airport because the municipality has switched it off; I suppose they need it themselves. Unfortunately, that means the ILS is not working; also, we have no money to buy fuel for the standby electricity generators. We will collect your suitcases shortly. Let us go to the car.'

As Duale looked at Mr. Do, he thought Mr. Do looked a pleasant man, even though his appearance was shabby. Mr. Do wore a tattered grey jacket and unpressed black trousers. Duale followed him through a throng of people, all of whom seemed to be pushing their neighbours. At last they reached the car, a black Russian limousine which, Duale thought, had seen better days; their luggage had already been loaded in the back. The drive to the hotel took the visitors through a network of rice paddies, where the peasants were planting rice in the rain; they were used to spending most of their waking hours standing in water up to their calves, their backs bent. Rain or shine, they wore their conical straw 'coolie' hats.

Now the car was crossing an iron bridge which spanned the Red River. Looking down, Duale could see a barge loaded with coal. About a hundred labourers were toiling to unload the barge; most of the workers were stripped to the waist and their blackened torsos and faces glistened in the rain; when the sun would come out later, their sweaty bodies would still glisten, this time from heat. From a distance, the sight reminded Duale of a swarm of ants hard at work; some were labouring on the pile of coal, while others swarmed up a steep bank towards some heavy trucks. Many staggered under their loads. What would Pieter Breughel the Elder have made of that scene, Duale thought. His picture would have been a masterpiece.

At last the car reached the city of Hanoi. Its streets were full of people, but there was a total lack of bustle. Instead there were men doggedly pulling heavy carts, their eyes staring ahead and seemingly unfocused. There were few cars to be seen and just the odd motor bike. As their car weaved its way between the people, no one reacted; the pedestrians simply ignored the lone car.

In the hotel Mr. Do showed Duale and Joe Wilkins their rooms. The walls were dirty and cracked. Mosquito nets hung over the beds. 'Make sure you use them when you go to sleep,' Mr. Do said, adding 'we have quite a lot of malaria around here.' What Mr. Do did not mention was that when the guests of the Socialist Republic of Viet Nam would go to bed, before falling asleep they would hear countless rats moving about the room and gnawing in bursts at the uneven wooden floor. Walking into the bathroom, Duale tried the taps; he was not surprised that no water appeared. The water would probably be delivered in the morning, he thought.

Duale sat on the bed and meditated. He realized that he had entered a country still reeling from the effects of a war that had come to an end only two years previously. The misery and hopelessness through which he had just driven were real. There was no possibility of a 'quick fix'; the wretched misery would persist for years. Little outside aid was available, and the country was governed by an absolute and rigid communist system. He wondered whether the deadliest effects were felt mainly in the cities; after all, in the paddies life had gone on in the same way for centuries. Did those who planted rice and reaped their harvest interest themselves in what system was used to govern the country? It was incredible that these were real people. They were part of humanity to be sure, but they were so far removed in so many ways from those who lived in developed countries that it was impossible to relate to them.

Duale was disturbed by a noise coming from the door. A piece of paper had been pushed into the room. A message from Mr. Do stated that Duale and Joe would be picked up the following morning at 8a.m.

It was, in fact, 8.30 before the car arrived. Mr. Do asked to see Duale on his own in his room; Duale led the way. Mr. Do closed the door.

'Would you please give me a travellers cheque for a hundred US dollars; I have already brought you some *dong*, that is the Vietnamese currency, so that you can buy some things in the town. This is a sort of personal thing that I have done. The *dong* which I am giving you are extra, so you will not be short of money.'

It was only about three days later that Duale came to understand that he had become involved in a black market transaction. He had been given an exchange rate which equated to some ten times the official rate. This meant that a vodka he ordered in the hotel would not cost in dong the equivalent of one US dollar, but 10 cents. He found it incongruous that a country which had got the better of the Americans should value the US dollar at a rate which was at least ten times the official dong exchange rate.

The main meetings followed a two-day inspection of the civil aviation facilities. Speaking to one of the larger meetings, Duale described the wretched state of what he had seen. Much of the mainly Russian, occasionally American, equipment dated from the late fifties or early sixties. Throughout the civil aviation organization there was a basic lack of civil aviation English. There were no crash, fire and rescue vehicles. Then Duale came straight to the point.

'So if anyone here finds himself in a crash – and I have no doubt you are having accidents – don't worry; just relax. Nothing will be done; there is no possibility that you will be rescued. Yes, you will die!'

The chairman found it impossible to contain himself. 'Dr. Duale, the government of Viet Nam is socialist. This means that we pay very good attention to the lives of our citizens. You are our guest. We do not expect criticism. The meeting is ended. Tomorrow is a public holiday and this will be a leisure day for you. You will enjoy a guided tour in the morning; in the afternoon you will be flown to Dien Bien Phu, where you will be conducted around the national monument which celebrates the victory of the Vietnamese over the French colonialists in 1954. I am sure there are no further questions.'

The following morning Mr. Do arrived with a guide. 'Is there anything in the city you particularly wish to see, Dr. Duale?'

'Well,' Duale responded, 'I would like to leave the tour to you. There is just one place I would like to see; that is the main church in Hanoi.'

The guide's face took on a mystified expression. 'But Dr. Duale, I must say that is a strange wish. We are communists. There is no religion here. No one goes to church. We use some of the churches as garages for the government trucks or the city buses.

What is left of the church is very far away! Surely you have a better, a more interesting, wish?'

Duale might have accepted the guide's word if the man had not said that the church was located a long way away. There could be no reasonable doubt that the main church would be found near the centre of the city.

Duale smiled and said, 'It is very nice of you to let me choose. I know it won't be interesting – but let us see the church, please.' The guide looked annoyed; Mr. Do seemed embarrassed.

Within five minutes the car was parked before the church. 'I will just get out and look at the garage,' Duale said. He walked past the statue of the Madonna and straight through the massive front doors of the church. As he opened the inner door, waves of music swept over him. He advanced a few paces and took stock of the situation. The church was packed and the entire congregation was singing the creed of the Mass. He went a little further forward and then stopped; he had met a wall of humanity. He could not approach the main part of the church because the aisles were full of people, each person pressing against his neighbour. When the singing came to an end, the people prayed; some were weeping and tried to prostrate themselves in supplication. They must be praying for deliverance from communism, Duale thought. He would never forget the intensity of these wretched, poverty-stricken churchgoers.

Duale turned round and forced his way through the pressing throng; at last, he regained the warm, sultry air outside the church.

'Thank you,' he said, 'I found that very interesting.' The tour continued. This was the humble house where the saviour of Viet Nam, Ho Chi Minh, worked on behalf of his people. The mausoleum for Ho Chi Minh had to be visited; Duale was instructed by one of the guards to take off his hat as he passed the deep-frozen corpse of the national saviour.

The morning passed quickly. Back at the hotel, the guide asked Duale to have lunch. He would be picked up again at 2p.m.

'May I please mention that I did not come here for leisure,' Duale said firmly. 'I have no wish to fly to Dien Bien Phu,' he added.

The guide dealt with the statement in terse terms., 'I am acting under instructions, Dr. Duale. You will either go in a voluntary way, or you will be escorted by the military; you may take your choice.' Duale ordered lunch which, according to the menu, would cost the equivalent of six US dollars; he ate happily, knowing that with his inflated wallet he would need to pay the equivalent of only sixty cents.

Duale decided to be gracious; he had no wish to become involved in a contretemps. In addition to Mr. Do and the guide, the deputy minister for transportation accompanied Duale on the flight to Dien Bien Phu. On arrival, the small group was welcomed by one of the defenders at the great battle. For three hours he escorted the group around the site. He knew every detail of the battle, pointing out by name the various hills which had been tactically used, either by the French or the Vietnamese.

He described the way in which the battle had been won. 'You see,' he said, 'the French always thought we were not very clever. And their strange behaviour at Dien Bien Phu showed that. How else could you explain their stupidity in trying to hold this area which has many hills and is surrounded by mountains. They even parachuted reinforcements to support their General de Castries. They must have thought about the possibility that we would bring our big guns to the crest of the mountains; but they thought we could never manage to do it. Of course it was difficult to haul the guns up and it took many days. After that it was quite easy. We could shell them whenever we felt like it. Our Russian friends made sure we had plenty of ammunition. The French General had 10,000 troops; so it would take some time to overcome them.

Please walk over here. This is where the French had their headquarters. There was a fortress here and the commander with his high-ranking staff had a huge oparations room underground. In the end, all who were left of the French contingent took refuge in the fortress. We demanded their surrender; they refused.

So over several nights we dug a tunnel; at last it reached the big room under the fortress. We gave them a last chance to surrender; they were very stubborn. They thought they could hold out until more reinforcements came; they are such proud and overbearing people. They always want to be superior, and as usual they underestimated us. We wired our explosives in the tunnel. At dawn one morning we pressed the button. That was the end!'

'Now I think we should have some lunch, Dr. Duale,' the

deputy minister said, 'let us go to the little restaurant.' The minister was good-looking and struck Duale as a man full of dynamic energy. He was probably a little over 40, and he spoke French with a beautifully cultured accent. When they sat down at a simple table, the minister said, 'My name is Ngo Nguyen; you can call me Mr. Ngo. I heard you speaking French, so I will also speak the same language; it is easier for me. In Viet Nam when we converse with foreigners we tend to speak either French or Russian, depending on our training and background. I liked your summary yesterday, when you described our out-of-date civil aviation facilities. I am sorry the chairman was offended. Constructive criticism is always helpful. I was impressed by the way you reacted, or should I say by the way you did not react; you are an excellent diplomat! Our Vietnamese colleagues should have understood that if you do not know what is wrong, then how can you put things right? We want the best and we must work to achieve it. When everything is in order, then we can reclaim our airspace. With other countries operating it, we feel we are back in the colonial times.

In an hour or so we shall fly back to Hanoi. We're near the border with Laos here, and the flight back is only 300 kilometres. Tomorrow you and Mr. Wilkins will fly to Ho Chi Minh city, formerly Saigon, which takes about three hours on a daily service from Hanoi. After you have seen the facilities there, I would like you to return to Hanoi and visit me. If you have the time, you can draft an agreement of co-operation between our civil aviation administration and TASS. I think it is important we co-operate. One of our many problems is that we have become isolated, so we don't know how we compare with other countries. We are, so to say, left out in the cold. TASS may help us to bridge the gap.

You are certainly a well travelled man, Dr. Duale. And I'm sure you have learned a lot along the way. Incidentally, where is your next stop?'

'I will spend a day in Geneva before returning to Chicago. And thank you for talking openly, minister; we always say in TASS that if you really understand a problem and face up to it, then you are already halfway to solving it. It's clear you under- stand the situation. We look forward to visiting Ho Chi Minh city. Before leaving Hanoi, I will certainly call on your office. I will leave the draft of an agreement with you, so if you have any questions or wish to propose amendments, simply write to us.'

'I have been to Geneva a few times' Mr. Ngo commented. 'When we were negotiating with the Americans, I used to start from there. It is a beautiful city. When you leave us, Dr. Duale, you are probably booked to fly from Bangkok. Instead, we would like to offer you a direct flight to Moscow with Aeroflot; as you know, it is the largest airline in the world. We'll book the onward connection to Geneva. It will be quicker for you and the costs will be met by my government. I will ensure you are treated as a VIP, of course, so you won't be bothered by the customs or immigration. If you will accept this token of our appreciation, it would make us very happy.'

Duale was taken aback. In accepting the gesture, his main thought was not to offend the deputy minister, who was evidently a force within the government. When TASS was dealing with Viet Nam, it was important to keep the key people 'on side'.

'Minister, this is a generous gesture, which I am happy to accept. Any savings we can make in our travel costs means we can use the money to assist other countries like Viet Nam. Thank you.'

Duale returned to his rat-infested room for one more night before leaving for Ho Chi Minh City early the following morning. When he boarded the domestic flight to Ho Chi Minh city he felt as though he was boarding a bus. Women sat with their children on benches which had been installed along the inside of the aircraft; they had no seat-belts. As he vainly looked for his own seat-belt, he noticed the grubbiness of the interior of the cabin. The door to the flight deck was hanging ajar and as they took off it swung open violently. As far as he could see, not the slightest attention was paid to flight safety.

On arrival, Duale and Joe Wilkins were driven to various facilities so they could assess the effectiveness of what was in place to ensure safety of flight. Although the equipment was old, in general terms it functioned quite well; what was of equal importance was the fact that the operational staff were much more efficient than those in Hanoi. They were interested in what they were doing and anxious to discuss how things could be improved.

The director of the airport asked Duale and Joe to accompany him to an area adjacent to the airport. When they tumbled out of the minivan into the scorching heat, the director said, 'I think this will interest you. This used to be the command centre of the US forces in Viet Nam. It was designed to be indestructible, and there were many rooms below ground. Three months ago we destroyed all the buildings, and this flat area, which is almost a square kilometer, is available for our use. We are planning that the aviation area control centre will be built here. When we are ready, we would like to have TASS's technical advice regarding the equipment we should buy to meet the needs of our system. Dr. Duale, would you please include this work in your proposal to the deputy minister.'

So news travelled fast in Viet Nam, thought Duale. The deputy minister had already been on the phone to the director of the airport.

'Very well, director,' Duale responded. 'If we have seen most of the main installations, I would like to return to the hotel with Mr. Wilkins so that we can work on the proposal. Would you be free for some supper this evening? We would be honoured if you and two of your senior colleagues could join us.'

The director smiled and nodded, 'Thank you. We will meet you at 7 p.m.'

During the short drive to the hotel, Duale noticed that there was much traffic, mostly motor bikes or three wheeler mini-cars; everyone seemed to be in a hurry. In contrast to the staring, hopeless-looking inhabitants of Hanoi, people were going about their business with a firm purpose and good humour. To Duale they looked natural; what a pleasantly refreshing contrast with Hanoi, he thought.

The supper was a delight and, for once, Duale found himself amongst men whom he sensed were truly from the aviation fraternity. They discussed their problems knowledgeably and laced their narrated experiences with gentle humour. They often smiled or laughed quietly. They were not only enjoying themselves; they were enjoying their polite, good humoured visitors who, on this occasion, were their hosts.

At one point the director moved his head closely to Duale. 'Dr. Duale, you know we hate those communists in Hanoi. They make life very hard for us. And they starve us of up-to-date information. Down here we are not suited to be communists. We are too dynamic and too happy; we like to enjoy ourselves, and our women especially have a lot of *joie de vivre*. The communists don't like that – they are horrible, and very cruel! We feel we live in a different country, and they know we want to keep it that way. They banned all sorts of things we do, but we ignore them as long as we can get away with it. And I'll tell you something else. The Americans thought they lost the Viet Nam war; well, we don't agree. They stopped the communists from attacking other countries, including Thailand. The more the communists can be stopped, the better! The Americans made a lot of mistakes here; but they did not really lose the war.'

Duale felt it was time to pay the bill. This time it was the equivalent of 120 dollars; using his supply of *dong*, he paid twelve.

On returning to Hanoi the following day, Duale called on the deputy minister and left a draft of the agreement for his consideration. Mr. Ngo thanked Duale effusively, commenting that in his country it would probably have taken six months to produce such a document. 'Yes, I will study it as a priority,' he said smilingly. 'I will try and despatch it to Chicago within seven days. I see you have signed it. I hope I will be able to add my signature. Where the foreign exchange will come from, I am not sure. But it must come from somewhere!' True to his word, Mr. Ngo signed the document a few days later and sent it to Chicago.

On learning that Duale would leave that evening, the deputy minister proposed a short official lunch; this would be attended by Duale and Joe Wilkins, as well as some senior members of the civil aviation administration. Because the lunch was offered at short notice, several of the top officials could not attend due to their busy schedule; Mr. Do explained that at least three would be attending communist indoctrination courses.

The lunch passed off as a typical official lunch, with brief speeches of praise being made on an ad hoc basis, each speech ending with yet another toast and the consumption of more brandy. There was a seemingly interminable wait for the main course. Duale quietly mentioned to Joe that there was a severe shortage of food in Hanoi; perhaps the fatted calf would need to be caught and then killed. Joe Wilkins smiled.

While Duale continued his smalltalk, he and Joe became

conscious of the howls of a dog. The noise seemed to come from the street below. The howls grew louder and more desperate by the second. Suddenly there was a bang – and a dying whimper. Duale and Joe looked at one another.

'It sounds as though they killed it!' Joe commented.

Forty-five more minutes passed before the main course arrived, served by pretty Vietnamese women in long, silk, pastel-coloured, fitted dresses. It was a meat course; the dark meat had been shredded and was tough to eat. Duale turned to Joe.

'I hope this is not the fatted dog, Joe. Eat as little and slowly as you can; and wash it down with plenty of brandy. The alcohol should help!'

Back at the hotel after lunch, Duale was happy. This had been quite a successful mission, and TASS would become heavily involved in Viet Nam. Eventually, this would mean enhanced safety for civil aviation, especially on the busy Hong Kong to Bangkok route.

That evening he would be leaving for Moscow, *en route* to Geneva. He had arranged for Joe Wilkins to maintain his ticketing arrangements to return to Chicago via Bangkok. After Duale's stop in Geneva, he would meet Joe in Chicago. All Duale needed now was his passport with his Russian entry visa. With the help of the hotel receptionist, after an hour contact was made with Mr. Do. The passport would be brought to the hotel at 4p.m. As soon as Mr. Do handed Duale his passport, Duale thumbed through the pages.

'Dr. Duale,' Mr Do said with a look of triumph on his face, 'the visa for the USSR is on page 5.'

'Thank you, Mr. Do,' responded Duale, as he looked for the visa, 'I appreciate your excellent efforts.' The writing surrounding the date on the visa was incomprehensible; but the date itself was very clear. It was the wrong date.

'Mr. Do, the date is not right; this date is one day later than the day I enter the USSR.' Mr Do looked confused and then gathered himself,

'I am sorry. Please don't worry, there is no problem. We will give you a letter written in Russian, explaining that there has been a clerical error. I will arrange it.'

Duale was not happy. He had seen too many Russians in

North Korea and Viet Nam. Apart from their tendency to become horribly drunk in the evenings, at times when they had been consulted during Duale's discussions they had often been difficult and rigid in their ideas. They had struck him as uninspired bureaucrats.

'I am not happy, Mr. Do. I don't want to take an unnecessary risk,' Duale explained.

'Well,' Mr. Do responded, 'it is up to you. Mistakes like this are frequently made. We just issue a letter and there is no problem. We have never had a problem, Dr. Duale.'

Duale accepted this statement at its face value; he could not know that what Mr. Do had just said was, at best, a half-truth. After a few moments of hesitation, and with a feeling of resignation, Duale responded,

'Very well, please arrange for the letter; I will leave on the flight tonight. Thank you.'

When Duale entered the Tupolev, he was told that it was 'free seating.' He soon realised that this meant every man for himself. The aircraft seemed to be full. A stout flight attendant approached him.

'You are Dr. Duale. We kept a seat free for you. It is the last row at the back, on the right; the one next to the window. You know that in the event of an accident it's the passengers at the back who have a bettter chance of survival. We want you to be a survivor!' The flight attendant treated Duale to a masculine smile.

Suddenly there was a tremendous roar as the aircraft left the threshold and lumbered down the runway. Well, thought Duale, whether I like it or not I am on my way to Moscow. At full power, the aircraft was the noisiest Duale had ever flown in; perhaps when the captain reached his cruising altitude and throttled back, it would be quieter. Unfortunately, Duale would be disappointed.

In an effort to banish the engine noise which was crashing through his head like a sledgehammer, Duale tried to detach himself from his surroundings; soon he was musing on his Viet Nam adventures. He had been trying to function in a war-torn country, a country in which the communists not only wanted to achieve unification under a communist regime; if they had thought they could succeed, the communist hordes would have swept into other countries in south east Asia. Then again, he thought, how could a country like Viet Nam, which possessed a rich culture extending back at least 2500 years, have succumbed to the communist system? During his days in Viet Nam he had seen first-hand the effects of the current system which had caused an incredible degree of human degradation. Perhaps the forbears of that unspeakably rude customs official, for example, had participated in one of the highest civilizations in Asia. And where today were the Taoists, the followers of Confucius or the Buddhists? There had been no sign of them. But what he had seen, had shocked and deeply saddened him.

As he returned to reality, he was reminded that his seat was hard; and the cabin decor struck him as old and faded. Shortly after take-off, dinner was offered. This consisted of a piece of cold chicken. Duale asked for a glass of white wine; after ten minutes and two reminders, the wine was brought. He asked for another one. 'Do not ask again!,' the flight attendant barked at him above the din, 'you have had enough!'

Early the following morning, Duale disembarked in the capital city of the Union of the Soviet Socialist Republics. He made a mental note never to fly with Aeroflot again, and hoped his hearing had only been temporarily impaired. Soon he was standing in the immigration line. When his turn came, he handed his passport and the letter to the tall immigration officer, a handsome man attired in military uniform with piercing, light blue eyes. The officer studied Duale's passport for several minutes; then Duale could see he was making a telephone call. 'If you have any questions, officer, just let me know.' The only response that Duale received was an incisive stare from those light blue eyes.

'Dr. Duale, I understand you are to stay in Moscow for one night to connect with your flight to Geneva tomorrow morning. As you know, you have entered the USSR illegally. May I please see your ticket; thank you. Now kindly come this way.' The officer ushered Duale through a door which led down a short passage; at the end were double doors.

'Go through please,' Duale heard the officer say. He went through; immediately he heard the double doors slamming behind him. Feeling apprehensive, he decided to return; he tried to open one of the doors, then the other. Both were immovably locked. He felt very much alone.

Then he heard a voice. 'Welcome to Moscow, Dr. Duale. You will be spending some days in the transit hotel. We will keep your passport and ticket. Please enter the small bus and we will take you to the transit hotel.'

He walked through some snow and boarded the minibus. He was the only passenger. On reaching the transit hotel he walked into a small lobby. As he had entered, he had noticed two soldiers holding submachine guns; apparently, their job was to control the doorway. After another five minutes he had been escorted to his room. He asked the man how long he would have to stay in the hotel; the response was non-committal.

'That depends.'

Duale wandered around his new home. The window pane carried a sign in four languages: '*It is forbidden to open the window. If you need fresh air call for room service.*'

Duale went downstairs and asked at the counter how long he would have to stay in what, he now realized, was euphemistically called the transit hotel. A man said it was difficult to say; it depended how long it would take the legal department to review his case. Now it was time for lunch and Duale should go to the dining room. There he would be allocated a certain table, which he should use at all times. He should avoid talking to others.

To take his mind off the situation in which he found himself, he began to draft his consultancy reports. As he was writing, he heard a crescendo of noise on the landing outside his room. When he opened his door he saw about 30 young men milling about and shouting at one another. They were dark-skinned and many had long hair. Eventually he found their leader, who seemed to be the only member of the group who spoke English. 'Where have you come from?' Duale asked him.

'I am a tour leader. These people are from Sri Lanka. We advertise in Colombo that they can travel cheaply to East Germany and find work. Aeroflot brings a plane load of these workers to East Germany every week. When they arrive, they are usually told that unfortunately for them no work can be found. However, they are then infiltrated to western European countries and they are told to find some sort of work. If they are challenged, or if they have problems, they are advised to make a lot of noise. In this way, somehow the west European countries accept them, especially Switzerland. Even if they cannot be given work, they have the benefit of the social insurance system. It's quite clever, don't you think? And it gives the western Europeans a real headache!' he laughed raucously. Incredulous, Duale returned to his room. He had thought he knew something of the world in which he lived. How silly of him!

When Duale woke up on the third morning of his stay in the prison which went by the misnomer of the transit hotel, he felt worried. The fact was that no one in the outside world knew where he was; if he disappeared, then it would be without trace. As far as the USSR authorities were concerned, they could say they had never seen him. He would simply vanish! He wondered if he should try and escape. Looking out of the unopenable window, all he could see was a carpet of snow. Even if he got out, where would he go? In his desperate situation, all he could do was hope he could maintain a reasonable level of mental stability.

As he went down to breakfast, someone from the desk addressed him curtly.

'Be ready for departure in fifteen minutes. You can catch the next flight to Geneva.' Duale saw no point in asking questions. Within ten minutes he was standing at the door, the armed soldiers sitting on either side of him. The minibus dropped him at the passenger terminal building. A tall, blue-eyed Russian immigration officer approached him.

'Dr. Duale, we are pleased to see you. You can go to your flight.'

'Thank you,' Duale said. 'I will need my passport and ticket.' The blue eyes focused on him with some intensity.

'Unfortunately, we have mislaid your passport and your ticket, Dr. Duale.' Duale was beginning to feel his temper.

'I don't understand. You must return my property; it is legally mine!'

The officer was unmoved. Tilting his head towards Duale until his pink cheeks almost rested on Duale's face, the officer smiled and said, 'You have a very nice pen in your pocket!' So he wants me to bribe him, thought Duale. He is a swine! They have imprisoned me. Now they can send me to Siberia; they can beat me! I will never part with my pen.

Fortunately for Duale, he did not express his thoughts with the spoken word. Instead he responded, 'Yes, this is a beautiful pen and it is unique; it is very valuable. Your government has looked after me so well! May I offer you a small token of my appreciation, officer? I hope you enjoy it. Now my plane will be leaving. Would you please make a special effort to find my passport and ticket? It is so kind of you!'

Within a minute, Duale was holding his passport and air ticket. He trotted to the departure gate and just caught his flight. As he sat in the aircraft *en route* to Geneva, he felt relieved and tired at the same time. As his thoughts re-lived the way in which he had been treated, he felt tears welling up. What a vile and horrible system, he thought. His experience at the hands of the communist government had been frightening; he had been the victim of treatment meted out by a system which was, in fundamental terms, evil, in whatever guise it might be camouflaged. Duale developed a feeling of contempt for communism, especially the brand which was practised in the mother country, the USSR.

When he left the air terminal in Geneva he felt liberated. Over and over again he thought how he despised the communist system, an unnatural system kept in place by sheer brute military force. He told himself to erase communism, and all the evil it represented, from his mind. He tried his very best, but it was not enough; it would haunt him forever.

Duale's consultation in Geneva was soon completed. He loved the quiet, clean surroundings and what he felt was the civilization of the discussions which were held on certain aspects of arbitration. After a good night's rest, he found himself boarding an aircraft for Chicago. In contrast to his recent experience, he was treated courteously and with humanity. And everything was so clean!

When he walked into his office, he felt he had been away for a year. His mind was full of his experiences, not least his success in reaching agreements on TASS's support in the communist countries of North Korea and Viet Nam. Mary Piggott came in.

'Welcome back, Dr. Duale. Did things go well? The CEO would like to see you at 10 o'clock.'

'Well done, Duale!' were the effusively welcoming words of Al Willis as Duale entered the office. 'I have already received the Viet Nam agreement, fully signed.'

'And I have the North Korea agreement in my briefcase. It is also fully signed,' Duale responded.

'Fantastic!,' Al Willis said. 'You have a half hour to tell me the highlights. I will study your reports later. After that, Duale, all we have to do is to get the committee, including our American friend, to agree everything. And we're home!

Yes, Duale, we shall be in heaven basking in glory! All I can say is you deserve it! And it makes me feel so good! The credit is really yours. The only little part I can claim is that it was I who decided to keep it a secret mission; and it paid off!'

Just for once, Duale thought, the CEO looked relaxed and not too unhealthy. He thought it better to leave him this way; certainly, soon enough he would find out the reality.

Chapter Seven

One Man's Destiny

'Dr. Duale?'

'Yes, Anna!,' Duale interjected, 'whether I hear your voice on the telephone like now, or I hear it when we are together, there is only one voice in the world like yours. How are you, Anna?'

'Well, thank you, Dr. Duale,' Anna responded coolly. 'I was about to say that as you know, the CEO will be meeting with the Executive Committee at ten o'clock this morning. One of the items on the agenda requests the committee's approval to start TASS's work in North Korea and Viet Nam. The CEO would appreciate it if you would kindly meet with him at nine-thirty in his office; I believe he wants to discuss the approach to gaining the go-ahead of the committee. I hope you have received the papers on this agenda item, Dr Duale?'

'Yes, I have the papers,' Duale replied, 'I will certainly be with the CEO at nine thirty. Thank you, Anna.'

Duale had been expecting the CEO's summons and his papers had already been assembled. As he left his office for the elevator, he briefly looked out of the window. An early Spring snowstorm had developed and the flakes were swirling between the high buildings. He could see that already about four inches of snow had accumulated on ledges. He walked to the window; looking down he could see miniature-like pedestrians plodding through the snow, their bodies leaning forward into the strengthening wind.

'Good morning, Duale. Let's sit by the table.' Willis was in his usual happy frame of mind; or was he? Duale had noticed the CEO hurriedly putting a small bottle into his pocket. So the CEO was taking pills. Al Willis, a perceptive man, flushed a little more than his ruddy complexion normally tolerated; then he said, 'Duale, I haven't mentioned this to anyone else, not even to my secretary, Anna. I saw a doctor the other day. He told me to change my lifestyle. I have to lose weight and get more exercise. He prescribed some pills to reduce my blood pressure. I keep a glass and a bottle of water handy, so I don't have to ask Anna.' He poured half a glass of water and quickly sank the pills. 'That's better,' he smiled, 'now let's get down to business.'

'Do you have any particular ideas, Duale, on how we should process the committee's agreement on North Korea and Viet Nam?'

'I suggest,' Duale responded, 'that you treat the initiatives as routine, in the context of supporting air safety. Although you might consider hinting that because of the complications in dealing with these countries, the agreements reached were something of a *tour de force* for TASS, it will probably be better to keep any discussion quiet and low-key. Let us hope that, in fact, there will be very little discussion.'

'Exactly.' Al Willis nodded his head slowly in agreement. 'That is precisely what I had in mind. I will deal with the item routinely. I would like you to sit in on the meeting. If we get an unexpected problem, I will invite you to clarify the point. Now I think we should go down to the meeting room; it's five to ten. Let's keep our fingers crossed, Duale.' Willis was smiling benevolently. For his part, Duale felt that the matter was in good hands. Yes, the CEO's face was too flushed, but the main thing was that he was calm and gave a strong impression that he was in charge. What would happen, Duale wondered, if the American Richard Spargel became difficult; perhaps they should have discussed their tactics a little more fully. In any case, it was too late now. They were on their way.

Duale watched the Executive Committee in session as the various agenda items were taken in turn. He was fascinated by the CEO's technique; not once did Willis overtly disagree with any of the many statements made by the committee members, even though the interventions often indicated disagreement with the recommended course of action. The CEO was full of praise for every statement made; they all deserved 'serious consideration if we are to agree on a meaningful decision.' And so it went on. The CEO could smile or 'take note of grave consequences' at every turn; and on demand. In whichever direction the wind blew, he was sure to be there. Then suddenly, after perhaps twenty minutes, Willis would look serious. Then he would sum up the discussion, subtly giving weight to those points which supported the recommendation; as far as the contras were concerned, in fairness these were rewarded with a mention. But it ended there.

'So, gentlemen, I take it that we are agreed on that agenda item and we shall proceed accordingly. Thank you.' He would scan the faces of the committee – some were happy, others less so; the most important thing, however, was that silence prevailed.

'So let us deal with the next item, please. I believe it should be straightforward.' Willis looked at his watch and his faintly startled facial expression indicated that things had been taking a little too long to discuss. He hoped this message to the committee would be noted. 'Yes, I am sure you have all read the papers on our breakthroughs in North Korea and Viet Nam. We have had successful visits to these countries, led by Dr. Duale. The proposal is that we should lose no time and put in hand whatever needs to be done to raise civil aviation safety standards in these countries. Do we have any comments, or do I take it that the committee agrees? In which case we can pass on to the next agenda item.' The silence which ensued lasted ten seconds. Then the CEO's gentle statement: 'Fine, then let us pass on....' was neutralized by the sound of a throat being cleared and a stronger voice which reverberated around the committee.

'Yes, I have something to say!' It was Richard Spargel Junior.

Al Willis looked up and turned his good-natured face in the direction of the intervention. He found himself looking at a stern countenance; when Willis looked at the eyes, they seemed to be riveted on him. At this moment, he felt a rush of blood in his head and, briefly, he felt weak. He closed his eyes and told himself to be calm. After all, so far nothing had been said; so why jump to a conclusion?

'By all means,' Willis said, 'but let us not take too long; our discussions are taking a little longer than scheduled. I am sure your comments will be to the point under discussion.'

Spargel opened a file and gave Willis a quick glance; Willis thought how mean Spargel looked.

'Yes,' said the American, 'my first point is a question. When TASS is to engage in sensitive matters, it is normal procedure that the committee is consulted. Why were we ignored on this occasion, Mr. CEO?'

'The committee is never ignored,' Al Willis clarified. 'TASS exists to support safety of air navigation. The consultancy visits to North Korea and Viet Nam were mounted to achieve a basis for action by TASS, in accordance with its mandate. This is routinely what TASS does. Now the committee is being consulted regarding the appropriate way forward. Does this answer your question?' From his detached observation point, Duale sensed the first signs of the CEO's capacity, on very rare occasions, to be confrontational; this was one such occasion.

'No, it does not!' was the instant response. 'There could never be anything routine about visits to North Korea and Viet Nam. The United States has sacrificed thousands of lives trying to protect countries from communism. In recent years, two of the main aggressors have been North Korea and Viet Nam. How can TASS claim to be apolitical when we are now supporting these countries? As far as I am concerned, we are being very political. Perhaps we are involved in treachery to our own country, the United States; maybe we are traitors! And I think the reason this committee was not consulted before the visits was because, Mr. CEO, you wanted to avoid our reaction. I would go further; you wanted the visits to be kept secret. Could we hear the truth, please?'

Duale was doing his best not to look anxious; he looked straight ahead and waited. There followed a long silence. At last, Duale looked up. Richard Spargel sat at the table with a look of solid determination on his face, almost as though he would soon be ready for the kill; the American's head turned and he glared at Willis. Duale also looked at Al; there was a nervous half-smile on his face and the complexion was blotchy. Then the features became slightly contorted as the blood rushed back into the hardening vein structure. A trembling hand made a gesture to the chest. The silence continued.

'I think,' Willis weakly announced, 'that we have a crisis of confidence. Before I comment on what has just been said, may I ask the committee members one question. I wish to know which members share the distrust expressed by Mr. Spargel. I also wish to find out who regards the TASS visits to North Korea and Viet Nam as politically motivated by me, rather than apolitical. Please feel free to speak. Thank you.'

To Duale, the silence which met Al's invitation to speak seemed interminable. No one spoke. Although Duale hoped the silence was a positive sign, he could not ignore the supercharged atmosphere which pervaded the meeting room. It was only when Al Willis started to speak again that Duale realized there was something wrong; the pitch of his voice did not sound normal and sometimes his words were lost in his throat, as the huskiness gained the upper hand.

'Mr. Spargel,' Willis said in a staccato burst as his breathing became a series of audible pants, 'I think the situation is clear. You have expressed concern on behalf of the committee about my actions. But the committee does not share your concerns; no one has supported your assertions. So this discussion is between you and I. No one else wishes to be involved. I think it should be obvious that there is a difference between discretion and secrecy. I have employed the usual degree of discretion. When TASS travels to other countries, our visits are self-evident, and they cannot be secret. May we end this regrettable discussion on this fact? '

'No!' responded the American. 'Because I do not think we should be involved with enemies, and I am still convinced you wanted these visits to be kept secret. In fact, a few weeks ago when I went looking for Dr. Duale (which Richard Spargel always pronounced 'Dweel' instead of 'Doo-ahli'), I realized he was absent; so I enquired regarding his whereabouts. I was told he was on a secret mission! So I put the CIA on to the job. They soon found the TASS team and caught up with them in Tokyo. Someone leaked the news to the newspaper in Tokyo; after that, all Asia knew where they were. But the committee was kept in the dark, Mr. CEO! I even have a copy here of the agreement made in North Korea; I must say, speaking as a legal man, I find it quite good.' Richard Spargel threw the copy of the North Korea agreement down the table in the direction of Willis; then he laughed, as though his ace of spades had trumped the CEO's highest card. Duale's eyes widened as he stared incredulously at the agreement. Then the image of the CIA Russian flashed through his mind.

Willis was speechless. Duale noticed that the blotches on his face were becoming more pronounced. His CEO suddenly seemed like a remote island. Their eyes met. All Duale could see were eyes which were weakly bloodshot; the surrounding distraught face heaved up and down with each desperate pant. Al looked in Duale's direction and blurted out, 'Speak'.

Duale spoke. 'Gentlemen, I appreciate the opportunity to clarify the situation under discussion. I can only reinforce the correctness of what the Chief Executive Officer has explained. I find no reason to repeat the truth. May I also mention, please, that the meaning of apolitical is simply that political considerations will not, repeat not, be taken into account; I have no doubt that TASS's trustees would confirm this interpretation. Certain members of the committee may wish to regard civil aviation as a national, domestic business activity. Unfortunately, however, those who maintain such an attitude have to come to terms with the fact that civil aviation is in fact a global business, and safe air navigation cannot be confined to certain countries only. Finally, I should observe that members of this committee are recruited to serve the interests of TASS, which is a trust. They should have no official link with their governments, nor should they share TASS information with any government without the express agreement of the CEO, who may wish to consult the committee on any given matter before he arrives at a decision. Thank you, gentlemen.'

This time there was no silence. Spargel immediately returned to the attack. 'Dr. Duale, were you involved with a supposed secret visit, or not. You have spoken with crisp eloquence. Goddam it! Now I demand a direct answer.'

'With respect,' Duale rejoined, 'may I again explain that my name is pronounced 'Doo-ahli' and not 'Dweel.' As far as alleged secrecy of the visits is concerned, I assumed that the CEO had already consulted the committee. For me, therefore, the matter was never an issue. I hope this is clear. May I also add...' Duale's statement came to an unnatural end, as the even tone of his voice was interrupted by a brief choking noise and a solid thud. All looked in the direction of the CEO. He was not visible, simply because he had fallen in his chair to the floor. His left hand held his small bottle of pills; the clearly visible white of the knuckles reflected his vain, final desperate grasp at possible salvation. Within seconds he was surrounded by the helping hands of the committee; except for Duale and Spargel. Duale had nimbly reached the telephone and had already dialled for emergency help.

The American sat at the table, unblinking, as though he had been turned to stone.

Within five minutes the emergency team had lifted the heavy body of Al Willis onto a stretcher, and two minutes after that Al Willis was on his way to hospital. The emergency operation was formidably impressive and had been performed to perfection. But human perfection is not always enough.

Al Willis was dying.

The members of the committee were silent as they dispersed. Although they could not know the fate of Willis, each feared the worst; and this would be confirmed to each of them within a few hours. There was no further discussion in that sombre atmosphere. Eventually the meeting room was empty; except for Duale and Spargel. Duale glanced in the direction of the American, who maintained his unmovable, stone-like grimace.

Duale slowly walked to the door and took the elevator; instead of returning to his office he called at Al's office complex. There he found Anna, who was sobbing; she looked up.

'He was a wonderful man. Even if he survives, which I doubt, he will be an invalid. It is the end of him. Why couldn't you tell the truth Duale? You knew everything was supposed to be secret. So why did you say that you assumed the missions had been cleared? That was not true, Duale. Maybe it was fate; perhaps he was supposed to die. But if he wasn't, then the shock of you not supporting him was the stroke which killed him. The poor man is probably dead by now, and if you had told the truth he might not have had his heart attack. Poor man!'

'How do you know what goes on in meetings, Anna?' Duale asked.

'My office is plugged in to all important meetings, whether they are in the CEO's office or in the committee's meeting room. I keep records so the CEO has an actual record of what has been said and by whom. And you are definitely on the record, Duale! Not that it makes much difference now.'

'Anna,' Duale said quietly, 'you are distressed. We must have some hope. You know, it has been snowing all day. There's probably a foot of snow out there by now. I'm not going to take my car out of the garage; it's too risky. Why don't we have a snack supper around the corner and then we might feel a bit better.'

'Maybe we should,' replied Anna. She put on her mink coat and leather boots and told Duale to meet her in the lobby. Five minutes later they had stepped into the snow.

Duale, wearing his large rubber overboots, took Anna's arm, which was just as well because she immediately slipped on the first step and found herself sitting in the deep snow, Duale still clinging to her arm; at least, his hold had broken her fall. Feeling slightly shaken, they gently navigated the now invisible remaining steps and descended onto the sidewalk.

The wind was howling and huge clouds of blowing snow swirled around them. A few deserted cars littered the street; with the thunderous wind, the snow was being packed against these minor obstacles which lay in the path of the relentless storm.

As Duale and Anna plodded their way forward, there were few pedestrians to be seen; most had been allowed to travel home some hours before. This was not the first time that the great metropolis of Chicago had been paralysed by a winter storm, nor would it be the last; but for some illogical reason, Duale was always surprised when the city was brought to its knees by a winter storm. Duale wondered whether the little restaurant would still be open and, as they rounded the corner, he was relieved to see the dim light of its window. As they closed the door behind them, they felt as though they had just escaped from the clutches of an uncontrollable giant.

'I think I will have a plate of spaghetti and a coffee, Anna. What about you?' Duale enquired.

'I can't eat – all I want to do is cry,' said Anna. And she began to sob.

'That's no good, Anna. I need some carbohydrates, which is why I will order spaghetti. Why don't you have some vitamins and protein. What about a salmon or tuna salad? If you like we can share.'

'Okay,' Anna said, 'a salmon salad will be fine; and some coffee, please'.

The two sat in silence, waiting for the order. At last, Anna turned to Duale and said, 'Who are you, Duale? I mean who are you really? You look nice and you do your job to perfection. Your professional relations are perfect. Al once said you were the most loyal and trusted man in TASS. Then suddenly you start telling half-truths, or you omit the most important facts from a situation. You are not quite a downright liar, Duale, but you are not totally honest, are you? We used to live together; so I should know you, or I should feel I know you. But there is something strange about you. If only I could put my finger on it!'

Duale seemed to be meditating; he did not respond straight away, but just looked ahead.

'Please say something, Duale,' Anna pleaded.

'Right,' Duale said firmly. 'Anna, I don't know who I am. And if this sounds amazing, then ask other people who they are. I think most of us are in the same boat. Each of us is born with a nature and our nature has certain qualities. I think I'm typical; I have some quite good qualities and a few bad ones. Then we can take stock of what we do with our qualities and what degree of importance we attach to them. In my case, I want to reach the top of my profession and stay there; that has always been very important to me. I prefer to be liked, but I don't need to be popular; and if I become unpopular in following my profession correctly, then so be it.

Then sometimes I think that as I move up the ladder, it is more difficult to be a good person; I mean I may be the subject of temptation because of the circles in which I find myself. Others who work at a lower level may not be given opportunities to do wrong; that is also a consideration, don't you think? This doesn't sound very nice, but I think it's probably true. And then I love women, Anna. When we lived together, sometimes I felt I was oversexed; and I thought you were too! But then I thought, what's wrong with that; what's wrong with a healthy sex life – nothing at all! But for me, Anna, there is one overriding element in my nature which takes precedence; and please don't ask me why. Whatever happens, whatever the situation, at all costs I must survive! What else can I tell you, Anna?'

Anna looked at Duale; she had stopped weeping. 'Well,' she said, 'I think you have told me a lot. For once, Duale, I have the feeling you are being honest. I know you better now, the way you do things becomes much clearer. One more question, though. Do you want to be the CEO, and will you tell half-truths, if necessary, to get what you want?'

'Anna – if the next CEO is a weakling, then I would prefer to do the job myself; and if I need to omit certain facts to improve my chances, then I will do it. If he is a competent person, then I will happily work with him. I hope that's the end of the interrogation, Anna. Incidentally, I am upset about Al, and I hope he pulls through. In many ways he was an excellent man; his problem was that he ignored his health. No CEO anywhere can afford to do that. I am afraid he paid the price. You were right, what I said in the meeting room didn't help; but our poor old CEO was on the way out regardless. I have no pangs of conscience about that – not that my conscience often bothers me! And if you are horrified, Anna, I am sorry; but that's the way it is – period!'

Duale escorted Anna in the blizzard to the nearest metro station and gave her a kiss on the cheek as he said goodbye.

'Thank you, Duale.' For the first time that day Anna was smiling. 'I don't know why, but I feel better. Thank you. You are special!'

'Night, Anna. You feel better because you have some food in your stomach. And you also found out some of my weaknesses; of course you feel better!'

* * *

Within a month of Al's death, the TASS's Board of Trustees had arranged to place a large advertisement in newspapers of high standing and aviation journals worldwide. The new CEO would need to have twenty years of high-level experience in the aviation industry. Although sound academic qualifications were a prerequisite, the Board made it clear that a proven track record of achievement was regarded as of primary importance.

Duale, as the senior director, was asked by the Board to be acting CEO in the interim. He slipped into the role with ease and handled the Executive Committee with consummate diplomatic firmness. He gave up appealing to Richard Spargel to stop calling him 'Dr. Dweel' instead of 'Doo-ahli'; if someone on the committee wished to make a point of pronouncing his name incorrectly, then why constantly rub the American up the wrong way?

One of Duale's first acts was to re-open the discussion on TASS's proposed involvement in the modernization and upgrading of civil aviation safety in North Korea and Viet Nam. Richard Spargel sat at the table with a sullen expression on his face. To Duale, he seemed exasperated that he could no longer indulge in patriotic rhetoric by hurling accusations against his former target; he seemed to accept only reluctantly that his target was no longer available. When comments were invited, Spargel had nothing to say, and the go-ahead was agreed without any further questions or comment.

Soon the summer recess of 1977 was upon the Executive Committee, which meant that Duale could direct TASS's affairs single-handedly until the committee would reconvene in September. Instead of performing as an interim stand-in, Duale grasped the opportunity to carry out a review of all of TASS's main functions. With the help of a small internal working group, the results of the detailed survey were summarized in a report and recommendations for reform were proposed. Duale, who had decided he would not be an applicant for the CEO vacancy, forwarded a copy of the entire report to the Chairman of the Board of Trustees, expressing the hope that the detailed document would help the new incumbent CEO.

When the Executive Committee reconvened in early September, the members were refreshed and lively. Richard Spargel, especially, was in good humour. He had let it be known that he expected to be appointed CEO, and he looked to his colleagues for support. His attitude to Duale, whose name he continued to pronounce wrongly, was polite but condescending. After all, an organization of any size needed legal men, but in this case it was only to keep TASS's nose clean. Legal men were there to give informed advice; but they would never become effective decision-makers. It was true, of course, that Spargel was a lawyer by training, but he was different; he was a decision-maker! At meetings of the committee Spargel became uncharacteristically co-operative, often congratulating Duale on his initiatives as well as on his polished presentation of work in hand.

What the American did not know was that every other member of the committee had also applied for the CEO vacancy; and they gave no inkling of their aspirations. After all, why compete in public; it was so much easier to humour the American. In any case, although the committee members wanted the record to show that they were applicants for the CEO post, they inwardly hoped that they would not be successful; they were

113

much happier asking questions or making wise observations than actually taking hard decisions.

At the end of November 1977, the committee received word that the Chairman of the Board of Trustees would attend one of its sessions at 10 o'clock in the morning. The Chairman would summarize the Board's findings on the applications received for the post of CEO. In addition to the Executive Committee members, TASS directors and their deputies were requested to attend.

On the appointed day, Duale received the Chairman at TASS's impressive entrance and escorted him to the CEO's office. The Chairman was a man of about 65, and had a long record of successful participation in a wide range of commercial and industrial activities. He had officially retired from business some three years earlier and had immediately been asked to chair TASS's Board of Trustees. He conducted himself with an air of quiet confidence and dignity. After a short exchange with Duale on the continued growth of TASS's activities, the Chairman suggested they should go down to the meeting room. On his arrival at precisely ten o'clock, all present stood up; Richard Spargel seemed to be beaming in the direction of the Chairman. Once the Chairman had taken his seat at the head of the table, the committee members and senior staff resumed their places.

In the tension which everyone present felt, the Chairman spoke.

'I wonder if you might agree with me when I comment that I find the atmosphere in this room to be what we might loosely call 'pregnant'! Do you agree, gentlemen?' There was a short ripple of quiet laughter around the table; the polite expression of humour seemed to contribute to a lowering of the tension temperature.

The Chairman went on, 'Well now, let me come to the reason that I am here. As you know, the Board of Trustees regards the vacant CEO post as most important in terms of TASS's continued effective functioning. I would like to officially pay the deepest respect to the late Al Willis, an outstanding man in all respects. He is now part of history – and I must say a good part. May God bless him!

Now we must look ahead. We have received over one hundred applications for the post of CEO. And rest assured, gentlemen, we have given each and every application full and exhaustive consideration. The Board has agreed that, for one reason or another, none of the applicants meet the requirements for TASS's CEO. Given this fact, we have decided that provided he is prepared to accept our offer, Dr. Duale should continue to act in the capacity of CEO for a further six months. On completion of this period, if the Board continues to be satisfied with his performance then he will be confirmed in his appointment for a period of five years. If not, the Board will re-advertise. Apart from many other considerations, the Board is pleased that TASS has at its head not only an oustanding administrator but also a lawyer, and an aviation lawyer at that. I am sure this will enable the CEO to keep TASS's nose clean.

Before I leave you to continue with your work, I want to make two points. First, acting as an interim CEO, the performance of Dr. Duale has been outstanding and we expect him to be confirmed in this appointment in six months' time. I look to the committee members in particular to support Dr. Duale, and therefore TASS, to the fullest extent possible.

Second, the Board is not entirely happy with the way in which the Executive Committee is operating. We see transcripts of your meetings; there are too many questions which are irrelevant. It is not the job of the committee to make the life of the CEO miserable. It is your job to make things happen; this is done by approving positive initiatives expeditiously. The Board finds it no co-incidence that so much was achieved by TASS during the summer months, when the committee was in recess. It begs the question whether TASS needs a committee. On balance, the Board still believes in using a committee so that the CEO's burden can be so to speak shared, at least to some extent. But unless the attitude on the committee becomes more positive and action-oriented, then the Board will look very carefully at how best TASS should be managed; we insist the management must work positively rather than that it is hindered by unnecessary questioning. I hope I have made myself clear.'

The Chairman paused and looked around the table until his eyes rested on Richard Spargel; there they stayed, as he looked hard at the American for several seconds.

Then he said, 'Now, Dr. Duale, do you accept in principle the Board's proposal that you should become TASS's new CEO?'

Duale looked the Chairman calmly in the eye, 'Thank you,

Chairman. I accept with pleasure.'

'Good' was the response, 'let me now get out of your hair, so that you can all get to work. Good morning, gentlemen; and good luck!'

The Chairman moved towards the door and insisted on showing himself out of the building, leaving Duale to be congratulated by his colleagues, each in turn offering their solid support.

Six months later the Board of Trustees confirmed, in the nature of a formality, Duale as CEO of TASS. Duale had just turned forty-eight. Although he continued to perform with consistency and imagination, he was under no illusion concerning the feelings of certain committee members towards him. He recognized his main adversary as Richard Spargel. Duale decided that this potentially lethal competitor had to be neutralized.

'May I speak with Richard Spargel, please. It is Dr. Duale here. Thank you. Mr. Spargel, yes it's always good to hear your voice, even on the telephone. I was wondering if we could meet sometime? I would like to discuss a point with you and it's not so easy on the phone. Would you like me to come to you? You will come here? How nice of you! This afternoon at three – perfect. I am looking forward to seeing you.'

Duale had had a busy day with virtually continuous meetings with directors and high-level visitors. Now it was three o'clock.

'It's really very nice of you to come to my office, Mr. Spargel. Some coffee, or tea?' As always, Anna had slipped into the room. 'Thank you, Anna. Yes, tea please.'

'Thank goodness the snow has gone; somehow, in Chicago we always seem to have to wait an eternity for the Spring. I must say, every day I am reminded that we live in the 'Windy City.' At least we are seeing a little more of the sun these days; and we have more light in the mornings and evenings.

What I would like to discuss a little with you, Mr. Spargel, is that from time to time you have mentioned that you are in touch with the US administration in Washington. It struck me that this connection could be useful for TASS. I would prefer any contacts we have to be informal. I hope you won't mind me being straightforward; it's my nature, I suppose. I just feel that it might be useful if your contacts could be mine as well, naturally for the benefit of TASS.'

Spargel looked at Duale and tried to disguise his surprise; he wondered what game he might be playing. Then he took the bull by the horns.

'Well, I find your curiosity interesting. I must say your feelings are in total contrast to your suspicious predecessor. I keep the administration informed, because the left hand has to know what the right is doing, if you see what I mean. All this talk of TASS being apolitical is rubbish! If you don't keep your finger on the political pulse, you're dead in the water. What about if I arrange for you to visit Washington so that you can make a presentation on what TASS is doing. I think they would appreciate that. And you would meet my contacts. How would that be, Dr. Duale – or should I say Mr. CEO?' Richard Spargel was chuckling.

Three weeks later Duale was standing in front of an informed, high-level civil aviation audience of technicians and administrators in Washington. Before commencing his presentation, he had been personally introduced to the top administrators by Richard Spargel. The presentation went well. After almost an hour, Duale had reached the closing stages.

He said, 'This presentation would be incomplete without reference to Mr. Richard Spargel Junior. His contribution in assisting with the management of TASS has been invaluable and I have no doubt it will continue. His wealth of professional knowledge is vast, and I might mention that one of our concerns is that he is simply too good for us; yes, we recognize that one of these days he may be tempted away by the offer of an even higher level post. As you know, TASS is apolitical and Mr. Spargel has always observed our working criteria in this respect admirably. So to finish on a personal note I would like to say to Mr. Richard Spargel Junior 'thank you!''

Shortly afterwards, just as Duale was making a sign to Spargel that he would like to leave, the most senior official present asked Duale if they could talk for a moment in a small adjacent room.

'Dr. Duale, were you serious when you praised Richard Spargel at the end of your presentation?'

'I am always serious, sir. I do not believe in false flattery, which serves no useful purpose. Indeed I was serious. We are very proud of Mr. Spargel. We appreciate him!'

'Thank you,' was the response, 'it was good to meet you and we were impressed with your presentation. None of us had any idea that TASS was mandated to be apolitical. It makes a lot of sense for civil aviation development. Keep up the good work. And keep in touch!'

A month later, Richard Spargel was put through on the telephone to Duale. 'Could you spare me a minute or two, Dr. Duale; yes, two o'clock will be fine.' At two o'clock sharp a beaming Richard Spargel Junior entered Duale's office.

'I wanted you to be the first to know. I have been offered Assistant Secretary in Washington, which I will accept. You know, Dr. Duale, when we look back it was a sort of rewarded virtue. I arranged for our trip to Washington; but while you were there you praised me, and I am sure this tilted the balance in my favour for this new job. Between us, I was the favoured candidate for TASS's CEO; the trouble was the Board of Trustees wanted a non American. So they disqualified me and gave it to you, even though your record is a bit suspect somehow – you know, the French connection but being educated in England. Strange. No hard feelings, Dr. Duale. Now you have helped me. It's amazing how things turn out, don't you think?'

'Absolutely,' Duale rejoined, 'and congratulations! You are a great loss, but you so thoroughly deserve advancement. You have so much to contribute!'

On the evening of the late-afternoon farewell reception for Spargel, Duale invited Anna and her husband to a champagne dinner. He thought he also deserved a celebration for ridding TASS of the American. Anna's husband was travelling, which meant that he could not attend. However, he gave his confident permission for Anna to have dinner with Duale alone. Both Anna and Duale felt it would be a romantic dinner, although both agreed in advance it should not become too romantic.

Neither need have worried. The dinner was superb and the view was uniquely magnificent. But the young romanticism of yesteryear was lacking. Duale could only think of his work; and he was preoccupied with his next moves as an accomplished manipulator of situations and the people who were associated with them. While he was not conscious of aging as such, he had matured into a well-rounded personality. Although he could not deny his occasional surge of sexual hunger for Anna, he recognized its impracticality; in any case, he was now more likely to seek sexual enjoyment with a younger woman. Even this possibility tended to be of academic interest to him simply because, more and more, he was lost in thought on some aspect of his work. This meant that his time for flirtation was correspondingly less.

As for Anna, she was not only thoroughly competent in her work. She was happily married and fulfilled in love with her husband. She would never risk indulgence and irresponsibility which would put her happy marriage at risk. She had no wish to offend Duale, but the fact was that his occasional advances no longer had any romantic content for her. In a nutshell, as the years passed the lovers were becoming good friends, their friendship based on mutual trust and recognition of each other's strengths and weaknesses.

※　※　※

As 1978 progressed, TASS went from strength to strength. Globally, and especially in Asia, civil aviation continued its rapid expansion. The number of passengers carried by some of the major international airlines again topped a twenty per cent increase. The strain on many developing countries to maintain safety became an almost intolerable burden. The only constraint on TASS's expansion was lack of financing for the training of staff and upgrading of facilities to improve civil aviation operational safety. TASS's growth seemed to know no bounds, unhindered as it was by a lack of political intervention of the type which had previously been encouraged by Richard Spargel. What had been 'rubbish' to Spargel was the liberating secret of success for TASS.

TASS was lauded throughout the world for its apolitical functioning. It would eventually become a symbol of what could be achieved for aviation safety by professionals who knew what they were doing and who could work without the intervention of a politically-appointed management.

In other fields of human endeavour, articles appeared in professional journals citing TASS as an international centre of excellence. Each of these articles begged the question: in the interest of extinguishing what was perceived as an obstacle in the path of worthy, life-saving work, how could self-righteous, often ill-informed, political appointees – who were strong on rhetoric and hypocrisy but frequently woefully lacking when a constructive approach was called for – be excluded from practical fields of human endeavour?

In June 1978 Duale received an internal report from TASS's head of contracts. Al Willis had previously put in hand the project for a new TASS building in downtown Chicago. Bids had been received from four short-listed construction firms. The approach favoured by the Board of TASS was that a new headquarters would be built in an area close to the site of the existing office block. The new building would be constructed within a period of two years and would be leased to TASS for 100 years. The new building's plans had been supplied to the selected bidders.

The report which Duale began to study summarized the results of analyses of the four bids. Two of these were recommended to be disqualified on the grounds that they were, in basic terms, non-responsive. The remaining two were judged to be good and almost equal in merit. Marginally, one was recommended above the other on apparent cost grounds, although it was conceded that depending on the timing and amounts of certain payments to be made, the order of preference might justifiably be reversed. The preferred firm was Schwartz Inc., and the second Giovanni; both proposals were of excellent quality. Duale called the Head of Contracts and told him how much all the good work was appreciated; Duale would need to digest the details and he would be in touch again within a week or so.

Early the following Saturday morning, Duale answered the telephone. 'Good morning. Your name is Mr. Giovanni? You are inviting me to lunch today. As it happens, I am free, yes. You will pick me up at 12.30. Thank you.' It was only after Duale had replaced the receiver that the name 'Giovanni' struck a chord; yes, Giovanni was probably one of the bidders. Now he remembered, Giovanni was the less preferred bidder.

The large black chauffeur-driven car appeared outside Duale's apartment building at exactly 12.30. Soon he was sitting in the luxurious back seat listening to Giovanni. Giovanni's family had come to Chicago from Toronto twenty years previously. They had won several major construction contracts and Giovanni was very keen that his firm should win the contract for TASS's new office complex. If necessary, they would be open to negotiation and they might find a way to reduce their price.

Now it was time for lunch and Duale found himself sitting in a superb seafood restaurant. Duale liked seafood, did he not? Giovanni hoped his homework was correct. Yes, Duale loved seafood. What Duale did not mention was that he was becoming increasingly distracted by the waitresses; each was beautifully dressed in a see-through white blouse and a fitted costume. As he eyed one and then another, one seemed more beautiful than the next. 'We can arrange one of these for you, Dr. Duale; just say which one,' Giovanni said in a quiet voice.

Duale was taken off-guard, 'I beg your pardon? Oh, no thank you, Mr. Giovanni.'

Giovanni continued talking throughout the meal about his experience in construction. He was ready to do almost anything within his power to obtain the contract. When the meal was over, Giovanni asked Duale to accompany him in the car for a half hour to a luxurious development of weekend houses.

Giovanni explained that each house was of the highest quality construction and included a garden of one acre. After looking over three houses, Duale mentioned that it was really high time he returned to the city.

'Of course,' Giovanni responded, 'incidentally, which of the three designs did you prefer?' 'Well, I think the first,' Duale answered. Giovanni spoke briefly with his chauffeur and they made for the car.

In front of Duale's apartment building, as Giovanni said farewell he repeated his hope about the contract.

'Anyway,' he added, 'whether we win or lose, I want you to have a memento of our meeting. These are the keys to the first house you liked; these are the title deeds. My lawyer will call you on Monday and he will arrange the transfer, Dr. Duale. I enjoyed our meeting and I hope we meet again!'

Duale took the elevator to his apartment and mused. Was it a trap? He thought not. If he accepted the bribe, would he be corrupt? Yes. So what! So long as no one would be hurt by his acceptance of the bribe, then why worry. What about setting a bad example? Well, the acquisition would be kept secret. In any case, even when it became known, he had certainly been working long enough at a professional level to be able to afford a country house.

And he was a bachelor; so of course he could accumulate money.

On Monday morning Duale asked Anna to arrange an appointment for the Head of Contracts. That afternoon, Duale spent two hours discussing the merits of both of the acceptable bids. Duale explained at some length that cost was not the only factor to be considered; what was of much greater importance was the value offered. If one really looked at the fine print and the details, Duale had no doubt which firm offered the better value. Eventually, the head of contracts agreed, commenting that the merit of the bids was in any case about equal. If the CEO preferred the order of merit to be adjusted, that would be absolutely no problem. The report would be modified and this would be reflected in the summary.

And so it came to pass. After all the correct audited procedures had been strictly followed, TASS acquired a new building. And without the involvement of any auditors, Duale acquired a country house. All he was asked to do from time to time was sign on the dotted line, which he did with pleasure. As for the accounts, Giovanni knew they would be 'taken care of' by his accountant's efficient, well-oiled system.

At the beginning of 1979 Duale took stock of the situation. He had just received a letter of appreciation and encouragement from the Board of Trustees; the letter was signed by the chairman on behalf of the Board.

As CEO of TASS Duale felt that he was on top of his job. He had arranged for Richard Spargel to be kicked upstairs; other potentially lesser trouble-makers on the Executive Committee had been contained. Once or twice Duale had found himself in danger-ously deep water, but somehow he had extricated himself.

He had a reputation for being dynamic, actively competent and confidently strong in character. As he managed to survive crises in the committee, challenges to his authority became less frequent. As far as he was concerned, he was gradually consoli-dating his position of power; he did not hesitate to exert this from time to time, although always just sufficiently to achieve his purpose. As far as others who observed him in action were concerned, Duale seemed to merit a nickname he had earned along the way. More and more, Duale became known as The Survivor.

Chapter Eight

Tashi's Homecoming

Shastri was standing at Tashi's bedroom door. 'So how is the packing going, Tashi? I can't believe that in twenty-four hours you won't be here any more. Imagine! All that way back to Bhutan. If our business here goes well, perhaps my father and I could visit you in a year or two. You've become part of our family; I feel you are my brother. Can I help you with anything?'

Tashi looked with brotherly affection at Shastri. He smiled; but Tashi's smile, usually so confidently effervescent, was lifeless. Tashi slowly turned his head and looked out of the window; the smile faded. Now he seemed to be musing. It was mid January 1979 and, as he took in the scene, it seemed to reflect his feeling of sadness. He looked up at the featureless grey blanket of cloud; as he glanced downwards, he was struck by the bare, leafless trees and the patchy wet grass as it tried to absorb the drizzle which permeated the heavy air. Inside his room, the already somewhat empty atmosphere seemed to accentuate the gloom.

He looked again at Shastri. 'I have just about done my packing, Shastri. I was just thinking. I should be so pleased to be going home. Perhaps when I arrive in Bhutan, I will be pleased. But for some reason I am so happy in England. Truthfully, I am really sorry to be leaving. Yes, Shastri, we are like brothers; and I love your family. You have been so kind to me and you are the best friend I have. I know I have been privileged to have stayed in England all these years; and at Dulwich and Cambridge I had a wonderful education. I will never forget this amazing experience.'

'I know you have enjoyed it here,' Shastri rejoined, 'but not everything was perfect. Tell me, Tashi. What did you like – or not? Do you think England is on the right track? Or do you think they are heading for problems? You've had a great education and you are pretty well informed; so I am interested in your impressions, Tashi.'

'Well,' Tashi responded, 'that's a tall order! Let me think a second. All right, here goes. You'd better sit down, Shastri. It will take a few minutes to give you my impressions.'

Shastri slid into an easy chair and looked expectantly at Tashi. Tashi did not disappoint him. 'As I was saying, Shastri, it's not that easy. But let me talk about just a few things. Whatever I say, I don't mean to be critical in a destructive way. I have been a guest here for almost ten years; as I said, I was privileged and I will always be grateful. Nothing will ever change that.

First, Shastri, in an unusual way I see certain common areas of outlook between England and Bhutan. England is an island; Bhutan is an isolated mountain kingdom. We both have close relationships with big neighbours. England has been accused of being a poodle of the United States; Bhutan has to ensure friendship with India. Both of the small countries like to kid themselves that they have this 'special relationship' with big brother. Both know that when the chips are down, the big brothers will do exactly what they feel like doing – regardless! I suppose to some extent because of their relative geographic isolation, both seem to be, at heart, conservative in their outlook. How else can you explain the problems the poor British have in coming to terms with Europe. Physical and electronic communications have improved tremendously and this part of the industrial revolution is still going on; but the majority of English people still look at European countries as though they are thoroughly foreign. That's quite an achievement, Shastri! Conservative values in Bhutan are even stronger, although in their case religion plays a more decisive role.

Which brings me to religion. Personally, my religion has always been very important to me. If I didn't have my religion, I would be lost as far as values are concerned. As for religion in England, I think they are in deep trouble, and it will not be long before they are lost. I am convinced we all need a religion. It doesn't matter too much which one, you can argue about the pros and cons *ad infinitum*; but we need to respect a god or gods and the values which they represent.

You know, Shastri, England is becoming an ungodly country – and nobody cares. There are lots of churches for sale. Then there are cults springing up all over the place. But they will never replace a religion; in fact, sometimes they do more harm than good – look at the United States. I think the situation is sad. Maybe the church and its form of worship needs an overhaul; perhaps something will need to be done about the schools' curriculum. But unless something is done, and soon, I honestly believe the country's population will degenerate into a superficial, materialistic society where nothing matters and only the so-called strongest survive.

And what pleasures can the strong and 'successful' look forward to? Maybe a bigger car than the neighbour's, or a new kitchen? This is not a very inspiring basis for living the short span of time we have on this earth; that's my opinion anyway. There is of course some religion; and there is also some culture. But it isn't deep enough. People sometimes say that such things are personal and should be followed at our discretion. I don't agree. If you don't educate people in basic terms, how can they develop their religion and culture through their own efforts? In the majority of cases they can't; it's as simple as that. If they are not careful, in the end the British will lose their soul.

I should stop talking. But let me quickly say two more things. My first point is that they have an awful pollution problem here and with all this road construction there will be more cars – and more pollution. The Germans sometimes call their traffic congestion 'Blechlawine' – metal avalanches. In ten years' time, it will be worse here.

Second, I think England has become too democratic; it sounds dreadful to say such a thing, doesn't it? But I think some of the unions have taken advantage of their strength and they are blackmailing the government and the people. The last two or three governments have tried to make them see reason and what has been the result – a disaster; it's getting worse. I think this woman Margaret Thatcher has the right approach. If she can get the conservatives elected, she will probably solve the problem. The population is being held to ransom and it's getting worse. When you look at the unions, you can see how power corrupts!

Oh, I forgot one thing, Shastri; immigration. The British really 'played cricket' over immigration and they were incredibly fair. But I think it was misguided. Enoch Powell talked a lot of sense. You know, some of his best friends were Nigerians, and they said they thought the British should never have let in so many foreigners who were labelled 'British.' I met some of those Nigerians and they said it would lead to a lot of racial trouble. I found it quite interesting how they went out of their way to say they never regarded Enoch Powell as a racist; the man was trying to apply common sense and find a sensible, practical solution. To be fair, I think it is amazing how well, so far, the British have managed the problem they created for themselves. Let's hope it works out all right in the end. But you know all this immigration will change English society; it's just a matter of time. Have I shocked you, Shastri?'

'Well, not exactly; but I have to admit I never associated you with getting involved with the British in this way. I don't agree with everything you have said, but I don't think we have too much time to go on discussing, Tashi. I had no idea how articulate you are! Once you are settled again in Bhutan, you will feel happy and I am sure anything you do will be a great success.

My father will take the family out for dinner this evening. He wants you to have a good send-off. I will drop you off at Heathrow tomorrow morning, Tashi. Let's hope we will say *au revoir* and not a final good-bye. We both have our lives ahead of us; we should definitely keep in touch.'

Neither of the friends had been looking forward to their parting at Heathrow; separately, both had decided the previous night that their parting should be brief. As soon as Tashi had checked in, he turned to Shastri; they hugged one another and Tashi, his eyes full of tears, said in a quiet voice, 'Thanks for everything. Now we must get on with our lives. Good luck, Shastri. Let's hope we will meet again one of these days. Au revoir!.'

Tashi enjoyed his flight to Calcutta; with his knowledge and experience of flying, he could easily imagine every phase of the flight of the huge jet. He had planned his stay in Calcutta to be a mere two days. The scenes of poverty and hopelessness of his visit of ten years previously had indelibly imprinted themselves in his remembrance and he had hoped to avoid a rekindling of the horror. Turning a blind eye whenever possible to dreadful everyday scenes of human degradation, he managed to maintain his equilibrium.

Soon he was again on his way, this time in a heavy cross-country vehicle which uncle Gyeltshen had sent with a driver to a *rendez-vous* in the city. And so he progressed generally northwards, reaching the Bhutanese border near Phuntsholing.

Tashi remembered the intense heat of the summer during his journey in 1969. Now it was winter and the dust and heat of the plains had been transformed; the weather was pleasantly warm and the green landscape reminded him of a quilt as he admired the crops and a mass of ephemeral vegetation.

At the border, feelings of anticipation began to excite his well-formed body; his chest and arms were positively tingling. How would uncle Gyeltshen be? And what about his beautiful mother? Would she still be good-looking at the age of 41? Seen through her eyes, would she still look upon him as a child; or would he be allowed to grow up? Suddenly, so many questions were appearing in his mind's eye. But he should be patient; it would still be some hours before he reached Paro. From there, it would take another three hours to drive to Thimphu.

'We need to see your papers!' Tashi was jerked out of his thoughts by the strong voice of a Bhutanese immigration official. 'Bring them into that building over there.' Tashi had carefully made sure that all his identity papers were in good order. 'You may proceed. We must caution you to be very careful on the road. The government has had some problems with the Lhotshampas. There have been attacks on government officials and some buildings have been damaged. Keep your eyes open and be prepared to drive fast and escape if you are held up. Report to the police when you arrive safely in Paro. Have a good journey.'

Tashi reached Paro at dusk and called at the police station. At the higher altitude the air was fresh and he looked forward to a meal and a good sleep. At last, he would again be lying under Yak hair blankets. Although he had expected to fall asleep quickly in the house of uncle Gyeltshen's friend, the darting thoughts returned. Would he be loved as part of the family? Or would he be regarded as someone apart, the product of a foreign educational system? Had uncle Gyeltshen made enquiries about a job for him? When would he start, what would he do – what could he do?

Tashi rose early and said his prayers. He knew that uncle Gyeltshen would make sure the house in Thimphu would be purified in preparation for Tashi's arrival. Tashi was anxious to lose no time in giving thanks to *Mahakala* and the *Yulha* for having looked after him throughout his almost ten years' absence.

When he had said his prayers, Tashi asked the driver to take him to Paro airport. The runway, air traffic control tower and passenger terminal building had all been constructed. The buildings were painted in lively colours, using Bhutanese motifs. In the early morning sunlight, the colours seemed to reach out towards him; somehow he felt that the colours represented a welcoming gesture.

He remembered the dust and abrasive noise of the construction which had assailed and shocked his senses in 1969. Now this mountainous kingdom in the Himalayas had an airport. Tashi felt proud. His country could truly take its place in the international community. And what a final approach for the aircraft through the mountains! Perhaps one day he could fly on that approach; or then again, perhaps not.

The drive to Thimphu would take a mere three hours. As the road wound its way along the side of the mountains, Tashi noticed the wintry brown landscape and the rushing torrents of the rivers; sometimes he noticed a heavily-clothed woman struggling across a swinging suspension bridge, her body bent double with the weight of firewood. He recollected that he had watched precisely the same scene ten years previously; apparently, at the peasant level, in contrast with the construction of the airport, nothing had changed.

Thimphu came into view. It seemed bigger than when he had left. If people from the mountains were coming to live in the town, what would they do, Tashi wondered. Here at last was his house. The walls were white and the wooden features had recently been meticulously repainted. In the clear mountain air the mix of strong, bright colours was beautiful; everything was so spotlessly clean! Now he was truly home. He was bursting with anticipation; but for some reason he also felt uncertain. Tashi wondered why he felt apprehensive. He was prepared for the known; but suppose there might also be an unknown? Although his mother would be expecting him on that day, she could have no idea at what time he might arrive; Tashi could hardly expect to see his welcoming family at the door. He should just go in; which he did.

Tashi entered. He was struck by the silence. Then he turned

into the main room. His uncle Gyeltshen was sitting in a large easy chair, apparently looking in Tashi's direction; but he made no gesture. Tashi took a few steps and stood before his uncle. 'Uncle Gyeltshen. It is wonderful to be home! I think you were expecting me today?'

Gyeltshen took a few quick breaths and responded, 'Tashi! How wonderful to hear your voice. Let me look hard at you. Yes, I think I see you; I am not sure. But I am sure of one thing; you are so handsome.' Then Gyeltshen began panting.

At last he explained, 'Unfortunately, Tashi, I have had a bit of a health problem. It started with a recurrence of an earlier illness. Also, for the last two years I have been losing my eyesight; sometimes I see better than at other times. But I am so pleased you are back. We have plenty to talk about. I have been working on your future. Let us talk tomorrow; perhaps I will feel better.' Gyeltshen managed a wan smile, which seemed to fade before it could take hold on his wizened face.

Tashi was bemused. This was not the uncle Gyeltshen he had known ten years previously. If only he had been warned. Tashi tried to collect himself, 'Uncle, I have to unpack and say my prayers. May I ask, is my mother at home; I had hoped to see her.'

Gyeltshen tried his best to appear alert, but failed the test miserably. Then he spoke in a slow, low voice, 'Your mother, Tashi? Yes, she will come. After you left Bhutan your mother took courses. When the UN established itself in our country they gave her a job as a secretary. She was very good at her work. After five years she was made senior secretary. Then last year she was promoted to administrative assistant. She works hard. She sent a message that there are some visitors from the World Bank; they are discussing how to develop hydroelectricity in the mountains. She is busy with them and will come home very late, perhaps at twelve o'clock. Tashi, I am sorry. It must be the excitement; now I must sleep.'

Tashi watched his uncle slowly put his head back; within half a minute Gyeltshen had fallen asleep.

As a man of twenty two, Tashi was not easily discouraged. He was in good physical and mental condition, keen to use his education and start his professional career. Now, quite unexpectedly, he found himself looking with compassion at a fading uncle. And his mother was nowhere to be seen. She was too busy to welcome him at home. Had Bhutan already become a victim of the Western pressure-of-work syndrome? Tashi decided he'd suffered enough shock for one day. The best thing to do, he concluded, would be to say some prayers and go to bed.

Perhaps because of the time change between London and Thimphu, Tashi slept lightly; for short periods, he simply could not sleep at all. From to time he found himself opening his eyes; the features of his room were illuminated by soft, diffused moonlight. Looking out of his window, he could see the silhouettes of the mountains; the brilliance and clarity of the moon seemed almost unreal. He looked at his watch; it was 2a.m. Then he was suddenly aware of a presence.

'Did you feel my hand on your shoulder, Tashi? I'm sorry I could not be at home when you arrived. I wanted to see you as soon as possible. Now I can see you very clearly. I have never seen the moon shine so brightly; the whole room is light, especially where your head rests on your pillow. This is a good omen, Tashi. Welcome home, my Treasure!'

The gentle voice of his mother was unmistakable. Tashi jumped out of his wooden, creaking bed and embraced his mother. Then he looked at her in the glorious moonlight. He was immediately struck by her beauty. She might be his mother, but this did not prevent him admiring the sheer beauty of her physical form.

'I am so pleased to see you,' Tashi said. 'You look wonderful. It is late; I have never seen the moon so bright. I looked at my watch without any problem. And I see you clearly. But mother, if you are working again in the morning, you should sleep. Before you leave, I want to say I am sorry uncle Gyeltshen is not well; when I saw him I felt so sad! But seeing you now makes me feel much better!'

Tashi embraced his mother again; she smiled warmly, and then turned to leave. At the bedroom door, she said, 'You are right, Tashi. I must get in a few hours' rest. But I must say two things: first, you are now grown up and you have a good education. Although you will always be my son and my Treasure, I am not going to treat you like a child, because you are not a child. I think we should become friends and support each other; and we should share our pleasures and our problems.

Second, uncle Gyeltshen. He is not well, and sometimes has problems concentrating. Sometimes he is bad-tempered. We will always be kind to him and listen to his ideas, but you only have to go so far, Tashi. First you can do your duty and listen; then *you* will decide how *you* will handle the situation. You are a man and you can have a mind of your own. I am sure you will take the right decisions. I will see you again in the late afternoon. Goodnight my Treasure!' Tashi was suddenly alone in the moonlight. He said a prayer; and fell asleep.

When he awoke in the morning the sun had risen over the mountain and it streamed into his room. He washed and shaved, and after brushing his thick, black hair, he went downstairs. Gyeltshen was sitting in his chair dressed in traditional Bhutanese costume; a servant was helping him pull on the second silk-embroidered shoe. Tashi noticed that his uncle was staring in the direction of a window, but apparently was unseeing.

'Good morning, uncle, it's Tashi. I'm sorry I got up late; I seem to be still half on English time. May I help you with anything?' Gyeltshen slowly turned his head – his eyes continued to stare and they seemed to be trying to search for Tashi, who now was standing directly in front of him.

'Ah, yes, Tashi,' Gyeltshen replied. 'Good morning, Tashi. I can't really see you, unfortunately. Perhaps in a few days my sight will be better. I want to talk to you, but it won't be as it was ten years ago, when I was much healthier. Apart from my eyesight, I can't always breathe properly. So I will be brief. Are you there, Tashi?'

'Yes, uncle.'

'Good,' Gyeltshen went on. 'I know you will lose no time in applying to join the civil service. I have of course already left your details with the Planning Commission, and His Majesty's office also is well informed about you and your academic achievements. It is important that your education and knowledge of Europe are used properly in the Kingdom.

Tomorrow you will call on various ministerial offices in the Thimphu *dzong*. I have a schedule here, showing those people who will talk to you. I suppose the main possibilities will be science and technology or international relations. Of course, it also depends whether they have a vacancy; all the posts in the civil service have to be properly funded from the Government's budget, as you know. Let me know the outcome in due course. Oh, and please pay attention to your national dress. His Majesty is very keen that we always wear traditional Bhutanese dress, especially when visiting government officials.

Now I must sleep for an hour; I feel very tired. I have put on my best clothes because this afternoon a minister will be visiting me. We are having a general discussion about the development of our country; if we think that certain adjustments are needed, we will draft a note for His Majesty's attention. I will eat with you in the early evening, Tashi. Then you can tell me something of the foreign countries you visited. But now I must sleep; I cannot over-strain myself.'

Tashi wandered into the garden. So this was his uncle Gyeltshen, a man who had doted on him and loved him more than most fathers love their children. Certainly, Tashi thought, uncle Gyeltshen was terribly sick. He had struck Tashi as a puppet, desperately trying to play a role which was patently well beyond his capacity. Poor man, Tashi thought, he had become physically degraded and this had affected his mental capability. A tragedy.

Over the next few days, Tashi met a number of government officials; without exception, they were courteous and knowledgeable about the Kingdom. Each was anxious to impress Tashi with the part their ministry was playing in the Kingdom's ambitious development programme. They spoke eloquently about the possibilities for Tashi's participation, although all emphasized that education would never be a substitute for experience. Tashi should understand that if a place were found for him in the civil service, several years would be needed to acquire the basic experience to perform his work with competence.

On two or three evenings Tashi walked around the centre of Thimphu. In contrast to the sleepy little town of the sixties, now there were pockets of noise and merrymaking; there were even a few neon signs. Few of the Bhutanese he saw wore the prescribed national dress; disappointed, he recalled how everyone had somehow looked much cleaner and smarter ten years ago.

Tashi walked into a small restaurant and surprised himself by thinking how pleasant the loud music was. He noticed groups of outsiders sitting at the tables. He discovered they were consultants from Switzerland, Austria or England. Although they all spoke English, Tashi conversed in German, and French also. Suddenly he had a link with the world outside. The foreigners enjoyed talking to Tashi, and for his part, Tashi felt less remote from the other world to which he had grown accustomed.

About two weeks later, Pema, Gyeltshen and Tashi had almost finished their evening meal. Tashi had been talking of his experiences at Cambridge. Feeling stronger after the meal, Gyeltshen decided to press Tashi on the subject of work.

'Now, Tashi!' he said in firm tones, 'where have you got to? When do you start working? Bhutan needs all your education. I know you have met the civil service people, so when do you start?'

Tashi looked his uncle in the eye; again, he was confronted with staring, unseeing eyes. 'Uncle, at the moment I can't say when I will start working, or what I will do. I know you won't be happy to hear this. The problem is that I cannot properly identify with my countrymen. The people I have met have all been very nice, and they know a lot about the Kingdom. They think they also know a lot about countries outside Bhutan, but this is not the case. I often found their knowledge incomplete and their attitude unrealistic. Although everyone wants things to move ahead quickly, I am afraid with the conservative attitudes you find everywhere around here this cannot happen.

I've thought of leaving Bhutan and working perhaps in India, or even Europe. I'm not ready to take such a step yet, but I may be forced to. In any case, I have decided....'

'You have decided?' interrupted Gyeltshen testily, 'I don't understand. I am the one who has mainly paid for your education. I expect results. You are here to work for your country, I have taken that decision. Now I need to hear when you will start working. That is all that interests me. If you are a man, Tashi, I will treat you like a man. Answer me!' Gyeltshen's head sank until his chin touched his chest and he seemed to slump in his chair.

'May I speak, or do you wish me to be silent, uncle?' Tashi was unruffled by his uncle's intervention. Pema looked at her son; it had been she who had told Tashi he was no longer a child, but even Pema was astonished to watch her son respond so coolly. Was this what an education in England had taught him? Her son was 22, but he could already conduct himself in a thoroughly controlled, mature manner.

'Just speak,' Gyeltshen growled in a low voice.

'Thank you, uncle. I concluded that I have become confused in trying to see where I can best fit into my country's future. Part of the problem is that I am a product of two worlds – Bhutan and Europe. Of course, I must work, but as far as possible I want to be sure that I am contributing in the best way. I have therefore decided to go on a week's retreat to the monastery I visited just before I left for England. I am leaving tomorrow morning.

Thank you, uncle, for all the good things you have done for me; I am sure the investment will prove worthwhile. We just need a little patience. Good night.'

Gyeltshen did not answer. Pema said, 'Gyeltshen, you have to accept that you are dealing with a man. Tashi is no longer a child. It is better that he takes his own decisions. Please promise not to treat him like a little boy. Can you hear me, Gyeltshen?' Gyeltshen was breathing heavily; he had already fallen asleep.

As Tashi retraced the paths of ten years previously, he thought how little had changed. Certainly Thimphu had grown, but once he was outside the town it all looked much the same. He was not quite as physically fit as before, though. In any case, the three days' walk would help improve his condition. He also hoped the stay at the monastery would help his confused state of mind and restore his mental health.

The walk was arduous, partly because it was winter. Tashi was lucky there was no snowstorm *en route*, even though from the cold, swirling mist it was evident that the atmosphere was near to saturation point. It was often slippery, and he had to pay constant attention to the conditions. Each morning he had to negotiate patches of ice; as the day wore on, the ice melted and he found himself sometimes slipping on mud. The last thing he wanted was to fall and hurt a limb in such a remote area.

At last he reached the monastery. Some of the lamas remembered him as a boy, and they gathered around to listen to tales of life in Europe. Tashi described his visits to the Tibetan Centre in London, and told the lamas that he could not imagine any adequate form of substitute for Mahayana Buddhism that might exist in the outside world.

After three days of intense prayer and meditation he felt that he had really returned to the country of his birth. Images of the other world were fading from his everyday thoughts.

On the sixth day of the retreat, Tashi took advantage of some fine weather to retrace his steps of 1969; he walked along the mountain ridge which extended from the entrance of the monastery. As he wandered in search of the rock where he had rested as a boy, a feeling of inner happiness began to take hold within him; he felt strengthened by an indomitable sense of well-being which transcended earthly anxiety and apprehensions.

Now he relished the familiarity of the wet moss and the ferns which brushed his calves. Then he saw the rock. Instead of sitting on it, he knelt and stretched his forearms over it, his hands clasped. He closed his eyes and raised his head to heaven, then prayed to the *Yulha* and the great mountain god *Odopa*. Again he gave thanks to *Mahakala* for watching over him during his travels. He cried out, 'O great and merciful Lord Buddha, guide me so that I may follow what is best for my country. Please help me!'

At that moment an ear-splitting crash of thunder signalled the beginning of an electric storm. Huge droplets of rain pelted Tashi's face, but soon the rain had turned to ice and snow. Before he reached the monastery, the dull, brown landscape had been transformed into a magical, white mountain kingdom. Tashi knelt in front of an altar; at that moment he was overcome by a profound feeling of contentment. He also knew that the solution to his dilemma was at hand.

It would soon be time to leave. As on the previous occasion, before leaving Tashi received a message that the abbot, the *Neten*, would like to see him. The abbott said 'I am so pleased to see you, Tashi, after all these years. You have become a fine young man and you have made excellent academic achievements. Come and sit next to me.' Tashi was moved by the abbot's friendliness and down-to-earth attitude. 'I think I know why you are here, Tashi,' the *Neten* went on with a smile. 'You have been educated in another part of the world. Perhaps now you are not sure which world you belong to; you feel unsettled. Is this not so?'

Tears welled up in Tashi's eyes. How could the abbot of a monastery perched on a remote Himalayan mountain-top know Tashi's problems? How could a man so permanently engaged in prayer and meditation, totally involved with Buddhism – how could he have such incisive vision? To Tashi the abbot looked the same, perhaps even a little younger, as when they had met ten years previously.

'Yes, *Neten*, you are quite right. I would like to serve the Kingdom, but each time I look at possibilities, doubts enter my mind. I accept that time will be needed for me to become a fully competent professional, yet I have been highly educated in England and I would like to use this knowledge without delay. I also wish to maintain physical links with the outside world. Can you advise, *Neten*, please?'

'Yes, Tashi. All you need is faith! I believe you have faith. Do the following. Leave here after final prayers in two hours. Then you have three days on your return journey to consider the options open to you. If it snows, you may have a month!' the abbot continued with a smile. 'In any case, I can guarantee that, strengthened and supported by our prayers, by the time you reach Thimphu you will have reached a decision. That decision will be in the interest of Bhutan; and it will also suit your aptitudes. Ten years ago I said you would become a great servant of the Drukpa. Soon you will start on that path, and your good works will not only be seen within our country; you will represent all that is good about our Kingdom internationally. Now, tell me, Tashi, do you have faith in what I have told you?'

'I have faith in your advice, *Neten*. Thank you. I cannot express my appreciation properly as I am so deeply humbled. I promise that I will follow your advice – and I will have faith! Good-bye, *Neten*.'

Tashi followed the abbot's advice on the return journey, his concentration only interrupted from time to time by the need to avoid slipping either on the ice in the early mornings, or later on patches of shallow mud. As he neared Thimphu, he recalled the noise and dust of the road construction work. Now he could see the finished product – a tarred road sweeping its way towards the mountains in the north.

When he arrived home in the late afternoon, the sun was already disappearing behind the mountain. The temperature would rapidly drop, and soon it would be below freezing. Pema was at home and Gyeltshen was resting in his chair. Pema embraced Tashi:

'It's wonderful to see you. I've been looking out for you.' Then she whispered, 'Uncle Gyeltshen is not in a very good mood, Tashi. He keeps saying that it's high time you started work. Try and reassure him; at least say something will be decided soon. He is so irritable!'

'Good evening, uncle. It's Tashi. I am back. Are you awake, or resting?'

Gyeltshen's head turned slowly; Tashi could see the unseeing eyes. Gyeltshen smiled and said, 'Tashi, I have been waiting patiently for you. Do you not agree that I have shown great patience? But my patience is wearing thin. Have you decided what you would like to do. You have so many choices!'

'Yes, uncle, I have decided. As you know, the Kingdom has an airport at Paro, which is hardly used. The only aircraft which sometimes land at Paro are from foreign carriers. Bhutan needs its own airline. The Kingdom should form a small airline. I will train for the ATPL, which means the Air Transport Pilot's Licence. I will be successful, and I will help to make the airline a great success. This will be my contribution to the Kingdom's development. I have no doubt that His Majesty will welcome the initiative. Tomorrow, uncle, you and I will discuss how to have the project approved as soon as possible. However, if you do not wish to discuss it further, this will be absolutely no problem. I can proceed on my own.'

Gyeltshen sat bolt upright in his chair and furtively looked in Tashi's direction. His lips trembling, he said, 'Tashi, I think I am beginning to recognize your features; you are so handsome! I was not expecting this. But, you have taken your decision and I respect it. Of course, we will work on the project, and we will succeed. It makes total sense. You already have flying licences. If it is a success, you will travel all over the place, and so maintain contact with your other world. It is a splendid idea. I have not felt so well in five years!'

Tashi turned his head and looked at his beautiful mother, her smile showing her feelings. The tension and stress of the long discussion on Tashi's future was at an end. Contentment would again prevail in the house. Tomorrow there would be discussion and action. Now was time for supper – and prayers.

Chapter Nine

Himalaya Airways – The Embryo

'So I take it, gentlemen, that based on the papers made available to us by the Minister of Communications, we are agreed that the Kingdom should, in principle, establish an airline.'

As Chairman of the government's Planning Commission, His Majesty was reflecting the unanimous decision of its members. For this particular meeting, in addition to the commission, several outsiders were present, including two ministers. His Majesty continued: 'We certainly have an airport at Paro. We know it is rarely used. Now we need an airline, but how do we do it?

Before I pass this question to you, I wish to emphasize that I see the existence of an airline rather in the nature of a double-edged sword. Certainly, it will speed up physical communication between our country and the outside world. It will also help to give our country an identity in the eyes of the world. There is much merit in having our own airline.

However, we have to consider the financial outlay. When we prepare the government's budget, we have always made it our business to make ends meet. How can we finance an airline? Another aspect we must think about is how we protect our people from outside influence. Some countries use their airline to fly in tourists; the Kingdom of Nepal is an example. But our policy is different. We already keep the number of tourists as low as possible, within one or two thousand a year, and limit what they can see. This is our policy, and I do not want any airline to change this. I am sure you agree?.' The Commission members slowly bowed their heads. His Majesty looked around the table, 'I wish to invite comments; they can be positive or negative, as long as they are constructive.'

There was silence. His Majesty looked at each member of the Commission and the invited outsiders in turn. All were dressed in traditional costume, based on what Buddhist clerics wore in the seventeenth century. Each wore a sash, the colour indicating his rank. Their colourful, knee-length tunics had been perfectly pressed and the deep cuffs were spotlessly white. Their boots, made of hide and cloth, were beautifully decorated and embroidered, with the background colours of orange, red or black indicating their high rank. The king's boots were ornamented in yellow, a colour uniquely reserved for His Majesty; as befitted royalty, the upper sections of his boots were decorated with appliqué, which depicted a dragon.

The king was used to the polite hesitation from members of his government and bureaucrats – a combination of reverence and cultural tradition. For their part, the ministers and officials knew what to expect. After a few minutes, the king said, 'Well, I think we should have a discussion. Minister of Communications, how do we establish an airline at a cost we can afford?'

The minister, who had been appointed by the king from the nobility, was a middle-aged, portly man who exuded benevolence, charm and good humour. Although he would never earn a good reputation within his ministerial field, he compensated for his lack of professional understanding by having an uncanny gift for finding the right people with the right knowledge. He first looked at the king and lowered his head in respect; then he looked around the table with a quizzical expression.

'Your Majesty, colleagues. If I may say so, I believe we are today witnesses to a momentous decision. Our country will have its own airline. This will mean that we can take our independent place in the international arena; we will no longer have to rely on our friends as far as air transport is concerned. However, before we do in fact reach this point, as you have so rightly pointed out, Your Majesty, we have to establish our airline.

In the papers I circulated two weeks ago, I outlined possibilities. From the financial viewpoint, others are more qualified to address this than I am. However, I would like to observe that we receive ninety-eight per cent of our foreign assistance from India. With this in mind, I would propose that you, Your Majesty, address the President of India to ascertain whether we may be granted help and financing on concessionary terms from that quarter. Then perhaps we should consider the UN. They have a business-like attitude to providing assistance to our country; they may have some good ideas. If they cannot themselves help, they may have access to a development bank which would be able to find funding, either as grant aid or, more likely, through a concessionary loan. Of course, the more capital the Kingdom itself can raise, the less onerous and burdensome will be the financing terms.

Then, Your Majesty, I would like to touch on the subject of staffing. As you know, at this time the government of India looks after air traffic control at Paro airport; in fact, the controllers are drawn from the Indian military. We do maintain the airport, although apart from the immigration and customs most of the work is checking the condition of the runway and buildings; then we make repairs as necessary. In other words the work is semi-skilled manual labour. But from all I have read, the operation of aviation and an airline is highly professional; to participate effectively, you need a good education and sometimes years of training. Your Majesty, your Kingdom simply does not have the human resources available which could be trained and adapted for aviation or airline operations. It is not pleasant, but we have to face this fact. Only when we know what is required to overcome the problem will we be able to initiate the necessary action..

May I finally mention that during the last ten years, a son of Bhutan has been educated in England. He took an honours degree in physics at Cambridge University. He is Tashi, the son of Pema; he has been in the care of his uncle Gyeltshen. Tashi has taken two flying licences in England and has been strongly commended for his knowledge of aviation and his ability to pilot aircraft. If you wish, Your Majesty, I can call him to explain more about aviation and the basic requirements for the operation of an airline. He is immediately available outside our meeting room, in case you wish to raise any questions with him, Your Majesty. Thank you!'

His Majesty smiled good-naturedly at his noble Minister of Communications.

'Minister, I should like to record my appreciation for your contribution to our discussion. You are older than most of us here; and I am reminded from time to time that you show us in your modest way that you are often wiser. Minister of Finance, Minister of International Relations, please liaise with one another and then with me on the subject of funding, whether we may be looking at a gift, grant aid or concessionary financing. When you are ready, you will prepare letters for my signature. If technical and costing studies are to be done first, arrange this through the UN. But let us be as speedy as possible.

Which reminds me, many years ago an organization called the Trust For Air Safety Support gave us a legal consultant who drafted our aviation law; at least that was a step in the right direction. At that time we could not go forward because we had no airport and no airline. Now we have our airport and we have today decided that we will have an airline. Minister of Communications, please arrange for the draft aviation law to be reviewed and updated, as necessary. In addition, we shall almost certainly need a manual to explain the meaning of various aspects of the law, the intention in implementing its provisions and how the law should be applied. Thank you.

Now, I think most of us should be feeling slightly exhausted from our deliberations. We were all required to read and study the excellent background papers prepared by the Minister of Communications. We had to take the recommendation to establish the airline very seriously, which I believe we have done. The minister has called this a momentous decision – he is right, it is a momentous decision. I have no doubt that it is the right decision! Now, it is proposed that we listen a little to Tashi the son of Pema. In principle, I think we should; but do we have the energy to absorb what he might tell us? He has just come from Europe and he is up-to-date. I am sure what he has to say will be interesting. The question is, do we have him today, or another time. May I have your view, please?'

As was customary, the participants sat silently, their heads slightly bowed. The king said, 'I will not ask our Minister of Communications what he thinks, because he has already told us. I suggest we ask questions and listen to the responses for fifteen to thirty minutes. I trust this will be agreeable? Perhaps we shall learn something. Minister, kindly call Tashi son of Pema.'

Tashi entered the meeting room, wearing traditional Bhutanese dress. He walked to the head of the table and bowed before His Majesty. The king looked at Tashi with pride.

'We are proud of you, Tashi son of Pema. I have received a note from your uncle Gyeltshen. You are not only clever; we have

141

plenty of clever people. You have applied yourself and met all your challenges. Now you are home. And there will be more challenges for you!' he added with a smile. 'Do not feel nervous. We may look impressive, but unfortunately when it comes to knowledge, some of us may be found wanting. Come and sit next to me. Then you can see your audience. Tell us about the operation of aviation, then focus on what we will need to do to make an airline a reality for our country. The floor is yours!'

Perhaps Tashi should have felt nervous, but at the age of twenty-two there was not the slightest chance that any thought of being affected by the assembled company should enter his head. Tashi knew that he had a solid education, he knew that his knowledge of foreign countries was probably greater and certainly more current than that of those present. He also knew that in the field of aviation he was unique within his country; apart from anything else, he had the ability to fly an aircraft. In plain language, although he was a man who conducted himself with impeccable modesty, at the same time he was self-possessed.

Tashi looked at his watch. For fifteen minutes he spoke about domestic and international civil aviation. He did his best to explain the meaning behind such terms as 'licensing of professional staff,' 'air traffic services,' 'flight operations,' 'airworthiness,' 'aviation meteorology,' 'aeronautical communications,' 'airport construction' and 'aviation security.' He explained that many books had been written on each of these subjects, and each field was progressively becoming more complex. He talked briefly about the history of aviation and the constant urge which over the centuries had driven people to develop the art and science of flight; he briefly discussed aviation's dynamic progress.

For another fifteen minutes he talked about the airlines. Tashi explained that one of the main east-west routes for the airlines ran south of Bhutan; the traffic density was relatively high at certain hours of the day, and the annual expansion was running at the rate of twenty per cent each year.

He named the main carriers operating in Asia, and he explained how they had started their operations. Some had inherited a nucleus of an airline from colonial times. Others had modelled themselves on successful foreign carriers; in fact, a few had actually imported foreign advice and expertise, not only to help establish their airlines, but also to put in place all the complex financial and administrative systems to assure success. He tried to give some dimension of the scale of operations worldwide when he explained that by 1990 it was estimated that at least one billion people would be boarding an aircraft each year. After a half hour, Tashi finished.

The king seemed to be musing; at last, he turned and looked at Tashi, then around the table. Two of the listeners were staring at Tashi with their mouths open; others simply focused on him and fixed him with stares of amazement. The king spoke, 'I think, Tashi son of Pema, that today we have not only taken a very important national decision. You have introduced us to another world – the world of flight. It is clear that we are ignorant and that we have much to learn. I have been informed that you intend to continue with your flying to gain a licence to fly large passenger-carrying aircraft. I wish the record of this meeting to spell out that the government strongly supports this course of action.

You will proceed as follows. For the next three months you will work in the office of the Minister of Communications and you will be our internal adviser with respect to the assistance we are seeking, as well as any studies which will need to be undertaken, including a long-term plan covering the training of Bhutanese nationals to eventually manage and operate civil aviation in the Kingdom. Using your knowledge, I ask my ministers to ensure that you review and comment on all papers and important letters which may be drafted relating to the kingdom's civil aviation development.

Once this phase is completed, you will do whatever has to be done to gain your flying licence at the required level; the government will meet the necessary supporting cost. Once you have done this, you will return to serve your country. Where will you train for the licence; will you need to return to Europe, or can this step be completed in Asia?'

Tashi was beginning to realize that he was becoming part of the decision-making process, but he also became conscious of feeling somewhat inadequate. He responded in a quiet, steady voice:

'Your Majesty, I am not quite sure where I will be able to progress to the full pilot's licence. Preferably, I would like to obtain it in Asia. I thought of approaching Thai Airways first.'

The king spoke directly to the Minister of Communications: 'Minister, we should support the application. I will leave you to arrange this. I think it is very appropriate that Tashi goes to Thailand for training. In the main, the Thai people follow the Buddhist religion and their values are similar to ours. If you need extra support, I am prepared to write to His Majesty the King of Thailand. I will leave this to your discretion, that is whether to draft a letter for my signature.

'Do we have any questions, or have I made myself clear?' The king looked up and saw the familiar bowed heads; silence prevailed. 'The meeting is ended. Thank you for your participation and I look forward to early action. And I hope in due course to see you again, Tashi son of Pema.'

Tashi followed the example of others who were present; he stood up and bowed towards His Majesty. The king left the room and the participants returned to their offices; in most cases, they were followed by assistants, their arms bulging with files.

At home, Tashi found his uncle in a state of excitement and full of anticipation. After Tashi had related the day's events, Gyeltshen smiled and said, 'A lot of progress was made today, Tashi. So all that work we did to help prepare the papers for the meeting has rewarded us. I have spent most of the day in meditation and prayer. I knew all would turn out for the best. Now you have to follow through on everything. If you are accepted for training in Thailand, again your mother and I will be alone. But at least from time to time you can visit us; or perhaps we could visit you? Bangkok is not so far away, especially if we are courageous and use the airlines.'

The next day Tashi received a message from the Minister of Communications. The minister would receive Tashi at 3p.m. 'Yes,' the minister explained, 'I have cleared your appointment internally. I would like you to start tomorrow morning. The office next door will be reserved for you as long as you work with us, Tashi. Your first job will be to draft a letter through me to the Thai airline people to find out if they will take you.' The minister leant over his desk and looked Tashi in the eye with a good-natured smile. 'Tell me, Tashi, do you seriously think it is better for you to train with the Thais; rather, for example, than go back to Europe?

Surely you will get better training in Europe or the United States? We have to make sure you have the best. Do you not think that the Thais are a little new at the game? How do they rate in civil aviation?' The minister chuckled, exuding confidence in his profound ignorance of one of the great airlines of Asia.

Tashi gathered himself. It was obvious the minister had not considered the possibility that, as usual, Tashi had done his homework. After all, without research, how could he have been in a position to make his recommendation in the first place? 'I would like to reassure you, Excellency, that with Thai Airways I will be in good hands. With your permission, I would like to give you a few facts about civil aviation in Thailand.' The minister nodded; he seemed to be listening intently.

Tashi continued, 'The first powered flight in Thailand took place in 1911, just over seven years after the first powered flight in the United States by the Wright Brothers. His Majesty Rama the Sixth arranged for three army officers to travel to France to learn more about aviation. They took flying licences the following year and returned to Thailand with aircraft. So the history and tradition of Thai civil aviation goes back a long time. In 1917 Thailand sent a military force to Europe, and this force included 340 aviators. During the 1920s and 1930s, regular air services for passengers and mail were established in Thailand; there was even an emergency air ambulance service. In 1927 the Thais designed and built their own aircraft at a factory outside Bangkok; it was called the 'Boripatra.' Then after the second world war three separate airlines were established in Thailand for domestic and international services.

Although civil aviation expanded quite rapidly, the expansion accelerated from 1959, when the Thais signed a co-operation agreement with the Scandinavian Airlines System. The co-operation went on for 15 years and was very successful. In the first year of the link-up with SAS, Thai Airways carried 83,000 passengers. By 1970, the number of passengers had increased to 500,000 and the airline made a profit of more than one million US dollars.

The airline terminated its SAS agreement about five years ago; now it is investing in more aircraft and negotiating more international routes. It is generally accepted that Thai International will link up with the domestic carrier Thai Airways within a few years. The airline is planning to become the third largest in Asia, and it expects to be carrying at least 7,000,000 passengers in ten years' time, by 1990. By then the airline is planning to have about 50 passenger transport aircraft, mainly from Boeing and Airbus. Thai International has a staff of about 14,000. In each year of its operation, the airline has made a profit; these days its profits are very large.

Finally, perhaps I might mention, your Excellency, that Thai International has a very good safety record. The airline looks after its own maintenance of the fleet and its standards are high; that is certainly why it has 65 other airlines as customers for their maintenance work. It also has a wonderful training centre with simulators and the most up-to-date training aids. Altogether it is self-sufficient; for example, it even has a large flight kitchen which is used by 27 airlines. The kitchen produces about 30,000 meals a day.

I hope, Excellency, I have given you enough information to convince you that my judgement is sound? I believe that if it is feasible it is much better to train in Asia, because when Himalaya Airlines is established the airline will operate within Asia. Thank you for permitting me to explain.'

The minister was speechless; when Tashi looked at him he noticed that he was no longer smiling. Tashi began to feel embarrassed. 'Do you need further information, Excellency?' The response was quick and to the point.

'I am more then convinced. Draft the letter to the Thais as we have discussed. I will see you tomorrow. Thank you, Tashi.'

Tashi could not help noticing the respectful way in which the minister addressed him.

Although the intention of the king had been that Tashi should assist within the Ministry of Communications for three months, in fact by the time all the initial actions had been completed seeking assistance and support for the establishment of Himalaya Airways, almost six months had elapsed. As it happened this schedule fitted in well for Tashi's further training, because after a few enquiries from Thai Airways, Tashi received a letter stating he had been accepted for employment with the airline as a trainee first officer, and he should report in Bangkok for duty on the first day of September.

Again, Tashi was on the move and saying his goodbyes. This

time, however, neither he, his mother nor Gyeltshen felt the wrench which had been the case ten years earlier. Tashi's mother was increasingly busy with her UN work, and his uncle had become relatively inactive due to his health. As for Tashi, he was not only an adult; he was accomplished and mature for his age.

There was also the general realization that, as far as Bhutan was concerned, the world was shrinking. The flying time from Paro to Bangkok was about four hours, including the stopover in Calcutta. Especially in an emergency, the family could soon regain contact. The days of the long drive in cross-country vehicles, not to mention resolving the Indian visa situation, were almost history; when the airline would start its regular service, memories of the long journeys over land for the Bhutanese to make contact with the outside world would fade.

Tashi spent three years in Thailand. With Thai Airways he completed 750 hours on turbine propeller aircraft. He gained vast experience in a variety of weather conditions, ranging from upcurrents caused by great heat to the relatively stable air when approaches were flown over water. High winds, tropical torrential rain and, sometimes, the dry air of drought constantly seemed to produce a mix of something different, which in turn meant a new challenge. He became accustomed to rough air caused by turbulence, and how to minimize its effect on the aircraft, as well as on the discomfort of the passengers. Once or twice he experienced windshear, and tried not to be terrified as he took what corrective action might be possible. Sometimes, especially from December to February, the weather was wonderfully clear and visibility seemed magically infinite; at other times the weather conditions reduced visibility to what seemed an impenetrable dark curtain.

Destinations such as Chiang Mai, Nan, Lampang, Phuket and Hat Yai became part of his everyday existence. Now he was doing a professional job to the absolute utmost of his ability. His airmanship was superb, and he was utterly reliable.

In early 1981 Tashi received word that the Managing Directors of Thai Airways and Thai International wished to see him; he should come to the office of the Managing Director of Thai International at 9 o'clock the following morning. Intrigued by the summons, he duly arrived at the secretary's office at ten minutes before nine. He was welcomed with a warm smile by, he thought, the most beautiful girl he had seen in his life. Perfectly formed, she seemed to glide towards him dressed in her pale green Thai silk dress. He simply could not take his eyes off her; the girl seemed not the slightest embarrassed and simply smiled at him. She explained that the Managing Directors would receive him at exactly 9 o'clock. She was sure Tashi knew their names: Air Vice Marshal Putchong of Thai Airways and Air Vice Marshal Anurak of Thai International.

Tashi watched the digital clock ticking towards the hour. The secretary slowly stood up and smiled at him; Tashi thought she looked like a rose which had just come into bloom. She walked over to him and smiled.

'Khun Tashi, kindly come this way.'

Tashi followed her to some impressive teak double doors; as he stood before them, they smoothly opened. The secretary said, 'Managing Directors, Khun Tashi.'

Tashi moved towards the men, both of whom were smiling; Tashi sensed how relaxed they seemed. Tashi's head was slightly bowed and his hands were raised vertically to eye level, the fingers of each hand gently pressed together; the Air Marshals adopted the same courtesy. One said, 'My name is Putchong; this is Air Vice Marshal Anurak. Please sit down, Khun Tashi.' Tashi took his seat, ensuring that his feet were as inconspicuous as possible; from the cultural aspect, under no circumstances should they point in the direction of his hosts.

AVM Putchong opened the discussion. 'Khun Tashi, are you happy with Thai Airways; how is your training going?'

'Gentlemen, I am happy flying with Thai Airways, and I believe my training has been good. I find the whole experience rewarding and personally satisfying. Yes, sir, I am very happy.'

AVM Putchong went on, 'Good; the reason we asked you to join us today is that we wanted to hear from you personally how you feel working in our country. As you know, you are the only member of staff who is from the Kingdom of Bhutan. We feel we have a special responsibility towards the Kingdom, and we therefore are taking a personal interest in learning about your progress.

I have a report here which covers most aspects of your technical competence, as well as your personal qualities. We want you to know that in all respects you are very highly thought of; for our part, Khun Tashi, we are proud of you.' AVM Putchong smiled benevolently at Tashi.

Tashi said simply, 'Thank you, sir'.

Now it was the turn of AVM Anurak; he cleared his throat and looked at Tashi. Tashi thought AVM Anurak's expression seemed more serious and business-like than that of AVM Putchong. To Tashi's relief, he gave a hint of a smile as he spoke.

'Khun Tashi, we are all very pleased with your progress. Now you have 750 hours flying experience; with your commercial pilot's licence hours of 250, this makes a thousand. To reach the air transport pilot's licence you will need at least 1500 hours. You should also have command experience; so this will mean that you will need 3000 hours altogether. Especially for the latter phase, there will often be a check captain sitting in the jump seat behind you; he will not be there to make things difficult for you, as you know, but to help you.

Up to now you have flown various types of turboprops. We think this is the right time for you to convert to jet aircraft. From the first day of next month, you will transfer to the payroll of Thai International. Arrangements have already been made for your conversion training in the simulator centre; you should report there for further instructions. We will continue to watch over your training and we are confident that within the next year or so you will have your ATPL. Once you have it, as I mentioned we would like you to build on your experience by continuing with an additional 1500 hours or so. Then you will be ready to return to your country. Do you have any comments or questions for us?' Tashi noticed AVM Anurak quickly glance at his watch; it was three minutes to the half hour.

Tashi was ecstatic. He had often felt that his peers and colleagues went out of their way to be pleasant to him; but he had little idea that his flying ability and his personal qualities were held in such respect. Tashi, an inherently modest person, looked at these captains of industry with a solemn expression.

'Gentlemen, I know you are both extremely busy. I would like to express deep appreciation for the interest you are taking in my training arrangements. I will report at the training centre as instructed. You may rest assured that I will always apply myself to my work with total dedication. May I just say again, thank you!'

The three men stood up; their hands returned to the eye position and Tashi bowed slightly towards the Managing Directors as a mark of respect. Then he withdrew towards the big teak doors; they opened. He cast a final glance at these two airline chief executives; they were gently smiling at him as he left their presence.

As Tashi strode towards the door to leave the secretary's office he felt as though he was walking on air. But he soon regained mother earth as he literally bumped into the secretary as she was escorting an elderly man to the teak doors.

'Khun Preeda,' Tashi heard her say; and the doors closed. Tashi was embarrassed, 'Please forgive me for bumping in to you,' he said, 'I think I was a bit overcome by the interview with the Managing Directors. I should have watched where I was going. I hope I didn't hurt you or something. I am terribly sorry.'

The secretary was smiling and the glow of her smile warmed Tashi's soul.

'No you didn't hurt me, Khun Tashi. I am probably tougher than I look! So you will start with Thai International; that will be nice.'

Tashi could not take his eyes off the beautiful creature before him; he knew he should leave, but he could not persuade his legs to make a move. The secretary was still smiling at him; he looked into her eyes and found himself beginning to feel intoxicated. Feeling dry in his throat and increasingly helpless, he said, 'I know I must leave... er... I know it sounds a bit strange... er... I wondered... er... whether we could have a coffee or a drink sometime? You look so nice! I mean, you seem to be so nice.'

Unlike Tashi, the secretary was not flustered in the slightest. She gently responded:

'Khun Tashi, I love to be with strong, handsome, healthy men. You have made a delightful suggestion. I should love to spend some time with you. We can meet at teatime one day, if it's convenient for you.'

Tashi said, 'Would it be convenient for you to meet me in the lounge of the Dusit Tani hotel at 4.30 the day after tomorrow? I will be flying most of tomorrow, but the next day I am free.'

'Yes, that suits me perfectly,' the girl replied, 'and I am looking forward to talking to you. Perhaps you will be able to tell me about the Kingdom of Bhutan; it must be very beautiful. You had better know my name. I am Khun Patsri; our name is chosen according to our birthday. I am sure you have lots of work to do; so have I. I am looking forward to the Dusit Tani. Good-bye, Khun Tashi.'

The beautiful creature slowly opened the door. Then her hands were brought to eye level and she gently bowed towards Tashi; he returned the gesture. The door closed behind him; Tashi valiantly tried to return to the real world.

That night and the following one were restless for Tashi. It seemed that instead of really resting, all he could do was dream of Patsri, the most beautiful creation of womanhood in the world. He dreamt of touching her and kissing her; he dreamt of gently undressing her. And he dreamt of making love with her. In an extraordinary way, he was intoxicated by everything he knew of her. Then he would ask himself what, in fact, did he know; except for the way she looked, he had to admit that he knew nothing about her.

But his attempts to reason were to no avail. He had to hold her; he must look after her. Patsri had to understand that he was the only man in the world who could adore her for the rest of her life. Then the torment of his waiting to set his eyes on her would start again. And so Tashi convinced himself that he had fallen in love; he hesitated to face the fact that there was practically no substance behind his emotions. He was simply infatuated with Patsri.

Tashi arrived at the Dusit Tani hotel a quarter of an hour before Patsri was due to meet him. He sat in the elegantly furnished, spaciously airy lounge and glanced from time to time at the entrance. At precisely 4.30 he caught sight of Patsri and jumped up; she immediately saw him and smiled. She was dressed in a perfectly cut, white linen suit and matching high-heeled shoes. Tashi returned her smile and said, 'Khun Patsri, you look stunning! Oh, I'm sorry, I cannot contain myself.'

'Well,' Patsri responded, 'thank you for the compliment, Khun Tashi. You seem to like the way I look, but beauty may only be skin deep, you know. Khun Tashi, you must learn to be careful when it comes to women! But I think you are quite safe with me.' Patsri chuckled and seemed to smile affectionately at Tashi. Then she thought, 'I know nothing about this man. I had better find out who he is.'

During the next four hours, each found out a great deal about the other. Tashi was a member of a noble family in the Kingdom of Bhutan. Patsri's father was a major general. Tashi had visited various European countries. Patsri's father had sent her to a finishing school in Switzerland where, like Tashi, she had studied French and German; she had also visited England and spoke English fluently. Both had attended a university; Patsri had taken a degree in economics at Bangkok's prestigious Chulalongkorn University. Both were keen on sports; Patsri loved tennis. When Tashi explained the rudiments of archery to her, she was enthralled.

At about eight o'clock, Tashi wondered whether they might be hungry after all the conversation. Patsri smiled and replied, 'That is a very nice idea. I hope you will not misunderstand if I mention that I don't want to feel in any way that I have to repay a debt.' 'Not at all,' Tashi commented, 'Let us have some dinner.'

'Are you a good Buddhist, Khun Tashi?'

'Well,' Tashi responded, 'I do my best. My religion has always been very important to me. We follow the Mahayana form of Buddhism. I know that in Thailand the predominant form is Hinayana, although a minority do follow Mahayana.'

'You know, Khun Tashi,' Patsri interjected, 'that is a real co-incidence. Our family also follow the Mahayana form. Is it not amazing that in following our separate lives, today we have found that we have done so many things in common?

You probably know that in Thailand many of my countrymen, and women, lead very loose lives. They are often promiscuous. When you think about our religion this seems to be a contradiction. In any case, I take my soul and my body very seriously. To me, there is a certain sanctity which has to be respected, without compromise. I don't want any Tom, Dick or Harry to think he can play around with me. When you look around, how many of these loose women are happy in the end? I think it is sad that most become unhappy; many catch some disease. It can be tragic. But when I meet the right man, Khun Tashi, I will belong to him. And I will love him as no other woman could ever love him!'

As they parted, Tashi said, 'Khun Patsri, you probably feel I am an innocent youngster and I should know more about women. Unfortunately, this is one area of my education which has been neglected. You seem much more mature than I am. What I am coming to is that if you might be able to find a little time so that we can go on talking, this would make me very happy. But if that's difficult for you, I quite understand.'

There was a silence as Patsri looked at Tashi; she smiled and her eyes met his. She said, 'Khun Tashi, the evening went in a flash. We may be from different countries, but we both have such similar backgrounds. It was wonderful talking to you. I should love to see you again. You have so much more to tell me, especially about Bhutan. Give me a ring soon. Goodnight, have lovely dreams!'

Tashi was entranced; and he felt weak. Eventually, he summoned enough strength to go home, and he slept like a log. It was only a matter of time before infatuation would become true love; which it did during the following year. By this time, the two had reached the point where there was no turning back; both felt that each had a responsibility to make the other happy. And each would ensure that it would be like that forever.

When Tashi thought of marriage, he hesitated before saying, 'Patsri, if we were to marry what would you do in a country like Bhutan? How could you think of giving up your job in Thailand; it is wonderful for you here.'

Patsri burst out laughing, 'You are so sweet! Don't you know what marriage means, Tashi? It means being together and staying together. Wherever the husband goes, his wife must be with him. It's so simple, you funny little boy!'

Tashi was married to Patsri in a short religious ceremony, followed by a long and sumptuous reception. Uncle Gyeltshen and Tashi's mother were invited, and Pema represented the family; her beauty and bubbling personality competed with each other in winning her many instant friends. Towards the end of the celebrations, Patsri's father quietly told Tashi that all arrangements had been made for a short honeymoon; the major general had discussed the period of absence with AVM Anurak, who had happily agreed. The major general had arranged for the wedding suite to be available in the Dusit Tani hotel; the following day, the couple would be picked up at noon and flown to Phuket to spend a week in the best hotel.

'Well, here we are again, Tashi. Do you remember when you

invited me for tea, and I stayed for dinner?' Patsri smiled and threw her hands around his neck; her skin felt like Thai silk – soft and warm. He felt her beautiful body pressing against his broad chest. He thought how lucky he was that Patsri was not of small stature, like the majority of Thai women; she was of medium height and matched his height perfectly.

'Patsri, I love you beyond what I can say. But I am not experienced with women. I have been excited sometimes, but you are the first woman I ever wanted to sleep with; can you believe that?'

'Of course I can, Tashi. Because you are unique; and I love you for it. You know, from the moment you set eyes on me I always had the feeling you wanted to eat me.' Patsri laughed. 'I admired you the way you held yourself back. Now you can eat me! You can love me all night, and tomorrow, and the day after, and forever! Don't be nervous – just love me in any way you want to. I know you will always be tender with me; that is your nature. I will make you the greatest lover on earth. You are the tops at everything you tried; and our love together will be no exception. You can undress me, which is not so simple for the uninitiated,' Patsri was laughing again; 'and then I will undress you, which is very simple! Then we will have our bodies to play with; and you can stay inside me for as long as you like. Tashi, I belong to you! I love you so much!'

Tashi graduated in love-making from student to intermediate during the week's honeymoon. He did not indulge in the stupidity of imagining that he could graduate in instant love; to reach perfection would take several more years. He often reminded Patsri that the honeymoon was by far the most beautiful and enjoyable experience of his life. As for Patsri, the more Tashi loved her, the more she yearned for more. Would they make babies? Both hoped so.

Shortly after the marriage, Tashi sat for his final tests and examinations, culminating in the award of his Air Transport Pilot's Licence. He continued to excel as the perfect pilot, whether flying or during simulator training with six-monthly checks. Now his destinations included most of the major cities of the world. Whether flying to Auckland or Amsterdam, to Los Angeles or London, to Paris or Perth his professionalism and rational judgement were maintained at the highest level. For his last 250 hours with Thai International, he was sometimes given command responsibility, and proved to be an exemplary captain.

The crews on Thai International jumbos included a relatively high number of flight attendants. Since they were there to provide the best possible cabin service, to a significant extent they were the 'face' of the airline. They fulfilled their role perfectly. Each was dressed in the traditional Thai *chidladda*, consisting of a silk fitted jacket and long skirt. The pastel shades of these hand-made Thai silk *chidladda* enchanted the passengers, as the attendants looked after their every need. During take-off and landing, the attendants wore a contrasting sash over the *chidladda*, which introduced a more formal tone to their charming appearance. If the cabin purser was a woman, then sometimes she wore a slightly different jacket which had a stand-up collar, called a *ruen thon*. These lovely girls treated Tashi with the deepest respect; they also felt a warm affection towards him. Sometimes, before or after a flight he would indulge in the pastime of comparing the most beautiful of these girls with Patsri. Invariably, Patsri won. Tashi thanked the gods for having given him the most beautiful wife in the world.

In early 1983, at the age of 25, Tashi returned to the Kingdom of Bhutan. Before leaving Bangkok, the Managing Director of Thai International held a special ceremony to bid him farewell. Certainly, Tashi had learned a great deal and had matured into an airline captain at the height of his professional knowledge; he had an uncanny talent in applying what he had learned. As the Managing Director had pointed out to the assembled guests, Tashi had also contributed much by his example. He had become an inspiration to all those who aspired to work in aviation. As the Managing Director handed Tashi a scroll which recorded words of appreciation of the airline, he emphasized that it was Tashi who had set the standard. He would always be remembered for that. He epitomized perfection.

For the return journey to Thimphu, Tashi was flown by Thai International to Calcutta. There he boarded a turbine propeller aircraft of Himalaya Airways. The captain, a tall, husky Sikh, introduced himself. 'I expect you heard that Himalaya Airways started operations about a year ago. It sort of operates, but there are many things that have to be put right. What we have at the moment is an embryo; but you have to start. I am sure once you are on board, things will get much better. They don't always listen to me. But this is your country; they will pay much more attention to you. And you can tell them some home truths that a foreigner wouldn't dare to do!'

Financing had materialized from various sources, including from the aircraft manufacturer, and three turboprop aircraft had been delivered. The staff of the airline were drawn mainly from India; TASS had sent a civil aviation consultant to assist the government in steering the development of the airline and its supporting infrastructure.

The captain had heard a great deal about Captain Tashi, and he was looking forward to working with him as a colleague. Visibility for the flight was perfect, and every moment was a delight for Tashi, especially the approach into Paro through the mountains.

On landing, Tashi was taken to Thimphu; now the car stopped in front of his house. Gyeltshen was sitting in his chair looking towards the mountain. When Tashi entered, Gyeltshen turned and looked Tashi in the eye.

'Oh, I am so happy to see you! I heard you might come today. At last I see you, Tashi!' Astonished, Tashi stood before his uncle.

'Uncle, you seem to see me – what about your eyes? What happened, uncle?'

'Yes, my dear Tashi. I took the flight to Calcutta on Himalaya Airways and had my eyes examined. Then I had two operations, mainly for cataracts. Now I see; not always perfectly, but well enough for most purposes. I can certainly see you very well, Tashi. But I want to see your wife; where is she?'

Tashi explained that Patsri would stay in Bangkok with her family until she received word Tashi had suitable living accommodation. He also wanted to look into the possibility of her finding a job. The Kingdom was incredibly beautiful; unfortunately, however, one had to be practical. Patsri would need to find something challenging to do.

Shortly afterwards, Pema returned from the UN office. 'So my Treasure is home again, Captain Tashi! You are so clever. And you know, Gyeltshen, he is not only clever with aeroplanes. He was very clever to find his beautiful wife; she is adorable. I heard Tashi say she will come soon. Don't worry, Tashi, we won't keep you to ourselves. We want you to be the happiest married man in the world. But until Patsri comes, may we spoil you? Let us have dinner. Afterwards, you will sleep peacefully; and you can dream of Patsri!'

Chapter Ten

Another Man's Destiny

It was five o'clock in the morning of the last day of February 1983; Tashi's digital alarm clock was doing its gentle best to awaken him by playing short, high-pitched Chinese tunes close to his bed. Tashi opened his eyes; the blackness of the night was being transformed into a dark grey, which would soon lighten as the sun began to rise above the Paro mountains. Tashi smiled. This was the day. Provided the weather conditions were good, his beloved Patsri would arrive in two hours.

He lit a candle and then a pressure lamp. Soon a kettle was boiling and he was sipping some tea. Now it was time to say some prayers. First, he prayed to the local deities, the *Yulha*. Then he implored *Mahakala* to keep a watchful eye on the Himalaya Airways aircraft which would bring Patsri to Paro.

He quickly dressed and made for the control tower. As he approached it he admired the brightly coloured paintwork of the traditional motifs on the walls; he thought how quaint and old-fashioned this modern building would seem to foreigners. He climbed the stairs. 'How are you this morning, Gurcharan? What's the news?' Tashi asked the Indian air traffic controller.

'The news is good, Tashi. We have been in radio contact with Calcutta. Visibility there is good. We have told them we have a fine morning; so they can fly visual flight rules, yes VFR. The scheduled arrival time is in one hour fifty minutes.'

About two hours' later Tashi's sharply tuned ears were the first to pick up the distant whine of the turboprop's engines. He could see the small aircraft descending through a giant cleavage in the razor-edged mountains. His thoughts began: 'Turn left, reduce altitude – now turn right.' Captain Singh had flown this approach a hundred times. Within minutes, and after a perfect landing, the turboprop was parked in front of the terminal. The first passenger to appear at the top of the steps was Patsri. Dressed in a suit of dark blue Thai silk, she briefly looked at the small group which was waiting to welcome the few passengers. Within seconds she had seen Tashi. With her large, widely spaced eyes resting on him, she waved and smiled. Seconds later she felt Tashi's strong arms holding her. 'I love you so much, Patsri. I will never let you go!' he said.

'What's this tear doing on your cheek, Tashi?' Patsri asked.

'I suppose it's emotion, Patsri. I can't help it. In an aircraft, I am always as cool as a cucumber. With you, I am just out of control.

I have a small house here in Paro, which I use when I have a lot of flying to do. Then there is a larger house in Thimphu, where we will live. Once you get used to the altitude and the low humidity, I think you will be very happy in Bhutan. I have the use of a car which belongs to the airline. Let me show you the little Paro house.'

Patsri looked adoringly at Tashi and smiled. 'Everything is wonderful, Tashi. For me, the only thing that matters is that we are together.'

The Paro house was constructed of local stone. Tashi explained that the coldest part of the year was drawing to a close. In the depth of winter the snow-line had extended down to the town, and for some days there had been snow on the ground. Tashi had bought some locally-woven carpets and these added a splash of colour to the drab furnishings. As Tashi was showing Patsri the small rooms, they entered the bedroom. Tashi had placed two beds and a chest of drawers in the room. Patsri smiled gently at Tashi. Tashi took her face in his hands and kissed her lips.

'Remember, Tashi,' Patsri said quietly, 'what I told you? With me you don't have to keep control of yourself. I belong to you –and to no one else. Just love me.'

Tashi felt a dryness in his throat. Within seconds he had undressed Patsri and he was kissing her beautiful body.

'Take your clothes off, Tashi. It's too one-sided,' Patsri said.

Tashi's trousers fell to the floor. Patsri opened his shirt and it was gone in a flash. Then Tashi showed Patsri how deeply he loved her. Eventually, with Patsri's soft and supple body caressed by Tashi and their legs entwined, they fell into peaceful slumber under a sheet and a warm Yak's hair blanket.

When they woke up they continued love-making. But this time, instead of sleeping in the after-glow, Patsri suggested that they should travel to their house in Thimphu. She walked to the front door and looked up at the mountains. In the midday sun the crests were white with snow; below, the forest of fir trees followed the folds of the mountains like a never-ending carpet. 'What beautiful scenery, Tashi. It's like a Shangri-La.'

'If you can believe it, Patsri,' Tashi interjected, 'when I was a youngster, I was brought here by my uncle Gyeltshen. We had to drive to Calcutta so I could catch the plane to England. I told you how much I enjoyed the school there. At that time, the airport was under construction and the lower part of the forest was completely grey with dust. I was very upset at the time. But now it has recovered and it looks beautiful again.'

'You must have been an adorable little boy,' Patsri said. 'And what is that fortress over there?'

'You remember I told you about our *dzongs*? That is the Paro *dzong*. It is a fortified monastery dating back to the first half of the seventeenth century. Next time you visit Paro we can visit it. I'm sure the priests will be happy to see us. In the old days, the monasteries were sometimes attacked, so they are strongly fortified. In fact, this one has niches by the side of the spiral staircases. If the defenders were under attack and the attackers managed to intrude into the *dzong*, the defenders used to crouch in the wall niches and club the intruders as they passed. These days the country is peaceful, at least up here. Thank goodness we have the monarchy and the hereditary system; it has kept things very stable for us.

It will take about three hours to reach Paro. Shall we go? This will be the most romantic drive I have ever had.'

'For me too, Tashi. I am sure I will love Bhutan. As long as I am with you, I will be happy anywhere.'

The journey to Thimphu was becoming routine to Tashi, but Patsri marvelled at the rushing torrents which charged their various ways between the great mountains. On the way to their house in Thimphu, they passed the house of Pema and Gyeltshen. Pema hugged Patsri and told her that neither she nor Gyeltshen would ever dream of involving themselves in the young lives of

Tashi and Patsri. But if the youngsters might ever need some advice or help, their first point of call should be Pema or Gyeltshen. Gyeltshen shook Patsri's hand and seemed lost in thought; he simply stared at her. At last, he smiled and said, 'Tashi, you told me that you have married the most beautiful creature in the world. You are right!'

The final stop that day was the house where Tashi and Patsri would live. Built on the side of a small hill, its white walls and generous overhanging roof gave it a similar appearance to Pema's house. Like Pema's, it was also well protected by the deities. As they entered the front door, Tashi pointed out the phallic paintings on the walls, explaining that these were there to encourage fertility. Patsri's laugh was at the same time effervescent and gentle; then in a bubbling voice she said, 'I don't think I need to be reminded about fertility, Tashi. Our eyes only have to meet and in no time you are giving my fertility another chance! I wouldn't be surprised if I'm already pregnant.'

Patsri was still gently laughing when she turned and looked at Tashi. Their eyes met. Tashi smiled and mentioned something about re-consummating their marriage in their new house. Patsri laughed again, and her fertility was given yet another chance to prove itself.

The following morning, Patsri and Tashi walked in the long grass outside their house. The air was clean and fresh; the sky was a deep azure. Patsri turned to Tashi, 'Standing here with you, I feel I'm in heaven. It is so beautiful, I can hardly take it in. You know, we can plan a garden; it would look very pretty with grass and some flowers.'

Patsri suddenly became pensive, 'I know it can't last forever, I mean just eating and making love. When do you go back to work, Tashi?'

'I have three days leave from my duties. We are only seven pilots in Himalaya Airways. There are four Indians, two Swedes and myself. If one of us is off, the others certainly notice it. In any case, I will be flying to Calcutta or Delhi the day after tomorrow. Then I will be due for a free day. It may be a bit difficult for you at first, Patsri, but you can always spend as long as you like with my mother and uncle. I will be introducing you to quite a few people in the next few weeks, and soon you will have plenty of friends.

They will all adore you the moment they meet you. Remember, Patsri, I am your husband!'

Tashi smiled; Patsri kissed him and pressed her body against his. 'I don't need reminding, you funny little boy! But seriously, go and do your work. I am very self-sufficient, Tashi. I can read or talk to your mother and uncle for as long as it takes. And we musn't forget the garden. So don't worry. And when you come home, we will make up for all the lost time!.'

At that moment a messenger delivered an envelope for Tashi. The Managing Director of Himalaya Airways wished to see Tashi in the afternoon; if it might be convenient, Tashi should bring his wife too.

The Managing Director was a middle-aged man who had been personally appointed by His Majesty. He cupped his hands and gently bowed to Tashi and Patsri. 'Well,' he said 'if I may say so, we are proud of you, Tashi. You are doing a good job with the airline. We will take a look at your performance in a year or so to see if we can reward you with a step-up in your career. We do have some teething problems, but in due course I will ask how you think we can overcome them.'

Turning to Patsri, he said, 'Khun Patsri, you probably know we have a good business relationship with Thai International. I was talking to the Managing Director in Bangkok recently and he told me about you. He was full of praise not only for your husband, but also for you. I am afraid we cannot compete with our Thai friends when it comes to salaries. But if it might interest you, I would be happy if you worked here as my Executive Secretary. I have a secretary, and you would decide on the division of work. Naturally, you would be the senior, and I am sure my secretary would learn a lot from your experience.' He smiled, then added with a chuckle, 'Of course, you would need to promise not to share any of our secrets with your husband.'

It was not long before the lives of Tashi and Patsri developed a pattern of work and pleasure. The epitome of professional relia-bility and predictability, Tashi's attitude to his work was exem-plary. As for Patsri, with sensitivity and diplomacy she had arranged with the Managing Director that she would work every other day; the volume of work could normally be handled within this working period. As for pleasure, with Pema's UN contacts,

Gyeltshen's noble friends and through Patsri's status as the right-hand person of the airline's Managing Director, within six months both Tashi and Patsri found themselves frequently invited to dinners or parties. Patsri loved to entertain and her dinner parties, which centred on Thai cooking, became a welcome addition to the social life of Thimphu. At evening functions she always wore her perfectly fitting Thai silk clothes, which enhanced her beauty.

By mid 1984 Tashi had established himself within Himalaya Airways as the ultimate professional. The senior pilot, Captain Singh, had developed a deep admiration not only for Tashi the pilot, but for Tashi the man. After a bumpy flight from Calcutta, Captain Singh turned to Tashi as they entered the terminal building. 'Thank you for that, Tashi. It was great to have you next to me. That was a rough ride wasn't it? I will never get completely used to the upcurrents we get in these mountains – amazing! Incidentally, Tashi, do you remember when your wife first arrived in Bhutan, she was the first to leave the aircraft; that was because I told the passengers to remain seated while our VIP disembarked! I did that out of respect for you, Tashi. Now I think it's time we did something more concrete. I've just written to the Managing Director. I recommended he should make you Chief Pilot. You deserve it. And you would be able to achieve much more than I can; remember, I'm partly an outsider.'

They continued walking to the car which would take them to Thimphu. Tashi did not respond for some seconds. The informal way in which Captain Singh had discussed such an important topic had thrown Tashi off balance. Then he said, 'That's very considerate of you. Thank you. You know, I have a lot of respect for you too.'

Captain Singh stopped, smiled at Tashi and shook his hand. 'Good luck, Tashi. I have something to do here in Paro, so you will be travelling alone to Thimphu today. All the best to Patsri.'

It was a week later that Tashi was asked to call on the Managing Director. 'Well, Tashi,' he said, 'I wonder if Patsri kept her word. Do you know why you are here, or perhaps your wife has already told you?'

Tashi was quick to respond. 'I hope I haven't done anything wrong in any way? If I have unknowingly contravened any rule, I can assure you, sir, I will put things right immediately.'

The MD smiled and looked Tashi in the eye, 'On the contrary, from the reports I have, you seem to be perfect in every respect. We are proud of you, Tashi. I hope you will accept the responsibility from tomorrow of becoming the Chief Pilot of Himalaya Airways.

There was a long pause while Tashi tried to take in the implications of what he was being offered; then he said, 'Managing Director, thank you for your confidence. I recognize the great responsibility, especially at this particular juncture in the airline's development. I accept the appointment. I undertake to do my best.'

Over the next three years, Tashi transformed the airline from the Paro-Calcutta-Paro 'milk run,' to an airline which flew scheduled routes to several regional destinations, such as Delhi, Bombay, Dhaka and Kathmandu. His training with Thai International stood him in good stead, and he fully understood the crucial importance of aircraft maximum utilization. Now, scheduling took on a new meaning; the airline's scheduling had to dovetail with the departure and arrival times of several other airlines in the region.

He also had to tackle the thorny issue of maintenance. It would be years before the Kingdom of Bhutan would begin to produce engineers. Even when trained engineers began to come off the 'assembly line,' the airline invariably found itself competing with other fields for their services. The Kingdom was developing in so many ways that the available national professional resources required to meet a multitude of challenges were, in fact, becoming relatively less as development expanded. There were one or two mechanics who could be trained to undertake basic engine checks, and these were sent to India and Thailand for training up to the level where they would be granted a licence. But for the foreseeable future, the aircraft would need to be maintained abroad, mainly in India.

Like every other aspect of the operation of the aircraft, money was involved, and most of this would be in foreign exchange. Now Tashi found himself appealing to his minister to stand firm against the Minister of Finance who, like all finance ministers around the world, saw his job as reducing costs. In 1985, it was only when Tashi threatened to ground the aircraft and resign that the necessary foreign exchange was released to ensure a minimum level of maintenance to assure safety.

From time to time, Tashi used to discuss the status of civil aviation development with the director of the Kingdom's civil aviation department and the TASS consultant. The tenor and pattern of these meetings were always the same. The first half hour was taken up with acknowledging the progress which had been made here and there; this was followed by a three hours' catalogue of deficiencies, together with expectations which had not yet been met. And how long would it take to put everything in place so that the Kingdom could confidently participate in the operation of safe aviation, using its own national resources? No one was prepared to give an estimate.

The simple fact was that the training of human resources was a complicated and, especially in the case of civil aviation, long process. It was one thing to have made an arrangement with Thai International that simulator checks and training could be undertaken with Thai in Bangkok. But it was quite another for the Kingdom to provide the human material to be trained. The only comfort that was mentioned from time to time was that Bhutan was not alone. Behind their facades of effectiveness, many developing countries suffered in varying degrees from a lack of minimum civil aviation safety standards. Even where legislation had been introduced to cover the operation of aircraft, who really understood the implications of the laws promulgated? Who could write explanatory manuals to explain the true intent and meaning of the legislation? And who, in the dynamic world of civil aviation development and technological change, had the expertise to keep the legislation current? These were just some, amongst many, questions that would remain unanswered for years.

It was in late 1985 that Tashi received a message from his Managing Director that he should attend a meeting to be convened by his minister in the Thimphu *dzong* the following week. In his note, the minister explained that he wished to compile a civil aviation progress report for His Majesty. The director of civil aviation and the Managing Director of Himalaya Airways would be present. In turn, they would ask some of their heads of divisions to contribute to the overall presentation. As Chief Pilot, Tashi should report on the progress of the airline's operations. Tashi's presentation was by far the most impressive. He spoke clearly for 20 minutes, spelling out the most important achievements; he also drew attention to the need to give priority to human infrastructure development. He explained that until Bhutanese nationals had been trained to take over professional functions, the need to employ foreigners and the consequent drain on foreign exchange would persist. Although he recognized the government's important policy decision to operate an airline, in purely financial terms there would be no possibility of making an operational profit for the foreseeable future. The fact was that Bhutan was one of those countries which the UN system had placed in the category of 'least developed country'; yet the government had decided to make the operation of its airline a priority. Not only would the existence of the airline ensure the free flow of passengers and goods to and from Bhutan; the need to respect national pride was of overriding importance. Unfortunately, this situation had to be paid for; if the necessary funding might not be made available, then the government would have no option but to ground the aircraft. This was an inescapable fact.

Tashi then explained that one way to reduce the deficit would be to increase the utilization of the aircraft. Another possibility would be to examine whether a different type of aircraft might be more cost-effective. As Chief Pilot he had both of these points under constant consideration. Tashi did not think that the time had come to increase the frequency of flights between, say, Paro and Calcutta. However, once the country's development projects gained momentum, then this would mean more passenger traffic as the number of consultants and representatives of foreign firms visiting Bhutan increased. As for acquiring more cost-effective aircraft, this question seemed to be academic, since Bhutan could not afford new aircraft and it seemed beyond the realm of reality to imagine that any country would grant aid in the form of an aircraft, plus the associated expense of its operation.

As Tashi was nearing the end of his presentation, he was interrupted by his Managing Director, who stated with some force that one point which had not been covered was the possibility of negotiating traffic rights between Delhi and Kabul. Normally, this question would not arise; however, the Managing Director had learned that pilots were becoming increasingly apprehensive about flying into Afghanistan. Perhaps airlines might agree to an arrangement under which Himalaya Airways would operate a service to Kabul under a type of sub-contract arrangement.

Tashi was taken aback. The Managing Director fell silent. He seemed to smile slightly as he rested on his laurels; he was anxious to demonstrate that he also could produce ideas. Tashi turned to look into the minister's eyes.

'Minister, I would like to clarify that it is quite correct, as my Managing Director has stated, that the possibility of expanding service into Afghanistan has been discussed. I should like to emphasize that I have proposed absolutely no action in the matter because of the politically unstable situation in Afghanistan. I also strongly have in mind that the safety of the aircraft should not be put at risk; we have heard that some flights into and out of Kabul have been subjected to small arms fire from the Mujahidin. As Chief Pilot, one of my basic responsibilities is to ensure the safety of the aircraft. My strong advice to you, Excellency, is that at this time there should be no consideration whatsoever of expanding service to Afghanistan; the risk is much too great! Thank you, Excellency.'

In August of 1986, Tashi was asked to call on the minister, accompanied by the airline's Managing Director. The minister explained that His Majesty had received the civil aviation development report with appreciation. Tashi's contribution had been singled out for its clarity and frankness. The minister then addressed Tashi.

'During your presentation, you will recall that one of the matters which was raised focused on the possibility of increasing utilization of the aircraft by negotiating for rights to fly into Kabul. The government has considered all the implications of this suggestion and we have had discussions with our friends in other countries. They have no objection to this proposal. So the next step is for us to visit Kabul to discuss the matter, that is if they will receive us. If and when we can arrange a visit, I will let you know. I hope the visit will be in the next three months.

In any case, this is preliminary information; but you should start making preparations. You will need to decide the routing and where you can re-fuel. Of course, you will file the flight plan. When we make our visit, the travelling party will consist of the

Managing Director, myself and you as Chief Pilot. You will be in command of the flight; I suggest you ask Captain Singh to travel with us as the first officer.' The minister looked at Tashi. Instead of sensing, as he had hoped, Tashi's excited anticipation, the expression which met his was uncharacteristically blank.

Tashi was dumbfounded. He received the minister's instructions in amazed disbelief. But culturally there was little Tashi could do; he could not express his anxiety about flying into the heart of the Mujahidin. A multitude of thoughts were flashing through his mind; if the Indian pilots, for example, with their relatively large jet aircraft were having problems with small arms fire, then what might happen to a Himalaya Airways twin-engined turboprop? The more Tashi's thoughts stayed on the subject, the more anxious he became; he continued musing.

The silence was interrupted by a question from the minister, 'I hope, Managing Director, that I have made myself clear. Do you or Captain Tashi have any questions; otherwise the meeting can be terminated.'

The silence continued, until Tashi responded, 'Minister, your instructions are clear, thank you. I will do my utmost to assure the success of the visit. My only concern is the safety of the aircraft and the passengers. During our earlier meeting I expressed my anxiety. I am sure you have taken this into consideration, Excellency.'

The minister slowly sat upright; his good-natured expression had turned to stone. Tashi found himself looking directly at the respected orange sash of nobility which crossed the minister's expansive chest; the minister placed his elbows on the desk. The deep white cuffs of his traditional tunic were raised as his hands met at their fingertips under his puffy chin. Looking directly at Tashi, his eyes narrowed; then he commented, 'A policy decision in this matter has been taken by the Royal Government. You are not involved in any way with such a decision. You are responsible for the technical aspects of the visit. We have every confidence that you will perform your technical work to perfection. The government acknowledges there may be a safety risk; it has been decided that this is so small that it should be discounted. Thank you for attending this meeting. You may now leave.'

At home that evening, Patsri smiled at Tashi. 'Tashi, we love one another. So we have to communicate. I have just made you a beautiful meal. I thought you would enjoy the meal and then after that you would enjoy me! Instead, you ate very little and you are lost in thought. My darling Tashi, what is going on?'

Tashi did not smile. He raised his head and spoke in a solemn tone, 'Yes, Patsri, we do love one another. You know, we always agreed we would never discuss things which you are close to in the office. But you must know by now about the Afghanistan trip. I have absolutely no problem with the flying side. But I am worried about the safety of the aircraft around Kabul; we are very vulnerable during the approach and take-off from Kabul. The minister said the risk is small. Of course, I could not tell him directly, but I disagree.'

Patsri stood up and blew a kiss at Tashi. 'Look,' she said, 'fate is fate. Probably, everything will be all right; and we will pray to the deities to look after the passengers and the aircraft. Stop worrying about things which are outside of your control and cheer up. I need your love, Tashi.'

Patsri gently pressed herself against Tashi. Tashi smiled; then she kissed him.

'Now, Tashi. I have a special announcement. I'm pregnant, my darling!'

Tashi looked at Patsri and seemed astounded. For her part, Patsri was relaxed and smiling.

'Don't look so astonished, my darling. Did you think you were impotent?' Patsri started laughing. Then she kissed Tashi again. This was more than enough to ignite the spark.

'Tashi, every time we make love, I enjoy you more. You must never stop loving me! Don't stop! And just before the winter starts we will have the little one. Then I hope we will make another one.'

In mid January 1987, the Himalaya Airways turboprop took off from Paro airport with Tashi as the pilot; Captain Singh sat attentively in the first officer's seat, muttering 'perfect' every few seconds as Tashi manoeuvred the aircraft through the mountains *en route* to Calcutta. The aircraft flew its scheduled route onward to Delhi. For the flight to Kabul, there would be only two passengers, the minister and the airline's Managing Director. The Delhi-Kabul sector was flown without incident, to Tashi's relieved surprise. Once in Kabul, the minister led discussions with the Afghan authorities and agreement was reached in principle that Himalaya Airways could operate into and out of Afghanistan. The timing of the introduction of the service would depend on a number of factors; so this was left as 'to be mutually agreed'.

The Bhutanese party had been in Kabul for two nights and they were looking forward to leaving a war-torn country; the ugly scars borne by so many of the city's buildings in Kabul seemed somehow to be at their worst in the depth of winter.

The estimated time of departure for the flight was 11a.m. However, at the last minute the head of the Afghan delegation decided that the Bhutanese representatives should be accorded an appropriate farewell. The Bhutanese were invited to an early morning concert, and this was followed by visits to the Dar ol-Aman palace and Babur's garden. The hosts pointed out with pride some of the relics of the Mughal empire, most of which dated from the 16th and 17th centuries.

The long lunch which was then served seemed endless. The Afghans made many speeches; apart from praising the visitors and thanking them for providing what was termed a 'bridge of understanding,' there were repeated statements about Moslem fundamentalism and the many benefits it brought to the followers of Islam. After each speech the Bhutanese minister thanked the speaker in a non-committal way.

At 3 o'clock in the afternoon, Tashi whispered to his minister and the Managing Director that he would file an amended flight plan; he asked whether the departure could now be scheduled for 4p.m. If the minister felt it might be later, then Tashi's recommendation was that the flight departure should be delayed till the next morning. He mentioned that should any problems be encountered, then it would be safer to have the benefit of daylight, than be caught in the dark. The minister's response was short and to the point, 'We will leave today. If necessary, at a quarter to four I will announce that we have to leave; and we will leave. Under no circumstances will I put up with another night in that hotel! You can leave for the airport now; we will follow you.'

Tashi soon reached the control tower and he entered the briefing room. His amended flight plan was filed, which he handed to the briefing officer. Looking somewhat anxious, the briefing officer said, 'Thank you, Captain Tashi. I must tell you that the Mujahidin are making more gains around the city. Sometimes, they shoot at landing and departing aircraft. It is possible you might have a problem this evening. We will employ our normal technique. As you depart, you will see tracer bullets around the aircraft. If we know where the fundamentalists are, then we will try and frighten them with mortars. This type of action on our part usually confuses them; by the time they recover, the aircraft is out of their range. So if you see tracer, don't worry, it's just a distraction. Good luck!'

It was 4.30p.m. when Tashi received clearance to depart. He released the brakes and applied power. Although the turboprop was doing its best to respond, Tashi knew that at an altitude of almost 6000 feet above sea level it would take longer to become airborne than would be the case in the lowlands. At last he had the speed to rotate and the aircraft lifted off from the remarkably even surface of the runway. He felt grateful to the Russians for all their excellent work in upgrading the airport. His intention was to climb away as steeply as his speed would safely permit.

Suddenly he saw the tracers; they seemed to be reaching towards the aircraft. Now he could see red, green, yellow and other colours; the tracers were all around him. Then there was a solid thump as something hit the aircraft; Tashi heard the minister's voice,

'What is happening? Gods! Have mercy on us!'

With the impact, the aircraft shuddered and it seemed to be thrown askew as it tried to lift higher into the atmosphere. Tashi treated the aircraft's attitude as a stall; for a few seconds he stopped climbing and eased the aircraft's nose slightly downward. By applying the rudder controls, the aircraft had soon regained its equilibrium. Now Tashi could continue climbing. He wanted to speak to the tower, but he stopped the moment he realized that his communication system was no longer functioning. At that moment, his eyes caught sight of the navigation system panels. Not only had the instrumentation glass shattered; a few flicks of the main switches confirmed his worst fears. The entire navigation system was out of operation.

Tashi looked at the altimeter; it read 3500 feet and indicated that the aircraft was still climbing. Then he looked at the compass;

thank goodness, he thought, that the compass is separate from the navigation system's electronics. Whether it was working properly he could not tell, but his take-off heading was indicated, which was comforting. Then Tashi carried out the standard cockpit check; the main controls seemed to be in order and the oil pressure of the engines appeared normal.

Shouting above the roar of the engines, he asked Captain Singh to bring the two passengers to the flight deck. Then he shouted with a solid, controlled voice, 'We have a problem. We were shot at on our departure. We have no navigation system. Normally, as the commander of this aircraft I would immediately return to the airport. However, I regard this as too dangerous. The main controls of the aircraft are functional and the compass may be serviceable; in any case, soon it will be dark and we can cross check the direction in which we are flying by observing our position in relation to certain stars. From the indications available, the basic electrical system is functioning; it does not seem to have been damaged. But of course we have no electronics.

If you agree, minister, I will maintain a south east heading, in other words we may be lucky and pass over Lahore, Faisalabad or Multan; we might even reach Delhi. If things had been normal, we would have diverted to Peshawar or Islamabad. But without an effective navigation system, the hilly terrain could be dangerous. Also, Islamabad has quite a lot of domestic and international traffic; so I think it will be safer if we avoid those terminal areas, if possible.

We have two main problems. First, it will soon be dark. Second, the briefing office in Kabul could give me no information about winds. In general, strong winds blow off the Himalayan mountains and these could cause the aircraft to follow a much more southerly track. The trouble is we don't know what the winds are doing. And I do not want to risk flying on a more easterly heading because we must keep clear of the high mountains. Do you understand, minister?'

His Excellency, clad in his traditional Bhutanese clothes, was silent. He stared at Tashi. His mind was boggled by Tashi's calm, matter-of-fact attitude. Here were four men who might have been killed a few minutes earlier by Mujahidin bullets or by the aircraft crashing; and here was the commander explaining the situation and asking for the minister's agreement to do what seemed to be the sensible thing, given their plight. The minister wanted to respond, but all he could produce was a trembling of his lips, which he could not stop. So he just nodded at Tashi, returned to his seat and, with closed eyes, began to say his prayers. Once he was sitting down, his legs uncontrollably opened and closed like a jackknife, the sides of his knees repeatedly banging against each other. He lapsed into a type of meditation. Naturally, not for one moment did the minister dwell on his stupidity in ignoring Tashi's sound advice that the mission to Kabul would be potentially dangerous.

For the first part of the flight, Tashi followed the Kabul river. At about 6 o'clock he and Captain Singh found themselves agreeing that below them was the junction at which the Kabul river joined the mighty Indus. At this point both agreed that Tashi should steer in a slightly more south easterly direction which, they hoped, would result in their track crossing the points of either Lahore or Faisalabad. As dusk fell 40 minutes later, both felt confident that within an hour the lights of the metropolis of Lahore would come into view. What they could not know in the darkness was that a strong northerly wind was sweeping across Pakistan, which would carry their aircraft well south of the intended track.

At 7.30 Tashi made a routine check of the control panel. Yes, his navigation system was out. But what was this? He turned to his first officer, 'Captain Singh, we are losing oil pressure in the starboard engine. It must have been penetrated by a bullet. This is an emergency. I will feather the engine and we will make an emergency landing within the next fifteen minutes using one engine. I will activate the 'Mayday' distress signal; but I doubt that it will transmit. Tell the passengers to prepare for the emergency landing and instruct them on their sitting position.' Tashi felt not the slightest fear in the dangerous situation. Throughout his life, he had never failed a testing situation; confident in his knowledge and experience, the possibility of failing the test which was imminent never remotely occurred to him.

As Tashi finished his instructions, he and Captain Singh simultaneously caught sight of a strip of silver below them. 'Captain Tashi,' shouted Captain Singh, 'that is the Indus. That's my country, the Punjab; if we are very far south, it could be Sind

Province. We are well south of our track. But this may help us. Along the river the land is flat. You see those lights ahead? There is a small township. I would guess that there are irrigation channels for two or three miles or so either side of the river. You are the commander and you will decide. But it should not be too bad for an emergency landing three to four miles away from the river, near that township. I will tell the passengers to prepare for the landing.'

'What about trees?,' Tashi asked.

'They always plant trees in the township,' was the response, 'but away from the river there are usually only small bushes. Sometimes there are rocky outcrops; we can't do anything about that. We are in the hands of the gods.'

From that moment Tashi withdrew into his own world, the world of flight. Descending to about 1,500 feet, he flew directly over the lights of the township. In the darkness, he could not identify the buildings; all he could see were the faint lights divided by the wide, silver ribbon of the Indus. As he left the lights, he banked the aircraft gently; he did not want to risk demanding too much from the single, remaining engine. Continuing his descent he flew at 500 feet along the outskirts of the little town. Against the starlit sky ahead he could see no barrier of hilly land. As far as he could ascertain, the land seemed reasonably flat. This was the best he could do. He again made a wide turn and flew towards the strip of nothingness parallel with the side of the township, about five miles from the river. He shouted, 'Prepare for the landing. We are on final approach.' He switched on his landing lights and was relieved to see the darkness ahead lightened. But where was mother earth?

Although Tashi flashed a glance at his altimeter, he did not fully trust it. After the Afghan bullets, he could not be sure it was working properly. Tashi reduced power and strained his eyes for some sign of land. According to his altimeter, the aircraft should have been on the ground. But they were still in the air. He was losing speed rapidly. If contact with land were not made in three or four seconds, then he should expect a stall, especially as he had applied full flap. The aircraft began to shudder; Tashi gently eased the nose forward. As he did so, the aircraft dropped. Tashi hung on and tried to steer straight; if a wing dipped, it would probably make contact with the ground, with catastrophic results. After another three seconds, there was a loud crack as the turboprop hit the ground. Immediately, the aircraft was leaping into the air again. Down it came – bang! Tashi cut the power and the aircraft did its best to remain stable as its wheels raced across the bumpy terrain.

'I must keep the nose up,' Tashi told himself; his concentration on the final stage of the procedure was intense. He applied a little brake; gradually, the aircraft slowed. Then it stopped. Suddenly, all was quiet.

Captain Singh broke the silence, 'You are a genius, Captain Tashi.' There was no response; in the darkness, no one could see that Tashi was slumped, unconscious, in his seat. Then Captain Singh heard the minister's voice reciting his prayers.

'How are the passengers? Are you hurt?,' Captain Singh asked. Both responded at the same time; they were not hurt.

'Captain Tashi, you seem to be leaning over. Can you speak?' There was a strange silence. Captain Singh loosened Tashi's harness. Then he felt his way into the cabin. He opened the main passengers' exit door. All was quiet and still. After a few seconds, he saw a lantern approaching. A voice, speaking in Punjabi, shouted in the direction of the open door,

'What happened to the big bird? Is anyone alive?'

Captain Singh recognized his mother tongue and responded in Punjabi, 'We have a problem with our aircraft. We need medical help for the pilot. Where are we?'

'This is Mohenjodaro. I will call for help.' Then all was quiet again.

An hour later, Captain Singh heard the straining engine of a minibus; help had arrived in the form of a nursing orderly and some municipal workers. A town councillor was in charge of the rescue. Captain Singh, the minister and the airline's Managing Director were helped from the aircraft. Tashi, groaning in semi-consciousness, was gently carried to the car. The small group then set off for the town, where Tashi was laid on a bed. Captain Singh said he would stay with him. Five more hours elapsed before Tashi began to regain consciousness. Captain Singh was at his bedside.

'I think we had an aircraft problem; or am I wrong? I have a terrible pain in my back. Is there a doctor here?' Tashi asked.

'There soon will be,' Captain Singh responded as comfortingly as possible. 'All you can do for the moment is rest. But if you can't rest, or you prefer to stay awake, then I will tell you where we are and what we are going to do.'

'Yes,' Tashi said, 'talk to me. It will make me feel better.'

Captain Singh began, 'There must have been very strong winds from the north to bring us down here. The main thing is that we have survived, and I'm sure you will be fit again soon. As you know, Punjab means 'five rivers,' all five draining into the Indus River, almost two thousand miles in length; it starts in Tibet and flows first along and then through the Himalayas. In the late spring and summer the Indus becomes very full, because it picks up huge amounts of water from the melting snow. Down here the water is probably quite low because the snow won't melt for a few months. Are you still awake, Captain Tashi?'

'Completely, and what you are explaining is very interesting,' Tashi replied.

'Okay,' Captain Singh continued, 'Now let me say something about Mohenjodaro. Actually, the town is in the Sind Province of Pakistan, which is just south of my area, the Punjab. I can communicate with the people here quite easily. The only historical fact I know about Sind is that when the British General Napier at last gained control of the area, he sent a message to Queen Victoria. He just wrote, 'I have Sind.' Whether he felt he had sinned, nobody knows.

In any case, Mohenjodaro is one of the oldest cities in the world, Tashi. The Pakistanis often say it is older than the Egyptian civilization; nobody seems to be sure. But there is general agreement that the Mohenjodaro Indus civilization extends back to at least 2500 BC, so it is about four and a half thousnd years old. There has been quite a bit of excavation. For example there was a citadel, which was about 40 feet high, with fortified towers; it had assembly halls for religious and ceremonial functions. Then there were many houses with courtyards; they even had small bathrooms and there are clear signs of proper sanitation and drainage systems. Quite a number of stairs have been found, so they probably had an upstairs. All the buildings were made of mud and brick and they were originally plastered with mud. Mohenjodaro never received the publicity of the Egyptian civilization, but it is very interesting. Are you still awake, Captain Tashi?' This time there was no answer. Captain Singh lowered his head and heard Tashi's breathing, which seemed to be steady. Then he felt Tashi's forehead; it was warm, but not hot. He looked at Tashi with compassion: 'Yes, let him rest. It can only do him good. Poor man! There's definitely something wrong with him. Probably, after the first touchdown, when the aircraft bounced and then came down hard with a bang, that the damage happened. For God's sake, I only hope he recovers.'

Three weeks later, things were quite different. The Pakistan government had organized an air ambulance to bring Tashi to the Aga Khan hospital in Karachi. There, Tashi was told that his vertebrae had been displaced in two places; he was also suffering from concussion and loss of memory. With his neck in a cast and his body held rigid by a harness, at the request of the government of Bhutan he had been flown to Calcutta for further treatment. Now he was lying with a reasonable degree of comfort in a hospital bed in Calcutta. Pakistan's Civil Aviation Authority had arranged for a small aircraft to lift Captain Singh and the two passengers to Hyderabad, where they had connected with a domestic flight to Karachi. The flight home via Delhi was straightforward.

Recovery of the turboprop was another matter. At the working level, the Indians and Pakistanis demonstrated their capability to co-operate. A technical group composed of airworthiness engineers and pilots surveyed the aircraft. They agreed it could be made serviceable after replacing some equipment, together with repairs. In mid February it was towed to the airstrip outside Mohenjodaro, where Captain Singh made the first test flight. He flew to Karachi, where it was thoroughly checked by the maintenance specialists of Pakistan International Airlines. At the end of February, Captain Singh flew the turboprop to Calcutta where, after final checks, it would gain a certificate of airworthiness. In mid April 1987 it re-entered service with Himalaya Airways.

'My darling, dearest Tashi, you must get better soon. I want to take you home. I want to love you and I want to make you happy. We shouldn't worry about anything in the future except that we belong to one another.'

Patsri had flown from Paro to Calcutta and had taken up residence in the hospital. She spent her time at Tashi's bedside.

Although she always looked beautiful, in her pregnancy Tashi thought she looked nothing less than angelic; the deep warmth of her expression and her sheer beauty were stunning. She went on, 'You remember, I told you that your mother came to see me when your uncle Gyeltshen was given the news about the accident?'

'I don't remember, Patsri. I wish I could remember more. 'Tashi's voice was quiet, almost wistful.

'Yes,' Patsri continued, ' I was in the garden and the new roses had just been planted. The garden already looks beautiful. When I was told about the accident, I just knew you would survive. And you did! The only thing you must do now, Tashi, is get better. We are going to have a lovely life together!'

Tashi smiled weakly; Patsri smiled with love. Then Tashi watched the tears steadily falling over her cheeks.

'Don't cry, Patsri,' Tashi pleaded, 'we shouldn't worry. I will not get better soon, but I will in time. You know, there may be a reason why all this has happened. We must be patient. Perhaps in time we shall know the answer.'

At last the orthopaedic specialists agreed that Tashi could leave the hospital and return to Bhutan. He was becoming more mobile and, to Patsri's relief, his memory was becoming more reliable. Once home, he physically and mentally exercised himself to such effect that many thought he had made a complete recovery. Although Tashi had his secret doubts about his eventual fitness, he continued with his exercises and, as the weeks passed, he became stronger.

In early September Patsri gave birth to a boy, named 'Little Tashi.' The birth was not difficult and from the beginning the baby was healthy. His parents loved Little Tashi, and tended to his every need. Grandmother Pema and great uncle Gyeltshen doted on the little one, just as they had with Tashi. Like his father, it would not be long before the helpless creature learned to help himself. Until the arrival of Little Tashi, neither parent had any idea how active a baby boy could become.

Tashi's physical condition improved steadily, and his sexual activity, always a good barometer, increased by leaps and bounds. Even Patsri would soon be convinced that all would shortly be again normal with her beloved Tashi. Yes, she hoped they would make another baby.

In December of 1987 Tashi announced he wanted to be medically checked to find out if he was fit to fly.

'You know, Patsri,' he said, 'you are the only woman in the world I can love. And I feel that for me flying is the only work I can enjoy. If I have to train for something else, I will. But it is only flying that makes me feel fulfilled. I love you; and I love flying.'

'So, Captain Tashi, I am afraid that is my decision.' Tashi was listening intently to the conclusions of an aviation physician in Calcutta. 'Let me assure you, whoever you consult in aviation medicine, the conclusion will be the same. You have made a good recovery from your injuries; but you will never get significantly better than you are today. You will never pass all the aviation medical tests. This means one thing, Captain. You have reached the end of your active flying career. You will, in time, almost certainly be authorized to carry out flight checking work. You can certainly become expert in the field of flight operations. On medical grounds, however, you will never be authorized to hold a pilot's licence. This sounds cruel, but I think it is better to be realistic. You have to know how you stand. I will be writing to your government Ministry of Communications, for the record.' The physician stood up and held out his hand. Tashi shook it and looked the physician unsmilingly in the eye.

'Thank you, doctor. Good-bye.'

Fortunately, one of Tashi's many excellent qualities was that he was a realist. Others might have been devastated when they heard the news. But Tashi was not shocked. He knew that the aviation medical regulations were strict and watertight; there was practically no room for judgemental discretion. He was not happy with the physician's news, but now he knew where he stood. If he was to continue in aviation, then his participation would be indirect, that is he could help and support other pilots. His flying days were now history.

'We have to come to terms with the reality, Patsri,' Tashi explained on his return. 'Our personal lives are unaffected, but now I must plan for a re-orientation of my working life. I have no option. I had a message that the minister wants to see me tomorrow. I had better make sure my clothes are in good shape; he is strong on traditional dress.'

'You look fantastic, Tashi,' Patsri said admiringly the next day.

'I will call you 'the courageous one,' my darling! Now I am going to kiss you. You should always wear traditional dress. By co-incidence it is exactly one year ago that you saved the passengers and the aircraft in that unnecessary accident. It is ironic that the very minister who put you in an impossibly dangerous situation, and whose life you saved, should have asked you to call on him today. If he wants a celebration, tell him you don't feel well and come home. You will be much happier with me in bed, Tashi my love!'

'Come in, Tashi. Let us sit over there. We can have some tea. How do you feel?' The portly minister was at his benevolent best, and smiled at Tashi like a good-natured headmaster who was settling a young boy into his first day of school. Then he went on, 'Tashi, we have not seen much of one another over the last months. I did not have the opportunity to tell you that I owe my life to you. And if my debt is to *Mahakala*, then you were the instrument he chose when my life was in danger. I still frequently think about that fateful trip.

Now I want to talk about your future. As you probably know, I have received the medical report from the aviation physician. I suppose you know that your flying days are over?'

'Yes, Excellency, I know the position.'

'Right,' the minister went on, 'what I want to tell you today is that with the agreement of His Majesty, from tomorrow you should start work in the office next to mine. You are to be promoted to Chief of Flight Operations, and you will have a free hand to do whatever may need to be done at any time to enhance the flight safety of Himalaya Airways.

You will always be assured of a responsible position within His Majesty's government up to the date of your retirement. I hope you will feel that His Majesty's Government has done what it can to alleviate a situation which must bear heavily on you. If at any time you need an approval or advice on any matter, then you will not need to make an appointment; ask my secretary if I am free and walk straight in to talk to me. Is that understood?'

'Thank you, Excellency. I appreciate your consideration.' Tashi stood up and bowed slightly. The minister cupped his hands. Before taking his leave, Tashi slightly raised his head and looked the minister in the eye. It was unfortunate, Tashi thought, that the minister was not looking at him; instead, his eyes were cast downward at the desk which separated them.

With mixed feelings, Tashi began work the next day. On the one hand, he was revered as a national hero; he was commonly called 'the flying tiger.' On the other, he was under no illusions concerning the bureaucracy of the government. As the months passed, he would experience frustration with delays in having his recommended course of action approved. He found the atmosphere of the Thimphu *dzong* stifling. Enormous effort was expended by countless bureaucrats in writing minutes and memoranda. Decisions on small matters were often delayed for months. As a commander of an aircraft used to taking quick decisions, Tashi felt choked by the endless administration of government.

One April day in 1989, as the winter was slowly giving way to spring, Tashi came home at about 5 o'clock. This was the routine which, in contrast to his challenging and exciting flying days, had been forced upon him. Patsri and the little one welcomed him and Patsri showed Tashi the roses which were beginning to bloom. Her garden would soon be a splash of glorious colours as the warmth of the sun encouraged her plants and bushes to flower. Patsri kissed Tashi and he thought how beautiful she looked as the shadows of a nearby tree flickered in the breeze across her lovely face. Soon the sun would sink over the mountain and dusk would fall.

'Living here with you and our little one is all that anyone could ask for. For me, Tashi, this is heaven and you have made it all possible. I love you my darling!' Patsri smiled at Tashi and kissed him. Soon it would be time for Little Tashi to go to bed and the parents would chat, or perhaps read to one another.

After dinner, when Little Tashi was asleep, Tashi looked at Patsri; his expression was so serious that she was startled. 'What's the matter, Tashi? Why do you look so serious. Is something troubling you?'

'Yes, my darling,' Tashi replied. 'Everything in our family is perfect. But outside it is a different story. Let me explain. For the last fifteen months I have been doing the flight operations job. In spite of the bureaucracy, I have done many things. I doubt that I can do more at this stage. Himalaya Airways is a small airline. We still rely mainly on expatriates. It will be another two years, at least, before trained people will start returning to the Kingdom.

Then they will need work experience. So there is not much more I can do for the next two or three years which will be significantly productive; we simply do not have the human resources which can benefit from my work. As the UN keeps reminding us, we lack absorptive capacity.

Today, Patsri, we received a package from TASS. Amongst all the papers was an advertisement for a flight operations specialist. The man will be based in Chicago. From time to time he will have to travel to developing countries to assist them in maintaining flight safety. I am not fully qualified for the job; ideally I should have more hours and another two years' experience in what I am doing now. But you never know, Patsri; depending on the other applications, I may be able to compete. How would you like to go to Chicago, Patsri? If you are dead against it, I won't apply. But if you quite like the idea, then I will. Of course, whether we actually go depends on TASS.'

'I think you should try, Tashi,' Patsri was relaxed and smiling. 'It will be a great challenge, that's what you need. Yes, write to them and see what happens.'

'Fine, I will try. I have no idea what will happen. I'll mention to the TASS consultant what I'm doing. He might put in a good word for me; he seems to be knowledgeable and competent.'

At the beginning of August 1989 Tashi received a letter from TASS stating that he had been successful in his application. Tashi had just reached the age of 32. TASS would be organizing the flight to Chicago as soon as he and his family were ready to travel.

What the letter could not say was that Tashi's application was one of 140 received by TASS. Under the normal selection criteria his would not have been shortlisted; there were several applicants who were much better qualified than he in several important respects. But the way in which recruitment for TASS was handled did not correspond to normal practice. The CEO, one Duale, insisted on seeing all the applications for every professional post. And his consideration was not usually apolitical in accordance with TASS's mandate. Duale was a political animal. If he felt that filling a post with an applicant from Bhutan would improve his image, then TASS would have the services of a Bhutanese, regardless of the stronger qualifications and experience of others from less exotic countries. One way of gaining support for his position was to recruit from various countries around the world. With subtle, gentle reminders from time to time, the civil aviation administrations would write to TASS to express gratitude for TASS's excellent professional help; some of the letters even singled out the CEO for special mention, lauding his dynamic leadership. Duale ensured that, without exception, copies of these letters were sent on to the Chairman of TASS's Board of Trustees who, in turn, sent copies to members of the Board.

Before departing for Chicago, Tashi made his peace with his minister. Although reluctant to let Tashi go, finally the minister said, 'I do not know why this should be, but in a strange way I feel I have a debt to repay to you. Now I will do my best to repay and I will recommend to His Majesty that we let you go. Captain Singh will take your place, that is once our people return to the Kingdom after their training. I am sure you will be an excellent representative of Bhutan in North America. Good luck, Tashi; and remember, if you are not happy in Chicago you can always come back and continue working here.'

The day before departure, a great party was held in Thimphu, attended by more than three hundred people, including Pema and Gyeltshen. The atmosphere was electric. A clever and great man of the Kingdom was about to travel half way around the world. He would bear the heavy responsibility of representing all that was good about Bhutan. Before the party the master of rituals had cleansed the house of Tashi and Patsri. Then lamas had been brought to lead the chanting of prayers. The deities were begged to look after Tashi and his family. *Mahakala* was singled out to keep watch over them. Friends brought small presents to Tashi and Patsri, who were praised for making the great sacrifice of leaving the beautiful Kingdom for the unpleasant substitute of life in the so-called developed world.

Tashi's virtues were extolled. The 'flying tiger' would again set out on his travels. Wherever he might go, he would benefit mankind through his professional knowledge and his help to those in need. And so it went on, the chanting reaching crescendo after crescendo late into the cool night.

Towards the end of the long flight to Chicago, Patsri became excited. 'We have so much to enjoy, Tashi. It will not all be easy, but we will be happy together. I wonder what Chicago is like?'

'I wonder what the CEO is like?' Tashi replied.

'Oh yes,' Patsri wondered, 'who is the CEO?'

'He is called Dr. Duale. By training he is a lawyer. I am sure he has an interesting background; I would like to know more about him. After all, he is the CEO of an important air safety support set-up, and he will be my boss. I wonder, what he's like?'

'There's not long to go till we arrive,' Patsri said. 'You'll soon find out !'

Chapter Eleven

Father and Son: One Moment of Truth

Patsri heard the bell and went to the door of the apartment she and Tashi had moved into on the previous day. 'Oh! My darling Tashi. This has been the longest day of my life. There is so much to do, but you have no idea how I missed you all day. The little one has just gone to sleep. Why did you have to ring the bell? Wait! You can't answer until I kiss you.' Patsri threw her arms around Tashi's neck and kissed him.

As the tenant of the next apartment passed behind them, looking straight ahead with a mock look of concentration on his face, Tashi whispered, 'Let's go inside and close the door, Patsri. I rang the bell because I forgot the key. We probably made too much love last night, so I couldn't think properly.' Tashi smiled lovingly at Patsri, then said, 'We'll soon develop a routine and you won't feel so lonely. Once I get to know a few people in the office, we can invite them. Everyone I met so far has been very nice, I must say. The staff seems to be predominantly American, but there are plenty of other nationalities. Apparently, the CEO wants it that way.'

'Now,' Patsri said, proudly eyeing her handsome husband, 'tell me about your first day in your new job, Captain Tashi of Bhutan.'

'Well,' Tashi said, 'it didn't turn out quite as I had expected. After all, what does one expect on the first day? Nothing much, except an office, an introduction to the supervisor (if you're lucky) and background reading. But it wasn't quite like that. First, I met a personnel man. He went out of his way to be extra welcoming. He told me that the personnel division had been directly instructed to make sure I was happy. The CEO, Dr. Duale, had told them that

185

he was very concerned that the first member of staff from Bhutan should be happy. I was told that if at any time I needed something, including advice, I shouldn't hesitate to get in touch with the personnel director's office. I must say, I thought this was a nice gesture.

Then, when I was introduced to my immediate boss, his name is Mike Wilson, he gave me two hours of his time, which again impressed me. He knew all sorts of things about my professional life. He must have asked for a briefing paper from the TASS man in Bhutan; apparently, I got a pretty good write-up. My boss has a good understanding of the situation in Bhutan, as far as flight safety in concerned. He also told me a lot about TASS; he gave me an assessment of its strengths and weaknesses. And he was happy to answer my questions.'

'And what did you ask him?' Patsri interjected.

'Not too much, I thought I should read and do some work before I started asking too many questions. But I did ask him about the CEO. I was a bit confused by the answer. Apparently, he is knowledgeable and highly efficient, but he has a tendency to get into arguments with his Executive Committee, though he usually wins; I was told they call him 'The Survivor.' In any case, it doesn't worry me. As long as I can get into my work without too much interference, then I will be happy. One thing that came through very clearly was that there's a tremendous amount of work to be done in the field of flight safety. With the never-ending expansion of air traffic, especially in Asia, I'm sure we shall be busier than ever. I wouldn't be surprised if in a few months they will ask me to go on some overseas trips to some of the weakest flight safety countries. In any case, I certainly don't need to get involved with the CEO on the work front, at least I doubt it; my boss will look after that. It wouldn't surprise me if I never meet the CEO; TASS is quite big, you know, and I am a very small cog.'

Gradually, their lives developed a loose routine. Tashi made sure he was at his desk in good time each morning; as the days passed he made rapid progress in understanding the parameters of his job. He normally returned home by seven, but occasionally stayed longer to finish work. Patsri was busy with Little Tashi. And she loved to cook. Almost every day, time had to be found to explore Chicago to track down the best fresh food so that she could surprise Tashi with yet another succulently prepared meal.

In his own way, Little Tashi seemed to enjoy these excursions just as much as his mother. He sat in his pushchair and chatted to her. He could not yet speak intelligibly, but his mother always pretended to understand; and this made him happy. In the early days of November the 'Windy City' seemed to close in as the temperatures dropped and the daylight hours shortened. The blue sky, when visible, had taken on its somewhat faded winter hue, and the late autumn leaves were whisked into whirligigs by gusts of the chill wind. But Patsri was not discouraged by the approach of winter. Although she had been brought up in the warmth and humidity of Thailand, she had become conditioned to the cold temperatures of Bhutan.

On her return from one of her walks with the little one, as Patsri crossed at the lights in front of the apartment building she felt the contrast between the life she had led in Thimphu and her new life in Chicago. That evening, with Little Tashi already tucked up in his warm bed and after she had served Tashi yet another delicious meal, Patsri became pensive. She was sitting on their new off-white sofa, which was the perfect backdrop, Tashi thought, for his stunningly beautiful wife who, at this particular moment, struck him as a supernatural goddess. If only, Tashi thought, he had a camera; he could capture the expression on Patsri's beautiful face, a countenance which at once reflected both deep intelligence and serenity. Above all, he was enchanted by her widely-spaced brown eyes. Tashi asked Patsri what she was thinking about. The beautiful face turned to him and Patsri smiled gently. 'I was just thinking, Tashi, how different things are here. It's funny, both Bhutan and Thailand are called 'developing countries'; and certainly in Bhutan the GNP is very low compared with the industrialized countries. But as far as our lives in Bhutan were concerned, in so many ways we were much richer. When I walk each day, I see someone you might call the 'average American.' Yes, on average they are materially very well off. Let us not talk about the poor – they are so terribly poor in this country! But too many of them look worried. And they are always in such a rush. Often they don't have time to feed themselves properly; all they have time for is some fast food at lunchtime and a tin, or something already prepared, in the evening. I think you could be excused for thinking they are often unhealthy. When I walk about every day with Little Tashi, there are so many dreadfully fat or pale-looking people on the streets. If you turn on the TV and look at the advertisements put on by the pharmaceutical industry, you might think just about everybody needs some sort of medicine or drug. I suppose 'success' with all this advertising is reached when you have converted an otherwise normally healthy person into a hypochondriac. The population seems to be pathological when it comes to dosing themselves with some sort of drug. It is something amazing.

And the traffic pollution is awful. When we wait at the traffic lights, sometimes I put a handkerchief over Little Tashi's nose. Thank goodness our apartment looks over the water; it is so beautiful and we don't have to put up with traffic fumes. I don't mean to single out Chicago; but I expect it's typical. I suppose the basic question is how do you manage development in a large city. In my country, Bangkok is one of the worst examples of how not to manage the city's development; the pollution and traffic congestion are terrible. Such a pity!

'Then there is this security thing. Today George, you know our very nice janitor, gave me a sketch which shows where we can walk safely at night and the areas where we have to be very careful. But don't worry, Tashi, we are going to enjoy Chicago and North America. We should explore as much as possible. And why don't we introduce ourselves to western classical music? The Chicago Symphony Orchestra is famous.'

Tashi's expression became solemn. He took Patsri in his arms and tenderly kissed her. Ever so gently he slid beneath her supple limbs and sat her on his lap. Then he kissed her again. 'Are you telling me you are unhappy, Patsri? You know, the minister in the Kingdom told me I could go back and carry on working there at any time. The last thing I want is for you to be unhappy.'

'Not at all, Tashi!,' Patsri rejoined, 'I am just thinking aloud. Remember, you have all sorts of people to discuss things with in the office. I only have you to talk to. On the streets each day I see hundreds of people, but nobody says a word to me; in any case, why should they? So sometimes I will have to talk to you, my darling. It's as simple as that. Now, Tashi darling, tell me what you think of my impressions.'

'I think your impressions make a lot of sense, Patsri. My main reaction is that we shouldn't be too hard on the Americans. In certain respects they have been hugely successful; certainly in technical and material matters they have overcome enormous challenges. Their record when it comes to quality of life is not so good, especially when you move downwards from the upper and middle classes. The average American would be horrified to hear a reference to a class system; which is silly. Their class level is defined by personal wealth and income; and they are very conscious of this type of class. That's a big difference in outlook to ours, or in comparison with the Europeans for that matter. We place a much higher value on culture and a well-rounded education; as you said, we might be poorer in a material sense, but in certain cultural respects we are much richer.

If you looked at the relative life-styles in that way, Patsri, you might reach a rather different conclusion. But I would certainly agree that it would not be that easy to find in North America such clear, beautiful air and the gorgeous scenery as we are lucky enough to have in our Kingdom in the Himalayas. Those mountains, Patsri, are so unbelievably beautiful!

Now, it's high time I took you into bed, my darling. I musn't bash my brains out too much; I had a message from the CEO's secretary this morning that tomorrow afternoon I should attend a small welcoming party in the CEO's office. It won't last long; I am sure he has much more pressing things on his mind. But it will be interesting meeting the big man.'

Tashi looked into Patsri's eyes, eyes which to him had such profound expression that he felt he would never be able to fathom their depth. He stroked her neck as she inclined her head towards his. Patsri whispered, 'I love you so much, Tashi; you are my world. I feel so safe with you.' She pressed her lips against his mouth.

'Patsri,' Tashi responded, 'we are wasting time again!' He carried Patsri into the bedroom and undressed her. Then he laughed and said, 'Thank goodness for the central heating!'

'How do you feel this morning, Captain Tashi?' Patsri enquired over breakfast, 'Are you in good shape to meet the CEO – or are you a little jaded?' she added with a chuckle.

'Well, since you asked me so directly, my darling,' Tashi

replied with a smile, 'I must say that I feel refreshed and my head is as clear as the air in Bhutan. And I am not at all exhausted! I feel I have had the perfect preparation to meet the CEO.'

Tashi set off for his office with a jaunty step. He was fortunate that the TASS building was within walking distance. He noticed a thin mist which hung over the water and he thought how this would soon be blown away in the Windy City. Once he reached his office, he lost no time in getting into his work. As usual, the day passed in a flash.

At ten minutes to 4 o'clock Tashi left for the CEO's office. As he passed the office of his division chief, he left word with the secretary that he was *en route* to the CEO's welcoming drink; he would mention his return on the way back, he hoped in a half hour or so.

At the CEO's office he was welcomed by Anna; he noticed there were already one or two other newcomers in the ante room. 'Captain Tashi,' Anna said with a relaxed smile, 'we are so pleased to see you. My name is Anna. If ever you need anything from this office, just call me. Lines of communication in TASS are there to be used. We don't want unnecessary bureaucracy.' Tashi thought how pleasantly Anna talked to him; and she was good-looking into the bargain. After the arrival of two more newly-recruited staff, Anna opened the door of the CEO's office and asked the small group to enter. Just inside the door a tray of drinks was offered to the guests. As Tashi took a glass of mineral water, he glanced beyond the tray and found himself looking into the eyes of a pretty blond girl. For a split second, the blue of her eyes reminded him of the early morning Himalayan azure. She smiled at him with a warmth that made him, with his innate shyness, feel slightly ill at ease. And he could not ignore the fact that physically she was very attractive. Caught off-balance, Tashi tried to hide this unexpected impact on his emotions. He looked around him; he counted four men and two women. They all seemed to be at least ten years older than himself.

Then Tashi noticed the CEO, who was standing up behind his desk; Duale looked at each member of the group in turn before walking across the large Persian carpet. He held out his hand to Tashi.

'You must be Captain Tashi of Bhutan. I am singling you out

because you are obviously the youngest here; so it's easy to identify you. Welcome to TASS and to Chicago. I am sure you will be happy, but if anything bothers you at any time you can consult the personnel people. If they can't help you, then call my office.'

'Thank you, sir,' Tashi responded, 'I will certainly bear that in mind, thank you. I hope I won't need to bother anyone.'

As Duale turned to shake hands and chat with each member of the group, Tashi watched him closely. For a reason which Tashi could not explain, he suddenly felt a kinship to Duale. Duale took a few paces backwards and stood in front of his desk; then he cleared his throat, which served to indicate to the newcomers that he was about to speak, which he did:

'On behalf of the Trust for Air Safety Support, I would like to say 'welcome' to each of you. I know you are busy, so I will be brief. You come from all over the world; we even have a newcomer from the Kingdom of Bhutan, Captain Tashi. You have different backgrounds, but there is one thing you all have in common. Each of you is at the peak of your professional competence. Each of you has been selected by me to work in TASS; I have personally signed your employment contracts. As CEO I wish to demonstrate, in a practical way, that I have placed my confidence in you. In return, I expect to receive your loyalty. In this way you will be serving TASS in the best possible way.'

Duale looked benevolently at the small group; he smiled slightly as though he wanted each to feel at ease. For their part, the newcomers found him to be a mildly fatherly figure. It was a fact of life that any CEO needed to be mentally and physically tough; at this particular moment, however, Duale gave a convincing impression that he was a gentle, caring, friendly creature. Then he carried on: 'As CEO, I look upon TASS as a family; I have heard that in certain respects some regard me as the father of TASS. In any case, in every family there has to be a head, as well as a code of good and ethical conduct. As CEO of this Trust I do my best to set an example; I try to show I believe in morally sound, decent conduct. I hope you will at all times follow my example. Like me, set your sights high; if you do, I have no doubt that in due course you will be rewarded.

Now I must leave you to get on with your important work. Just before we break, let us have a photo taken, for the record.'

Within a few minutes the group photo had been taken, Duale had shaken hands with each of them, and all were back at work.

A few days later, Tashi found a copy of the group photo on his desk, which in turn triggered the writing of his monthly letter to his mother and uncle in Thimphu. Tashi wrote how impressed he had been with his CEO; he also passed on Patsri's judgement that, from what Tashi had related, her intuition told her that Duale's representation of himself was simply too good to be true. She had tried not to be cynical, but if she were to be honest, then she could not ignore her conclusion.

'Oh, Lord Buddha!' exclaimed Pema when she opened Tashi's letter. Gyeltshen looked up sharply for a man of his age; in Bhutan, a man of sixty was regarded as old.

'What has happened, Pema?.'

'My Lord Buddha! I am looking at a photo of Duale; and Tashi is standing next to him!' Pema's hand was shaking nervously as she tried to read Tashi's letter. Gyeltshen took the letter from Pema and read it aloud. When he had finished, he turned to Pema and said in a low voice.

'Now we have to choose, Pema. We can say nothing and hope that Tashi and Duale will never know their true relationship. Or we can be more honest and explain the fact to Tashi. The first course avoids the issue; the second course is honest, but we cannot tell what the consequences will be. What shall we do, Pema? You are the mother. It is your decision!'

Pema did not hesitate in her response. 'We shall tell the truth to Tashi and pray to the gods that they should reward our honesty by giving Tashi good judgement. When Tashi was young we decided to shield him from the truth; even then he found out. Now he is a man of the world. It is right that he should know the truth. He is wise and he will know how to deal with the situation.' That afternoon Pema wrote her letter, imploring Tashi to use the information with wisdom and discretion.

'You look bemused, my darling,' Patsri laughed, 'tell me the secrets; you are reading with such concentration!'

'What can I tell you, Patsri. This is the monthly letter from Bhutan. My mother and uncle Gyeltshen are quite well, although my uncle is getting a bit old. I always concentrate when I read something. Why don't we have some tea, my angel.'

To Tashi's relief, Patsri went to make some tea. 'Yes,' he thought, 'I am bemused. I may tell Patsri sometime, or I may not. Why worry her? And I don't really need to do anything. The CEO doesn't know that he is my father. The best thing is to do nothing.'

Although Tashi did his best to forget, he found he was attempting the impossible. At night in particular, when he had time to think, he found himself becoming more and more curious about Duale. What sort of man was his father? Was he a decent man, and if so, why had he not married his mother? Fortunately, Tashi was a busy man, and the demanding technical tasks he was asked to tackle every day helped to dim any thoughts he might have about his father.

For just over a year, Tashi kept his enquiring mind at bay. It was in early 1991, however, that he realised he was losing the battle. Since his arrival in Chicago, Tashi had applied himself with great energy, and was already highly regarded within TASS for his excellent work. He began to think he might be working too hard. One evening he confided in Patsri, 'I don't know why, but I don't feel quite as I should do these days. I think I should go away for a few days and think through a few things. TASS has a travel agent in-house and they will organise a hotel for me.'

Patsri tried to smile, but felt tears slowly making their way over the contours of her high cheekbones. 'Is it my fault, Tashi? Have I done something wrong, my darling?'

'Of course not,' Tashi quickly replied, 'it is about something in the office. When it is all settled I'll tell you, but I need to get away to make sure I am doing the right thing. There are times, Patsri, when one needs to be alone. We may need to pray or meditate; or we might have to think about something very deeply. The important thing is that there are no distractions. Please trust me, Patsri. In the end everything will be fine.'

Tashi pulled a white handkerchief from his pocket and gently wiped the tears from Patsri's cheeks. She smiled and kissed him. Patsri seemed to be struggling to speak, then said, 'All right. Go when you are ready, sort yourself out and come back. But don't leave me for too long, my darling.'

'Well, Tashi, if you need a rest, you need a rest.' Tashi had been talking the following morning to his boss Mike Wilson. 'That's fine by me. I suggest you take a week off and get some warmth into your bones. Incidentally,' Mike Wilson asked, 'have you seen the CEO during the last few days?'

'No,' Tashi replied, 'in any case, as you know I would never see him without you being present.'

'I just meant,' Mike explained, 'whether you might have seen him in the building. You know, our Duale is a bit of an odd fellow. Sometimes he seems to withdraw from us. A week ago, I needed him to sign off on something and his secretary just said he was 'away.' When I mentioned that it's normal for the CEO to let us know if he is going away, she explained he was on a three day trip. He had been invited to the White House in Washington and then he was going on to see 'his friends' the top people in the UN. Of course, Tashi, he can do what he likes. But he is often away and I for one cannot imagine what good his political visits can do for TASS. After all, we are an apolitical Trust.

I have another concern. If Duale is often away, how can we expect initiatives from TASS to help keep international aviation safe? Up to a couple of years ago, he was always calling meetings to focus on weak areas in the developing world and then he would challenge us to come up with ideas for a solution. But these days we hardly see him in the office. It's not healthy from the point of view of our work, nor do I think it's good for TASS's image. If this goes on, I'm afraid TASS will lose its way, simply because we'll have lost our leadership, not to mention our apolitical image.

Now today I called the CEO's office, and again Anna told me he is 'away.' I could hardly contain my exasperation, and I unthinkingly asked where he had gone. Anna said she didn't know, which of course is nonsense. That woman knows everything!'

Tashi noticed that Mike was suddenly blushing; his reddened face took on a sheepish expression. He went on.

'Tashi, I don't usually let rip like this. I treat you not only as an excellent colleague; you have become a very good friend. Apart from yourself, I wouldn't risk talking to anyone in confidence. I know I can rely on you not to pass any of this on; I wouldn't like anyone to think that I'm being disloyal. I don't mean to be; I think I am just raising legitimate concerns. Maybe it's best if you just try and forget what I said, Tashi. Is that all right with you?'

Tashi responded without hesitation, 'Of course, it's all right,

Mike. You know you can rely on me. I wouldn't dream of taking it further. In any case, thank you for agreeing to my little vacation. So I will be off next week and look forward to seeing you on Monday week, refreshed and ready to go.' The two men shook hands and Tashi left the office.

Shortly afterwards, instead of working as usual through his coffee break, Tashi took the elevator down a few floors and visited TASS's travel agent. The following Monday he boarded an aircraft for Florida. On arriving at Fort Lauderdale he drove a hired car to Pompano, where he would be staying in a good hotel that gave TASS employees a discounted rate. Now I've arrived, he thought, I have to do my best to put my work behind me for a week and come to terms with my situation.

His mind was awash with a multitude of thoughts, one line of thinking following hard on the heels of the next. Am I going to carry on in TASS and pretend that Duale is not my father? If he is to know that he is my father, how should I tell him? And if I do tell him, do I leave it at that; or do I ask him why he broke contact with my mother? After all he slept with my mother! And then I have to try and assess the fall out, yes the consequences, of each course of action. If he knows, will he treat me as a son; or will he see me as a possible impediment that might be best removed? And if I challenge him to support my mother, how will he react?

At one point, he thought how he could cope instantly with every flying situation in which he found himself; in his profession he was supremely confident. But in his personal relationship with Duale, that is if he chose to enter the relationship, he would feel unsure, perhaps insecure. On balance, he thought, it would probably be safer if he had no relationship at all; that would be the easy way out. As he was drifting into slumber, Tashi told himself he had to try and resolve the dilemma. Eventually, all his thoughts would be arranged in some sort of order; and from this order, the various consequences of each possible action would become clear. Then he would take a decision on which course was best. None of the consequences of the possible decisions would be clear-cut, but once the decision had been taken, he could put the issue behind him... he hoped. The torment would come to an end and he would resume his normal lifestyle. Then he fell asleep.

Tashi awoke to brilliant sunshine streaming into his room. He got up and pulled the curtains back. Looking out of the large picture windows, he could see a swimming pool surrounded by palm trees, whose large, light green leaves moved slightly in the gentle breeze. Below were lawns divided by clean concrete paths; and in neat flower beds deep red cannas injected a splash of colour into the idyllic picture. Looking over and beyond the pool and gardens, Tashi saw the sea.

Everything here is so perfectly quiet and calm, he thought, if I can't sort out my thoughts here, then I will never manage. Before going down to breakfast, he said his prayers, then called Patsri and reassured her that all would be well. If possible, he'd even come home before the end of the week. 'What's that Patsri? Of course I love you. I adore you. Just be a little patient. Everything will be fine. Just give me a few days.'

Feeling rested, comfortably warm and altogether in harmony with his beautiful surroundings, Tashi went down for some breakfast. Although the hotel called the breakfast room a 'coffee shop,' Tashi could see that he was about to enter a spacious dining room. Once inside, he paused and briefly looked for a vacant table; as he cast his eyes around the room, he suddenly found himself looking at Duale. Almost in disbelief, and certainly confused, Tashi's immediate reaction was to leave; but his intention was neutralized by a charming waitress who spoke to him.

'You must be Captain Tashi of TASS. Please follow me, we have a nice table for you which has a view into the garden.' To Tashi's relief the table was some way from Duale's, on the other side of the room. When he sat down, he found that when he turned his head he was looking at Duale's profile. At least that is better, he thought, than looking at him head-on!

Tashi was trying not to be flustered; although in any case this would not have been in his nature, he nevertheless felt that he was consciously trying to keep the lid on a rising feeling of excitement which seemed to be gripping him. He had been surprised by a new situation. What to Tashi was a quite extraordinary co-incidence could, in fact, easily have been explained by TASS's travel agent. When TASS staff asked for vacation accommodation, the agent normally chose from three hotels who offered TASS discounted rates. In this case, Duale and Tashi had asked for accommodation in the sunny south, each unknowing of the other's plans.

Tashi quickly took stock of the situation. On the one hand, he had no wish at this stage to meet Duale; on the other, he could not help feeling curious about Duale's presence in the hotel. He decided that his breakfast would be short and he would then retreat to consider his next move. A pretty, smiling waitress poured some coffee. As Tashi began to sip from the cup, he slowly turned his head and looked in Duale's direction.

What he saw gave him a start. Duale was tenderly pushing a swath of beautifully brushed, wavy blond hair to one side and he was kissing the neck of a blond. And while Tashi's amazed glance lingered, the blond turned her head to press her lips against those of Duale. Yes, Tashi thought, I recognize that beautiful face; I last saw the face in the CEO's office. She was offering me a drink!

At that instant, Tashi decided that he had had enough for one breakfast. Even if he might be short on food, what he had seen had been a feast for the eyes. Without hesitation, he got up and strode out of the dining room. He thought of going to his room, but for some reason he discarded the idea. Some hidden voice urged him to stride out of the hotel and go for a long walk. Which he did.

Tashi could not know that Duale had seen him; nor would he ever know that Duale would immediately call TASS's travel agent and explicitly instruct the manager that when Duale was staying at a TASS-approved hotel, under no circumstances were other TASS staff to be booked into the same hotel. And if the CEO's instructions were ignored, or overlooked, the manager would lose his job; adopting an angry tone, Duale hoped the manager clearly understood?

'Absolutely, sir!' was the immediate response.

Although Tashi had no particular goal to reach in his walk, he nevertheless strode along the sidewalk as though he had great purpose. What he had seen had emotionally charged him to such an extent that he seemed to be almost blindly walking at an ever-increasing pace. Soon he had reached the outskirts of Pompano and he turned towards the seashore. The warmth of the day was pleasant as he reached the sand. A gentle breeze touched his face as he took off his sandals and walked through the edge of the surf, the refreshingly cool water gently washing over his feet. Now his pace had slackened; at last he stopped. Standing alone in the shallow water, he looked along the coastline and then out to sea.

Slowly he was collecting himself. Now it was time to think.

First, his thoughts turned to his mother. Although his mother had never related the details of her affair with Duale, she had told Tashi that she loved Duale. For his part, Duale had even discussed marriage. Tashi dwelt on this fact. He tried to imagine how Patsri would feel if Tashi simply broke contact with her; he imagined that she would be devastated. In her isolation and loneliness what might she do? It must have been a terrible experience, he thought, for his mother to have been left high and dry by a man who professed to love her. Thank goodness for his uncle Gyeltshen, Tashi thought.

Next he thought of Duale. The fact that a man of sixty, who happened to be his father, was necking with a young blond in the dining room was, he recognized, of no direct concern. But the fact that his father had never contributed one iota to the upkeep of his mother was, for Tashi, altogether another matter.

Tashi's thoughts had tended towards the 'let the sleeping dog lie' option. Now things were different. Duale, he mused, had been earning his CEO salary for years; and he could afford a lifestyle which enabled him to enjoy certain luxuries in his life including, for example, vacationing with young women. He probably indulged himself in other ways. And what was Duale's attitude to Tashi's mother? Well, Tashi thought, Duale had enjoyed her as a young and beautiful girl, just as one might appreciate a fresh, tender rose blossom. Then Duale had gone away. And he had left his rose to wither and suffer in her loneliness.

The more Tashi mused in the warm, watery sand, the more incensed he became. It took him one more hour of hard thinking to reach his conclusion on what, for him, was the right course of action. And it was about midday that he stepped out of the surf and took a few paces to the dry sand; there he brushed the wet sand off the soles of his feet and slipped into his sandals.

In contrast with his walk from the hotel, no longer was he filled with confused, directionless emotions; even an innocent onlooker might have noted the stride of someone possessed of a quiet, but determined, resolve. Tashi would confront Duale. And if Duale had left the hotel? This would make not the slightest difference; in that case, he would tackle Duale in Chicago.

As Tashi strode through the entrance of the hotel, he heard a voice, 'Good afternoon Captain Tashi.' Duale was holding out his hand so that Tashi could take it; Tashi, taken off guard, hesitated. Duale continued, 'I had no idea you were on vacation; normally I know where our professional staff are. I saw you in the dining room at breakfast time, but you didn't greet me. You probably thought I was preoccupied with the young girl. I have no idea who she was; in any case, as far as I know she has left the hotel. Being a bachelor, I'm normally happier to have someone to talk to at meal times. Come and sit down and let's talk for a bit, if you have time – or are you on the way to a *rendez-vous?*' Duale chuckled.

'No, Dr. Duale, I am not on my way to a meeting. I can talk as long as you like.' At this point, Duale asked Tashi how his work was progressing; Tashi was impressed by Duale's knowledge of flight safety, especially the relative lack of it in certain developing countries. And he was surprised that a man with a legal background should show such detailed knowledge of a field in which he had no practical experience. After about an hour, Tashi decided to take the initiative.

'Dr. Duale, you have been asking me quite a few questions; would you mind if I raised one or two?'

'Well,' Duale responded, 'within the TASS family we not only have to be good, we have a duty to be democratically fair. That has always been my credo. At least when you ask me questions, you are guaranteed the truth when I answer.'

Tashi glanced at Duale; he would never forget the benevolently relaxed, self-satisfied look on Duale's face.

Tashi spoke. 'In your early days with TASS you advised the Kingdom of Bhutan on their aviation legislation. As far as I know, your work was greatly appreciated. During your stay you were very busy. But you also found time to make some personal acquaintances, especially with a young and beautiful woman called Pema. Am I correct so far, Dr. Duale?'

For a legal man, Duale instantly committed a blunder, the seriousness of which would have profound consequences not only on the life of himself, but also on the life of Tashi. Without hesitation, and smiling broadly, Duale responded, 'I never divulge secrets, but I suppose there are exceptions and we are talking about a long time ago. Yes, Pema and I enjoyed one another enormously!'

So, Tashi thought, the man has no trouble in admitting his

relationship. He continued, 'Did you ever wonder what happened to Pema?.'

This time Duale's expression changed from one of happy self-satisfaction to a slightly thoughtful look; Duale was beginning to wonder where these questions might lead him.

'Well,' Duale replied, 'I must admit that I don't usually spend much time wondering what might have happened to old flames; a conquest is a conquest, then it's all over. Of course, in developing countries, as you know usually it is not exactly a conquest; they are much hungrier, if you see what I mean – poor devils!' Duale let out a short snort of a laugh before continuimg, 'In any case, you're a man and you know that, in basic terms, a man is a hunter. I hope you know what I mean, Captain? In any case, one can't go through life wondering what happened to one's various conquests. I must say I was greatly infatuated by Pema; she was a fine and beautiful woman. But like all of them, I lost contact in time.'

Tashi became pensive, but only for a few moments; resisting any form of distraction, he said, 'May I tell you what became of Pema, or do you have no interest in such things, Dr. Duale?'

'Look, Captain Tashi,' Duale rejoined slightly testily, 'we are having an off the record chat; soon I must leave you for a meeting. But of course, if you would like me to know about Pema, er... yes... I mean, it could be interesting. After all, I knew her quite well.'

'Thank you, I will come to the point immediately. Pema had a baby nine months after you left her. The name of the baby was Tashi... which means you are talking to your son. Have I made myself clear, Dr. Duale?'

Tashi began to count the seconds during the ensuing silence; eventually he gave up. His resolve strengthening, Tashi wanted to look Duale in the eye; to his dismay, Duale's eyes were closed. The smug, self-confident figure opposite him had metamorphosed into a creature that resembled a scarecrow. Duale seemed lifeless. Now the creature slowly opened its eyes and tried to speak; as the mouth twitched, all that became audible were short pants.

Tashi continued, 'Something that has become of grave concern to me, Dr. Duale, is that over the last thirty years you have totally failed to provide any support whatsoever to my mother. My mother has told me of your professed love for her; you even told my mother you would marry her. She has shown me some of your beautiful letters. Yet, your love was apparently inadequate to motivate you to ensure she received even a little support.'

'Stop!' Duale exclaimed, 'that is enough! That is the end of the discussion; I will not listen to one more word. You can leave!'

Tashi was not in the slightest affected by his CEO's instructions. His expression took on the same determination which Captain Singh had seen when he and Tashi had found themselves in difficult flying conditions. And here was Tashi sitting in Florida, again in the pilot's seat and fully in command of the situation. He knew, and Duale was beginning to understand, that Tashi had a particular objective. And one way or another, the objective would be reached.

Tashi coolly rejoined, 'I understand your emotional interruption. However, in your own interest, Dr. Duale, I strongly recommend that you hear me out. The alternative will be that you learn the rest of what I have to say in a written memorandum which I will address to the Board of Trustees, as well as to members of the Executive Committee; naturally, you will receive a copy. I can assure you that in the inevitable enquiry which will arise, your image will be greatly damaged, perhaps irretrievably. At least the hypocrisy of your overall approach will be fully exposed. I would like to hope I might be wrong, but unfortunately I assess your situation as hopelessly indefensible.'

Again Duale interrupted Tashi; with his eyes narrowing in hatred he said, 'If you think you can blackmail me, you will be surprised. I am not called 'The Survivor' without good reason. I know how to survive, Captain, and there are those who tried to cross my path and paid the price. I hope I have made myself clear.' Duale stopped looking at Tashi and turned his head to look at the lawns.

Tashi decided to make a final attempt to transmit his message. 'Dr. Duale, this is my last try to finish saying what I must say to you. May I finish without further interruption? Or do you prefer to receive the copy of my memorandum?'

Duale slowly turned to look again at his son, a son whom he already regarded as the devil. Now he was beginning to feel weak again. With a heave of his panting body, he quietly responded in a tone which Tashi thought sounded like someone who was in a state of nervous exhaustion: 'Finish'.

'Thank you. As I was explaining, over the last thirty years you have failed to support my mother. I believe this was wrong; and after you have reflected on the subject, I hope you will also agree. Regardless of any view you might hold, I now require that you visit my mother in Bhutan, and not only apologise for your singularly inhumane conduct – you will reach an agreement with her under which you will pay her an appropriate lump sum, and you will make periodic payments to help support her living costs.'

Duale looked at Tashi with a grim expression; his eyes seemed to be getting larger by the second. Tashi continued, 'I fully understand you will object to my requirements, and I have no intention of sitting here while you waste our time protesting the very reasonable course of action which you must take. I will only say this. You have ninety days to complete the required action. If you fail, I will ensure that this despicable part of your history is made known to those who can assess whether your personal qualities are appropriate for someone who not only holds high office, but whose work is mainly concerned with the Third World and its development. The recipients of the detailed memorandum will draw their own conclusions, and it is these people who are in a decisive position to remove you from your office. Thank you for your patience, Dr. Duale.'

'Duale, my darling, where have you been?' questioned the shrill voice of the beautiful breakfast blond. Taken slightly aback, her blue eyes moved from Duale and were suddenly looking into Tashi's relaxed young face. The blond turned again to Duale. 'Oh, I am so sorry. I didn't realise you had a friend with you. We promised to meet – remember? See you soon, honey!' Then she was gone.

Tashi stood up and looked at his downcast adversary. 'In spite of our personal problems, Dr. Duale, you may rest assured of my loyalty to TASS and my dedication to my work. On the work front there is no problem. As far as your personal problem is concerned, as I told you, you have ninety days to repair the situation. In your own interest, I hope you succeed.'

As Tashi took his leave, his impression was of a face that, above all, epitomized sadness. As Tashi finally left him, Duale seemed to have relapsed into a trance-like state; he simply gazed at the lovely hotel garden. If Tashi had asked himself whether Duale's face reflected anxiety, he would have concluded that there was little trace of worry in the countenance. And Tashi would have been right. Unknown to him, Duale was already meditating on his options for survival. This was not the first time in his career that disaster had threatened to engulf him; nor would it be the last. Certainly, his image had been injured. Now he was considering how best not only to survive; he would move quickly to control the damage. He would fully regain his unassailable position, unfettered by threats.

Tashi resisted the temptation to return to Chicago that evening. He called Patsri to tell her that, fortuitously, he had begun to resolve the problem rather sooner than he had anticipated. He would stay two more nights.

'You sound much better than when you left, Tashi,' Patsri said, 'Until you come, my darling, I will dream of you holding me in your strong arms. I love you!'

The next morning Tashi went down for breakfast. Would he again see Duale? In any case, he was not in the slightest concerned. Now that he had implemented his course of action, where and when he again saw his father was of no concern to him. The waitress poured his coffee,

'I saw you talking to Dr. Duale yesterday, Captain Tashi,' she said, 'he's a wonderful man isn't he? You know, just after you left him he moved out; he said he had matters to attend to in Chicago. He was so enjoying his vacation. Something serious must have happened to take him all the way back to Chicago.'

'Yes,' Tashi commented, 'it must be something serious.'

After breakfast Tashi retraced his steps of the previous day. This time, however, he walked much more slowly. Above all, he felt delivered from the torment which had plagued him for over a year. He admired the cleanliness of the wide boulevards and he was fascinated by the palm trees which ornamented them. Later he walked in the shallow surf for about three miles in the glorious sunshine. His mind was clear, which freed him to admire the azure of the sky and the harmony of movement of the small waves. And he loved the feeling of mildly abrasive sand which filtered between his toes.

The following afternoon Tashi had returned to the snow and cold of Chicago. As he left the busy baggage hall of O'Hare, he suddenly felt a gentle jolt. 'Now I can start living again.'

Patsri kissed him and he suddenly realised what he had been missing. When they were home, Patsri hugged Tashi and pressed her head against his chest. He looked down lovingly at her beautiful head. Then she looked up at him and smiled, 'Before you kiss Little Tashi goodnight and take me into bed, tell me one thing. Have you solved the problem, Tashi?'

Just for a moment Tashi looked thoughtful. Then with a relaxed, mild and open countenance he replied, 'Patsri, it is quite a difficult problem and I have done my best. Our religion teaches us patience and faith in what is right and good. Whether the problem has been solved, I am not sure; but I am hopeful. I will know for certain, one way or the other, in ninety days – yes, Patsri, in ninety days'.

Chapter Twelve

The Rekindling

'You don't look as happy as you should, Dr. Duale,' Anna mentioned, as she tried to check that Duale had all his papers for the Executive Committee meeting, 'is everything all right? Or is something troubling you?'

'Everything is fine,' Duale responded; although he looked worried, he tried to produce a brief glimmer of a smile.

'Dr. Duale,' Anna went on, 'I have checked all your papers against each agenda item; they are all in order – except I didn't find anything about the staff. According to the agenda two are to be let go. You did not give the names; did you dictate something on that? Have I missed something?'

'No,' Duale said as he gathered up the papers and prepared to leave for the meeting, 'you didn't miss anything. It's a small item and we don't need more than an oral explanation. Thank you Anna; now I must go down.'

As Duale passed Anna and left the office, Anna had a feeling that she was looking at someone who bore a remarkable likeness to a person she had seen only a few days ago. Yes, she mused, it is quite extraordinary that his features seem to resemble an older version of Captain Tashi's. This led to her next thought; it was well known that doubles exist all over the world and these two were not exactly doubles. But the likeness was interesting. With her mind full of thoughts about the busy day ahead, Anna returned to her desk.

'Thank you, gentlemen,' Duale looked around the table at the Executive Committee, 'I thank you for your understanding and constructive discussion; give and take is so important. So I hope you will agree that we have disposed of item number eight. Before we come to Any Other Business, I would just like to quickly dispose of a formality, which is item number nine.

If I may briefly explain. As you know, to meet our ever expanding work commitments, we have to take on new staff from time to time. The last batch has settled down quite well. Unfortunately, however, there are two members of staff who have not made the grade. One is a woman; although she is well qualified as a statistician, she has an impossible personality. She constantly argues with her colleagues and although we have made every possible allowance, she has proved to be basically unsound, that is she is time-consumingly unreasonable, undisciplined and spiteful.'

'That's enough, Mr. CEO,' interrupted an American member of the committee, 'I suggest we don't waste time, get her out!'

Duale looked around the table, the epitome of understanding and patience; after a short pause, he enquired, 'Do I take it that the committee supports me on this point? If you do, we shall issue the notice and TASS will be free of her within a month.' Each committee member sat silently and gently nodded. 'Thank you, gentlemen.'

Adopting a thoughtful expression, Duale went on, 'The second case is more clear-cut. You may recall the recruitment of a man from the Kingdom of Bhutan, by name Captain Tashi. I have to accept some responsibility here. He was not the strongest candidate; but I was keen to develop a more international image for TASS. The fact is my experiment has failed; he is a nice man, but from the all-important aspect of knowledge he is a failure. With your agreement we will replace him as soon as possible, almost certainly with someone from the developed world. Do I have your agreement, gentlemen, please?'

There was a short silence, which was broken by the Italian. 'Mr. CEO, before we endorse this I think we need more information. I have seen some of Captain Tashi's work. I am not an expert in flight operations, but I was impressed by the way the report was written and the detail which Captain Tashi included. What precisely is the problem; maybe in his division there is a personality clash. I think we should not be too hasty.'

While the Italian had been talking, Duale had noticed the American briefly leaving the table to make a telephone call. Now he was again seated. The American spoke, 'Mr. CEO, I will be brief. I worked for twenty years in the field of flight safety. I do not regard myself as an expert because I am not current. But I know the parameters of the job. I must say, up to today I had the impression that Captain Tashi was doing a good job. From the few short conversations I have had with him, I was impressed. I am sure everyone here will agree with me when I say we should not spend too much time on this; the Trustees have told us to be more efficient, which means that we should do our work as quickly as possible. Normally, in cases where doubt arises, we would have asked for a written report. To save time I have asked Captain Tashi's supervisor to come down and tell us the details of Captain Tashi's shortcomings.'

At that moment, there was a knock on the door and Mike Wilson entered. 'I was asked to attend for some clarification on Captain Tashi, Dr. Duale,' he said.

Duale quite suddenly found himself in a position where he seemed to have lost control of a meeting which he was chairing. Worse, he was on the point of being exposed as a patent liar. His ice-cool mind was trying to function at a frantic pace. Before anyone had the chance to speak, he said, 'I think there might have been some good-intentioned misunderstanding. It is clear that I have misjudged the feelings of confidence that committee members should have in me. I believe the right thing for me to do now is to get back to the beginning. I withdraw my proposal and the committee will receive a report on the subject in due course. Only after you have agreed with my judgement and endorsed my proposal, shall we move to replace Captain Tashi. We are short of time, Mr. Wilson; and you are a busy man. So please return to your office and the committee will finish its work. Thank you, Mr. Wilson.'

As Mike Wilson moved to the imposing door of the meeting room, a strong voice rang out from the table, 'Stop! Just come back here for five minutes, Mr. Wilson, please.' The American said, 'Mr. CEO, we seem to be getting into a complicated situation; I cannot imagine why. There is no reason to waste time.' Turning to Mike Wilson, he said, 'Please sit next to the chairman and give us a five-minute summary of Captain Tashi's knowledge, performance and character.'

'I prefer a reasoned written report,' interjected Duale.

The American looked at Mike Wilson, 'Please speak. When we

have heard what you have to say, if we need a written report then we can say so.'

Slightly confused, Mike Wilson spoke. 'On all three counts I would give Captain Tashi an A plus. He is the best flight operations man I have ever met. His knowledge of his field knows no bounds, his performance is nothing less than excellent and his personality is perfect for his work, that is to say the ideal combination of convincing persuasion, based of course on knowledge, linked with firmness. He is a wonderful man and in my judgement TASS is extremely fortunate to have his services. I can answer any specific questions committee members may have.' Then he added, 'I hope Captain Tashi is not thinking of leaving? That would be a dreadful loss!' Mike Wilson sounded concerned.

Duale broke the bemused silence, 'Thank you, Mr. Wilson. I have recommended that we find someone more expert than Captain Tashi. I must admit my judgement was based almost solely on my assessment of his shortcomings in the legal aspects of his work. In any case, it is clear that you and I will need to discuss the matter further. As I stated earlier, for the moment I am withdrawing the recommendation. Any further consideration of this issue will be based on a written assessment. In view of the time spent on the matter, the meeting is adjourned. Thank you.'

Without more ado, Duale left the room. The American was musing – and he was smiling, just a little. He thought that if Duale had been a Buddhist like Captain Tashi, Duale might have been reincarnated as a dog. And if he had been a dog, then his tail would have been well down between his legs.

As Duale took the elevator to his office, he knew he had suffered a reverse and he wondered how this would undermine the committee's confidence in him. He also knew the suggested report on Tashi would never be written. For their part, most members of the committee sensed this too. The issue of Tashi's contrived departure, neatly wrapped behind a facade of correctness, was dead. All that was left were the damaged image of Duale as CEO, the disappointed surprise and doubts of the committee, and the incredulous confusion of Mike Wilson.

When Duale reached his office complex, Anna was waiting for him. 'Dr. Duale, you have a visitor,' Anna told him in a somewhat cold, detached tone of voice. 'Do you mind me mentioning that I find the likeness between you and Captain Tashi to be quite striking.' Duale stopped and his eyes flashed at Anna, 'What do you mean?'

'I don't mean anything, Dr. Duale. I thought it might cheer you up; as you know, Captain Tashi is very handsome!'

Feeling troubled, Duale entered his office and closed the door. Sitting in front of his desk was the Florida breakfast blond. Duale held out his hand to greet her. 'Is that the best you can do, honey? I have a sort of present for you. You'll recognize it when you see it. But you'll have to earn it, Duale.' The blond opened a huge, shiny plastic skin bag and took out a small object wrapped in tissue paper, the paper held in place by coloured ribbon. 'This is for you; but you only get it if you kiss me, honey.'

Duale looked at the pretty, honey-coloured, smiling face, the beautiful blond hair, the skin-tight, short navy-blue dress and the perfect legs. If things had been 'normal,' he thought, he could meet her somewhere outside the office; and he would do justice to her body. But at that particular moment, for Duale things were far from normal. His life seemed to be caving in; it seemed only a matter of time before he might be destroyed under a heap of accusations and non-confidence motions. Now he had this girl in his office.

Yes, he quickly thought, she would have to leave. She seemed intent on giving him a present; and she wanted to be kissed. He kissed her. She pulled him towards her and whispered, 'Duale, you are a great lover. My darling, we should see one another again sometime.'

'Of course,' Duale replied.

Then she went on, 'You have been a good boy. Now you get your present.'

Smiling with mock anticipation, Duale undid the ribbon and opened the tissue paper. He was staring at a denture. He went on staring at the teeth; it slowly dawned on him that they belonged to him.

'Of course, I realized I had lost them, but I didn't know where,' he said, 'Now I remember, they were in the closet.'

'Dear Duale, it's a pity you're so old, because you make love better than most youngsters. Remember when you had to leave Florida in a hurry? You were a bit forgetful, my darling. Anyway now your teeth have come home! Enjoy!'

For Duale, the silence which followed was hurtful; and the pain was made worse by the relaxed, blue-eyed, smiling face opposite his. Duale took the easy way out. He pressed himself against the blond and put his arm around her slim waist; then he started laughing.

'If only,' he said 'we had more time. We could enjoy one another forever! But I am busy; and I am sure you are too. *Au revoir*. The moment I get a chance, I will be in contact. And thank you for the present!' Then, thank God, she was gone. As he briefly looked at the teeth, he chuckled – yes, he thought, there was no escaping age.

As the hours and days passed like the unrelenting ticking of a clock, Duale found himself increasingly lost in thought. What should he do about Tashi and Pema? If he did nothing within the ninety days, he knew that Tashi would act. Duale continued his long bouts of musing. He wondered whether he could shrug the whole thing off? But how could he? Would the committee, and by extension the Board of Trustees, disbelieve Tashi? After Duale's exposure in the meeting room, he soon reached the conclusion that his position was virtually indefensible; and it might soon be untenable. The committee would put two and two together; they would even brand Duale as an unethical and heartless manipulator who would lie, which he had, to remove a perceived threat.

And what was at stake? As a man who had spent years building his career, his reputation would be the first to suffer. He was associated with many captains of industry in the aerospace world. As head of an apolitical organization he had nurtured the friendship of many who held high political office. He was known to the White House, as well as in the higher echelons of the UN. After all, he had reasoned, one day he might need political support. Now he could envisage that this too might disappear with his professional image. And what about his lifestyle? He held the respect not only of TASS's staff, but also of a large segment of society. He enjoyed his cocktail parties and his many invitations to social events; and he loved meeting beautiful women, some of whom would later happily return his affectionate attention. He invariably travelled first-class to destinations all over the world. Sometimes he was received by ministers of Third World governments; he was accorded deep respect and his views and advice were highly valued. He was a Very Important Person.

Was all this hard-won achievement to be thrown to the wind because of an affair by a young man with a Bhutanese girl? Was he to disappear from the world scene and quickly vanish into obscurity. No! There must be a solution and Duale was more than adequately experienced to find the way out of a situation which seemed to be inexorably closing in on him. The torment continued to plague him for weeks. Until he reached his decision.

'Anna,' Duale said one morning, shortly after reaching his office, 'please arrange an appointment for Captain Tashi to meet me in my office. He will ask to be accompanied by Mr. Wilson. Explain to Mr. Wilson and Captain Tashi that I wish to see Captain Tashi alone.' The following day, Tashi found himself standing before Anna five minutes before the appointed time.

'My goodness, Captain Tashi, you are so like the CEO. Such similar features, yet each of you comes from a different part of the world. Incredible! But you know they say we all have a double somewhere; I wonder where mine is?' Anna laughed gently. 'Dr. Duale is ready to see you, Captain Tashi. Just go in.' Anna was smiling and Tashi again thought how relaxed Anna was; and she was so nice to him.

'Good morning, Captain Tashi. Let us sit over there.' Duale had resumed his mode of fatherly benevolence. In any case, Tashi thought, it was pleasant to talk with someone who seemed affable, whatever qualities might be lurking behind the facade.

'Good morning, sir,' Tashi responded.

'Yes,' Duale went on, 'you remember our discussion in Florida?'

'Yes, Dr. Duale, I remember it very well. In fact, it was only today that I noted a circle on my calendar. You are at the halfway mark; there are 45 days left.' Duale had not expected such a forthright statement, but realised there was little he could do. The Florida discussion had shown the fruitlessness of Duale losing his temper; Tashi was not to be intimidated. Duale had no intention of repeating the Florida scenario. Duale knew that he was on the losing end and the sooner he capitulated the better. He was under no illusion; with Tashi, Duale had met his match. He felt defenceless in the face of the raw truth.

He lost no time in coming to the point. In a quiet, measured tone, he said, 'I would like to thank you for being available today. As you can imagine, since we last met in Florida I have been giving a great deal of thought to all the points which you made. There are of course different ways to interpret the events of thirty years ago, and I would not agree with some of the so-called facts as you presented them to me. Nevertheless, two points are undeniably factual. The first is that I fell in love with your mother, and even considered during that period that I might marry her. The second fact is that, unknown to me at the time, otherwise I am sure I would have done something to support your upbringing, the woman I loved had a child; and that child is yourself.

So with these facts in mind I should come to the point. I believe that it is certainly correct that, albeit *post facto*, I should try and make amends. Therefore, in principle I agree with what you have proposed. I will now take the necessary actions to give effect to your proposal. I intend to visit Bhutan within a month in the course of an overseas travel schedule. Will you kindly write confidentially to your mother, Pema, to let her know that I will make contact with her and that we should do our best to reach an equitable settlement. I have no doubt that we shall succeed. That will then be the end of this particular unhappy chapter. If you agree, Captain Tashi, with what I have proposed, I have to ask of you one condition. If you accept the condition, then I will proceed. If you do not, I will do nothing.'

Tashi had been listening intently, welcoming Duale's statement. In any case, he thought, Duale's actions would speak more loudly than his words. But what condition might be injected into all this? Then he responded, 'Dr. Duale, so far so good, as they say. The right actions depend on you in any case; we shall see. I was not expecting to hear anything about a condition. But of course I might be willing to consider any reasonable suggestion.'

'The condition is as follows,' Duale continued; his attitude of benevolence had changed to one of straightforward negotiation, 'if I pursue my actions and successfully complete them, then in return I require you to remain silent concerning our relationship. This will extend, for example, to a straight, unequivocal denial in the event, however unlikely, that you are challenged to admit that I am your father. In other words, there shall be no relationship between us at any time. Do I make myself clear?'

'Yes,' Tashi responded, 'You have my word that I will never under any circumstances mention to anyone that you are my father. If I am challenged, I will never admit it. I can assure you that my word is my bond.'

* * *

In March 1991, a month later to the day, Duale found himself looking at the huge mountains of Bhutan as the small aircraft positioned itself for the unique approach into Paro airport. Although winter would soon give way to spring, deep virgin snow still carpeted the higher elevations, and Duale began to feel light-headed as he tried to take in the scene of majestic beauty which unfolded before him. He recalled his visit to the Kingdom in the fifties, and he was relieved that, as far as he could see from the aircraft, little had changed. As he looked down at the small villages which dotted the mountains, in contrast with some of the countries he had just visited Bhutan seemed to have the same appearance as when he had visited the country some years ago. What a difference, he thought, to the situation in countries such as China, Thailand or Indonesia where explosive population pressures had caused sprawling, often ugly, townships to spring up.

'Welcome back, Dr. Duale; I am the director of civil aviation. This is the TASS consultant here, Mr. Bennett. He has work here in Paro today, but he will be available as you may need him in Thimphu tomorrow. We feel honoured that you should visit our small country. Please come this way. Once we have your baggage, we can drive to Thimphu.'

'Thank you, director,' Duale responded with a smile, 'we think that every country in the world, large or small, is very important when it comes to aviation safety. Safe international aviation relies on a global system. The Kingdom of Bhutan is an important part of this system.' The director had just met TASS's CEO for the first time, yet the atmosphere was already cordial; Duale's smile and relaxed way of speaking had reassured the director that he was talking to a man of the world, a highly-respected member of the international community.

After Duale's passport had been stamped by the immigration,

they made for the car. Duale bade the consultant *au revoir*; the baggage was loaded and the director escorted Duale to Thimphu. As the car wound its way through the Himalayan valleys, the director explained the programme which had been arranged for Duale's visit. There would be a number of meetings; the director also handed Duale three invitations to receptions where Duale would be the guest of honour.

'So I will say goodbye, Dr. Duale,' the director said in Thimphu about three hours later, 'we hope you will find the hotel room to be comfortable and not too cold.' He laughed. 'If you need anything, the hotel knows how to get in touch with me. Have a good rest for today and try to get used to our 7000 feet high atmosphere. I will pick you up at nine o'clock tomorrow morning.'

Left alone, Duale slowly walked to his room. He was yawning and tired; this must be a mixture of jetlag, intensive work and the altitude, he thought. By the time he had closed the bedroom door, he had decided he needed a sleep. He unpacked his suit and hung it in the wardrobe. He set his alarm clock and put it on the bedside table. Then he noticed an envelope which had been placed next to the lamp. Although he was decidedly sleepy, he vaguely thought that the handwriting was familiar. He opened the envelope. This is what he read:

> *Dear Duale,*
> *My son Tashi has told me you would like to see me during your visit to Bhutan; you will discuss a specific issue. I am arranging for you to be picked up at the hotel at 4 p.m. We can then drink some tea together and you can explain what you wish to discuss. I hope this is convenient.*
> *Pema*

Well, that is very good organization, I must say, thought Duale. If I arrive by 4.30, then by six o'clock the matter should be finally dealt with and put to bed. To be safe, I will get her to sign a piece of paper, he mused. Duale re-set his alarm for three o'clock and slept like a baby.

It was 4.15 when the driver stopped and motioned to Duale that he had arrived. Duale was looking at a charming house with white walls and a deeply overhanging roof. The garden seemed to be preparing itself for the Spring. He admired the mature fir trees; and here and there he could see young plants bravely breaking the surface, as though they were hoping to catch some of the warm rays of the setting sun. He slowly, somewhat hesitantly, approached the front door. There seemed to be no door knocker, but he noticed that the door was slightly ajar. Duale gently pushed the door and it creaked as it opened; he walked inside, his face betraying nervous curiosity, then through an inside door, hoping he might reach the living room.

Then he saw Pema. There are rare moments in everyone's life which remain engraved in the mind forever. For Duale, this was one of those moments. A perfectly proportioned woman, Pema was wearing a blue silk dress trimmed with white lace, a dress which hugged her beautiful body as far as her slim waist and then flared until it almost reached her ankles. Her widely-set, large brown eyes looked into his. Now she was approaching him; she seemed to float across the room. Pema held out her hand and gently smiled at Duale, 'Good afternoon Dr. Duale.'

Duale did not move; nor did he try to reply, simply because he knew he would not be able to utter one word. And he did not smile. He seemed mesmerised.

'I hope you are feeling all right, Dr. Duale. You look a little unsteady. Please sit down. We have bottled water; should I bring you a glass?'

Duale was incapable of collecting himself. He was in a state of deep shock. He had given practically no thought to his expectation of Pema's appearance. It had briefly crossed his mind that she would be in her early fifties, and at one point he'd hoped she would have weathered not too badly over the years. Now, after some thirty years, he was astounded to find he was looking at a beautiful creature who, to him, had changed little from the days when she was a young woman. He had loved the body which was coolly standing in front of him. Duale felt unsteady and a dryness in his throat was beginning to take hold. Above all, he could only stare at her. Still keeping his eyes on her, he slowly sat down. Now at last he tried to speak; with trembling lips, Duale stammered, 'G..g..good a..af..ternoon – Pema.'

Pema sat down opposite him; again, she smiled. 'We can have some tea. Before we approach the money subject which my finan-

215

cially-correct son is so keen to see settled, tell me about your life, Duale. Are you married; and do you have children, oh, I mean in addition to Tashi? Tell me about your work. Did you achieve everything you set out to do? Talk to me like you used to in the old days.'

For the next four hours Duale talked to Pema; and Pema conversed with Duale. She seemed to enjoy listening to Duale cataloguing some of his many achievements. And Duale was impressed with Pema's account of her work in the UN in Bhutan. Pema had no wish to cross-examine him on why he had failed to keep his promise to marry her. She knew this was an everyday happening, especially for young people. In any case, she thought, why dwell on the past; surely life is too short. She loved to hear Duale just talk; in that respect he was the same person who had held her spellbound so many years before.

Duale stood up. 'Well, Pema, I came to talk about money. I have been here for four hours and we haven't even started on the subject yet. Shall we talk now, or do you prefer another time? I promised your son that I would reach an agreement with you during this visit.'

'I think another time, Duale. Why spoil a perfect evening by talking about money. You need a good night's rest to prepare for your meetings. I will say goodnight and I enjoyed talking to you; it will be a lovely memory.' Duale watched Pema as she seemed to glide towards the door; he followed.

As Pema opened the door a shaft of moonlight illuminated her serene face. In the crisp air she held out her hand, 'Goodnight Duale, sleep well,' she said quietly. Duale gently took her hand and raised it; he wanted to kiss her hand. But Pema withdrew into the hall.

'You should go now, Duale. The car is waiting for you. You seem to be panting a little – do you feel all right?'

'Yes,' Duale said, 'I feel all right. It must be the altitude. You know the last time I saw you, you were wearing a blue dress; the colour was royal blue and I remember you wore a deep blue sash around your waist. Er... I will go now. Please let me know when I can see you again.' The door closed. And a feeling of emptiness came over Duale.

Duale had been looking forward to a long rest; instead, he

spent a restless night. Whether awake or sleeping, all he could see in his mind's eye was Pema. And he not only dreamt of her lithe, beautiful body. Especially when he lay awake, he realised that she was a woman who was widely knowledgeable and, certainly as far as her UN activities were concerned, an achiever. Duale admitted to himself that he was confused. He had come into a situation with set ideas and now he had found his judgement could not have been wider of the mark.

And what of his emotions? Although Duale was in his early sixties, his attraction to women was still strong. He was sometimes rebuffed; but on the whole women returned his affection. He was not sure whether he had ever really loved anyone. He loved women's bodies; but he recognized there was more to love than sexual enjoyment. Because he had never felt very close to anyone in his life, he wondered whether the capability to love in the widest sense was something that was simply beyond him. In fact, he knew no one with whom he felt close in a spiritual sense. Duale was a natural leader and a consummate performer in his work; at the same time he was a loner.

Now Pema was making him think again. As a young man he had enjoyed her. As a much older man he had just seen her again. He had been astounded to find that, in his eyes, she had changed very little physically. When people take sustained care to look after their appearance, not to mention their health, and especially where there is also an element of mutual attraction, as each grows older each seems to change little in the eyes of the other; this was something for which Duale had not been prepared. He had just learnt a curious lesson; and it was this that had caused Duale a shock.

Another fact of life which he had to learn was that, often, Asian women managed to retain a young and beautiful countenance well into their fifties; a shining example had stood before him in the beautiful form of Pema. As a person Pema had certainly matured and his four hours' conversation with her had passed in a flash. As he had said goodbye in the moonlight he had felt strongly drawn to her. Yes, he had not only admired her physically; to this was now added a feeling of care and affection, not to mention admiration and respect. He had wanted to kiss her hand, but she had withdrawn it. Was this because she had no time for him; or was she afraid that his affectionate gesture would lead to a rekindling of their much earlier relationship? Duale could not answer the questions which repeatedly surfaced; so he remained confused. Except in one respect. He was sure he was deeply attracted to Pema in the widest sense. What so many years ago had been a sexual desire had now been rekindled in a different form; this time, and for the first time in his life, Duale was experiencing mature feelings of love.

At nine o'clock the following morning Duale was picked up by the director of civil aviation and the TASS consultant. Four long meetings were held during the day. As always, those with whom he met were deeply impressed by the way in which he presented TASS's ideas. For his part, Duale was happy to receive reassurances from the eloquent government officials that aviation safety in the Kingdom would continue to remain a high priority. An agreement in principle was reached as to how an omnirange ground navigational station should be established and maintained near the top of a high mountain. Training of technicians was also to be expanded.

Duale normally found these types of meetings to be variations on a theme, regardless of which country he was visiting. Weaknesses in the aviation system in any given country were frankly discussed and solutions agreed. It was then up to the country to find the money and to implement the upgrading projects. Sometimes the officials would tackle Duale concerning a source for aid funds. They explained that in a world where money for expensive projects seemed to be getting scarcer by the year, the government would find it very difficult, in some cases impossible, to find the money needed. Perhaps TASS could help by supporting their efforts. Duale's response was invariably the same. TASS did not wish to get itself involved directly with governments' financing plans; and that was the end of that part of the discussion. However, once the financing was in place, then the administration could contact TASS and request support.

'Excellency, it has been a great personal pleasure, and privilege, for me to discuss various matters with you.' Duale was about to take his leave of the Minister of Transport and Communications.

'Thank you, Dr. Duale, for visiting our country. I believe we shall see one another later at a reception. It is something for me to look forward to.' Three hours later, Duale was escorted to the

Thimphu *dzong*, where he was received by senior officials attired in national dress.

As he entered the reception hall, the conversation became hushed as faces turned towards him and inquisitive eyes took stock of the Chief Executive Officer of the Trust For Air Safety Support. For his part, Duale was the epitome of pleasantness, good humour and patient humility. As he listened to those who were introduced to him, he could feel them warming to his presence. What a nice, polite and unassuming man he is, they thought; and he must be so clever.

'Now, Dr. Duale, I would like you to meet one or two members of the UN mission here.' The Secretary of the Ministry turned and asked the director of civil aviation to interrupt a lively conversation which was in progress a few steps away; the head of the mission and one or two others should meet Dr. Duale.

'Indeed,' the head UN man said, 'it is excellent you are here. This country needs a lot of assistance one way and another. Without safe aviation, of course, people cannot even reach the Kingdom. Dr. Duale, this is the senior of our local staff, Miss Pema. We are very lucky to have her. Miss Pema has worked for some years with the UN. Some say she knows more about the UN in Bhutan than anyone else; they may be right. I will just say she is worth her weight in gold. In certain respects I regard Miss Pema as my right hand.' The head of mission smiled as Pema stepped forward.

Looking beautiful in a hand-embroidered long dress, Pema said, 'It is a pleasure to meet you, Dr. Duale.' She seemed relaxed and full of self-confidence. Just for a few seconds Duale was thrown off balance. He talked to the UN people for a few minutes and told them he looked forward to discussions the following day; then he turned to talk to others. As the reception continued, from time to time Duale looked in Pema's direction; she always seemed to be surrounded by officials, almost as though she were holding court. He could see how much the officials were enjoying her lively conversation.

Shortly before leaving, Duale noticed that Pema was standing alone. He strode towards her and bluntly said, 'Pema, I have to see you and I have to talk to you. It's very urgent. When can I see you again? Perhaps later this evening?'

Pema's brown eyes focused on Duale's tense face and she smiled a little. She gave an impression of being slightly shy, but at the same time she seemed to be self-possessed and in control of a situation in which a man called Duale was pressing her to see him again. Duale was not sure whether she was feeling happy, or if perhaps her smile was one of pity. 'Please answer me, Pema!'

'Yes, Duale, I will answer. Now let me see. After the reception this evening I have a dinner and tomorrow there is another reception for you. What about 9 o'clock tomorrow evening, after the reception? I will send the car. We can settle the money business; I am sure we can do that very quickly and within the hour everything will be settled. At least our son, Tashi, will be satisfied. Then who knows, if we talk as we usually do, you might even stay another hour. Is that all right with you? Incidentally, I won't be attending the meetings in the UN tomorrow because I have to see my brother Gyeltshen; he is in hospital. Of course, I have given the head of mission a comprehensive written brief. So good luck with your meetings tomorrow, Duale. Good night.'

Pema held out her hand and chuckled, 'We are in a public place. Don't kiss my hand, just shake it courteously and leave.' Which Duale did.

Twenty four hours later, Duale was standing again in front of Pema's house, the moon flooding the whole area in silver light. He looked beyond the house and could see the silhouettes of the mountains behind. Surely, he thought, this has to be one of the most beautiful countries on the planet. He tapped with his fingers on the front door and pushed it ajar. Pema greeted him and said, 'Good evening, Duale. Please come in and sit down. I am still here alone because my brother, Gyeltshen, is lying in the hospital. He is not at all well and I think it is quite likely he will leave this world in the next few weeks. He is 63. He has led a productive life and he had great influence on our son, Tashi. He has also been a strong support for me since you and I knew one another years ago.'

'I am sorry, Pema,' Duale commented, 'I hope that whatever is best for your brother happens.'

'Shall I make you some tea? Or would you like something else?,' Pema asked. There was no response from Duale. Pema looked at Duale; just for a second, she thought how handsome he still was. She instantly forced the thought from her mind.

'Did you hear me? Do you feel all right? Are you staring at me – or are you thinking about something? If I may mention it, Duale, you don't seem to be quite yourself; you look a little odd. It would be nice if you said something... anything.'

After a few seconds, Duale did say something: 'Pema,' he said, 'I love you. I will look after you forever. It was only last night that I realised I have loved you for thirty five years. The problem was that after we parted, I never saw you until the other day. If we had met, I am sure we would have married, that is if you had agreed. As it was, for all those years I had to find another outlet and I pretended to be in love here and there; the reality was that I never loved anyone except you. I am such an idiot! I should have come back and we could have spent all those years enjoying one another.

Pema, I respect you for all the wonderful things you have done. They think the world of you in the UN here; I am sure in the Royal Government too. If it's not too late, I beg you to marry me. You are still so beautiful; and I know I do not exactly have the looks I had so many years ago. I look worse than usual because I have been awake at night, just thinking about you. Even if I were to live only for the proverbial three score and ten years, we could have several years of happiness together. Would you consider marrying me? Or should I follow Tashi's instructions, make some support payment arrangement – and leave you for good? Will you at least consider it? My darling Pema, just tell me – and I will obey.'

Duale walked slowly towards Pema's chair and took her hand; he kissed it. 'Oh,' he added, 'I have to make a sort of confession. Before I left Chicago, I spoke to Tashi and I told him that a condition of my making amends to you had to be that no one would ever know that Tashi is my son. You may know the term 'conflict of interest,' Pema?'

'I know exactly what it means,' interjected Pema, 'and I think it was wise of you to make that understanding with Tashi. Otherwise you could be accused of favouritism and, who knows where these things end – Tashi might lose his job. And I do understand that at the time you talked with Tashi, you really thought you would come here to make some financial arrangement; and that would have been the end of it. Poor Duale, how the best plans go wrong.' Pema laughed.

'In any case,' Duale went on, 'I had to tell you that because it is important. Dear Pema, for me the only thing that matters now is whether you will consider marrying me. Please don't just reject me; will you think about it? I beg you – please!'

Pema sat quietly and did not respond immediately. She was conscious of the fact that she was confused; she was also trying to control the tingling which excitedly ran through her veins. She did not raise her head to look at Duale because she knew he would kiss her; and then she might lose control of herself. Then she spoke: 'Duale, the first thing is that I don't want you to kiss me. And if you don't understand that I am sorry. So go over there and sit down. Duale, I am trying to think. I am very fond of you for all sorts of reasons. But at the moment I am in a state of confusion, so I am afraid I cannot respond to you properly. But I will not dismiss the idea of marrying you.

Perhaps I should; after all, we are not exactly young. But I will consider it. The problem for you is that I need a week to reach a decision. I have to think whether this is the best thing for us. And if I think it is, then I have to sound out some relatives to find out what their advice is. If all the signs are positive, then there are certain things you have to understand, Duale, about the religious factor. Do you know, Duale, what is involved in a Buddhist marriage?'

'No,' Duale immediately rejoined.

'Then let me tell you,' Pema went on. 'You have to understand, Duale, that from the day of my birth the Buddhist religion has been part of my life. I could never forego my religion, simply because all the teaching I have received and the rituals we follow would never allow me to simply walk away from them. Deities and demons, and many types of situations in-between, are part of our everyday life. We are strong on astrology, cosmic signs and philosophy; and for us certain rituals and symbolic actions have to be followed. At this moment certain deities are protecting me. At all costs, Duale, I must never offend them. If I do, not only I but my family is vulnerable to punishment; it may be an immediate punishment, or sometimes it could be something long term which will always remind us of our misdeeds. There is no point in trying to explain to me that this is irrational. Our faith in Buddhism is much too strong to be influenced by those who might hold different religious ideas. So what I am saying, Duale, is that if – 'if' is a short word with such a huge meaning – yes, if we were to be married, then you would have to accept that I will remain a Buddhist for the rest of my life. That means I will need to pray to Lord Buddha, I will need to meditate and if there is a Buddhist centre near where we live, then I will visit the centre regularly and pray under the guidance of the lamas, the priests and monks.

If we were to be married, there would need to be an important understanding between us that each of us should follow our religion. In my case, I am talking of several hours a week. Of course, you might not like the idea. Have I switched you off, Duale? Do you want to think about it; or do you want me to go on thinking about marrying you?'

Pema seemed relaxed and she chuckled. Duale watched her beautiful face and his eyes seemed to be riveted on her lips as they gently parted to reveal her extraordinarily white teeth. It did not take him long to respond.

'Pema, I suppose after all these years you find it difficult to take me seriously. What I have said is that I love you. If you will marry me, you can do whatever you like, for the rest of your life. What you have told me gives me no problem whatsoever. All I need to know is whether you will marry me. All I want is an answer, that is when you are ready. If I had my way, I would take you in my arms now and I would carry you back with me to Chicago. But I respect your feelings; of course you have to think about it.'

'Duale,' Pema went on, 'you are a very special person! You are unique – really. So I have to go on thinking; and I will.' Pema laughed gently. 'If – it's that little word again – if I were to marry you, the Buddhist ceremony would normally take about a day, possibly a little longer. It could vary I suppose if I am to marry a Christian. In the old days, weddings were very elaborate and they lasted about three days. Now it's different; there is a great big reception, a *Lhapsang*, and the religious aspect is not so strong. Of course, the priest is there to say the appropriate prayers, but the emphasis tends to be on the guests enjoying themselves and giving a good send-off to the wedded couple.

I think the best thing now is for you to go. Here are two books which describe and explain the main foundations and practice of

Buddhism; I don't need them back. I suggest you read them both. Then you might want to change your mind. Now you should go, Duale. Please don't touch me; I don't want to start something that I cannot finish. I believe you are leaving the day after tomorrow. Where will you be in a week, Duale? I promise to contact you.'

'I will be in the hotel, Pema.' Duale responded. Pema was mildly astonished; when would Duale stop surprising her, or himself for that matter? Then he went on, 'You need a week to decide. If we are to be married that takes another day or so. So I will stay for two weeks. If we are married, we can fly together to Chicago. Mr. Bennett, the TASS consultant in Thimphu, will send a message for me to my office that I am taking a holiday. My last one was cut short anyway. I think I have earned a few days after all these years, Pema. Contact me when you are ready – I will be waiting! Good night, Pema. I love everything about you; and you are so wonderfully serene. I won't kiss you. If you decide to take me on, I promise to more than make up for everything I should have been giving you during all those years. Good night, my darling!'

Duale turned and hesitated at the door. Pema was alarmed that he would take hold of her; she knew she would have no control over her emotions. The more she looked at Duale, the more she liked what she saw; as had happened when she had first met him, he was again becoming irresistible. Yes, he was certainly older, but he looked so distinguished; and he was still handsome! Her body tingled intensely. She simply looked at him; then in a slightly uneven voice which betrayed her rising emotions, she said, 'Quickly, go now, Duale – go!'

Then he was gone.

Chapter Thirteen

Marriage

It was six days later that Duale received a note from Pema. He had just finished his breakfast and had been musing on how chilly he had felt during the night; he would ask for another heater, he thought. He had also briefly told himself that the end of the week of decision for Pema would be reached the next day. He opened the note, which simply said, 'Sorry to have kept you waiting. Now you can come. Pema.'

Well, Duale thought, in Pema's note there is nothing there to generate much hope for me. Duale was a man who was used to getting his own way; for once, he thought, he might as well prepare for rejection. In any case, he agreed that was what he deserved. There would be no discussion; if Pema did not want to marry him, then he would have to respect her decision.

Feeling slightly empty, Duale left the hotel and followed the driver to the rugged cross-country vehicle; as usual, the clean-shaven man was wearing a traditional Bhutanese jacket of dark brown with deep, spotlessly white turned-up cuffs.

The short journey took them past the busy Thimphu market and Duale was struck by the large splash of colour which reflected the predominantly red clothes of the throng of noisy buyers and vendors; from a distance the scene reminded him of a modern painting. The German impressionist Emil Nolde would have done justice to all that colour, he thought. Soon they had reached the slope on the outskirts of the town and Duale could already see Pema's white house. The vehicle made its way up the narrow track and stopped near the front door.

'Good morning, Duale,' Pema said in a clear voice which to Duale was very much in tune with the crisp beauty and sunshine of the glorious morning. 'Be careful as you walk through the grass; try not to get too wet from the dew. Please come in. The living room is full of sunshine; it will be nice and warm.'

Duale took three long paces and jumped into the doorway; he briefly looked down at his shoes which had been lightly sprinkled with dew. He had already noticed that Pema was dressed in a long red silk dress; below the high neck he admired the intricate embroidery. When he reached the living room, Pema was standing by the window in the sunlight. Duale had admired many women in his life; some had been dressed, most had been undressed.

'You are the most beautiful woman in the world, Pema,' he blurted out. 'Oh, I am sorry. I couldn't help it. I shouldn't have said that, Pema. Forgive me.' Pema could see that Duale felt awkward and embarrassed; it was not characteristic of him, she thought, that he should be so apologetically unsure of himself.

Smiling at Duale, Pema said, 'I hope you have had a good rest, Duale. Did you read the books I gave you?'

'Yes, I did, Pema. In fact I have brought them back; thank you.'

'And how do you feel now about the idea of proposing marriage to a Buddhist woman?,' she asked. Pema was smiling even more, Duale thought; now she laughed a little.

'Well,' he said, 'now that I know more, I want to marry you even more strongly, if that is possible, Pema. I admire piety and I love the qualities of patient understanding and respect. And you are such a serene person; I think that reflects the philosophical aspect of your religion. The philosophical and cosmic elements of your religion are deeply rooted in a mixture of cultures. Don't ask me to understand the concept of the deities. After all, by upbringing I am a Christian, although I am afraid I do not practice it except on the main feast days such as Easter or Christmas. But we also have symbolic actions in our religion; that aspect is nothing new to me. What I am saying, Pema, is that although I will probably never be converted to Buddhism, I will certainly always respect the religion. What else can I say?'

'Do you still want to marry me and take me to Chicago, Duale?' Pema asked.

'Yes please!' Duale instantly rejoined. Pema thought he sounded like a schoolboy.

'Just listen to me, Duale,' Pema said. 'I do not want any recompense from you in the way of support money, in the sense that

Tashi would like to see. I would never marry someone because I felt his wealth or position would be of some benefit to me; nor for that matter that it might give me a special status. What I am saying is that I will marry you for love. For me that is the only thing which matters; there are many facets to love, Duale, but above all it includes your basic decency and your devotion to me – and to me alone. It is nice for me that you are so good-looking. Yes, I will marry you, Duale. And when we are married, I will love you and do everything in my power to make you happy.'

Although Duale looked much younger, he could not escape the fact that he was a man of 61. On a previous occasion he had tried, and failed, to analyze his character. After the death of Al Willis he had confided in Anna about his own personality traits and qualities; some were good, some were not so good. But there was a hole, some sort of gap, in his character; and as he went through his life he was sometimes reminded that there were certain aspects of his personality which were unknown to him. Today he was again surprised. To his disbelief and astonishment, tears rolled over his cheeks.

'What have I said, Duale?' Pema anxiously asked.

'I am so happy, Pema,' Duale replied through his tears. He was struggling, and failing, to control his emotions. I don't know what to say. I love you – and I always will.'

'Since we are to be married, Duale,' Pema interjected, 'you can kiss me.' Then she laughed. 'The rest will have to wait till we are married.' Duale took her in his arms and gently kissed her.

Then Pema continued, 'The marriage ceremony starts tomorrow morning. Because you are a Christian, the lamas told me the ceremony will be a little abbreviated. It will start at the hotel and you should be ready early in the morning. The hotel manager will help in having beer and other drinks ready at the right time. The best thing is for you to stand politely and quietly near the ceremony; Duale, you can put on the best suit you have with you. One of the guests will explain what is going on. With the shortened ritual, we should be together tomorrow, in the evening. You may be contacted by my brother's family and there will be a group of guests. Co-operate with them and enjoy yourself as much as you can. We will be able to leave for Chicago in six days time, Duale.

Unfortunately, my brother, Gyeltshen, is old and very weak. I am afraid he will not last long and he will never leave the hospital; they look after him well enough, but he can hardly eat, poor man. And he is barely conscious. In a sense, his passing will be a deliverance. In any case, you have read about re-incarnation. Of course, he has known about you since we first met. I think he understood the way we feel about one another, which I tried yesterday to explain to him; unfortunately, his mind is not very clear these days. No Bhutanese can ever understand why another Bhutanese would ever like to leave the Kingdom. For me, I know it will be a tremendous change. But I told him that with my UN experience, and listening to the radio or watching videos, I think I have quite a good idea of what life in the western world is all about.

In any case, he told me he is happy for us and he hopes we spend the rest of our lives in love and happiness. I will always remember him telling me, in such a weak voice, that he was happy that we would be married; he said he felt that any contribution he had made in his life to my well-being would now be taken over by you. You know, Duale, he told me that he thought I was a very special person.

Then my brother added, 'You will never find a better person in the world than your son, Tashi.' I thought that was such a touching thing to say; after all, Gyeltshen and I brought Tashi up during his early years. Then my brother said that he felt his duty had run its course. He said, 'I feel very tired; goodbye, Pema.' Then he fell asleep.

He might last a month; I suppose he could go on for a year. The only thing I am sure of is that he will never leave hospital. Poor Gyeltshen! It happens to all of us, doesn't it? I mean we are born, we live – and we leave this earth.'

Duale was saddened; he said, 'I am so sorry, Pema.'

Pema looked resigned. 'I thought I should tell you about him, Duale,' she said. 'He is a part of my life here on earth. I hope he doesn't suffer too much.' There was a pause, then with an air of finality: 'Now we have to think about ourselves and our marriage.'

The next morning, Pema prepared to participate in the marriage ceremony. She had consulted her family and the lamas had been asked for their co-operation; all had agreed that Pema was free to marry Duale. The priests carefully checked the astrological situation and calculated the precise direction in which evil might lurk. They advised that, at all costs, at no time during the wedding ceremony should anyone look into the direction from which evil, sickness or death might threaten.

It was at about six o'clock on the following morning; although the sun had not yet risen over the mountain, Duale could see the lightening dawn from his window. He had just had his morning bath. There was a knock on his door.

'Please come in; good morning, manager.'

'Yes,' the manager replied, 'it is a good morning, Dr. Duale. May I congratulate you? Part of the wedding party, the part which will support you, has already arrived. Could you please come to the restaurant. One of us will try to explain what will be happening during the ceremony.'

Slightly mystified, and surprised, that things should be happening so early, Duale dressed as quickly as he could and a few minutes later he was being introduced to various officials who had been drawn from the United Nations, the Ministry of Transport, and from the directorate of civil aviation. All wore Bhutanese traditional dress, and Duale felt uniquely different surrounded, as he was, by a group of people whose clothes bore no resemblance to his own; because he had met only one or two of the group, he found the situation bordering on the incongruous.

Duale noticed that almost all the men were wearing a sash over their bright, hand-made tunics; the colour of the sash reflected the high rank of each. One of the officials, whom Duale noticed was wearing decorated boots, stepped forward.

'Dr. Duale, I am the personal representative of His Excellency the Minister of Transport and Communications; my name is Nyima. On behalf of His Excellency and all of us here, we would like to congratulate you on your marriage to Miss Pema. Because you have no family here, in agreement with the priests, just for today we are adopting you. We have a deep respect for you and we hope you will accept our friendship, which is intended as a substitute for your family.'

'I am privileged, Mr. Nyima. I am in the hands of everyone present and I thank you all for your friendship and consideration.'

'Please come outside, to the steps of the hotel,' Nyima said. 'I would like to introduce you to a very old lama. He will tell you how times have changed. Up to about thirty or forty years ago, the religious component of the marriage was much stronger than it is today. Nowadays, the marriage ceremony is mainly a *Lhapsang*, which is a long party; the participants are the family and other invited well-wishers. Like all occasions, there are not only positive but also negative sides. The wedding is certainly a very happy event; at the same time, regrettably, too much attention is given to how much the family spends on it! The whole business of apparent wealth and extravagance takes on an exaggerated meaning. Too much attention is paid to status. For this wedding, there will be about a hundred guests; and believe me, they will be very spoilt – they have to be! Of course, the lama says prayers and follows a ritual at the family altar in the house. But the main activity is partying.' Nyima chuckled. 'So that will be your main pastime for today, Dr. Duale. The more you can be seen to be enjoying yourself, the more prestige and status the guests will accord Miss Pema's family.'

Duale stood courteously at the top of the hotel steps and listened intently; he also thought how warm the rays of the sun were becoming as the ball of fire slowly rose in the heavens above the mountain.

'Dr. Duale,' Nyima went on, 'I would like to introduce you to the lama; as you can see he is quite old.'

Duale found himself looking down at a small, old man with a wizened face; Duale was struck by his lively eyes which seemed to be riveted on him. Duale bowed slightly and held out his hand. The old lama, dressed in a faded saffron-coloured robe, took it and smiled a little; Duale noticed he had lost two or three of his front teeth.

'Yes, Dr. Duale,' Nyima explained. 'I thought you might be interested in the old type of ritual which used to be followed; although it is now something of a museum piece here, in fact it is still followed in certain remote village communities, especially in the west of Bhutan. I will ask the lama to relate the main points and then I will translate for you. If after five minutes you feel bored and you think this is not for you, then please say so and we will stop. On the other hand, you might find that what you hear gives you some background and an insight into the Buddhist marriage ceremony. When he has finished, we shall go to the house of Miss Pema. I understand that it is the intention to complete the marriage today; so they will start early with the *Lhapsang*.'

Nyima turned to the lama and asked him to relate the main points of the old form of the marriage ritual. Then Nyima started his translation into English for Duale's benefit; Duale admired the simultaneous interpretation ability of Nyima, who made notes from time to time before asking the lama to pause while Nyima gave Duale the English translation. Nyima started.

'About now, Dr. Duale, the monks would be erecting a mast with prayer flags in front of your house, which of course would have been this hotel.' He smiled before going on. 'There would be three rods to symbolize the three gems of Buddhism. The three jewels are the Lord Buddha, his teaching and the community of monks. The flags would be dedicated to the God of Protection, who is called *Dablha*, as well as the local deities, whom we call the *Yulha*. Then the lamas would have unrolled the *Thangka*, which was called the *Parkha*. It would have been of the classical type, with the twelve signs of the zodiac and the eight diagrams of Chinese science; they symbolize various elements such as earth, iron, water, wood or fire. There would also have been a representation of the cosmos.

The *Thangka*, what the lamas call the *Parkha*, was essential when it came to formalizing a marriage. It served two main purposes; to protect us, and especially you, against those influences in the cosmos, that is to say in the universe, which might be harmful to you, your wife or any of the guests; and then it symbolized the connection between the universe and the good order of mankind.'

Duale was already beginning to feel that what was being explained was beyond his full understanding, but he decided to mentally do his best.

'Then some servants would bring a huge bowl-like clay pot, which would be placed near the prayer flagmast. Within a few minutes the servants would have filled the pot with a special type of beer; it is made by certain old women. They use millet, maize or sometimes wheat for the fermentation. The beer bowl played an important part in the ceremony. It represented the God of Protection, the one I already mentioned, *Dablha*. At certain points, the marriage guests would be invited to drink from the bowl and the act of drinking symbolized our strengthened relationship with *Dablha*.

Then a stone would be laid against the prayer mast; this was the last object which was needed to set the scene for the wedding. The stone was also used as a symbol for the God of Protection. It encompassed male and female aspects of what is creative and productive on three levels, that is above, below and on the face of the earth. With all these objects which reflect various aspects and levels of Buddhist ritual, the marriage could begin.

The *Parkha* would be blessed and sanctified and then it would be brought inside to take its place at the altar. All these religious preparations should be completed before the cock crowed. If the cock crowed after everything was ready, then that would have been a good omen, Dr. Duale.'

Nyima looked at Duale and smiled; he wanted to make sure Duale was still listening. then he said, 'It must all be quite confusing for you. But Buddhist ritual is complicated and full of symbolism. I am sure you know that the Lord Buddha lived rather more than 500 years before Christ. So there has been plenty of time to develop an enormous mass of philosophical teaching.'

Nyima paused for a moment, then said 'Dr. Duale, should I go on, or have you had enough?'

'Far from it! I would like to hear you to the end, please, Mr. Nyima. What an incredible ritual used to be followed. I can understand there was a move to simplify it.'

'All right,' Nyima went on. 'During the next stage, everyone from your house would move in procession to the house of Miss Pema. The lama would head the procession; no one would walk in front of the *Parkha*, otherwise there would be a risk that demons and other evil spirits might set upon us. You would walk behind the lama and behind you there would be a holy man who would carry an umbrella; the umbrella is one of the eight Buddhist signs of good fortune. He would hold the umbrella over you to bring you good luck. Later, he would use it to hold over Miss Pema and yourself.

When the procession would reach the front door, they would find that the door would be locked. This would be intentional; the locked door symbolized that the guardian of Pema still had the right not to let her go. We used to have a saying that on the wedding day 'The bride's parents, or guardian in this case, are mightier than the king.' Then the door would be opened and we would all enter.

On the altar in the house there would be a lamp; the lamp would be fuelled by ghee. Do you know what ghee is, Dr. Duale?' Nyima asked.

'Yes, I think so,' Duale responded, as he thought back to his childhood days in Morocco, 'as far as I recall, ghee is heated butter; the froth is taken away and you are left with the ghee. I suppose your butter is made from yak milk.'

Nyima continued, 'Behind the lamp would be a cup of rice in which you could see three little sticks. These symbolized a connection with various deities and the five directions. I have to explain that in addition to the four main directions of the compass, we have a fifth; it extends from the earth up to the heavens. Now the priest would read out the text from the back of the *Parkha*; he would read about the planets and the elements (iron, fire, water and so forth) which could be found in each geographic direction.

Then the priest would chant; he would implore the gods that particular constellations should not show anger, nor should we suffer from the earth being rent asunder. Also that dissatisfaction and jealousy should be kept under control. All the elements should function normally. The whole world order of space and time should be stable and harmonious.

When this part of the ritual was completed, the priest would sing about the harmony we should seek between ourselves, our Buddhist religion and a universally natural world order. Every verse would end with a request for good fortune, well-being and prosperity. He would name the bridegroom as a mountain, that is you, Dr. Duale. And he would call the bride a snow leopard.

Then it would be time for us to eat and drink. The food would be pork and rice. Right in the middle of the ceremony there would be a clay pot; it would be there because under our religion we believe that when we would be invited to drink from it, the act of drinking would bring us closer to the deities who can protect us. In time, you would be invited to drink. The lama would chant something like this:

A pot of beer with twenty one straws,
We will drink the beer together.
We who today are gathered here,
We feel that all our lives are one.

'My goodness!,' Nyima exclaimed as he glanced at his watch, 'I am sorry, Dr. Duale, I have to interrupt the old lama. I had not realised how late it is. The *Lhapsang* must have been in progress in the house of Miss Pema for more than two hours. And here am I laboriously relating the old-fashioned ritual. I apologise, Dr. Duale; I think I have my priorities mixed up. After all, you are to be married! Of course, you must participate. I think we had better go now to the house. The wedding must surely be well on the way. Please follow me.'

Duale and his supporters walked through the fields with Nyima for about an hour; they followed narrow, grassy tracks. At last, the house came into view. When they reached the front door, the smiling face of Pema's aunt greeted the wedding party.

'Please come inside, Dr. Duale,' Nyima said cheerily. 'You will spend the rest of the day here. If you look at the altar, the lama is saying prayers; from time to time he may sing and bless us all, especially you and Miss Pema. Apart from that there will be plenty of food and drink; everyone will be having a good time at the *Lhapsang*.

Now, look over there. Those women are going to dance. When the dance is finished, they will stand in a line and sing. Try to enjoy it, Dr. Duale. You will only have this experience once; at least we hope so!' Duale began to feel relaxed and he enjoyed the dancing. He ate and drank a little, which strengthened him.

'During the *Lhapsang*,' Nyima was explaining again, 'the lama will call upon various gods to protect all those assembled in the house and to guarantee their safety. The *Lhapsang* ceremony concentrates on sanctifying the house and releasing the bride from the gods who have protected and guided her up to now. At the end of the *Lhapsang*, the priest will bless all those attending the wedding with a butter sign, which symbolizes protection. The blessing is important for us all because it will protect us against evil influences; these could be physical or metaphysical. Excuse me, Dr. Duale, I see you are looking around the room – are you looking for Miss Pema?'

'You are very observant, Mr. Nyima,' Duale commented. 'I was wondering if Miss Pema is in the house.'

'Don't worry, Dr. Duale, you will see her soon.'

Duale ate a little more and tried to take in the scene around him; above all, his impression was one of bright colours and a throng of happy people. Then Nyima spoke.

'Dr. Duale. The *Lhapsang* is well advanced. Soon you will be invited to sit near the altar with the lama; Miss Pema's aunt will also be present. When they invite you to drink a small mug of beer, do so; it has a symbolic meaning. There will also be a little singing. The bride's family has to ask the forgiveness of the house deities that the bride will be taken away from the house.' There was a short pause; Duale noticed how quiet it had become.

'Look to your left, Dr. Duale,' whispered Nyima.

Duale turned his head. Pema was approaching the altar. She was wearing a short black jacket; underneath, Duale's eager eyes caught sight of a long dress, which had been made from hand-woven cloth. Between long vertical strips, which were mainly of a crimson hue, there were small diamond shapes of various patterns, each intricately woven in yellow, blue and dark pink. Duale noticed a heavy gold necklace which set off her small, tender neck. On her wrists he could see beautifully engraved and decorated gold bracelets. Her face was serenely beautiful and he thought how dignified she looked; to Duale, Pema's being seemed to radiate an almost supernatural quality.

Pema slowly turned her head and treated Duale to a suggestion of a brief smile, before taking her place behind her aunt in front of the altar. The lama turned to face Pema; he blessed her. Immediately, her aunt chanted a few words in a loud voice.

'Dr. Duale,' Nyima whispered, 'The aunt is chanting that finally Miss Pema has left the protection of the Gods of this house and she will receive the protection of other deities. That is a brother of Pema,' Nyima went on, 'not Gyeltshen, poor fellow, who is so terribly sick, but another one. He will sing, asking for good fortune, and he will implore you to treat Pema well at all times. Then at the end he will turn to us all and tell us to be witnesses to what he is chanting. If things were to go wrong between you and Pema, then we should never deny that we were present today. In other words, we will have to agree that we were witnesses and we heard her brother say that you must treat her properly.' Duale listened as the interminable recitation progressed.

When the singing came to an end, Duale saw the lama take a length of white cloth, which he threw over the altar; he draped one end of the cloth around Pema's aunt. Pema got up and slowly stepped backwards towards the door.

'This is the moment when Pema finally leaves her family,' Nyima said in a low voice. 'The cloth is directed to the bride's family which is here and to make sure Miss Pema does not take any of the deities from this house with her.

Now we will be invited to a meal of pork and rice. While we are eating, a loud voice will cry out; don't be alarmed, Dr. Duale. Someone will be asking for the master of ceremonies to speak. When he does this, which he will do in a very formal way, he will talk about various aspects of the marriage and at the end he will declare you and Pema to be married. He will recite a wonderful poem; he will tell us that the stars are favourable, the sun shines warmly over the earth, he will say that you will remain married for an eternity, and so on. It is a very touching poem. That's not quite the end, Dr. Duale, but almost. Now we should all eat something and listen to the master of ceremonies.

After about an hour, the recitation came to an end. 'Now, Dr. Duale,' commented Nyima, 'we come to the final part of the wedding.'

The lama who had conducted the ceremony asked the wedded couple to come to the altar. Duale advanced towards the altar as directed and found himself standing next to Pema. He glanced at her; he thought how much he loved her.

The ever-present Nyima whispered, 'Dr. Duale, the priest is asking that Miss Pema should be fully accepted by the gods; we call them the *Yulha*. Because you are not a Buddhist, the priest is saying special prayers to *Mahakala*, the great God who specially looks after those who travel.'

After the priest had finally blessed the couple, he touched each with the butter sign. This signified that the bride would be fully received into her new surroundings; she would be protected by *Dablha* and the local *Yulha*. Provided she followed Buddhist teaching, she should have no fear.

Nyima turned to Duale and said, 'that is the end of the wedding, Dr. Duale. We have all enjoyed it very much and remember,' he added with a chuckle, 'we were all witnesses!' Duale and Pema laughed.

Then Nyima went on, 'We want to wish you both, from our hearts, all the very best, yes, for always. And we hope you will both visit Bhutan from time to time. Goodbye.'

Duale responded, 'Thank you for everything, Mr. Nyima. We all have interesting experiences as we go through our lives. For me, the marriage ceremony was fascinating and amazing – nothing less than unique. I will do my best to be a good husband; don't worry.' Then he shook Mr. Nyima's hand.

Pema turned to Duale, 'Duale, now we are both not only married, but we are bound under my faith with the gods. We have nothing to fear. We can be happy forever!' Pema smiled and Duale again noticed her look of deep serenity and happiness.

Pema looked at Duale and thought how well he had fitted into a ceremony which, in so many ways, had been alien to him. 'Duale,' she said, 'you have excelled yourself. I am very proud of you! Now I think we should say our good-byes and slowly leave the gathering; they will go on celebrating well into the night. When we are ready to leave, we can walk to the hotel. It will be a beautiful walk.'

About half an hour later, Pema and Duale set off for the hotel. Although Pema had expected to be alone with Duale, they soon found they had company. A few musicians walked behind them.

'Now you get something extra,' Pema laughed, 'you will hear some original Bhutanese horn and drum music.'

They slowly wound their way to the hotel. Duale thought how fortunate they were that the air was crisp and cool in the afternoon sunshine. As they followed the grassy paths, he noticed teams of archers competing in a meadow. When an arrow hit the small straw target, the successful archer and his team would let out howls of delight; Duale gauged the distance of the target from the archers to be about a hundred metres.

At last, the hotel came into view. As the couple walked up the steps and passed through the entrance they heard the voice of the manager. 'May I offer my congratulations! If I may, Dr. Duale, I would like to compliment you. I have been told that everyone was impressed with the way in which you conducted yourself today.

We are proud of you, especially now that you are united with your wife. Sleep well!' He gave the couple a warm smile.

Pema and Duale walked into the small, simple hotel lounge; they looked at one another in silence. Then Duale embraced Pema and kissed her.

'Now that we are alone, Duale, tell me what you thought of the wedding,' Pema asked.

'It was an incredible experience, Pema,' Duale replied. 'It's a bit early for me to analyze my feelings. Apart from the deeply religious and cultural aspects we witnessed, above all it made me feel so small and totally unimportant! In the context of the universe, we are like pinpricks, even nothing, Pema. Yes, I was overcome I suppose by the cultural depth of the wedding ritual. Now I can begin to comprehend the importance of your religion to you. As I said, Pema, in any case I will always respect what you want to do as far as your religion is concerned.'

'What do you think we should do now, Duale?'

'What do you think, Pema?' smiled Duale in return.

'I think, Duale, we are both thinking the same thing.'

Duale led the way to his bedroom. He kissed Pema as soon as he had closed the door. He gently took off her jacket.

'Do you like my dress?' Pema asked.

'You look very beautiful, Pema.'

'Thank you, Duale. Can you imagine, I had this dress made by hand thirty five years ago. I kept the dress in a wooden box. And now at last I have worn it.'

Duale looked at Pema's eyes and drew her towards him. He opened her dress and it fell to the floor. He caressed her body and fondled her firm breasts.

'Duale,' Pema whispered, 'I think I am going to be ready for you a bit sooner than I was expecting. We'd better get into bed. I know you will be gentle with me. We will just love one another all night. Then tomorrow we can start again.'

Which they did.

* * *

Until they left Thimphu, Duale and Pema enjoyed luncheon and dinner parties. It seemed that wherever they went, someone would approach them and offer good wishes. At last, as their aircraft climbed away from Paro through the cleavage in the giant Himalayan mountains, they sensed a certain finality; the beautiful mountain kingdom had been left behind. On their first leg of the long trip, Duale turned to Pema and said 'Pema my darling, we have just left one world; now you have to prepare yourself for another.'

At that moment, a voice said, 'Pema, Mother of Tashi.'

Pema looked up; it was the captain of the Himalaya Airways flight to Delhi.

'Pema Mother of Tashi,' the captain continued, 'we are privileged to have your husband, such an important man, and yourself on board – you are the mother of the most famous of our pilots. I hope you will enjoy the flight. I have been requested to give you this letter, which I understand is from your aunt; your aunt asked the UN people to pass it to me for you. If you will excuse me, I will return to the flight deck. Thank you Pema Mother of Tashi.'

Pema opened the envelope and read the brief letter; then she turned to Duale.

'It's just to say that my brother Gyeltshen has died. It is not a shock, Duale. As I told you, it was a deliverance for him. I suppose my aunt did not want to disturb the marriage ritual, nor delay my departure because of the funeral. How thoughtful of her. Don't worry, I am not greatly upset or shocked; it was inevitable and I recognized that. Now, let us go on enjoying one another. That is what Gyeltshen would have preferred.'

At Delhi, Duale and Pema boarded a jumbo and settled themselves into the first-class cabin. At last, as the big jet approached Chicago, Duale began to feel apprehensive. Suppose, he thought, that Pema suffers from culture shock; what would he do?

'All those lights look wonderful, Duale,' Pema said. 'I am so looking forward to living there. I have watched a few videos; but now this is the real thing!'

'Dear Pema,' Duale rejoined, 'I want you to be happy. If anything worries you, you must tell me and then we will do something about it.' Pema started to laugh.

'What is the joke, Pema?,' Duale asked.

'Oh, I was just thinking,' Pema replied with a chuckle. 'Chicago must be a little above sea level. When I think how virile you were at 7,000 feet, Duale, what is going to happen in

Chicago?' As the aircraft made a perfect landing, Pema and Duale were still laughing.

As soon as Pema had been shown Duale's apartment, she suggested they call Tashi and Patsri.

'Pema,' Duale replied, 'I have a special idea, if you could just wait three days, please.' Within three days, Duale had arranged a formal marriage ceremony at a registry office.

'Now,' Duale said, 'why don't I invite them to dinner. And then what a surprise for them!'

'What a wonderful idea, Duale. You always have wonderful ideas!' Pema kissed Duale.

'But first, Pema, I think I had better call my office... Good morning, Anna. Yes, I had a good trip, thank you. I will return to the office on Monday morning. Is everything all right; nothing urgent?' Anna sensed how lively and happy Duale sounded.

'Well, Dr. Duale,' Anna replied, 'as you know everything here is quite urgent; but most things are being looked after by your deputy. There is just one thing, Dr. Duale. The Chairman of the Board of Trustees called. He would like to see you in your office for a discussion. He didn't say what it is about; and he said it's not urgent. It would be helpful if you could let me know when it is convenient for you. You said Monday morning at 10a.m.? Yes, very well. I will call him this morning.'

'Thank you, Anna. Now would you just connect me with Captain Tashi in flight safety, please. Thank you, Anna. I will see you on Monday. If anything serious crops up, just call me at home. But only if it's very important. Goodbye, Anna. It's good to hear your voice again; now I feel I am really home!'

'Captain Tashi? Good; it's Duale here.'

'Good morning, Dr. Duale,' Tashi replied. He was slightly confused; the CEO had never called him directly before. And the CEO sounded so happy!

'Yes, Captain Tashi,' Duale went on. 'I thought I should let you know I am back.'

'I hope all went well, Dr. Duale? I have been trying to contact my mother, but so far without success.'

'Well,' Duale responded, 'I think that all in all we have a perfectly acceptable outcome. In fact, I was wondering if you and your wife might be free for dinner the day after tomorrow. I am sorry for the short notice, but in the circumstances I think the sooner we can get together the better. Shall we say at 7.30? Good.'

Tashi put down his phone. What was the CEO up to this time, he thought.

* * *

'Please come in, let me take your coats,' said Duale as Tashi and Patsri entered his apartment. 'In fact, I have a little surprise for you both. I hope you will be happy. Please go in.' As Tashi entered the living room, he stopped in his tracks. Was this really his mother, was he dreaming?

'You don't have to stare at me like that, my Treasure,' Pema said with a smile. 'I am real. Yes, it's me! I have married your father.'

For a split second, Tashi felt weak. Then he turned to Patsri, 'I will explain everything later, Patsri. You know my mother well enough – and this is my father.'

The evening proved to be a delight for all concerned. Even Tashi had to admit to Patsri afterwards that he had dropped his guard as far as his father was concerned. It was almost midnight when Pema could be persuaded to stop talking to Patsri; and only then on condition that mother and daughter-in-law would meet again within the next few days. Pema could hardly wait to see Little Tashi.

'Good night, my mother. Good night, Dr. Duale. We thank you for a wonderful evening,' Tashi said as he and Patsri made for the front door.

Then he quietly added, 'Dr. Duale, I am very pleased that things worked out so well. You have a reputation for solving problems. You seem to have succeeded again.'

'Thank you, Tashi,' Duale replied. 'You may or may not know that I am often called The Survivor. I try to live up to my name! Sometimes I must admit that I have to overcome considerable challenges. My thesis is that when a problem crops up, there is always a solution; it is just a question of choosing the right one. I should be more modest when I say that so far I think I have shown good judgement. Of course, I also needed some luck sometimes; it was very lucky that your mother and I fell in love. In any case, I

241

intend to go on surviving.' Then his expression became more serious, as he added, 'And I hope, Captain Tashi, you will also survive. Good night.'

Chapter Fourteen

Survival

It was a few minutes before eight on the following Monday morning. 'You are looking at yourself in the mirror, Duale,' Pema said, 'is there a special reason for that?'

Duale turned to his wife and smiled; then he kissed her. 'Yes, Pema, there is a reason,' he responded. 'Although it's not exactly special. It somehow became a routine with me. Before leaving for the office, I just like to check that my tie is straight and my hair is brushed. You know, Pema, the last time I looked at myself in this mirror, I was a different person. I mean I looked worried and anxious, although I did my best not to show it. In the office I seemed to be losing some of my confidence. I have to deal with TASS's Executive Committee; some of the members are always looking for ways to challenge or embarrass me. It can be difficult sometimes and you have to be very fit mentally and physically to cope. Now I feel happy and young again. I have to thank you for all this, Pema. When you think how we have been making so much love, in theory we should be exhausted. But I feel the opposite! Thank you, Pema.'

Duale was looking at himself again in the mirror; he liked what he saw. He was in good shape physically and his grey, hand-made suit fitted perfectly; he briefly noticed the hand-stitched borders of the lapels, the discreet tell-tale sign of the hand finished suit. In contrast to many of his age, he looked slim, supple and strong. He took his overcoat off the hook and buttoned it up to his chin. 'Good-bye, my darling. Let me kiss you. Patsri will soon be here to talk to you. I should be home again by eight this evening at the latest. Then we will have a nice dinner together. If you need anything at all, just call me.'

Duale put on his fur hat and pulled the side-pads over his ears. He took the elevator down to the lobby; then he strode out of the apartment and into the teeth of a cold, ferocious wind. Yes, he thought, Chicago always lives up to its name.

With his jaunty step he soon reached the TASS building. Just as he had done more than thirty years before, with the agility of a much younger man he leapt up the few steps and passed through the imposing entrance of what old-timers called the 'new' building. As he entered the elevator which transported him in a flash to his floor, the TASS staff smiled at him. One said, 'Dr. Duale, it's good to have you back. You look very well on your travels. Have a good day, sir!'

'Thank you, I am sure I will,' Duale responded as he walked to his office.

'Morning, Anna.' Anna turned on her swivel chair and stood up. She looked at Duale and gave him a warm smile. For a fleeting second, he thought he saw those irresistibly twinkling blue eyes; but then again, it was probably his imagination.

Anna said, 'You look wonderful, Dr. Duale. I think the trip and the vacation have done wonders. I am sure there will be a lot of dictation to all those movers and shakers you discussed air safety with in Asia. As I mentioned on the phone, the main thing this morning is that the Chairman of the Board will be visiting you at 10 o'clock. I have left the unopened confidential mail in the usual tray on your desk. I will let you know the moment the Chairman arrives, Dr. Duale.'

'Thank you, Anna. It's good to be back.' Duale looked into her eyes and smiled. This time, Anna thought, it was not his usual hungry smile; somehow he seemed more mature.

Duale stepped into his spacious office; the sun was streaming through the large windows and its brightness lightened the brown of the wooden furniture as the rays diffused throughout most of the room. Duale had learned many years ago that the CEO of a dynamic organization like TASS should never dare to feel contented, if only because it was the norm that the CEO's life was punctuated by unpleasant surprises; nevertheless, as he sat at his desk and took hold of his paper knife, it was with an air of self-assurance and confidence that he slit open the first envelope. Whatever he might read, he thought, the contents would almost certainly be a variation on a theme which he had successfully handled at some stage of his long career. As always, the unopened letters which Anna had left for him were marked *Personal and Confidential.*

As Duale opened each letter and read it, what he could not know was that three floors below Mike Wilson, who was the Head of Tashi's Flight Safety Division, had just asked Tashi to join him in his office.

'Come and sit down, Tashi. I want to talk to you,' he said. 'Tashi, prepare yourself for a blockbuster. Before I deliver it, let me give you a little background.

You know, from time to time we have talked about the way in which TASS is managed. I mentioned once that the CEO tends to get into arguments with the Executive Committee. Sometimes I am called in to give some background information on technical matters or flight safety statistics. Well, Tashi, I don't like being used as a tool by the CEO so that he can justify his actions. When I am to be called in, he always sits down with me in advance and more or less tells me what he expects me to say; invariably, he gives me a little lecture on what he loosely describes as 'loyalty.'

I might have been able to stomach it for a bit longer if the statistics for accidents were better. But if you look, Tashi, at the number of accidents for the last five years, especially for the non scheduled airlines – the charter carriers, the picture is not exactly encouraging. You don't need to be a genius to reach a conclusion that if airlines' operations keep growing, which they certainly will, then the number of accidents will increase. In ten years' time it could be serious.

I am the first to recognize that TASS is not here to solve every country's air safety problems; ultimately, this has to be the responsibility of the country itself. Having said this, Tashi, I do firmly believe that we could, and should, be doing much more. TASS is an apolitical organization and its mission is air safety. And we shouldn't confuse rule-making with helping countries to implement the rules. The mission of TASS is not to lay down safety standards; they already exist. Our job is to support implementation. Over the last few years I have become increasingly disappointed with our approach. You only have to look at the numbers for Africa and South America, not to mention Asia, to understand what I am talking about.

I have given a lot of thought as to whether we could have done

245

more. Whichever angle I approach it from, I get the same answer. Of course we could have done more – much more!

And what is the main obstacle? Again, Tashi, I always get the same answer. Our problem is right here in the house; and unfortunately it is right at the top. Yes, Tashi, our Mr. CEO one Dr. Duale is the problem. First, he is often away and undertaking trips he could delegate to a divisional head. Then he spends a lot of time on entertaining or cosying up with the White House or top people in the UN. And where is TASS in all this? To be blunt, Tashi, it is directionless. If the CEO spent a reasonable part of his time in managing TASS's affairs, we could be a much stronger and more effective Trust. I have tried to talk to him about it, but he's a stubborn man and very egotistical. I am afraid he will never change. He seems mainly concerned with surviving in his arguments with the Executive Committee. It's really pathetic, Tashi; and such a tragic waste of time. Let's face it, compared with the way things were when the CEO took over the job, TASS these days is not exactly brilliant. The CEO used to be just great; and look where we are now – it's just hopeless!

You know fifteen years ago, in the mid seventies, the then Divisional Heads of the Trust produced an analysis of failings in Third World civil aviation human infrastructure. We stated that we recognized that a major part of the problem was lack of financing for training, plus equipment. So we proposed that TASS should establish a financing arm specifically geared to upgrading civil aviation in the Third World. We had a great big struggle with the CEO on the subject. Eventually, he chaired about three meetings when the whole thing was to be discussed; but he decided to be a non chairman for this particular event. He left the last meeting early, telling us he had to catch a plane to Washington. So TASS missed the boat, again!

Or again, look at the legal system for civil aviation in various countries. You know that many countries do not have up-to-date laws in place. And what about the regulations, especially those relating to airworthiness of aircraft? There is an enormous amount of work to be done in this field. I know the countries have their responsibilities, but very often they don't have the right expertise. I know of several countries who asked for help from TASS. Our CEO is a lawyer; so he should know what has to be done. In fact,

TASS has hardly touched the subject in a number of countries. As I said, so many of them don't have the expertise to do the necessary and they have been crying out for our help. Well, up to now we haven't done much, have we?

Now I come to the point, Tashi. Because of the way I feel, I've resigned. You know, many years ago when I was learning the flight safety business, once I was a bit slow to finish some work. My boss called me in and said, 'Mike, either get on or get out!' I got the message and got on with it. In TASS, I have tried, but for reasons beyond my control, failed. So I am going to get out. I'm explaining this to you, Tashi, not only because I want you to be the first to know. It's mainly for another reason. Apart from any outsiders, there are three possible contenders in the house to take over my work; and you are the junior of those who will be considered. I want you to know that you are at least a head and shoulders better than the others. So I am recommending that you should be offered my job as the Head of this Division.

Let me explain something. The CEO will not wish to appoint you as the Head. Don't bother to ask me why because I won't tell you; just accept what I say. Because he will resist doing what is unquestionably right, I have spoken to the Chairman of the Board of Trustees and some members of the Executive Committee. I even briefed one or two Division Heads. I just told them I was resigning for personal reasons. Then I briefed them on who is the right man to take over. Now you have a lot of support, that is if you want the job. I advised the CEO not to advertise for an outsider because TASS will never find a better professional than you. I mean that, Tashi, in every sense of the word, including what I see as your unique ability to get results in the Third World. You obviously understand better than most the mentality and values of those who are there to make things happen in the developing world. So there you have it. I will be leaving in two months' time.

There was a long silence. Tashi stared at the surface of the table in front of him; sadness was taking hold. At last he responded:

'Mike, I want you to know that I am very sorry. I could never imagine working with a better person. I don't feel like dissuading you from resigning, because I know you would not have reached your decision without taking everything into consideration. If I am offered the job, I will take it because that is what you want. For the rest of my working career you will always be my example. Thank you for talking to me. I valued our relationship and it is something I will always cherish.' Tashi held out his hand and Mike Wilson took it in friendship.

Meanwhile, three floors above the flight safety division, Duale continued scanning the letters in the *Personal and Confidential* tray. So far so good, he thought, as his paper knife slit open the next letter. As always, before beginning to read the letter he glanced at the signature, which in this case read 'Michael Wilson.' I wonder, thought Duale, why he should be writing a letter.

'Dr. Duale?,' Anna's voice interrupted his concentration.

'Yes, Anna,' Duale replied on his intercom.

'The Chairman has entered the building and should be with you within two minutes.'

'Thank you, Anna. I am ready,' Duale replied. He put Mike Wilson's unread letter back into his tray, got up and strode to the door. As he opened it, he caught sight of the Chairman entering the ante room.

'Good morning Chairman. It is good to see you again.' Duale was relaxed as he shook the Chairman's hand; he had been looking forward to the Chairman's visit.

'Good morning, Mr. CEO. I am amazed how cold it is in our windy city; at least it's warm in here. And you have a great view, I must say.'

'Yes,' Duale responded, 'it is great. The trouble is I normally only notice it once a day when I come into the office. Then the first I know is it's dark outside. Every day passes in a flash. Shall we sit at the table over here? It's nice and bright without being in the direct rays of the sun.'

'That's fine,' the Chairman said as he moved to a leather easy chair and placed a file cover on the adjacent small table. Duale thought how 'normal' and alert the Chairman seemed; after all, the man was now about 78.

'Well, Mr. CEO,' the Chairman said, 'it's a pleasure to see you again. I have been wanting to talk to you for about a month; I gather you have been travelling on business and you also took some well-earned vacation. No doubt, we shall soon hear about the results of your trip to Asia? I wanted to mention one point and discuss another. First, as you may know, I am in my late seventies;

although I must say I feel energetic, I think I should make way for a younger man. So I will be retiring at the end of this year. The Board has already received my decision and we are taking steps to find a replacement. That's point one.' The Chairman looked at Duale's eyes in his usual direct way.

'Thank you for letting me know,' Duale said. 'You were instrumental in my appointment as CEO and I have served under you with complete confidence. Unfortunately for us as individuals, not to mention TASS's air safety mission, time does not stand still. You have had a wonderful career and, if I may say so, your period as Chairman was the crown.' Duale smiled and looked at the Chairman; then added, 'And thank you for all that support!'

'Good,' the Chairman continued, 'now I will come to the second point. It is rather delicate and I am sure I can rely on you for a constructive discussion.' The Chairman opened the file; he held a letter in his steady hand. Then he looked at Duale again.

'I have received an unusual letter from two members of the Executive Committee. At this time, I am treating the letter as confidential and personal to me. Depending on the result of our discussion, the letter will remain confidential, or it will be copied to the members of the Board. Let me explain.

About three weeks ago, while you were travelling, the letter appeared on my desk. Two members of the Executive Committee have expressed concern that because of your relatively long absences, the business of really managing TASS has fallen, so to say, into a state of neglect. They assert that TASS is in a position to do much more, but that your absences effectively negate their initiatives to propose how TASS could give stronger support to countries in need of civil aviation expertise.

Part of their thesis, if I may use that word, is that you should not spend time on visits to the White House or the UN. In other words, too many visits to Washington and New York. They also refer to too many cocktail parties; in essence, they suggest that such activities are irrelevant to TASS's work. They quote from the articles of TASS's Trust which, as you know, explicitly states that TASS will at all times operate as an apolitical organization. At the end of their letter, they call for your removal and the appointment of a younger, more technically current, man.

I have considered showing you the letter, but until I get a feel from you of your reaction, I prefer to be cautious. After all, if we are dealing with a storm in a tea cup, why should you have to waste time and energy defending yourself? So before taking the next step, I would like to listen to what you have to say. Then I will decide what to do.'

There was a pause. The Chairman looked at Duale and thought how mature and relaxed Duale looked. Outwardly, the only sign of a reaction from Duale was a slight raising of the eyebrows accompanied by a mild expression of dismay. Inwardly, Duale's brain was functioning at high speed; he was under no illusion that if the assertions gathered credence, then the outcome for him might be at best uncomfortable; at worst, he might lose control of the situation. That would eventually mean his end.

Duale spoke. 'Mr. Chairman, thank you for talking to me in confidence. All I can do is be honest in my response, after which you will deal with this unfortunate, and I believe unnecessary, intrusion into our work. My explanation is quite simple. At all times I delegate to the maximum extent possible. However, for the last two or three years we have taken initiatives which, if successful, will mean an intensive and long-term involvement of TASS in certain Third World countries. Most of TASS's staff are technicians; they are not practised in negotiating TASS Agreements. From time to time, I have tried to call on one or two Divisional Heads to travel to certain countries to conclude Agreements; they not only came back empty handed, but in one case the TASS man managed to have a quarrel about lack of safety. I then had to travel myself to patch things up. So I decided that where important TASS Agreements were to be discussed, I should handle such matters myself. I believe the results speak for themselves. Incidentally, in my absence my deputy regularly chairs meetings of the Executive Committee, so if members wish to pursue initiatives they are not in the slightest inhibited.

As far as calls on the White House, the UN and so on, are concerned, these are usually of short duration and certainly have never impeded our work. I make these visits from time to time simply to maintain good relations. It is true that TASS is apolitical; but it would be naive to believe that we can work in a vacuum. We cannot, Mr. Chairman. If we have good relations with the White House, or for that matter even with the Mayor of Chicago, when we meet problems in this country we can turn to such institutions for support and assistance.' Duale looked at the Chairman, whose head was slightly bowed. The Chairman's countenance, passive and thoughtful, gave no clue of a reaction.

Duale went on: 'Every action I take in any respect only has one aim in view: to assure the smooth functioning of the Trust. I am the first to agree that many decisions are judgement decisions. If others disagree, let them say so and we will reach a consensus. Of course, from time to time all of us, with the luxury of hindsight, conclude that we have made mistakes. I am no exception. But if we take an objective look at the big picture, then I think we can be proud that TASS is achieving its mission.'

The Chairman stood up; Duale noticed a faint smile. He held out his hand and Duale shook it, unsmiling. He personified humility and respect; at the same time his facial expression was of a man who felt wronged, if not directly victimized.

The Chairman said, 'Don't worry, Dr. Duale. I will personally deal with this matter today. I am always suspicious when people, at any level, write letters of complaint when the target is absent and unable to defend himself. At your next meeting of the Committee there will be two empty seats. Proceed with the Committee material you have and we will appoint replacements as soon as possible. I think there is no need to change your approach. My only suggestion is that you may consider taking an extra critical look as to whether you definitely need to be absent. I think things here will always move along better when you are in the chair; it is understandable that your deputy may be a little cautious in your absence. I think I have already taken too much of your time. I can see myself out, thank you.'

When the Chairman reached the door, he turned to Duale and said, 'Oh my goodness, I almost forgot; maybe I am getting old after all.' He chuckled. 'Yes, you have probably already learned that Mike Wilson in Flight Safety has resigned; he says it's for personal reasons. It's a pity – an excellent man. He came to see me about his successor. Of course, the Board does not usually get involved in such things; the staff appointments are your responsibility. However, I suppose you won't mind too much when I say that in my opinion, and from what I've heard, there can only really be one successor. Captain Tashi is the right man. I know he's not the most senior, but he's unquestionably the best. I will leave it to your judgement, naturally; but I suggest you appoint Tashi as Head of Flight Safety without going through the usual advertising route. It's a very important part of TASS's work and we should not entertain any unnecessary delay. We need continuity. The Board will support you in this too; I have sounded out one or two members quietly. So I will leave it with you, Dr. Duale.'

Again, Duale's outward appearance was relaxed and calm. Inside his brain, however, there was furious activity. Given the choice, he would never have entertained the idea of appointing Tashi to be the Head of Flight Safety. Deep down, he dreaded contact with Tashi; already, on more than one occasion he had gone out of his way to avoid contact with Tashi when flight safety was to be discussed. With Tashi at the helm of the Division, they would often meet. What a shame, Duale thought, that after satisfying the Chairman he was now placed in this difficult situation. He knew that the Chairman was not the sort of person who would easily accept what Duale would prefer, which was that Duale would 'consider' it. And if Duale tried this avenue, the Chairman might question why there was a problem. And if there might be a problem with Tashi, perhaps the Chairman might have second thoughts on the points raised in the letter of complaint.

Duale looked at the Chairman. Then he said, 'Yes, Chairman, it is unusual for the Board to get into the business of appointments. And I hope this will not create a precedent. Since you have expressed a view in this case, I am happy to accept you advice. Thank you, Chairman. Goodbye.'

As the door closed, Duale walked slowly to his desk. He suddenly felt tired and weak; the brightness of his office seemed to have lost its energy. He decided to get back to the letters. When he had finished reading Mike Wilson's short letter of resignation he thought, 'When I married Pema, that was supposed to solve the problem with that Tashi. I wanted to break contact with him as much as I could; I hoped that thorn in my side would get out of my life. How will I cope with that personification of perfection in everything he thinks and does? So did I achieve anything at all today? Yes, I still have the confidence of the Chairman; that's very important. Above all – I have survived!'

Duale pressed the buzzer. Anna walked in; after a few steps

she glanced at Duale and stopped in her tracks. Her easy assurance and gentle smile were replaced by a look of astonishment and concern.

'Dr. Duale, what is wrong? What happened?.'

Duale turned his head slowly towards her; with a grave expression he said, 'Nothing is wrong, Anna. I don't know why, but I feel troubled. I can't explain it, but I feel my survival is threatened. There is no reason for me to feel like this. The meeting with the Chairman went quite well.'

'Shall I bring you a coffee, Dr. Duale?'

'It might help. But I have a better idea. Let's go and have some lunch together, Anna. I feel like telling you some secrets.'

'Secrets, Dr. Duale?.' Anna teased him and smilingly added, 'You have secrets?'

'Yes, Anna,' Duale replied, 'I have secrets. I am just going to tell you one of them, not all, Anna. Let's go in ten minutes, if that's all right with you.'

After a short taxi ride, Duale and Anna were looking at one another across a luncheon table in a small Indonesian restaurant. The head waiter ensured that Duale's every wish was swiftly satisfied. The orders for lunch were quickly placed. Then Duale said, 'It's not exactly like old times, Anna; but it's still nice to be sitting here with you. If I didn't have you to talk to sometimes, I would feel empty and lost.'

'Thank you, Dr. Duale. I think all men in high places need to know that at least someone is reliable. I do my best to support you. And now you are going to give me a secret to chew on. I was looking forward to more than just one secret.' She laughed for a moment. 'I hope you won't be too selective. Who knows, I might be able to come up with some advice for you to consider.' Anna smiled and Duale thought how her charm had never deserted her.

'Well, Anna,' Duale said as the soup was served, 'here is the main secret. On my recent trip I have married a Bhutanese woman called Pema. Pema flew with me to Chicago. I fell in love with her years ago without realising it at the time. I should have married her then. Anyway, better late than never, I suppose. We are very happy together, Anna.'

Duale looked at Anna. Her smiling countenance had become more serious; she looked thoughtful. Duale said, 'Do you think I should circulate the staff that I have married?' Anna rested her spoon in the bowl of soup; then she rejoined, 'Is that the one and only secret; is that the end for today?' Now she was gently smiling again.

'Isn't that enough for one day, Anna? I don't think I have any more secrets for you.' Duale raised the soup spoon to his mouth. 'It's quite good isn't it? I feel better already,' he commented.

Then Anna spoke, 'I thought you might have told me another secret – about Captain Tashi' The tone of her voice was matter-of-fact.

Duale tried to gulp the soup he had sipped from the spoon. He almost managed; the residue burst through his lips and spattered the linen tablecloth. The head waiter was immediately at his side, 'Oh, Dr. Duale. I am so sorry. There is something wrong; I am sorry.' Within seconds a spotlessly new tablecloth had been placed between Anna and Duale.

Duale sat quietly and seemed to relapse into a brief meditation. Then he raised his head and looked across the table. Anna looked apologetic.

'Anna,' Duale asked, 'what are you talking about?'

'It's simple, Dr. Duale; at least for me with my straightforward mind it's a simple deduction. I always noticed the likeness between you and Captain Tashi; once I even mentioned it, and what an exaggerated reaction I got from you! Anyway, now you have told me of the link that has been missing up to today. Am I wrong?' There was a pause.

'You are quite right,' Duale rejoined; then he added, 'Perhaps sometime I will tell you the whole story. You know, when I decided to bring Captain Tashi on board, I had no idea he was my son. I am not sure what to do now.'

Anna was quick to respond, 'I suggest you circulate the staff that you have married – period. Keep it low key. It is not necessary to tell them anything about your wife, not even her nationality. As for Captain Tashi, he is a great success. Let him go on being a success, and if you are lucky the situation will resolve itself when you retire. If your relationship with Captain Tashi becomes known in the meantime, then you will have to explain yourself. If you are worried about the resemblance between Captain Tashi and yourself, did you consider growing a beard? I think it is important to try and forget your relationship with Captain Tashi; treat him as a good member of staff. The important thing is that both you and he produce good work for TASS.'

'You are probably right, Anna. Thank you. Now let us enjoy our lunch.'

The two chatted amiably for another half hour or so and they were just thinking of leaving after an espresso. Anna quietly said, 'Since we have been discussing secrets, Dr. Duale, would you be very upset if I got something off my chest. You won't be too happy with what I would like to say, but sometimes it is better to be straightforward; I am only thinking of you.'

'Well,' Duale replied with a resigned air, 'if you think it's in my interest, after all your good advice I should definitely listen. Don't be too cruel, Anna.'

With her totally open expression, Anna's blue eyes focused on Duale's face. 'You remember that flaming affair you had with the young American official. You pursued her from coast to coast. I always used to wonder what reason you would dream up next so you could visit her in her new location. You remember?'

'Probably, Anna, you are thinking of the girl who ended up in the White House?' Duale responded.

'Exactly – she's still there, but not for much longer. I know you liked to show that TASS had good relations with the White House; she was certainly a convenient excuse. She called today to say she would be moving to New York and she left her new address. I hope you won't be angry if I suggest that now that you are married, you break that particular relationship.'

'Oh, I agree, Anna. Even if she had stayed in Washington, I would probably not have met her again; in any case, if she won't be there, then there is no point in calling on them. She was the main reason for visiting, although I quite liked the image of being someone who frequented the White House. I was probably being vain. Consultations can take many forms, don't you think?' Duale laughed a little; then he went on, 'In fact, after my discussion with the Chairman this morning, I think he would be happy if I told him that my visits to the White House and the UN will be greatly curtailed from now on.'

It was six o'clock in the evening two days later that Duale replaced his dictaphone on the desk at the moment when Anna had walked in with his first day's dictation. 'You look a bit weary, Dr,' Anna said as she placed a folder with countless letters and memoranda in front of him. 'They are all for signature, please. I have asked Captain Tashi to call on you first thing in the morning; you may wish to hand him his promotion letter personally.'

'Thank you, Anna. The rest is on this tape.'

The following morning Duale received Tashi and told him about his impending promotion. He gave Tashi a letter to confirm what he had said. Then Duale gathered his papers and took the elevator to the main meeting room. The Executive Committee were ready for work. 'Good morning, gentlemen,' he said. 'I believe we are all here. I know you have been provided with papers for our meeting. Under the first item I will give you a brief account of what I was doing in Asia.....'

'Mr. CEO,' interrupted the American.

'Yes,' Duale went on, 'I will give you....'

'Mr. CEO,' this time the voice was stronger. Duale looked up and turned his head in the direction of the interruption.

'Thank you, Mr. CEO. Excuse me interrupting you. You mentioned that we are all here; unfortunately, my two neighbours are not here. It's unusual because they are normally punctual.'

Duale tried not to smile; yes, he thought, the Chairman had promised to move fast. And he had!

'Thank you, now I see that we lack two members of the Committee. I do not expect to see them again and I hope their positions will be filled soon. We can proceed, gentlemen.' The agenda was dealt with in record time. Duale implored more participation of the Committee; the response was silence, punctuated by the occasional muted, low voice as it said 'Agreed.' By the end of the meeting Duale was forced to conclude that the Committee had decided that their best hope for safety was to remain silent, except when they were asked for their endorsement of a particular point; this was their cue to say 'Agreed'.

'It is wonderful to see you, Duale my darling. Did you have another good day?' Pema asked, as Duale took off his coat and shook the snow from his boots.

'Before I tell you, Pema, let me kiss you and then let me ask you what happened? I mean, you look different.'

'I think that's wonderful,' Pema replied, 'men are not known for noticing details in their wives' appearance. I went shopping with Patsri and we bought some nice American clothes.'

'You look fantastic,' Duale commented, 'they fit marvellously!'

'Thank you, darling,' Pema went on, 'now you can tell me about your achievements.'

'Well, I've just had a very interesting three days. First, after some unfortunate misunderstandings between a couple of Committee members and myself, I seem to have managed quite well; the main thing is I continue in the good books of the Board of Trustees. I suppose there are some who would like me to make way for a younger man. The problem for them is that I know too much. As long as I have the support of the Board of Trustees, I can stay on as CEO for as long as I like. Who knows, I could even survive into the next millennium.' Duale laughed, 'To be realistic, Pema, in this business at my level you never know what might happen from one day to the next. In any case, for the moment I am still there; and the outlook is quite good.' Then Duale bit his tongue as he was about to say, 'If only I could rid myself of that devil; for some reason, he worries me...' Instead he said,

'Next, Tashi will be promoted as Head of his Division; this is wonderful, although we shall have to be careful to keep our relationship with him a secret.'

Duale took Pema in his arms and he kissed her; slowly, he lowered his head until his mouth found her neck. He went on kissing her. In a quiet voice he said, 'Pema, I can't tell you how wonderful it is for me to have you here when I come home. I want to love you. Do you enjoy me more before or after dinner?'

'Darling, you are amazing. You come home from a busy day's work and you have all this energy. When do you enjoy me most, Duale?'

'Well,' Duale replied, 'to be honest, the way I feel at this moment, I could enjoy you now. And then depending on how we feel after dinner, we could try again.'

'I think,' Pema rejoined with a chuckle, 'that is a thoroughly constructive idea, as they used to say so often in the Thimphu UN Office. If we both try hard, dear Duale...'

And they did.

Chapter Fifteen

Tashi's Vision

It was Spring 1996. Tashi had just driven with Patsri and Little Tashi from Geneva Lake; now they were home again. 'I loved every second of our trip; yes, every second, Tashi,' Patsri said as they left the car in the underground garage and made their way to the elevator. 'When we drove up the coast of Wisconsin, the lake looked so beautiful. With the changing weather, the colour of the water was amazing; every other minute its appearance seemed to reflect a different shade of blue or grey. It was unforgettable. And you know, those little flowers, especially the blue ones in the woods around Geneva Lake, they were so pretty. We must make more trips on the weekends, if you have time.'

'Yes darling, we shall make more excursions,' Tashi replied. His response seemed a little distant, Patsri thought. She decided to put Little Tashi to bed.

'I will give the little one some supper and see him into bed, Tashi. Then we can have a quiet supper together.'

Left alone, Tashi slipped into quiet thought. He was still quiet forty minutes later when Patsri's interrupted.

'So what is the great man thinking about? It's to do with the office, isn't it?' Patsri sat on Tashi's lap and kissed his ear.

'I've been thinking. I started off by thanking Lord Buddha for you... you look so incredibly beautiful – how do you keep that figure?'

Patsri pressed herself against Tashi and kissed him. 'Thank you, Tashi! Perhaps I am looking better than usual.' Then she smiled gently. 'My darling, I am expecting another baby.'

'What?! I think that's just perfect...! So Little Tashi will have someone to play with, how wonderful! No wonder you have this serene look about you.'

'Something else you'll notice in a few months will be my

figure... you'll have to get used to a few extra pounds. But it will be lovely to have another child. Who knows, then we could think of some more? Now, tell me what else you were thinking about.'

'Well,' said Tashi with a grin, 'perhaps after the momentous news I should postpone telling you? Believe it or not, it's about air safety, Patsri. I know I am a small cog in a big machine; I suppose since I became Head of the Division I am a bit bigger. I just feel that TASS is not doing enough. Or, to put it another way, TASS could be doing much more. You know, my predecessor became disenchanted and he blamed my father for poor leadership; that's why he resigned. I don't think anyone in the office has ever felt close to my father. He seems to have his own agenda, and that's about it. But over the last six months or so, he seems to have withdrawn himself from the TASS staff. We rarely see him; and when we do, we try and raise some long-outstanding issue – which leads to the end of the discussion! I am not the only one who has noticed this; other Division Heads are complaining bitterly. They say they write to him to get the go-ahead for something, but he simply doesn't reply. Of course, the atmosphere in the office is not very good; too many people feel frustrated. With that concentration of professional competence we could be moving ahead and really making a difference; instead, we are just held up because the man at the top is so unresponsive.

The other day I was looking at some accident statistics. In my opinion, there are too many. Of course, no one can be sure, but the accident rate seems to be on the increase. A lot of people say that if you want to transport a billion passengers a year, then if you have an accident somewhere in the world each week, then that's not a bad price to pay. I think this attitude is callous and not at all objective, Patsri. Air travel is much safer, statistically speaking, than road travel; we all know that. So what? Should we all relax and let those people be killed every year? Who knows, as the traffic increases it could get worse, much worse. I honestly think TASS could be doing more, especially for the developing countries. I wonder what our CEO really thinks about it? He has an amazing ability to ignore reality.'

Patsri turned her head and looked into her husband's eyes. 'Why don't you ask him? Why not try and lead him to do more of what you think is right. And if he convinces you that you are

259

wrong then you will accept that, because you are so honest, Tashi. Why not try? You don't have anything to lose, do you? Could he fault you for coming up with some fresh ideas?'

There was a pause; Tashi was thinking. 'You know, Patsri,' he commented at last, 'in theory you are right. The trouble with my father is that he is a complicated man. He only seems to have one priority, which is to survive. If I put some ideas in front of him, he may see this as a challenge to his own ideas, that is to the extent he has any. He may not want to have his boat rocked. You see, I don't think air safety is his priority; unfortunately, his priority is himself.

And there is another point. I can't ignore the CEO's nature. By the way, I am sorry to keep calling him 'the CEO,' but he doesn't regard or treat me in any way like his son; so how can I feel that he is my father? To all intents and purposes, uncle Gyeltshen was my father; and as you know I am very close to my mother. I know the CEO's conduct has improved a lot, at least outwardly, since he married my mother, but in a basic sense each of us is born with a nature. And I don't think our natures change. If we are lucky, the bad sides may not surface too often, perhaps never. There are people whose basic natures are not really put to the test; then there are others who have the potential to be bad, but they are somehow controlled. At work, for example, they are usually kept under control by a supervisor.

In the case of the CEO, he is in the top job. He is supposed to be monitored and supervised by the Board of Trustees. The Executive Committee is also there to help keep him on the rails. In practice, he manages to do what he wants. So in a certain sense he is out of control; and he exerts his power very cleverly. The point I am driving at is that if someone feels himself sort of cornered, then you have to be careful of the person's nature. In the case of my father, we know he has some unpleasant streaks. What I am saying is that if, however unintentionally, I were to upset him, or he perceived me to represent dangerous competition, then his reaction could be unpredictable. He can't help himself, Patsri; as far as I am concerned, he is a prisoner of his nature.'

Patsri became pensive, but tried not to show her anxiety. Then she said 'If that's the way you feel, Tashi, then why not forget it. You are doing your job and you are contributing to air safety. If you are doing the maximum within the system, that's the end of it – or not?'

'Not exactly,' Tashi responded. 'I could adopt that attitude in a narrow sense. But if I look at the big picture, then it is a different matter. If, for example, I were to conclude that by doing things differently TASS would potentially really save lives, then to be true to myself I have to say something. I think the best thing is for me to keep on thinking. I can also find out a bit more; I would like to hear about the experience of the other Heads of Division. After I have certain facts established, I can decide whether to try and do something to persuade the CEO to change TASS's policy for the better. If I succeed, then good; if I fail, then at least I will have tried.

While we are talking a bit about the office, there's one thing, Patsri, I have to explain. I am going to grow a beard.' Patsri gave a little start and turned her head, this time in astonishment, 'What did you say?'

'Yes, Patsri, from tomorrow I am afraid you will begin to notice the stubble.' Tashi chuckled. 'I haven't actually seen the CEO for a couple of months, which I must say has been rather pleasant for me. But last week, on two separate occasions and in two different locations, some colleagues remarked on the resemblance I have to the CEO. We have enough things to think about without people talking like that; in the end certain ideas about the CEO's relationship with me might gather momentum – who knows? In any case, I thought I should camouflage myself a bit. Can you stand it, Patsri? After all, the man might retire in a year or two. Do you mind too much, my darling?'

Patsri threw her head back and laughed; then she turned to Tashi and, as she hugged him, she kissed him. Still smiling, she whispered, 'From the beginning, my little husband, I told you that you can do what you like. In fact, I rather like the idea of a beard. I told you I was in the Art Museum last week and how I loved the European paintings. I think you will soon be ready for a portrait by Hans Hals or Rubens, or for that matter Rembrandt; or then again, Tashi, El Greco would have made a wonderfully dramatic portrait of you. It's a pity we are almost four hundred years too late! We must take some photos of you when the beard is there.

Now you can take me to bed, Tashi. Do you remember that

song about 'the beard in her ear'?' Patsri was still laughing as Tashi carried her into the bedroom. 'Please be as gentle as you always are; we must think of the little one. In a few months I'll give you an assessment of making love with you, first without the beard and afterwards, with.'

As their naked bodies came together, Patsri's laughing gradually subsided and she briefly thought how wonderful it was to feel the smooth skin of Tashi's face as he kissed her full breasts. Tashi said quietly, 'Thai women seem so much more emancipated, or liberated or something, than women in Bhutan.'

Patsri laughed gently, 'Is that so? So you know something about Bhutanese women after all, my darling? I am only teasing... whether I am emancipated or liberated I don't really know; and I don't need to know. All I am sure of is that I know what I like – and that happens to be you!'

The next morning, the sun had already risen and a few of its strengthening rays were forcing their way through slits between the curtains of the bedroom. Tashi could hear the quiet, regular breathing of Patsri, who still seemed to be sound asleep. He pressed his body against hers and he gently held one of her breasts; then he dozed.

'Good morning, my darling.' Patsri slipped out of bed and pulled on a silk dressing gown.

When she came back a few minutes later, Tashi said, 'Patsri, I don't know how you feel, but I sometimes, like now, feel I could just live on love. But then again, I suppose that would not be very realistic.' After a pause, he went on: 'To change the subject for a minute, I was awake a bit at night. I've decided to try and force my father to change his ways in the office. Although it's not common knowledge, it is very clear that we're on the brink of a technological revolution as far as global air navigation is concerned. It will affect every country of the world, including the developing countries, so TASS absolutely has to move on this whole business. When it comes to implementing the new system, which incidentally relies a great deal on satellites, TASS should be leading. All the Division Heads in TASS know what has to be done. As far as I know, most of them have written to the CEO asking for the go-ahead to adjust our working approach; and the adjustment is a big change from what we are doing at the moment. Because no one can get a response from the CEO, the initiatives we suggest are dead in the water. As far as the new technology is concerned, TASS is in a state of paralysis. So instead of being the leader, we are the laggard. This is unacceptable – after all, we are the Trust For Air Safety Support. Something positive has to happen – and soon!

I would like to try and sort out this mess. And if this means that because of the distraction I might not be as active as usual, I hope, Patsri, you will understand.'

'Of course I understand, my darling.' Patsri leant over and kissed him.

'Thank you,' Tashi said, as he gently pulled Patsri towards him. He felt the silkiness of her gown against his chest and as his body took her weight he thought how lightly she rested on him. A few seconds later, Patsri's gown had slipped to the floor...

'Tashi,' Patsri whispered, 'you are supposed to stop, not start again. When will you learn to control yourself?'

'I hope never!'

'Good,' Patsri rejoined, 'but you must try because we have to think of the next little one.' She kissed him again.

After breakfast, Tashi prepared to leave for the office. Patsri kissed him goodbye and said, 'Tashi, you always do the right thing. So start today and try and sort out that wayward father of yours. And if we have to sacrifice a little on the love-making, we can comfort ourselves that it can only be good for the little one. For the last three months we have to stop anyway. We'll survive!' Tashi kissed her, then he was gone.

Once in his office, Tashi lost no time in starting his consultations. He began with aeronautical communications. The Head of TASS's Communications Division looked Tashi in the eye; Tashi noticed that his colleague's face flushed, as he said, 'Tashi, the CEO is totally unresponsive. I can't get him to see beyond the end of the table of his Executive Committee. Apparently, all he wants to do is survive. I tell you, Tashi, I am desperate!'

'I agree with you, Tashi. There is a revolution going on in aerospace communications. It is quite probable that your field is affected as well. To my mind, TASS's whole outlook and thrust has to change. We have to educate the Third World in all this new technology. We should be leading. And where does leadership come from, Tashi? There is only one place – the top! I tell you, I have tried for two whole years to explain to the CEO what it's all about. And what is his reaction? The man is a blank, Tashi. When it comes to anything new, he's a non-starter. It's sad, but it's as simple as that! I'm sorry to blow my top, Tashi, but I am so frustrated! I feel like resigning.'

'No!' Tashi was quick and decisive in his cool, crisp response. 'You don't have to resign – yet. Gerry, give it a chance. I tell you what I propose to do. I will write a short memo to the CEO, explaining I have talked to various Heads of the Divisions, and we are all concerned about TASS's current technical policy in the light of technological developments. I won't alarm him at this stage; that might make him more resistant to bringing TASS upto date. I'll ask for some time with him to give him a presentation, then I'll ask when he intends to propose some initiatives to the Committee.

Hopefully, Gerry, we'll get a positive response. Before we're through, one way or another we'll shame him into doing something positive. After all, aviation safety is not some airy fairy pastime in which people indulge for fun. We are dealing with one of the greatest developments of the last hundred years, and we are here to do everything possible to assure the safety of well over a billion passengers yearly. So I think we have to be responsible in everything we do, Gerry. You are quite right; leadership in this whole business must come from the top. So give me a chance and I will get back to you.' Tashi got up, gathered a couple of files and strode to the door.

As Tashi opened the door, he heard Gerry's voice.

'Tashi,' he said, 'I don't want to delay you, but from the day you joined the Trust, I admired your thoroughly professional, objective approach. You know how to get things done. And after all, that's what TASS's work is all about, isn't it? This will come as a surprise, but frankly I would love to see *you* as the CEO. There will always be people who will jump to the wrong conclusion and say you are too young. The fact is you are not. I'd say you are the ideal age. You've had unique experience in the Third World and you are blessed with excellent judgement. In fact, I would say to be young with all these qualities is a great advantage because you have all that energy. Personally, I think you have everything it takes to make the perfect CEO. I tell you, within six months you would be at least twice as effective as the Survivor. Think about it, Tashi. Think about being a worthy successor to our played-out CEO. I am sure a lot of good people would support you.

If you decide to go for it, let me know. Some of us have the ears of the Trustees or members of the Committee. I'm sure we could do the necessary. Please think about it. If you told me you would seriously consider it, it could make the difference between me resigning out of desperation and disenchantment, or staying in the hope of a change for the better. Anyway, you'd better get moving. Good luck!'

Gerry was relaxed and he smiled warmly. 'Oh, incidentally, Tashi, I see you are sporting a beard. I must say it suits you. If you were older, you might look like a crusty old airline captain counting the months to his retirement. But being younger and at the top of your profession, it's quite different. See you soon; I can't wait.'

By mid 1996 Tashi felt well prepared to tackle Duale. He wrote a three-page memorandum summarizing advances in aerospace technology which he thought should affect TASS's working approach. At the end of the memorandum, he asked for a three hour meeting with his CEO so that he could make a presentation, during which he intended to recommend new TASS initiatives.

By mid September Tashi had received no response from Duale, nor had he seen him; so he decided to call Anna.

'Yes, Captain Tashi,' Anna responded, 'you are quite right. Three months is too long to wait for an answer. The CEO has been away, you know mixing work with his summer vacation. But he is back in town now and I will make sure you get some sort of response within the week. I am sorry about the delay, Captain.'

What a wonderful woman, Tashi thought, she is always so charming and somehow doing her best to protect her boss.

True to her word, Anna was on the line again, this time the very next day. 'Captain Tashi? Apologies for the delay,' Anna was relaxed and managing the situation, as always. 'I have spoken with the CEO. He has quite a busy schedule. Would it be convenient for you to meet with him a week today, that is at 2 pm in his office. He has reserved the afternoon for you. I am sure that, between you, you can solve all the aerospace problems of the world in half a day!' Anna was chuckling.

'Thank you, Anna, at least we can try. Thank you for your intervention.'

'That's fine, Captain,' Anna said. 'I must say it's getting quite difficu... oh, excuse me; I was being a little thoughtless. You're a deceptively relaxing person to talk to, Captain Tashi. I must be more on my guard! We look forward to seeing you next week. Goodbye, Captain Tashi.'

A week later Tashi got up a little earlier than usual. When he appeared at the breakfast table Patsri looked at him in admiration.

'This must be a very special day, Tashi. You are wearing your new suit. You look very distinguished with the beard.'

'Thank you,' Tashi replied, 'today could be quite important. I am meeting the CEO to try and shame him into doing something positive.'

'And what do you want him to do?' asked Patsri.

'I want to bring him into the real world, to do something for once. If he goes on clinging to the past, that will be the end of TASS. I think I'll go to the office a bit early to do some final homework. Wish me luck, Patsri.'

As Tashi left the apartment Patsri rushed towards him and kissed him. 'Goodbye my darling; and good luck. Of course I am biased, but if you ask me, I think you should be TASS's CEO. Then the right things would start happening!'

At five to two that day Tashi appeared at Anna's door. In his inimitably courteous way he said, 'Excuse me interrupting you, Anna. I have come for the CEO's appointment.' Anna smoothly swivelled herself around on her chair and looked at Tashi; her eyes widened the moment she caught sight of him. 'Oh, my goodness! Where did you get that beard from, Captain Tashi?' She looked confused. 'It doesn't matter. You'll find out for yourself. The CEO is expecting you; please go straight in.' Slightly perplexed, Tashi strode behind Anna and continued into the CEO's office.

Duale was writing a note on a file and he did not immediately acknowledge Tashi's presence. 'Good afternoon, Dr. Duale,' Tashi said.

Duale looked up and just stared at Tashi. 'What happened?' Duale asked. 'You have a beard. Come and stand by me in my personal bathroom over here. Look in the mirror. We look identical! I grew my beard to disguise our likeness; now we both

266

have beards! Shave your beard off tonight. Is that understood?'

'With all due respect, sir, this is hardly an official matter; I think you might agree it is something personal. Perhaps I could suggest that you may wish to consider shaving off your own beard? But as a gesture of good will, by tomorrow I will again be clean-shaven, so you will be saved embarrassment. Now, Dr. Duale, I know how busy you are. Shall I begin?'

Duale struck Tashi as irritable; he would probably be a reluctant listener, Tashi thought. Duale did not respond, but eyed him.

Tashi said 'I appreciate it that you have reserved the afternoon for my presentation. Thank you for studying my memorandum.'

'First,' Duale responded curtly, 'you must realise that I did not welcome your memorandum. I do not need to be told what TASS should be doing. That is because I know. Second, it is true I have reserved the afternoon for you. But if you can finish sooner, so much the better. I am extremely busy and I have only agreed to listen to you because we have a personal connection. I have very little interest in the subject of your presentation, yet I am prepared to listen. Please start.'

Tashi opened his file and briefly glanced at the first few lines of his notes. Then he started. 'I am afraid, Dr. Duale, that what I am going to present to you cannot be hurried. There is background and there is context. I can only be grateful that as the CEO of TASS you show endless patience.' Tashi looked up with a faint smile; all he saw was an unsmiling, bearded face, from which eyes of steel seemed to fix on him, as though they would pierce him like laser beams.

With a look of empty resignation, Tashi cleared his throat and started. 'My presentation, Dr. Duale, is divided into two parts. The first part deals with the flying and navigation side; the second chiefly with ground facilities. But may I start with a few statistics. In 1956, which you will remember was the year when, amongst other things, you drafted the civil aviation law for the Kingdom of Bhutan, the number of passenger embarkations recorded by the then scheduled airlines of the world was 68 million. In 1977, the year that you were appointed CEO of TASS, the number had grown to 517 million. As you know, by 1990 the billion barrier had been broken. The statistics covering the freight picture also reflects enormous growth.

Now if we look at the flying side, which is my specialization, there are a good number of problems. Possibly, the greatest problem centres on the lack we often find of what one could term a safety culture. Especially since liberalization, at the chief executive level the main concentration is often directed to the bottom line, unfortunately with safety taking second place. There needs to be a change of focus in the culture of the airline industry.

The worst category for accidents is CFIT; I am sure you have heard the term, Dr?' Tashi raised his head – Duale commented, 'Of course I have heard the term – what does it mean?'

'Controlled Flight Into Terrain – yes, hitting the ground! In an effort to reduce the number of CFIT accidents, about twenty five years ago the Ground Proximity Warning System was developed and installed in aircraft. It didn't work very well, first as it couldn't 'see' very far ahead, which meant the warning tended to come too late, and second, almost in a psychological sense, pilots tended to rely much too heavily on the GPWS, rather than paying proper attention to their instruments and really controlling the aircraft. Now a new type of GPWS has been developed and installed in some aircraft; it 'sees' further ahead, so the pilot gets an earlier warning. It also displays warning signals in a very vivid way. But there are still too many CFIT accidents. Pilots have to regain something which too many of them have lost, that is a really deeply ingrained safety culture.

This leads me to the problem of pilot over-confidence and complacency. Especially with the military-trained ones, the pilots seem to have a feeling they are invincible; they know everything and they can manage anything they feel like doing. Their personal self-assessment seems to take precedence over their objective attention to safety. Now if you look at the global accident statistics for the last three or four years, Dr. Duale, I personally do not feel encouraged by the trend. I would hope you would agree with me.'

Duale interjected. 'I prefer not to interrupt you, but I must say I am not sure that I agree with you. Why should this concern TASS, Captain Tashi? TASS can only go so far. We can't spoon-feed the Third World forever. They have to help themselves. In any case, carry on.'

'Thank you. The reason I am highlighting the situation is

because so many of these accidents take place, as you implied, in the Third World. I would suggest this raises the basic question, which is whether TASS could be doing more? Surely we could not be criticized for some self-questioning within the Trust, especially if we found we could, in fact, be doing more to prevent accidents. After all, this is the mission of TASS.

As I said earlier, the second part of what I would like to present for your consideration focuses on the situation as far as communications and navigational facilities are concerned. Highlighting only the basics, the aerospace industry has, as you know, embarked on a sort of revolution...'

'No! I do not know that,' interrupted Duale. 'Why do you dramatize perfectly normal, evolutionary developments in air navigation? Please be more objective.'

'I am being objective, Dr. Duale. I do not intend to dramatize in the slightest.' Duale noticed the firmness in Tashi's voice, which was now replacing Tashi's accommodating and respectfully courteous tone. 'As you should know, the navigational and some communications systems which were developed fifty years ago have run their course to some extent. Navigational aids – NAVAIDS – are expensive in terms of purchase, installation and maintenance. Plans are being developed which in an ideal situation will provide for a so-called seamless air navigation system. This should happen in the next ten to fifteen years.

The basis of the new system primarily involves the use of a global navigation satellite system. To begin with, this will give worldwide navigation coverage, including guidance for non-precision approaches. This will mean that, using on-board avionics, aircraft will be able to navigate with a high degree of safety anywhere in the world. Later, augmentation systems, which are currently being developed, will safely support most precision approaches. The new system permits aircraft to automatically transmit data by satellite to an air traffic control unit where the aircraft's position, heading and speed are displayed.

At least for the early years, the aerospace industry will rely on the American Global Positioning System and the Russian Global Orbiting Navigation Satellite System. The US GPS is a constellation of twenty four satellites which operate in six orbital planes; each satellite orbits the earth every 12 hours. The Russian system performs operationally in a similar way. The accuracy and precision of these systems are remarkable; one hears references to a pilot knowing his position to within a few metres. The Europeans are also discussing something similar. I heard the other day it might be called 'Galileo'. There are no approvals yet, but if Europe decides to go ahead, then this will strengthen the whole concept.

What will all this mean for aviation? It means a lot, not just for the operators but for just about everybody. Once the technical integrity of the systems has been fully tested and proved for operational use, mandatory separation standards can be reviewed and reduced. This will produce much greater capacity, which will mean that for the busy routes, the congestion will be either eliminated or greatly reduced. In a sense, the biggest gainers will be the Third World. Once they have made their initial investments in the equipment for the ground stations, then that's about it. There are no huge installation and maintenance costs as is the case today; for example, when they need an instrument landing system.

As far as controlling, that is managing, airspace is concerned, there will be fundamental changes. The fact is that the advanced airborne equipment which is now coming on to the market is much more efficient than the current ground systems which are supposed to be supporting flight paths. So this will lead to the airline industry and their pilots exercising much greater flexibility when planning their flight profiles. The captain of the aircraft will decide how he intends to reach his destination, which is rather the opposite of today, where he is in the hands of the current rigid air traffic system.

The free flight formula which will be automatically applied for the pilot, essentially involves longitude, latitude, altitude, plus time. The captain will be told when he can depart and what route he should follow using his on-board equipment; this will be the best the system can offer in response to his request. During the flight he will be cocooned by two zones. The smaller zone, which is called the protected zone, must remain sterile at all times to assure separation. Then there will be the outer zone, which is called the alert zone. In this zone the aircraft receives enhanced monitoring; if it might be necessary, air traffic control will need to intervene so as to assure continued safe separation.'

Tashi paused and looked into Duale's eyes. Duale's eyelids

seemed to be momentarily fluttering; then his eyes opened a little more. And he yawned. Duale shifted in his seat a little and sat in a more upright position. Then he said, 'Captain Tashi. I am sure what you are saying is of interest to some people. I am more interested in organization, administration and legal matters. I have already received some briefing material from the Divisional Chief of Communications. So I have a grasp of what you are talking about; so far, I have heard nothing new. Now I think it would be better if you finish your presentation. As I told you, I am very busy. Or have you finished?'

Tashi was nonplussed; although he felt disappointment taking hold and gnawing within him, true to his character he persevered.

'Thank you, Dr. Duale. I will now come to the main part of what I wish to present to you and I am grateful for your close attention. As I mentioned earlier, we are at the beginning of an air navigation revolution. The established systems have run their course; increasingly, they will be found to be inadequate for day-to-day civil aviation operations. The equipment needed to support what will be regarded as the old-fashioned way will be replaced by different, less expensive equipment; the new systems will be much easier to operate and maintain. Automation will be employed more and more; and the transmission, reception and processing of digital data will become key to effective air traffic management.

My question to you, Dr. Duale, is what is TASS doing to help Third World countries to come to terms with what I call a revolution and what you regard as evolution? Have you sought the endorsement of the Executive Committee to initiate appropriate action to assist and support Third World countries during their transition to the new technology?'

Duale stirred in his chair and glared at Tashi. But Tashi was not to be intimidated. He went on: 'Or again, in the light of these extraordinary technical developments, have we assisted them with one cost/benefit study to help them decide which way to go, technically speaking, over the next ten or fifteen years? Have we advised them about the changing role of the air traffic controller and the need to review the training of these people? Have we explained that within a few years some professional-type work will fall by the wayside, while new jobs will need to be developed, especially in the field of automation, for which men and women will have to be trained? Have we told them that the navigational aids of today will eventually become museum pieces? There are several other important questions I could ask; but I have asked these questions because, as far as I know, TASS has done none of these things, Dr. Duale. I am very concerned....'

'So am I!,' Duale interjected in a loud voice. Now he was very much awake. 'Who do you think you are? Let me tell you – you are a revolutionary – yes, a revolutionary! Do you think I sit here without considering the briefings I am given? Do you think I am ignorant of the things of which you speak? You have been having consultations behind my back. Now I am wondering about your loyalty to TASS and to me personally; yes, your loyalty is certainly thrown into question.

Let me tell you, I have heard nothing new today. As far as I am concerned, all this noise about satellite systems is a storm in a teacup. Engineers always dream in technicolor; good luck to them! I deal with realities. TASS is TASS because I recognize that this new system you have been trumpeting about is a pipe-dream. It will never work. Can you tell me, Captain, what will be the legal arrangements under which the Americans and Russians will consider letting countries use their satellite systems? The Americans are historically impossibly legal in everything they do. From a practical point of view that will mean the new systems will never be operated as the users need them. Supposing there is a system breakdown, which might cause dislocation, even an accident – do you think the Americans will accept liability? And the Russians? Everyone knows they are short of money for repair and maintenance. So what will happen when they get system problems? The whole concept is ridiculous!

Even if some years down the line something happens, how will the Third World finance what they need to buy? Some people say TASS should help the Third World with financing. Why should we mollycoddle them? They are not children. If just for a moment I could bring you down from your world of dreams to mother earth, I would venture to suggest that perhaps you haven't even yet begun to think about how the Third World will finance what they need. Am I right? I want an answer!'

Tashi's eyes flashed at Duale. 'I am extremely disappointed at your comments, Dr. Duale, especially as they come from a much older man! I had been hoping to discern some realistic wisdom in your remarks. Apart from my disappointment with your generally negative attitude, I regret to note your ignorance of current technological developments which are already underway. I am surprised to hear your comments about the Americans, one of the world's leaders in aviation technology. What you have said about the United States is not only wide of the mark – it is wrong.

Turning to another aspect of this whole subject, if I had made my full presentation, which you will receive in any case shortly in writing, I would have touched on the question of the Third World's financing needs. The new system can only be completely effective if it is operated on a truly global basis. So the developing countries are crucially important players in the introduction of the new system. It happens to be a fact of life that by far the largest category of the world's countries are those of the Third World. In general, the Third World countries have little money for civil aviation development and, unfortunately, financing for civil aviation is rarely a priority of the development banks; so I propose to you that TASS should create a financing division exclusively to generate financing for Third World civil aviation safety projects. The creation of this division will reflect what is needed in the real world and...'

'Captain Tashi, I promoted you to your present position against my better judgement. I have had enough of you for today, and for that matter for the residual period of your work with TASS. I regard you as a revolutionary – and I must say a clever one. You know quite a lot and you have used this knowledge to try and interfere with my administration of this Trust. Normally, I would be more courteous and at least present a facade of patience and understanding. I would tell you that I would consider your points and get back to you. But since you have told me absolutely nothing that I have not already heard, I can tell you straightaway that, as long as I am here, nothing will change. I keep all major aviation matters under review. From what I know, at least up to the millennium there will be no basic change in TASS's working policies. Is that understood?

I see that you have been in my office for almost three hours. What a waste of time! Good afternoon, Captain Tashi. Incidentally, please don't waste more time by writing your long confirmation memorandum; surely you have more productive things to do?'

Duale did not accompany Tashi to his office door; instead, he turned to his confidential tray and slit open an envelope.

With Tashi already out of his mind, it was therefore with some surprise that his concentration was interrupted by Tashi's voice.

'You mentioned, Dr. Duale, that nothing would change as long as you are here. Now let me see, you are due to be considered for an extension to your appointment in about a year. Yes, that would be quite acceptable – at least I hope so. If you leave in a year, then the new, hopefully younger and better informed, man will be appointed from the real world. He should have just about sufficient time to make the basic changes in TASS's work to take account of the revolution in the new air navigation system.'

Duale raised his head. Very briefly, a questioning smile flickered across his face, 'Young man, excuse me when I repeat that you should leave. You should assume that I will be re-appointed in a year. You should not bother your head with thoughts of a new man. Can you think of anyone else who could handle this job? Of course not. Now leave!' Duale reverted to his confidential letter.

'Yes, Dr. Duale,' Tashi stubbornly responded, 'since you asked, I can think of a replacement for you. There is nothing to stop a new man offering himself for appointment. If he is the right man, then TASS will do what it is supposed to be doing. Aerospace, and therefore the world, will be all the safer for it! Good afternoon, Dr. Duale.'

'Don't leave,' thundered Duale. He got up and took a few steps around his desk. Tashi looked up at the bearded face and focused on Duale's eyes. For the first time in his life he felt he could actually see evil and hate. Duale continued, 'How dare you come to my office and lecture me on things with which I am fully conversant. How dare you engineer revolutionary, false information as a pretext to throw my lifelong dedication to aviation safety into doubt! If you continue spreading rumours of doubt, Captain Tashi, you will pay the price. I would not like to be in your shoes. By all means let someone who thinks he or she is better qualified than myself seek appointment. Whoever this genius might be, I can assure you the applicant will never succeed. To start with, however good the person might be technically, he will probably behave as a realist; but you see, this is not the way for a politician and....'

'Dr. Duale,' Tashi interjected, 'I have no intention of being lectured to by you. I consider you are seriously letting down the world of aviation and the international community, especially the countries of the Third World. By nature, when I deal with others, I do my best to be considerate and generous. So I will excuse your inexcusable work attitude by simply saying that you are probably too set in your old, dated ways to shoulder your responsibilities properly. When one becomes older, one should be wiser; unfortunately, in some cases this does not seem to happen! I am convinced you will be replaced, Dr. Duale. If the applicant has to make a brief excursion to become political, why should he hesitate? Fortunately, the type of political conduct which you employ to maintain your position in an apolitical Trust needs no training; you know, Dr. Duale, anyone can indulge in it. I have no doubt that the aspiring replacement will be successfu...'

'Shut up!' Duale angrily exclaimed. 'My boy, I have always said I am in favour of democracy, but there has to be a limit!' He laughed. 'Excuse me, I was just thinking of the opposition on the horizon, someone waiting to take my job.' He laughed again, this time more loudly.

To his surprise, Duale heard Tashi's voice again, this time with a question. 'Dr. Duale, perhaps you would permit me to ask you a simple question?' Without pausing for a reaction, he went on, 'May I ask, do you regard yourself as indispensable, Dr. Duale, as the leader of TASS's initiatives and effforts to support worldwide air safety?'

Duale briefly looked thoughtful. 'A strange question', he responded. 'I don't understand. Why do you ask such a question when you know the answer?' There was a short silence. Then Duale said in measured tones, 'Captain Tashi, what is the point of your question?'

Tashi looked directly at Duale. 'I have been reading recent European history, also a biography of General de Gaulle. He was not a very nice man – and he suffered dreadfully from an ego problem. Once at least he made quite a wise statement to the effect that the world's graveyards each have more than their fair share of

275

so-called indispensable people.' Duale watched a rueful smile cross Tashi's face. Tashi went on, 'In other words, there is a limited time and place for each of us – but unfortunately there are those whose ego gets the better of them. They simply cannnot let go and they refuse to move on and make way for a younger person. Pity!'

Tashi heard a pant. He watched Duale's face; the evil eyes were riveted on him. The face twitched. Duale walked back to his chair and pressed the bell. Anna immediately entered, but stopped in her tracks just inside the office. She looked with concern at Duale, then turned to Tashi in the icy silence. 'You look upset, Dr. Duale. Do you feel all right?' 'Ye...ye..yes, Anna. I feel ver...very well. Captain Tashi has overstayed my generous welcome. Please escort him from my office.'

As he prepared to leave, Tashi said, 'Dr, I appreciated our constructive discussion. I will of course be forwarding my full presentation in writing. I look forward to action from you. For reasons which I know you well understand, I strongly recommend that results are clearly visible within the next six to twelve months. Goodbye. Oh, just to clarify, I will be shaving off my beard, as you have instructed, sir, this evening. After you, Anna, please. I really don't need an escort; if I may, I will escort you to your desk.' Tashi gave Anna a relaxed, warm smile.

Anna preceded Tashi from the office; as Tashi drew the door to a close, he finally glanced at his CEO. Duale was slumped in his chair and seemed to have drifted into staring, unblinking medita-tion; he had gripped the paper knife and held it, motionless, as though it was a dagger. Poor man, Tashi thought, he is devoid of vision; and he is the exact contradiction – the opposite – of what the founder of TASS intended. This man, who happens to be my father, Tashi thought, is simply a consummate politician. There are some excellent political leaders in the world; it is such a pity my father is not one of them, although of course TASS is supposed to be apolitical. In any case, this obscures the fact. The fact is that TASS's CEO is an international disaster. The sooner he goes the better. He probably never was part of the real world. He only seems to know another world; his world revolves around his own survival. That's all – poor man!

Chapter Sixteen

Duale's Decision

'Duale!' Pema almost seemed to shout in consternation, 'what has happened? Are you having a heart attack or something? You seem to stagger. Duale you look grey; sit down. Tell me, my darling Duale, what is it?'

'It,' Duale blurted out, 'is your son. Tashi is a devil. He is a devil! And he torments me, Pema. I have the deepest suspicion that now he wants my job. Can you imagine that? I will fight him to the end – and I will win, Pema.'

There was a long silence. A look of sadness clouded Pema's eyes. At last she raised her head and looked at Duale, a man who quite suddenly seemed foreign to her; she tried not to feel frightened. In a calm and gentle voice she said 'Duale, Tashi is not only my son; he is yours also. I married you because I love you – and I will go on doing so. We must never let Tashi come between us. You must find a way so that he can get along with you. You are an older man and you must lead him. It is not the Buddhist way to quarrel. You must compromise and strive to establish harmony. Perhaps you treated him like a child; or am I wrong?'

'That is exactly what he is, Pema,' Duale replied, 'you cannot compromise with someone who is pigheaded, and wrong into the bargain. He wants TASS to get into the latest aviation technology, you know this whole satellite business; it's a waste of time and money – it's a fantasy!' Then his voice rose, 'I will never compromise with your son! I would give a lot never to see or hear of him again. He's a devil! That's the end of it!'

'Is it?' Pema quietly asked. 'Suppose he is right. After all, Duale, you are 66; Tashi is at least twenty five years younger than you. You have the experience, but perhaps he has more technical knowledge. Have you thought of retiring? Why do you always have to survive? No one can go on forever, there has to be an end.

277

Perhaps you should be thinking more realistically. Did you hear what I said...?'

Duale struggled to his feet and glared at Pema; then he thundered, 'Is this a conspiracy? Why are you supporting your son against me? Why should I retire? Unless some devil tries to cross me, I am perfectly fit in all respects. I worked and worked to reach the position I am in. Others tried to unseat me and I always survived. I told you, I will be there when the millennium dawns. My head and TASS's head will be held high. And as long as I stay we will enjoy our lifestyle, Pema. We are not invited next week to the Mayor of Chicago's reception because I am a nonentity. The Mayor knows who I am, just as hundreds, probably thousands, know me internationally. The top people at the UN called me the other day on a point. I am known in Washington. We have the house on Lake Geneva; that's where the top one percent of Chicago has a country house. Are you and I to give all this up just because a young devil has for his own reasons decided to torment me? He is like a Satan, Pema. But he will never succeed!'

'Goodnight, Duale. I don't want to see you again till you feel more rational. Have you ever thought of the fact that if it had not been for our son, someone whom I call my Treasure and whom you *dare* to regard as a devil, we would never have married? I will sleep in the guest bedroom. Goodnight. You will not feel lonely, Duale, because you have your ego to keep you company. I suggest you take a good look at your ego. And, just in passing, I think that living in retirement on Lake Geneva would be much nicer than living in the city where you go out of your way to make sure you are so terribly stressed.' Duale looked up to see a saddened face with tears falling over high cheekbones.

Pema left the hall of the apartment where she had welcomed her husband home. Duale sank into a chair and mused; now, he thought, it was as silent as it always had been until he had married. He felt lonely and vulnerable. He knew he was tired; but why, when he was convinced he was right, did he feel unhappy?

A week passed in the icy relationship before Duale managed to bring himself to ask for forgiveness. Caressing Pema, he told her that life without her love was unthinkable. To his great relief, Pema responded positively.

In an effort to break the ice, Duale had related the events of the week. There was one event, however, about which Duale had decided he should say nothing. That very day Duale had received Tashi's confirmation memorandum. Apart from summarising what he had explained to Duale, Tashi had also drawn Duale's attention to a recent statement from the insurance industry. Aircraft insurers were becoming increasingly concerned at the failure of the aviation industry to reduce the rate of accidents worldwide. With the projected increase in air traffic becoming a reality as each year passed, the insurers were predicting that soon the world should expect to hear of at least one large air transport crash every week. It was clear the insurers were already becoming anxious.

At the end of his memo, Tashi had emphasised the urgency of improving air safety, especially in developing countries. Tashi stated his recommendation in bold type: **TASS should lead the aviation world in supporting a higher level of aviation safety. Amongst other things, TASS should immediately become deeply involved in the transition to the latest satellite technology for aeronautical navigation.**

Duale had spent less than five minutes scanning the pages of Tashi's work before writing his instructions to Anna; 'No action. File.'

When Tashi called Anna the following day and courteously enquired if his memorandum had been received, Anna unconsciously committed one of the very few indiscretions of her career; she answered happily, 'Oh yes, Captain Tashi, the CEO has already passed it on to me. He has written on it 'No action; file'.'

There was a short pause, before Tashi responded, 'Thank you, Anna. Nothing else. Goodbye.'

Although Tashi seemed to be more and more absorbed by events in TASS, he did his best not to neglect his family. In particular, he and Patsri were awaiting the arrival of their new baby. It was on the first day of November 1996 that Patsri gave birth to a daughter. She had called Tashi at the office who, in his usual, well-organized way, was in a constant state of readiness to come and take his wife to the hospital. Patsri asked if Tashi could stay and hold her hand, which she found comforting in her labour. After the final great push, the pains of labour subsided. The doctor announced that Patsri had given birth to a girl. Tashi kissed his wife and whispered, 'I am so proud of you, Patsri. You have given us a lovely baby. You suggested a Thai name. Yes, Patsri, we can call her Sipang. Now you should rest. I love you, my darling.' As Tashi left the room, he turned to glance at his beautiful wife; she had already drifted into slumber. He paused for a few moments and looked at her face, which carried an ethereal smile of joy.

As Tashi walked into his office he noticed a note on his desk. He took the elevator down and knocked on the door which carried the sign: 'Gerald Strong – Head of Aeronautical Communications.' Tashi went in.

'Hello Tashi,' Gerry said, 'thank you for coming straightaway. I wanted to find out if you have made any progress with the CEO?'

'None!' Tashi replied with a certain emptiness in his voice.

'I see,' Gerry responded. 'So in TASS's interest, have you thought of applying for his job?'

'Yes I have,' replied Tashi.

'Good for you, Tashi,' Gerry went on. 'Now listen, at this stage keep quiet. Leave everything to me. I will mobilise the other Heads and we will get to the Committee and one or two of the Trustees. Don't start exposing yourself until I contact you again; do you understand, Tashi? Just forget about it for the moment. I'll get back to you in due course and we can sit down and discuss the reaction we get. OK? If we can manage this, Tashi, I think it would be fantastic. Incidentally, I know you wouldn't think of it; but when you become CEO, no favours please. What we are trying to do is for the good of air safety. That's the beginning and end of it. All we can do is our best. If we fail, I'll resign; and I think several other Heads will go too. But let's be positive; let's hope we succeed.'

'Thank you, Gerry. I will wait till I hear from you,' Tashi said.

'Goodbye, Tashi. Don't worry, everything will be all right. You are not only a breath of fresh air, Tashi; it will be like passing from a long night to brilliant daylight! See you!'

Well, Tashi thought as he retraced his steps to his office, it seems the die is cast. Gerry seemed very upbeat; they had better be careful. With my father you never know what might happen. Then, he went on thinking, why mention anything to Patsri; after all, this is all about work and she has her hands full with Little

Tashi and the baby.

It was a few days later when Anna spoke on the intercom, 'Dr. Duale, Mr. Henrikson, Member of the Executive Committee has just called,' she said, 'he would like to see you urgently this afternoon either within or outside working hours. You said 3 o'clock, Dr. Duale? Very well, I will ask him to come then.'

At precisely three Duale's door opened. With the onset of winter, the glorious view from Duale's office over Lake Michigan had become obscured by the misty gloom. Duale glanced briefly outside; he was reminded of the power of electricity as he noticed innumerable specks of light which were gathering strength around TASS's skyscraper, as the winter darkness inexorably closed in. Duale held out his hand, 'I must say, Mr. Henrikson, it is always a great pleasure to receive you. Of course, I have a duty to be impartial and perhaps I shouldn't say this; but I find discussing things with you is always so easy because, like me, you are completely straightforward. I think there is great merit in calling a spade a spade, instead of beating around the bush. And it is so much more efficient! May I suggest we sit over here. Coffee or tea?'

'Tea, please, Dr. Duale.' Duale pressed the bell and Anna repeated her routine; the tea was brought within minutes.

'I gather, Mr. Henrikson, you wanted to discuss something urgently?'

Alex Henrikson was, like Duale, an aviation lawyer. As usual, he was dressed in a dark suit. He was known for his good knowledge of aviation law and his crisp, effective interventions. Although he looked pleasant enough, in fact he rarely smiled. Duale regarded him as a worthy member of the Committee who gave Duale no trouble; in general, he was supportive of Duale during Committee meetings. Henrikson quietly cleared his throat and sipped his tea for a few moments; then he said, 'Dr. Duale, first I would like to thank you for receiving me at short notice. I know how busy you are and I will come to the point immediately; I will not take longer than necessary. As you have said, in me you have someone who calls a spade a spade. It is good to know we are on the same wavelength in that respect.

The reason I am here is simply to give you some information. I will leave you to consider it and you will decide to take some action if you feel it is needed. The fact is, Dr. Duale, for the last couple of years there have been voices of dissatisfaction regarding TASS's modus operandi, shall we say. Being the CEO, you are the one most affected by this development. At the working level, there is currently a fairly widespread feeling of disenchantment with your leadership. The Division Heads, in particular, consider that TASS is no longer in the forefront of aviation technology; in other words we tend to be a laggard instead of the leader.

I will reserve my judgement on this issue until I am better informed. As far as you personally are concerned, you are in the happy position that perhaps more information is fed to you on civil aviation developments than, perhaps, to anyone else in the world. In your case, you do not have to reserve judgement. If you do your homework, which I believe you do, you know whether TASS is leading. Personally, I have complete faith in your leadership, Dr. Duale. That is why I am here today.'

Duale sat opposite Alex Henrikson with an impassive look on his face. Inside his complex character, he was becoming increasingly curious about what would be said next. Alex Henrikson continued, 'Yes, now I come to the point, Dr. Duale. You have some opposition as far as your re-appointment is concerned. The TASS 'workers,' if I may call them that, are supporting the candidature of Captain Tashi, the flight safety specialist. They are sounding out members of the Executive Committee; it is quite possible they will be talking to some of the Trustees.

Normally, such a development would not be cause for alarm. However, what you should know is that in my discussions with other members of the Committee I have found strong support, in all respects, for Captain Tashi. There is a feeling, which seems to be growing, that TASS needs a younger man at the helm.

Of course, I do not subscribe to such a view. My assessment is that you are doing a first-class job and I am confident you will go on doing it. But I find myself in the minority, Dr. Duale, which is why I decided to seek this appointment with you. I will leave you to consider the implications.'

Alex Henrikson finished his cup of tea and prepared to leave.

'One minute, Mr. Henrikson, please,' Duale said quietly. 'I want to thank you for your loyalty to me and therefore to TASS, which I intend to go on leading. I will certainly consider this information. In the meantime, it is business as usual.'

Duale smiled and stood up. As he shook hands, Alex Henrikson produced a rare, brief smile and said, 'By all means work together with me on this. Rest assured I will keep you fully in the picture whenever I can get some reliable information. As you know you can rely on me a hundred percent.

Incidentally, Dr. Duale, while we are together, perhaps I should mention that when you eventually decide to retire, which I hope will not be for several years, I foresee that I myself will be a strong candidate for the CEO job. When the time comes, I hope our relationship will be even stronger so that you will have over-whelming confidence in giving me that all-important support at the time it will be needed. May I look to you for that, Dr. Duale?'

Without hesitation Duale responded, 'Absolutely. I like to feel our working relationship is already close. Goodbye, Mr. Henrikson.'

Although Duale had not been completely taken by surprise, mentally he had received a jolt. Although he was doing his best to remain calm, he slightly surprised himself by nervously standing up. For a moment he glanced out over the lake; he noticed it was becoming shrouded in mist. Then he began to stride around his office. From time to time, he looked out in the direction of the lake. In an extraordinary way, he realised that the misty scene was dispersing. He stopped. He continued peering into the fading mist; now the scene seemed to be lightening. Gradually, his mind's eye focused more and more strongly on an image; now he could see a face. It was the grave countenance of Joe Wilkins; near him, Duale could see an instrument landing system. Joe Wilkins seemed to be shaking his head. Duale was mesmerised as he watched the face slowly moving from side to side; then he saw Joe's index finger, which pointed directly at him.

Duale recalled that some thirty years previously it had been Joe Wilkins who had explained the importance of regular calibra-tion for navigational aids; if ground aids were not properly cali-brated, then accuracy would be affected, sometimes with disastrous results for a landing aircraft. Suddenly, he heard a siren; yes, he thought, that is the alarm to warn the technicians that the ILS was not working properly. Was he dreaming? Was he sleep-walking? No! He was awake. He felt confused. Duale contined his striding around the office.

Unnoticed by Duale, Anna had just entered in her usual discreet way. Duale, who seemd to be slightly dazed, was completing his third circuit of the office, every now and then casting a nervous glance in the direction of the lake. Then he almost bumped into Anna.

'You are thinking, Dr. Duale. It must be important. I was looking for a file; I will come back later.'

Duale gave a start; jerked out of his musing and thrown slightly off balance, he stopped and looked at the obstacle which had suddenly appeared. Then he said, 'Anna, I am very pleased to see you. Did you hear a siren?'

Anna looked perplexed; she felt a little embarrassed and laughed gently. Then she responded, 'No, Dr. Duale, I did not hear a siren.'

Duale continued, 'Yes, Anna, you are quite right as usual; I have been thinking. Now I have finished. Sit down; I have some dictation for you.'

It took Duale five minutes to dictate a note inviting all the Divisional Heads to a meeting a week later; although Duale had already decided on the outcome of the meeting, ostensibly the subject to be discussed would be the future orientation of TASS.

'It must be important, Dr. Duale,' Anna commented. 'You haven't met with all the Division Heads for more than ten years. I will make sure the meeting room is nicely arranged. Are there any supporting papers?'

'Thank you, Anna,' Duale replied, 'yes, that's a good idea. Please make copies of Captain Tashi's memorandum on the future work orientation of TASS; on the first page, take off my note to take no action and photocopy the clean page. I have changed my mind; I think the time has come for some action.'

A week later, Pema was watching Duale as he completed his morning ritual in front of the mirror. 'You don't need a mirror to reassure yourself, Duale. You really are the most handsome man in the world! You look young, handsome and vibrant.' Pema looked admiringly at her husband; then she continued. 'You have something special on today, don't you? What are you going to do?'

'Well,' Duale responded, 'I must say, Pema, you are very perceptive.' For a moment he paused for a thought, which he would keep to himself; he hoped that Pema did not have a woman's intuition as well. Then he continued, 'Yes, it is a bit special I suppose. I am going to meet with all the Division Heads. It should be quite interesting. We are starting at 10 o'clock, so I won't be home late. Have a nice day.'

'Good morning, gentlemen,' Duale seemed relaxed and good-natured as he looked around the table and briefly took in the face of each of the twenty Heads of Divisions. 'I do not intend indulging in a waste of our valuable time. But let me just say how pleasant it is for me to be sitting here with you. As far as aviation is concerned, TASS is fortunate that you probably represent the most knowledgeable and experienced technical group in the world, certainly at the operational level. If I may say so, I feel privileged to be your Chief Executive.'

While Duale was speaking, Tashi's eyes were moving from one face to the next; when he reached the Head of Communications, Tashi's eyes rested on Gerry's face for a moment. Gerry was looking at Tashi's eyes also; could Tashi detect a glimmer of a smile on Gerry's lips?

'Let me come to the point, gentlemen,' Duale continued. 'A few months ago, Captain Tashi wrote a quite excellent memorandum on how he saw the future orientation of TASS's work; I specially made time to receive him in my office so that he could make a presentation on the subject. In essence our work must, I repeat must, reflect current technology. And we must be seen to be in the forefront of the application of the latest technological developments. It's as simple as that.

As you can imagine, I have spent long hours studying Captain Tashi's memorandum. I regard what he has written as an excellent basis for further action. I only have one qualification. I believe we should go further. We absolutely must grasp all the latest developments with both hands. I also think we should be considering how we can best help the poorer countries in financing the acquisition of modern equipment. If that means that we have to establish a Financing Division, then we should do it.

As a start, gentlemen, I would ask you to do two things. First, please write on one page, that is so we avoid getting bogged down in lengthy memoranda, yes write on one page what changes each of you considers is required in each of your specialized fields, to ensure that TASS's work reflects the very latest in aerospace technological developments. As far as you, Head of Finance are concerned, I would like you to outline the merit, or otherwise, of expanding your responsibilities and developing a Financing Division. In addition, Head of Communications, I know you will pay due attention to the advantages to be gained by TASS in supporting the introduction of satellite technology in aeronautical navigation and communications, as you and Captain Tashi have already advised me.

Once you have done your research and drafted your summary page, with findings and recommendations please, send me a copy as well as to all the other Divisional Heads. We will then consider the next steps in a month's time.

Second, and perhaps I should have addressed this subject first, I would like our Head of Flight Safety, Captain Tashi, to organize an informal meeting or two to discuss the thorny question of whether we can agree on which country has the unenviable reputation as the least safe in terms of its operational aviation system, including the operation of its national airline. Depending on what you propose regarding changes in our work orientation, we may agree that TASS should start by doing whatever has to be done to convert whichever country we agree on, so that it becomes one of the safest in the world in which to fly.

Some of you may think I have been a little slow in bringing us together. You are of course entitled to your view. But I make no apology. Any possible changes have to be thought through; and I have been doing this for months. But now I am convinced that the time has come for positive action. There is no time to lose. I am sure you have read the statement from the group of aviation insurers a few days ago. Their forecast is stark! If something is not done about air safety, then as the growth of airline operations continues, the world can expect at least one major accident every week.

TASS will be instrumental in changing the situation and through its intervention air safety will be brought under control. We all have a responsibility to apply our technical skills to make this happen. My role is to implement TASS's operational policy and to co-ordinate your efforts. I have no doubt that together we shall succeed. I have no intention of allowing any hindrance to our efforts. The legacy of TASS will personify air safety to the ultimate degree.

Gentlemen, I am sure you are as busy as I am. If you have an important intervention to make, then do so now.'

Duale looked around the table for five seconds; all was silence. 'Good,' he went on, 'Let us meet again in four weeks on the same day of the week at ten o'clock. I will be looking for agreement on a recommendation that I can put to the Executive Committee. The Committee's endorsement will empower us to act. We shall then go forward. Thank you for being here today. I know I can rely on your total confidence on this subject; the last thing any of us would want is that public rumours begin to circulate about deteriorating air safety. I look forward to being with you in one month.'

Although Duale was not smiling, he looked his good-natured, benevolent best; at the same time, there was not the slightest doubt that, like a superb captain at the peak of his performance, he was fully in control of the ship. Duale got up and strode out of the room.

Tashi looked across the table at the Head of Communications; Gerry motioned gently towards the door. Tashi got up and made for the door. As he turned in the corridor, he heard Gerry's voice, 'Captain, may I have the pleasure, sir, of inviting you to drink a cup of tea or coffee in my office?' As he passed his secretary, Gerry said, 'No interruptions, please, Mary. If you could bring us a couple of coffees, that would be very sweet of you.' He smiled at Mary.

Once they were inside and Gerry had carefully closed the door, he said, 'So, Tashi my man, what did you think of that?'

'I don't know,' Tashi replied; then he went on, 'The only thing I do know is that the CEO is clever and he is a highly polished politician. Whether he will actually do what he says he will, only time will tell. I suppose we have to give him a chance. And if we do that, Gerry, then as far as my own position is concerned, we will have to be very careful. If the CEO produces, then let him go on being CEO. I am not in the category of a candidate who says, 'Anything you can do, I can do better.' I have no personal ambitions in that direction, as you know; my only consideration is the future of TASS. If we give him a chance, then it will be better to put your supporting efforts on hold. What do you think?'

Gerry looked at Tashi for a good half-minute, as though a flaw had become visible in one of his personal possessions. Then he said, 'Pity! You know, you have to admire the man; he has a wonderful sense of timing. He really is an incredible politician; have you ever witnessed a more convincing performance? But you know, Tashi, if he does come through, it will all be thanks to you – yes, only you, Tashi!

That aside, unfortunately, Tashi, I have to agree with you. We'd better wait. My only qualification is that I think we should only wait so long; otherwise we shall run out of time. Who knows, that could be the game which the CEO is playing? Anyway, he says he will meet with us again in one month, in other words in mid February. So why don't we give him till the end of March? If nothing much is happening by then, I will bring out the big guns. There is a lot of support for you in any case, Tashi; I can assure you of that. So in April and May we can consolidate; you will come into the open with your candidature in June, that is in time for the Trustees to consider appointing you in July. How's that?'

'It's fine with me, Gerry; I just want to repeat, I don't have a strong personal ambition. If the CEO comes through, then let us forget the past and support him in pushing ahead with the latest technology. Now I'm going to get back to my desk. I am all fired up with the prospect of better things in the future for TASS! And, let's face it, we will have our work cut out to identify the least safe country in the world as far as aviation is concerned.' Tashi quickly drank his coffee and seemed to almost run from Gerry's office.

Again, true to his word, in mid February 1997 Duale found himself chairing a meeting with his Divisional Heads. He handled the meeting with consummate ease. Each of the Heads warmed to him; all the participants could relate to the logic and rationality of the concise, balanced statements he made at various junctures. After three hours of orderly and thoroughly constructive discussion, Duale announced that he felt the time had come to sum up, which he did.

'Gentlemen, I have been impressed with our discussion and I would like to thank you for your participation. I will now endeavour to summarise our findings and conclusions. First, we have agreed that the least-safe aviation country on the planet is Styxia; and that in terms of our up-dated work approach Styxia should be our immediate target. In his memorandum, as you all know Captain Tashi has recommended that, on the basis of our support agreement, he visits the country as soon as possible to make an overview of flight safety measures and, if he considers it appropriate, to observe the performance of the pilots at first hand. Based on his experience and his report, we shall consider further steps to upgrade the aviation safety of the country.

That is the first, immediate step. Then we have the additional follow-up steps. These include costing the establishment of a new Financing Division and expanding the work of the Communications Division to ensure that, with immediate effect, TASS involves itself in satellite technology for civil aviation operations.

There are several other special initiatives we have discussed; I support all of these and they will be itemized to the Executive Committee. If what I have just stated reflects your views, gentlemen, I shall place all this before the Executive Committee and we will then proceed. I propose to give priority to Captain Tashi's initiative and my office will obtain the necessary clearance for Captain Tashi to undertake his visit in the near future. I suggest, Captain Tashi, you tentatively schedule your visit for mid to late April; that should be realistic.

Do we have any questions, or do we proceed as I have summarised?' Duale scanned his audience for a few seconds and then said, 'Good, thank you for your attendance...'

'Dr. Duale, I have something to say, if I may, sir?' It was Gerry.

'But of course.'

Gerry found himself staring at Tashi; after a few seconds he turned his head and looked at Duale.

'Mr. CEO. I found your summary to be admirable and I am sure we all support your excellent initiatives a hundred percent. There is just one point I would like to mention. I am wondering whether we are wise to endorse a course of action under which a TASS Head of Division travels alone to a country which we know falls far short of international aviation safety standards; after all, sir, this is a country which has had three accidents in two years. I would feel more comfortable if Captain Tashi were accompanied by, say, a navigational aids expert; or perhaps he needs an airworthiness man. To me, there is an obvious advantage in having two, rather than one, TASS technical people working in Styxia. As a basic principle, as far as our technical work is concerned, we have invariably sent a minimum of a two-man team to Third World countries. At least they have the opportunity to jointly mull over their work; the mere opportunity to talk to someone else in confidence has its advantages.'

Duale became thoughtful; Tashi did not think Duale looked happy. Then he said, 'Thank you. Of course, I have already considered this point. My conclusion was that we are responding to Captain Tashi's own proposal. He did not ask for a second man. I also took into account his superb competence; he has excellent judgement, so I believe we can be assured he knows how to look after himself. Just in passing, I could mention that I myself often travel to these countries alone. Of course, as you may imagine, I also considered the financial aspect. TASS should never be seen to be wasting money; we cannot afford luxuries. May I have your view on this, please, Head of Finance?'

The response from the Head of Finance was entirely predictable; devoid of mention of technical considerations, and as though his voice was speaking from an automatic, recorded tape, he simply said, 'I support your position very strongly, Mr. CEO. TASS should not be seen to be going overboard when it comes to spending money. There is no room in TASS for extravagance!'

'Captain Tashi, can we hear your view, please?' Duale was smiling at Tashi.

Tashi felt uncomfortable. And he did not like the smile which Duale had reserved for him; he had seen it before. He responded, 'Whether I go alone or have someone to assist me, rest assured I will do my best. I hope I recognize my limitations and I will work within them. If I am alone, this might mean that certain of my actions might be more limited than if I had, for example, a navigational aids technical consultant. In any case, from a technical viewpoint I will act with prudence. It is up to you, Dr. Duale, to decide whether I should be alone, or accompanied.'

Duale addressed the meeting, 'Captain Tashi will travel alone on his first visit, as I originally proposed. For subsequent visits, he will be accompanied by a specialist, or perhaps specialists, as may be justified. Thank you for your contributions, gentlemen. Once I have the endorsement of the Executive Committee for our proposed actions, I will get back to you. In the meantime, please carry on with your preparations to deliver TASS's revised work programme in its new format. I am convinced that our new orientation will lead to success as far as global air safety is concerned.' Duale stood up and briefly scanned the faces around the table; then he left the room.

Two weeks later, Duale met with the Executive Committee. After a short discussion on the item, he said, 'May I take it that I have your endorsement for the first step, and only the first step, in revising the orientation of TASS's work programme? At this stage, the proposal is that Captain Tashi travels to one of the weaker countries to review their flight safety capability. Depending on the results, TASS may need to expand its work to embrace other countries. I will of course refer back to you with future proposals as they arise.' The Committee members nodded their assent.

Then Duale heard Alex Henrikson clearing his throat. 'I would like to make a short comment, please, Mr. CEO. It is this. I think the Committee should congratulate you on your initiative; our appreciation should be conveyed to the Board of Trustees. I would also mention that, in due course, I believe TASS should become directly involved with satellite technology developments. There may also be merit in TASS establishing some sort of financing support for the Third World, especially for the weaker countries. I am sure you have this under review, and I have every confidence that you will take this whole re-orientation approach further as required.'

Duale thanked Alex Henrikson for his comments. 'I am only doing my job,' he said, 'however, if it is the Committee's wish, I will pass the essence of Mr. Henrikson's points on to the Board.' The members nodded.

At 3 o'clock on the first day of April 1997 Tashi made his way to Duale's office; Anna had called him to say that Duale would like to see him. 'Good afternoon, Anna,' Tashi said. Anna swivelled around; Tashi loved her warm smile.

'Good afternoon, Captain Tashi. Please go straight in. Dr. Duale is expecting you.'

'Do you know what he wants, Anna?' Tashi asked.

'I think it's routine, Captain Tashi. It's probably about your visit to Styxia.'

'Well,' Tashi commented, as he quietly approached Duale's door, 'I feel like a lamb going to the slaughter.' Tashi smiled briefly at Anna as he opened the door; as he went in he heard Anna say, 'You men take life too seriously. The world will still go on whether you're around or...' Anna's voice faded as Tashi closed the door.

Duale leapt up and strode towards him. 'It's good to see you, Captain Tashi,' he said. 'I will not keep you long; let us sit over here. Why don't you sit on the sofa; then you get the view over the lake. At last we seem to be into Spring; what a glorious day we have for a change.'

Tashi sat down and wondered what Duale would say next. He had become conditioned to Duale's benevolent approach and could not resist an inner feeling of suspicion.

'Yes, Captain Tashi,' Duale said. 'I wanted to tell you personally that I am very grateful to you. Our last discussion was not easy. But it served to jerk me out of a rut. I think it would have taken me longer to act, if we had not had that discussion.' Anna had discreetly entered and placed a tray with coffee in front of the men.

Duale continued, 'The main reason I wanted to see you this afternoon is to tell you that I have the clearance of the Committee to proceed as we have discussed; and the first step, of course, is for you to review the safety situation in Styxia. For the last few weeks, I have been in contact with the civil aviation authorities there and I have their agreement that TASS will carry out a flight safety survey which, to them, will be at no cost. Today, they confirmed they have processed your entry visa and it will be available at the airport for your collection on arrival.

If you agree, I would like to suggest you arrive in Styxia on about 20 April. Your work in the country should take, I would imagine, ten to fourteen days. So we shall look forward to seeing you back here in early May. I have been to Styxia twice. They are pleasant people, but they struck me as rather removed from the real world. In certain respects, I suppose they are. I am sure you will get on well with them. I don't quite remember, have you visited Styxia before?'

'No', Tashi responded, 'But I read a book on the little country.

Centuries ago the inhabitants thought they had some sort of link with Greek mythology – that's why it's called Styxia. Yes, I read there were nine rivers in the underworld and the river Styx was used to ferry the souls of the dead. I hope the mythology is not related to the present.' Tashi smiled a little; then he went on, 'Anyway, my work is very much above the earth, in the air – nothing to do with the underworld.'

Duale looked thoughtful. Then Tashi watched him turn his head; he was looking in the direction of the lake. Tashi followed his gaze and saw that a light mist was rising over the lake. Duale seemed to be focusing on an image in the mist; straining his eyes, Tashi tried to see what Duale was looking at. He saw nothing – only the mist. He briefly looked at Duale; a smile was crossing Duale's face.

Then Duale said, 'Captain Tashi if you agree with my suggested schedule, once you have the actual arrival date perhaps you could draft a fax with Anna to say when you will arrive and so on. Do you have any questions, Captain?'

Tashi finished his coffee and looked at Duale. Then he said, 'What you have told me is fine, Dr. Duale. I will do the necessary. I only have one question. You have said the Executive Committee has endorsed the proposed course of action. Does that mean they agree with the whole re-orientation programme, including TASS's involvement in satellite communications and financing support; or has the Committee endorsed only my visit to Styxia?'

Duale smiled, 'You really are on the ball, Captain Tashi. What you are actually talking about concerns my scope of work, in my capacity as CEO. In any case, the Committee has been informed and in general the members endorse the new course of action; they have given their immediate go-ahead for your visit as the first step in TASS's new approach. I hope that is clear, Captain Tashi. I am sure you will have a successful trip. Bon voyage.'

Duale stood up; as he extended his hand towards Tashi, he found he was looking at Tashi's back. Tashi was soon at the office door. Tashi turned briefly and said, 'Goodbye, Dr. Duale.' Duale smiled; he noticed the deadly serious expression on Tashi's face. As the door closed, Duale thought, 'Good riddance. I hope you have a lot of problems. Who knows, anything can happen – and I hope it does! Otherwise, we can always arrange another dangerous consultancy trip. You devil!'

Upto the day when Tashi flew out of Chicago, his time passed in a flash. For the last evening he had arranged for the neighbour's daughter to babysit the children, so that he could take Patsri out. Tashi had asked Anna where he should take his wife for dinner. Anna responded instantly, 'The Casablanca restaurant. It's on the 60th floor of a huge skyscraper. I will never forget it. I was taken to dinner there once by Dr. Duale, before he was married.'

As they stepped out of the elevator, Patsri squeezed Tashi's arm. 'What an amazing view, Tashi. All those lights round the edge of the lake. It's wonderful!' Patsri and Tashi were escorted to their table and as Patsri looked out, she noticed that the view was gradually changing.

'Oh, Tashi. You are wonderful! I have never been in a revolving restaurant before.'

'My darling,' Tashi said, 'this is the least I can do. We have been so busy for the last few weeks, I have positively neglected you. I suppose that's the way it is with most of us. But don't worry, I will make it up to you. Now we should strengthen ourselves. Take a look at the menu; choose whatever you like.'

As they enjoyed their meal, their conversation centred on the children. Then Patsri said, 'Where are you going, Tashi?'

'To a little country called Styxia. I'm going to make a general review; then TASS will help them upgrade themselves. But that will be later, the follow-up stage, Patsri.'

'How interesting for you, Tashi,' Patsri rejoined, 'and who is going with you?'

'I am going alone, Patsri. Obviously, I can't cover everything, but I should be able to make a pretty good overall assessment.'

Patsri commented, 'That's very unusual, isn't it? You don't usually travel alone in this age of specializations. Anyway, I'm never worried about you. You always do the right thing and you know how to look after yourself.'

The following evening Tashi left for the first leg of his journey and the next day he was sitting in a Tupolev heading for Styxia. At the airport he was politely met by the duty officer, who arranged for the entry visa to be stamped in his passport. Then a black limousine took him to the hotel, where he was met by his interpreter.

'Welcome to Styxia, Captain Tashi,' the interpreter said. 'My name is Boris. We know Dr. Duale well; he only sends his best men to visit us. Here is a work programme, which we hope you will find agreeable. You will be picked up tomorrow morning at eight o'clock. The temperature will be about minus 10 celsius; so dress warmly. You will be taken first to the Director General's office; our DG was a General in the military. In the evening there will be a dinner for you, which will be attended by all the heads of the various civil aviation sections. Now I will show you your room.'

The interpreter led the way. 'Here we are. Because your stay will be several days, we have given you another room, in here, where you can read or write. The refrigerator is full of bottles.'

'Well, thank you,' Tashi said as he explored the accommodation. He wandered into the bathroom, which he gauged was about the size of his living room in Chicago. 'I'm sure I will be very comfortable.' Wherever he had been in the former communist world, he thought, it was the same. The political system which represented the poor had built some of the most spacious hotels on the planet.

The following morning he was shown into the director general's sumptuous office. 'Good morning, director general.'

'Ah yes, you are Captain Tashi of TASS. You look too young to be a specialist for anything. How old are you, young man?'

Tashi smiled at the director general. Styxia's civil aviation organization co-ordinated the activities of everything to do with civil aviation, including the airline's operations, a hang-over from the communist days. Tashi took in the DG's appearance and bearing; he was a man of about fifty-five, Tashi thought, and his fresh face exuded energy. His blue eyes stared unblinkingly. The DG was wearing a dark blue tunic with brass buttons down the centre.

'I am 40,' Tashi responded crisply, 'and should I ask you your age; or would you consider that impolite of a youngster?' Tashi was relaxed and smiling. 'May I thank you for the arrangements to meet me and to escort me to the hotel?'

A long silence ensued while the director general eyed Tashi. Then the DG said, 'I understand you are a flight safety man. How many hours do you have?'

Tashi smiled; he decided to avoid answering for the moment.

295

There was a pause; the DG felt he could win a point or two, as he made a verbal thrust: 'You have not yet answered. I hope you are not being evasive.'

Tashi smiled again; then he said, 'Now it is your turn, General, to answer a question. You have a military background? Or am I wrong, sir?'

'You are right.' The General beamed at Tashi.

For his part, Tashi was not sure whether the smile was one of scorn; or was the DG becoming more relaxed? Tashi stared at the white teeth and wondered whether they were natural; on balance, he thought they were not. Tashi noticed two gold-capped teeth, one on either side of the mouth.

'General, I think we are going to get on well together. I can imagine you were a very good military pilot before transferring to the aviation authority.'

'You are right again. Yes, I retired from the military to take up this job. In the military I was a General; now I am a civilian. I am called the Director General of Civil Aviation. I will never get used to civilians; they never do what I command them to do!'

'So, General, I was right; you are a famous and great military man. If that is correct, then I seem to be making good progress – or not?' The General laughed.

'Good,' Tashi continued, 'now it is your turn to answer again, General. How many hours do you have?'

The military director general stared at Tashi. Tashi thought the smile was of a man who had no more challenges left in his life. His attitude showed he had achieved everything; and he knew it. The DG said with an air of finality, 'I have 5000 hours. Some military, some domestic, some international.'

'That's wonderful,' Tashi commented with a grin. 'I have 7000 hours. Now can we start to discuss the work programme, please, director general? If TASS is to help your organization in the most effective way, I will need to see all of your main facilities. Among friends, there is no point in hiding anything. You may be the best pilot in the world; but you are not one of the captains who is flying the airline's aircraft. The fact is that the airline has reported three major accidents in two years; as you know, there were two others which you did not report.'

The DG sat bolt upright; with a look of incredulity, he interjected, 'You seem to know everything!'

Tashi continued, 'We have to find the reasons for that. There is no mystery. Accidents don't happen by chance. There are reasons. If together we can put our fingers on the main problem areas, then together we can solve the problem. I hope you agree, General?'

'Yes, I do,' the DG said in a quiet, unassuming way. Now the facade had been replaced by realism. 'You are young, Captain Tashi, but I see you have experience. Yes, we need help. Go and make your review and I will instruct all my staff to fully co-operate with you. When you have finished, report back to me and we will discuss further. We have terrible problems with foreign exchange, which is why so much of our equipment is old. There is no money to buy new equipment and it gets more difficult to maintain the old rubbish. Then we have a staffing problem. On the whole, our personnel are well educated. But we don't have the money to pay them properly. So we often find that just when they are becoming experienced, they leave for a better job. You can't blame them; they have to eat. And in this climate if you don't eat, you get sick; you may die!

Yes, we have terrible problems; I suppose that is why we have accidents. As I said, do the review. That will be stage one; then we shall see if we can advance to stage two.'

In contrast to his earlier ebullient attitude, the DG sounded sad, almost morose; Tashi also detected a tone of desperation. Tashi stood up to take his leave. The DG walked around his desk and held out his hand, 'I enjoyed talking with you. You have brought some fresh air with you; you must leave the fresh air here, Captain Tashi. If you can do a good job, we might somehow manage an upgrading. Let us try! Have a good day, as the Americans say. I will be present at the dinner this evening.'

'Thank you, General. I will do my best. I will get back to you.' Tashi felt happily relieved as he left the warm office and, once outside, suddenly noticed the cold air striking his limbs.

That evening, Tashi attended the dinner which was offered in his honour in the hotel where he was staying. He was personally introduced by the DG to the heads of the various sections. Only the Chief Pilot of Styxia Airlines was missing; the DG explained he had decided to fly as captain on a new route. The Chief Pilot would return before the end of Tashi's survey. 'The man you just shook hands with,' the DG said, 'was the Head of Air Traffic Control. Now I shall introduce you to the Head of Airworthiness.'

A young, beautiful woman stepped forward with blond hair and sparkling blue eyes. In a quiet, shy way, the beautiful creature spoke, 'My name is Natascha, a Russian name I was given when our country was communist. I am pleased to meet you, Captain.' Tashi gulped and thought of Patsri; unfortunately, this was of little help.

The dinner followed the usual pattern. The food seemed to be incidental; there were frequent short speeches, punctuated by toasts and much merry-making. Tashi limited his intake of local brandy and various schnapps as much as he could, in contrast to the other participants who seemed intent on consuming as much alcohol as their constitutions would permit.

For Tashi, the single redeeming feature of the dinner was that Natascha was seated next to him. She seemed angelic in appearance and well-educated. She told Tashi that she had learned her English in school, after which she had attended a scientific institution in France, where she had studied physics. With this common element in their educational backgrounds, they found themselves absorbed in discussion for the entire dinner. The only interruptions were caused by the crescendoes of boisterous outbursts which sometimes drowned Tashi's voice.

Over the following days, Tashi carried out his work meticulously; he always aimed for, and usually achieved, a level of perfection. Each evening he would work long hours into the night as he made his notes and tried to piece together what to him had become an aviation jigsaw. As his task progressed, he focused on gaps and failings. Soon, he thought, the survey will be complete; then I can discuss the situation with the DG and leave for Chicago. Then TASS can follow up.

One evening, he was finishing yet another mediocre meal in the hotel's restaurant. His interpreter appeared and sat down.

'Would you like something to eat, Boris?' Tashi asked.
'Thank you, Captain Tashi. I will choose something from the menu. So at last your work is nearly finished. I will make an appointment for you to see the DG. What about the day after tomorrow?'

'Yes, that should be fine, thank you,' Tashi replied.

'So you have done a lot of work with us; plenty of things to put right, I suppose?' Boris continued. 'Incidentally, Captain Tashi, how did you find the Head of Airworthiness?'

'You mean Natascha? Well,' Tashi explained, 'I am not an airworthiness expert. But I have discussed her field with her, that is to the extent I could. In a nutshell, she is very well educated and knows some theory. But she has absolutely no hands-on experience. With airworthiness, experience is the key. She doesn't have any experience. So this means the airline does not have proper airworthiness controls, which of course is very serious.'

Boris let his knife and fork drop on to his plate as he let out a bellow of laughter; then he swigged some vodka.

'May I share the joke with you, Boris. What are you laughing about?' Tashi asked with a look of mild dismay.

Boris' laughter subsided and he smiled at Tashi. 'Captain Tashi,' he said, 'you mentioned that Natascha lacks hands-on experience. Would you like to find out the extent of her hands-on experience, Captain Tashi? I think you would learn a lot. When Dr. Duale was here we organized some hands-on experience for him. He loved it! You must be tired of your work; she could meet you in your bedroom in half an hour. And it would be courtesy of the airline.'

Tashi, who showed not the slightest surprise, looked at Boris for a few seconds. Everything Tashi had looked at had revealed the cancer of arrogant neglect, ignorance of basic technical norms and misapplication of procedures. And now the rotten aviation set-up wanted to thrust a beautiful whore at him. Tashi simply said, 'No thank you. Good night.'

Two days later Tashi was received again by the DG; this time he had arranged for the presence of the airline's Chief Pilot. Tashi made an excellent presentation and methodically ran through his list of failings. He was anxious not to be too blunt, because he had no wish to antagonize the DG who, in due course, would be a critical player in the game of gaining the government's agreement for reforms.

When Tashi had finished, he invited comments or questions. The DG expressed appreciation and looked forward to receiving TASS's report; there would have to be positive action to put things right.

'Chief Pilot, do you have any questions?' the DG asked.

'Yes,' the Chief Pilot responded, 'I do have one point. Captain Tashi, you have talked about the failings of some of the pilots in their procedures and lack of discipline on the flight deck; you also talked about the lack of an air safety culture, not to mention poor airmanship. I find this strange. Our pilots attend their simulator training at six monthly intervals and they pass with flying colours.

Because of my absence, I was not flight checked by you. I would like to suggest that before you leave you check me out on one of our regional jets? What about early tomorrow morning? I would like you to take back a more positive picture. I will prove how well we can fly.'

'That is fine with me,' responded Tashi, 'but on one condition. I do not know when your navigational aids were last calibrated. The engineers told me they were checked and adjusted a month ago. But the records were not produced. So I have limited my flight checking to routine flying on non-directional beacons and VORs; as far as the approaches were concerned, we only made visual approaches. There were no instrument approaches. I could flight check you on the same basis, that is without you demonstrating an instrument approach. Is that agreed?'

'Yes, I think so,' replied the Chief Pilot. 'I understand that what you are saying is that you can do the checking provided we have visual flying conditions?'

'Exactly,' said Tashi.

'Well, all right,' the Chief Pilot continued, 'let us do that. It is quite true the ILS was checked last month. I returned the other day from a new destination. I used the ILS when I returned. Of course, it's easy here because we all know the airspace and topography anyway, like the back of our hand.'

'That may be,' Tashi interjected, 'but there are some hills quite close to the airport. All the pilots should be thoroughly competent in instrument flying conditions. It's always useful to have some local knowledge; but you cannot rely on local knowledge as a substitute when you are making an instrument approach.'

'I see you stick to the letter of the law, or should I say the rule-book, Captain Tashi. Unfortunately, the way things are in this area of the world, sometimes we have to be a bit more imaginative. Anyway, I will meet you at the tower tomorrow morning at 0730 hours. Provided the conditions are half reasonable, you can check me out. I want to prove that, as far as I know, my procedures are perfect; then at least you can give me a positive flight check report. I think that would be very much in the interest of the airline.'

'Before I leave you, General, may I ask one question, please?' Tashi asked.

'Of course, Captain Tashi' the DG replied.

'It is just that I am a little curious,' Tashi explained. 'Although your airport is usable, I wonder why you chose to construct the runway so that the hills are quite close to the approach path? The hills could easily have been taken out of the picture if the runway orientation had been moved around another 15 degrees or so. What I would like to explain is that your instrument landing system is of a very old design. If the localizer should not be functioning properly, then it can give an aircraft a false course. If you study aircraft accident reports, one of the things we have learned is that in cases where there has been a problem of this type – and this especially happens with older equipment – usually you can trace a malfunctioning either to a complete lack of maintenance, or sometimes to incorrect maintenance. In the case here, if an aircraft deviates on to a false course, that could lead the aircraft directly into the hilly area, which would be dangerous, especially in bad weather. And in any case, as you know, it is in poor visibility that you have to rely on the ILS. Have I made myself clear, General?'

'You are quite right,' the DG responded. 'You know, all I can say is that small countries like ours are victims of corruption. We have very little foreign exchange. When it comes to help, beggars cannot be choosers. The consulting firm which gave us this advice, which we now know was bad advice, was from the west; the airport planning project was a gift arranged by one of the embassies. We learned later that the consulting firm's people were not much good; in fact they went out of business.

At the time they were awarded the contract to advise our Government on the construction of the airport, the firm paid a higher bribe to the top people in our Government than their competitors. So they were awarded the contract. It was as simple as that. Now we have a runway which does not have the best orientation. I hope that answers your question?'

'Thank you for your frankness, General. I am looking forward to completing my work tomorrow morning. Once I am back in

Chicago, I will prepare the final report and this will be forwarded to you under cover of a letter from Dr. Duale. Then TASS and your administration will go forward together. I hope I have the pleasure of meeting you on a future occasion, General. Goodbye.' Tashi offered his hand, which the General firmly took hold of. Tashi noticed the gold teeth again.

Tashi awoke the following morning to brilliant sunshine. He had asked for an early breakfast. As he munched the hard bread and drank the weak tea, he thought how nice it was that this was his last breakfast in Styxia. No doubt Styxia must have its beauty spots, Tashi thought, but he had not seen them; so he would take back only a memory of a land which resembled a moonscape with its vast gravelly, featureless plains, occasionally relieved by treeless, rocky hills.

He hoped the flight checking would be completed in the morning, which would mean that he would be able to leave Styxia on the late afternoon flight; this would connect with the trunk route to New York. All being well, he would return to Chicago on the following day, during the afternoon.

Tashi met the Chief Pilot as had been agreed. The crew comprised the captain, first officer and the flight engineer. The flight plan was filed and the latest meteorological reports were made available. After the captain had studied the weather data, Tashi asked for a forecast. The senior meteorologist replied, 'Well, I think you can see for yourself how things are. All of this is a high pressure zone and it should last for a day or two. There might be a little harmless cloud, but nothing to worry anybody. Our Chief Pilot knows his way around these parts. No problem!'

Tashi carefully watched the actions of the Chief Pilot and noted all the procedures followed; he was impressed with the thoroughness of the Chief Pilot's approach to the impending flight. Next, Tashi observed the Chief Pilot carrying out the numerous pre-flight checks on the aircraft. As necessary, technical records were consulted.

At last, they were ready to taxi. Following procedures in the strictest sense, the captain was given clearance by the tower to take off. Applying full throttle, the aircraft noisily accelerated down the runway. At precisely the correct speed, the captain rotated. They were airborne. Captain Tashi sat in the jumpseat behind the captain and briefly commented, 'Everything perfect.'

In accordance with the flight plan, the captain set the aircraft's heading to a certain VOR; twenty minutes later, the first officer reported that they were overhead. After three more legs had been successfully flown, it was time to return to the airport. Up to this point all manoeuvres had been perfectly executed.

'So you have the airport in sight, Captain?' Tashi asked, 'as you know, for a visual approach the runway must be in sight from a distance of four nautical miles. Do you have the runway in sight, Captain?'

The captain hesitated for a few seconds; then he said, 'I did have it in sight. But now we have a little cloud. But there is no problem, Captain Tashi. I know exactly where I am. I have already locked on to the ILS localizer and we have just flown over the outer marker. Everything is functioning perfectly. I know where I am.'

'Captain, I am sure you do,' Tashi interjected. 'But you remember our agreement. You must make a visual approach. If you cannot see, then you must climb and go round again. As you know better than I do, if the localizer is out of calibration you will be flying a false course; that could mean a significant deviation. And there are some quite big hills in the area. You are not to use the ILS!'

'I see no reason to waste fuel, Captain Tashi. I am not going round again. The approach is perfect. I will just duck under that cloud and we shall be down. If we go round again, the weather may be worse next time. Then what do we do? In theory I suppose we should divert, but that would be a waste of time. And you would miss your flight into the bargain.' The captain half- turned his head towards Tashi; he laughed.

'Captain,' Tashi was now speaking with a voice that was in command, 'Captain, the last consideration is my flight; I can leave later. I must instruct you to go round again. Climb away immediately and ensure you have adequate altitude to clear the hills. Immediately!'

'No,' the captain responded, 'I refuse your command. You are an outsider; you have no legal authority to give me orders. I am the commander of the aircraft. Keep quiet and everything will be fine. As you can see, I am precisely on the glide path; now we are passing over the middle marker. We will be out of this cloud any second. Then I will have the runway in sight. Keep quiet!'

The First Officer spoke, 'Captain, my advice is that we should go round again. If we meet similar conditions, then we should divert. Captain Tashi is right. We must follow procedures!'

'When I need your advice, I shall ask for it. I want no more distractions!' At that very second, the aircraft broke out of the swirling cloud. The captain briefly felt a surge of triumph racing through his veins. In contrast, Tashi was seized with anxiety.

'Oh my God!,' the captain shouted, 'where is the runway?' Then he shrieked, 'there is no runway'.

'Take off the flap and pull the nose up, Captain!' Although Tashi's voice was authoritative, he conveyed not the slightest tone of panic. 'Pull it up, Captain. There is a hill straight ahead. Turn left, Captain. Keep climbing! You must miss the hill!'

The aircraft began to vibrate. Bells rang out. Tashi knew a stall was imminent. The vibration became a judder. The hill loomed closer. 'Dip the nose a little, Captain, and keep turning left. When the vibration stops, do your best to climb away – but not too steeply. Just enough to miss the hill.'

Tashi noticed that the shoulders and back of the captain were saturated in sweat. 'Keep calm, Captain. You may just manage. Hold on. Concentrate!' Tashi shouted in measured tones.

During those agonizing minutes, no one could have understood better than Tashi that, ultimately, the question was whether the performance of the aircraft would, in effect, defy the laws of physics. Tashi had his gravest doubts. If only, just for once, he could have been wrong. But again, he was right.

As the captain tried once more to pull the nose up to avoid a huge spur which seemed to jut out of the hill, there was a violent judder. And the aircraft stalled. At that moment it was about 300 feet above the slope of the hill. The crew instantly knew there was not the faintest hope of the aircraft recovering from the stall. Although it was carrying virtually no load, after its final judder and one or two excruciatingly strong vibrations, the aircraft no longer had the speed and the lift, not to mention the power, to remain airborne; the physical conditions needed to enable the aircraft to fly had ceased to exist.

The jet fell, and hit the stony hillside. As it crashed, the fuselage broke into three sections. One of the wings was still attached to the fuselage; the other had been severed as the aircraft tore through the trees which had taken strong root in the hillside.

The tower air traffic controllers sounded the alarm. The response was pathetically weak. The airport was not equipped with the standard rapid intervention and crash rescue vehicles; this is mandatory at all major airports. After several minutes, a truck with a few helpers on board made its laborious way towards the crash site; although there was no fire, a cloud of dust was now rising above the canopy of trees. Shortly after reaching the airport perimeter, the truck came to a halt and the helpers went forward on foot into the hilly area. After about forty minutes, they noticed the first tell-tale signs of the accident; pieces of metal littered the ground. Ten minutes later, they reached the doomed aircraft. The scene was one of utter desolation. Two of the helpers clambered on to the front section of the fuselage and peered into the flight deck area. The captain and Tashi were strapped into their seats.

They were dead.

The contrast in their appearance was nothing less than remarkable. Blood was trickling through the pilot's thick matted hair, as well as from his mouth; his teeth were covered in blood. As the blood reached his sweaty shirt, the deep stain of the mixture of blood and sweat was steadily extending over the upper part of his body; soon it would congeal. As for the expression on his face, it was contorted in terrified, agonised desperation. In contrast, Tashi sat unblinkingly behind him in the jumpseat. He looked perfectly composed. There was no sign of blood, nor sweat for that matter. Above all, he seemed relaxed and at peace with the world. The expression on his face was ethereal.

Two days later, on the other side of the world, Anna had just reached her office. Duale arrived a few minutes later. 'Good morning, Anna. What a wonderfully clear morning. Is there a more beautiful place in the world than Chicago on a morning like this? The view from my office will be superb. Come in for a moment and let us enjoy it together.'

As Duale entered his office he heard Anna's phone ring. 'I will come in a moment, Dr. Duale. There is an urgent fax. Someone is on the way up with it. I will be with you in a moment.'

'Of course, Anna.' Duale was looking out over the lake. There was not a cloud in the sky; he was just thinking that he had never been able to see so far.

Anna walked in. Duale did not turn to look at her; instead he was intent on pointing out one or two landmarks. 'You know, Anna, I have never seen that lighthouse before. And today it is so clear. Do you see it?' He heard no reaction from Anna; so he turned his head towards her. Her lips were trembling and her face had lost its colour.

'What has happened, Anna? You are so pale! Sit down a moment. Now tell me, what is it?'

Anna's hands began to shake violently; she was holding the fax. Through her sobs, she tried to look at Duale, but his image was blurred through her tears. At last she said, 'Dr. Duale, please excuse me. I think I am going to faint. This fa... fax has j... just arr-rived. Captain Tashi, your son, D..Dr. D..Duale has d..died in...in an acc...cident.'

Then Anna took an unsteady step in the direction of a chair; as always, she did her best. Before she could reach it, she fainted; and she fell to the floor.

Chapter Seventeen

The Survivor Stumbles

It was eleven o'clock at night before Duale arrived home on the fateful day that he had learned of Tashi's death. As he turned the corner and headed for the apartment building, he tried to recall what he had been doing the whole day. He failed; just as he would fail again and again over the ensuing weeks. He knew that the fax had arrived first thing in the morning and he remembered that he had called TASS's nurse to help revive Anna. He had suggested to Anna that she should go home and rest. He remembered Anna's question:

'When you approved the record of the meeting with the Divisional Heads, why did you have the section about the danger of Captain Tashi travelling alone, deleted?'

Duale had answered dismissively, simply saying, 'The Trustees are interested only in decisions for action, not discussion!'

Although Duale had not planned Tashi's death directly, he had certainly recognized that Styxia's aviation was unsafe; if Tashi became involved in an accident, so much the better. Duale had been instrumental not only in having the least-safe airline in the world identified; it had been his decision that Tashi should work in Styxia on his own, deprived as he was of support. Now that the accident had actually taken place, in a sense Duale had been caught off balance. He could not claim to be happy, as he had expected. Instead, he found himself in a state of shock. Looking into the future, Duale's vision lacked clarity. All he could see was uncertainty.

He had been left alone; that he knew. But what had he been doing? He had certainly looked at a couple of files. But what else? His mind was a blank. He had not been conscious of his seemingly endless musing. He had sat motionless at his desk for hours, in fact almost 12 hours; and his keen mind, which as a matter of course worked like a tireless dynamo, had apparently simply stopped functioning, as though it had suffered a paralytic affliction at its energy source.

As Duale entered the apartment building, he was seized with deep concern. How would he handle Pema? What should he say? Or should he keep quiet? Why had he left it to the last minute to think of this? He had spent the whole day in the office. What had he been thinking about; what had he been doing? He had no answer.

His key turned in the lock; he went in. As he hung up his cashmere overcoat in the hall, he sensed how quiet things were in the apartment. Often he had heard Pema's voice welcome him; now all was silence as he peered into the gloom of the sitting room. He switched on the light and strode towards a small mahogany table on which he could see a note. He sat down and read it:

'Dear Duale,

Anna called me mid morning and she told me about my Treasure, our son. I am very distressed; although I am doing my best to be calm, the way I feel at the moment is that I can see no reason to go on living this life. I called you in the office but no one answered the phone. I waited all day without hearing your voice, which I do not understand. I am taking the flight at eight o'clock to Bangkok, from where I will travel on to Bhutan. There I will make Tashi's funeral arrangements. I believe Tashi has left our world because he was too good for it. I also believe he will be born again as a lama and that his next life will be a stepping stone to reaching the Lord Buddha's paradise. In the meantime, I hope his spirit will reside not far from the foot of the godly mountain.

I ask you to arrange immediately to have any remains of Tashi embalmed and sent to Thimphu. I expect them to arrive within the next 72 hours – I hope you will personally ensure this.

I wanted to take Patsri and the children with me, but Patsri has collapsed She is under sedation in the hospital at the moment. When she contacts you, please arrange for her and the children to follow me to Thimphu. I will make sure they are looked after. I think this is the best way.

I hope to return, alone, in about two months. Then we will have to see whether we have a future together. Anna has told me that it was your decision that Tashi should be alone with one of the least-safe airlines in the world. Until I hear your full explanation, Duale, I will not jump to any conclusions. In the meantime, I hope you continue to survive; as I understand it, this is what you want to do.

Now I must attend to more important matters. Tashi's funeral should have already started, which is why I had to leave immediately. As soon as possible, Tashi's soul must be cleansed and nourished, so that he will have the most successful next life which is possible.

Goodbye, Duale. Pema'

Duale re-read Pema's letter. Then he sank back into his easy chair and closed his eyes. He briefly wondered whether he was part of the real world; and if his world represented the real world, which he thought it did, then he was conscious of a change. But he could not define what, in a basic sense, had changed; just as had happened earlier that day in the office, he seemed to be looking at a new situation which was amorphously grey.

He fleetingly thought how Pema's letter was balanced, in spite of the poor creature being stricken with grief. But most of his thinking was directed at himself. How in fact did he feel? The short answer was that he did not feel very much. What he did notice was that the longer he sat in the chair, the better he felt. He was relieved that he had not been confronted by Pema. Although he would, as always, have put on the best face possible, he might have been found wanting. He felt grateful that he had not become involved in a face to face explanation. Eventually, Pema would confront him. By that time, he would be well prepared to counter effectively; in the end, time would be the great healer.

Duale turned his thoughts to TASS. Whatever might be said, Duale would explain that it was always easy to be wise with hindsight. Over the years, he had learned how to cope and turn the tables on those who dared to utter any inkling of criticism. Yes, as far as TASS was concerned, he felt confident.

Now that Tashi was dead, above all Duale was conscious of a

feeling of relief that Tashi would no longer be there to torment him. Duale went further; he had no wish to speculate, but he could not avoid mentally observing that in spite of his undeniably high level of expertise, Tashi had died on duty, whereas he, Duale, continued to survive. Surely this was a clear sign that the aviation world needed Duale – was it not? A hidden hand was almost certainly at work.

With these thoughts, Duale rose from his chair and put out the lights. Feeling more relaxed by the minute, he fell into a deep slumber; and he slept like a child.

While Duale slept, his wife was wide awake. Sitting in the inter continental jet on the long haul to Thailand, she sobbed from time to time in her grief. A flight attendant asked Pema if something could be done to help her. 'No thank you,' Pema replied, 'it is that I have just lost my son. If you could bring some water, that would be fine. I don't want any food, thank you.'

After a few hours, Pema slipped into a first fitful slumber, the first of several; each time she awoke she found herself consciously thinking, 'Where am I? Oh yes, I am flying to Bhutan.'

Eventually, Pema was conscious of the first, faint glimmer of rationalization, a coming to terms with the reality of life and death. Yes, she thought, Tashi was too good for this life. Throughout his life he personified perfection. It would only be a question of time before he reached paradise. And did Pema imagine that Tashi's paradise would take a certain form and that it would include particular characteristics? Certainly.

Pema closed her eyes. She thought of some of the great mountains which were described in Buddhist scripture. Within the snow-capped peaks of these mountains, the gods resided. And it would eventually be through the medium of the lotus flower that Tashi would be finally reincarnated into paradise. Pema had been instructed in the Mahayana teachings of the Sukhavati-Vyuha and she strongly accepted the concept of the final attainment of a life free of cares, a life without differentiation between the sexes and, above all, a pure life which had a supernatural power to move wherever it might wish.

Pema envisioned the Buddha Amitabha, who was seated on his lotus throne, supported by gorgeously plumed peacocks. The Buddha, who was sitting in meditation, resided at the highest level of a splendid palace ornamented with gold, the gold reflecting the Buddha's wisdom and teaching which stretched over a vast area.

Pema's mind's eye moved to the garden around the palace; the grounds were walled. The colourful flowers were fresh and here and there she could see ponds with beautiful lotus flowers. The trees were shining with gold decoration and in the crown of the branches she could see the sign of the Buddha, which symbolized the spreading of the Buddha's teachings far afield.

Pema's musing was interrupted; it was the senior flight attendant. 'Ladies and Gentlemen. We are approaching Don Muang, Bangkok's International Airport. Please fasten your seat belts. Thank you.' Pema mentally braced herself to contend with the present, real world. Her stop-over was brief and she would soon be boarding the regional jet which would fly her to Calcutta and on to Thimphu. She just had time to make a brief telephone call to Patsri's parents; as soon as Patsri's mother answered the phone, Pema broke down. Through her sobbing, she passed on the sad news and explained she was on her way to Thimphu for Tashi's funeral.

Meanwhile, half a world away, Duale had awoken to another gloriously clear spring day. He had decided to go early to the office. After the happenings of the previous day he wanted to return to his routine and review his files. The loss of Tashi would affect TASS's operations; but there should be a limit. Normality must be restored in the shortest possible time. As always, Duale should set an example. His first act, he thought, should be to look over Anna's desk and glance inside each of the several files which were lying there; perhaps he would discover an important matter which was awaiting his urgent attention. He hoped Anna would come soon; in difficult or complex situations he always felt reassured if she was there.

Wearing his lightweight coat, Duale left the apartment building and strode with his usual purposeful step towards TASS's headquarters. As he entered, he heard a happy 'Good morning, Mr. CEO' emanating from the security desk. He turned and smiled.

Duale had arrived at the TASS building about an hour before the normal start of the working day. As he entered the ante room from which Anna controlled the steady stream of visitors who would call on Duale each day, he stopped in his tracks. For a second he found himself looking at a man's back; he soon realised it was the Chairman of the Board of Trustees, who was sitting in Anna's chair. The Chairman swivelled round and, in contrast with the now-retired Chairman with whom Duale had worked for so many years, Duale felt a slight jerk as he found himself looking into the clear blue eyes and youngish fresh face of a stocky man, who was the successor. Duale was doing his best not to look shocked.

'Good morning, Dr. Duale.' Duale noticed the Chairman was not smiling. 'After the events of yesterday, I had a feeling you might be in a little early. I am sorry I did not personally contact you, but there was really no opportunity. We have an important matter to discuss. Shall we go into your office?'

'By all means,' Duale responded as he unlocked his office door.

As Duale followed the Chairman into the office he looked out over the lake. As had been the case the previous day, the atmosphere was crisply clear and he could see for miles. Today he had the Chairman at his side, instead of Anna; a thought flashed through his mind that he would have been much happier with Anna.

'It's a wonderful view, Chairman, don't you think?' There was no response. 'Shall we sit over here. We will feel a little warmth from the sun without being dazzled by the rays. I would like to offer you some coffee, but my secretary is not in yet.'

'Don't worry, Dr. Duale,' the Chairman commented, 'if she comes later we can perhaps have some then. But now I think we should get down to business.'

Outwardly Duale looked composed; inside, his stomach constantly reminded him that it was a different mattter.

'Well,' the Chairman opened, 'we have a sad, and I must say difficult, matter on our hands. It is not every day we have to cope with an aircraft accident involving one of TASS's staff, thank God. The reason I am here is to tell you that my office tried to call you yesterday because I wanted you to join the Board's meeting. Unfortunately, no one answered the telephone.'

'My secretary was not well, Mr. Chairman...,' Duale explained.

'No matter. The Board is very upset that we have lost Captain

Tashi, we all held him in the highest respect. In fact, something I learned only yesterday was that one or two Members regarded him as the ideal successor to fill your job. Did you know he was a possible candidate for the post?'

There was a pause; Duale judged it was the time for straight-forward innocence. With a thoughtful, slightly questioning look on his face, he quietly responded, 'Really? I must say I had no idea. Certainly he was very good technically. Whether he would have had what it takes to administer the Trust I could not judge. As far as I know, he had little experience in that respect.'

'In any case, Dr,' the Chairman continued, 'there is concern amongst the Board Members about this tragic accident. If you had been able to join us yesterday, perhaps some of these concerns might have been laid to rest. But you could not join us. The Members pressed very strongly for some immediate action. I have therefore agreed to establish an Inquiry to look into the events which led to Captain Tashi's visit, a visit which he was required to undertake alone to review the activities of what has been described as the least-safe aviation country in the world. I have nominated one of the Board Members to participate in the Inquiry and we shall be asking the TASS staff committee to nomi-nate an appropriate person from the workers. The Board feels that the Inquiry should include someone from the Executive Committee. Would you please consider this today and let me know by tomorrow morning who you think would be the best choice for the job?'

Although Duale was becoming deeply troubled, he gave not the slightest hint of the sinking feeling that was beginning to take hold within him. He looked the Chairman in the eye and responded, 'Mr. Chairman. I hope the Board is not over-reacting. Aviation should be safe; and it is safe when established practice is properly followed to ensure that standards are met. As you know, the *raison d'être* for TASS is to support countries in achieving safety. By definition, TASS's work is often a dangerous business. I have myself been involved in an emergency landing and a near miss; if it had not been for my Guardian Angel, I might well have lost my life in either of these incidents. Now we have a loss of life on our hands. If we apply the law of averages, some would say this was an inevitability. It is a fact of life that aviation accidents do happen; and the statistics show that the risk is relatively greater in developing countries.'

The stocky Chairman was not a man to waste time. 'I did not ask you for your views; I am here to put the Board's points to you, not to discuss other matters. What I have asked...'

'Very well,' Duale said, 'I don't need time to consider a nomination from the Executive Committee. There is only one totally objective member – and he's a lawyer into the bargain. His name is Alex Henrikson. Since you have already set the Inquiry in motion without consultation with me, I will leave you to make all the necessary arrangements for its work.' Duale stood up and walked to the door; he turned and said coolly, 'I trust that completes the points for discussion, Mr. Chairman?'

The Chairman made no movement, except to turn his head towards the window for a few moments. Then he said in a quiet voice, 'You certainly have a lovely view.' Then looking at Duale, he continued, 'No, Dr. Duale, the points I wish to make to you have not all been covered – yet. Do you prefer to stand up, or will you sit down?'

Looking perplexed, Duale rejoined the Chairman and sat down. He said nothing.

'The Inquiry will start its work tomorrow and the Board should receive its report within 30 days. We shall expect the full co-operation of all those who will be questioned, including yourself.' Duale's silence continued. The Chairman went on, 'Now, I come to what we may describe as the second initiative of the Board. As I mentioned, there is considerable concern amongst the Trustees regarding the circumstances of Captain Tashi's death. We are not confident of the capability of Styxia to perform the accident investigation properly. In your absence yesterday I contacted TASS's senior accident consultant; with his full agreement a fax has been dispatched to the civil aviation people in Styxia offering the services of TASS in helping to establish the cause of the accident. Specifically, we have offered the Head of the Aircraft Accidents Division and he would be assisted by the Head of Aeronautical Communications, Mr. Gerald Strong. Had we been able to contact you yesterday, we would have consulted you. As I mentioned, this turned out to be impossible; we were confident of your agreement in any case.

That is all I have to say. We will have the internal Inquiry report in a month, which I hope will put the matter to rest. The in-country accident investigation will take, I would imagine, several months; for that we are in the hands of the government of Styxia. I know you have a busy day ahead, so I will leave you.' The Chairman got up and approached the door; this time it was Duale who remained seated. By the time Duale looked up, the Chairman had left.

When Anna entered Duale's office a few minutes later, she found him in deep thought. When he looked up, he saw a form which he felt was something that resembled a shadow; as he focused on what had almost always been the twinkling blue of her eyes, all he could discern were two red-rimmed, colourless slits. But his overriding impression was that Anna looked frightened, almost hunted, and her posture seemed similar to that of a cowering dog.

The pale-faced Anna said weakly, 'Dr. Duale, I still feel weak and unsteady. But I thought you would have a lot of things to do; so I am here to help.'

'Anna,' Duale responded, 'you are wonderful! I really appreciate you. We do have some things to do, for example like circulating an obituary notice and I am going to ask you to make contact with Captain Tashi's wife. She is in the hospital and once she can travel we must arrange for her to fly with the children to Bhutan. My wife is already there for the Buddhist burial. Oh yes, Captain Tashi's remains have to be embalmed and sent to Thimphu.

Almost all the other things are being done by the Board. They seem to think they can take over my job. We must do a letter of protest and remind them that there is a deputy with whom they can consult if I am not available; there are established administrative procedures and the Board has ignored them. These little administrative things will not take long. Then we can get back to some form of normality. I detest over-reaction and busybodies getting into our hair. I will put a stop to it; and if they refuse, Anna, I will resign!

But somehow I don't think it will come to that. There will be attacks on me and I will let that phase work itself through. Then the moment of truth will come and I will answer everything that

315

will have been said. The Chairman and his Board will be disarmed. And that will be the end of it. Eventually, I will of course retire; but that will be at a time of my own choosing. You know, the Survivor has to live up to his name!' Duale laughed quietly.

Duale watched the wretched creature for a moment that was straining every nerve, with such limited success, to function; then he smiled warmly and benevolently.

'May I ask you a personal question, Anna?'

'Yes,' was the short, weak response. Anna was not smiling; on the contrary, she maintained a stony, unblinking look at Duale's desk.

'Anna, my question is when did you last eat?' The slits seemed to peer into his lively brown eyes. Then Anna lowered her head again; Duale noticed the cowering position.

'I think, Dr. Duale,' Anna responded in a steady, if weak voice, 'I think I ate some supper the day before yesterday; then my husband left on a business trip. Yesterday I had some coffee. Why do you ask?'

'You know, Anna, for all my faults, I am usually right. You are under-nourished and I am sure your blood pressure is too low; that's why you feel weak. May I suggest we go and have some breakfast. With my wife away, I only had a cup of coffee myself this morning; if I don't eat something we will be a pair of weaklings. That's not what TASS expects of us, is it? Shall we go?'

Fifteen minutes later the two were sitting down to breakfast in one of those little restaurants which specialize in huge American breakfasts. 'You already look stronger, Anna. How do you feel?' Duale asked, after they had each eaten a muffin and prepared for fried eggs, sunny side up, with a sausage and Canadian bacon.

'Thank you,' Anna replied, 'yes, you are right. I am beginning to feel stronger – and steadier.' There was a pause while Anna sipped her coffee; then the breakfast was brought. Anna did her best, but she realised that it would not be easy to eat; she had no appetite. Anna raised her head and the slits opened a little as she focused on Duale's face; her lips quivered slightly, which hindered her efforts to speak calmly. Then she said, 'How do I feel, Dr. Duale?' A flicker of a smile crossed her still-pale face. 'Well, I suppose I am very upset. I can't explain it, but the main thing I feel at the moment is fear; I feel frightened. I don't know exactly how or why Captain Tashi died, but I wonder if it could have been avoided. We are talking about someone who was your son, Dr. Duale. You manage to control your emotions much better than I do. I know you had a few problems with him. But I thought he was a wonderful man, he had so many qualities I could admire. Of course, I did not have a close relationship with him. But everything I noticed about him was positive. I just wish I could stop feeling frightened.'

'Do you feel frightened of me, Anna?' Duale asked.

'I don't know, Dr. Duale. If I could put my finger on it, it might help I suppose.' With a look of resignation, Anna poked at the sausage and cut off the end; she ate it.

Duale spoke, 'Anna, if you should ever have a feeling that your fear is related to me, I want you to know that you should never, at any time, feel frightened of me. As far as Captain Tashi's accident is concerned, you know this accident will be investigated and I hope we will learn exactly what went wrong. Today we don't know why the accident happened. In several months, we should know much more.

So why don't we finish our breakfast and get back to the office. We will soon catch up. Then you could go home and rest. Try and eat something this evening. Then have a good sleep. I am sure you will feel much better tomorrow.'

Duale leant across the little table and kissed Anna on her forehead. Anna sat up and looked him in the eye. Suddenly, she felt better. 'At last some colour is returning to your cheeks, Anna. Shall we go?' Duale suggested.

'Dr. Duale, since you asked me a personal question, may I ask you one?'

'By all means,' Duale responded, 'if it's too personal, I will talk around the question; over the years I've had plenty of practice at that!' Duale laughed. 'Go ahead, Anna.'

'Thank you, Dr. Duale.' Now Anna's voice was altogether stronger and assertive. 'My question is, how do *you* feel?'

There was a pause. Duale looked around the little restaurant and took in the red-chequered tablecloths; as a waiter passed, he asked for the check. Then he looked thoughtfully at Anna and said, 'I feel, Anna, that I am going through a difficult time in the office. I also feel I have a duty to the international community to

317

survive. But I also recognize this may not be possible. I have no feelings towards Captain Tashi and the accident. When we travel overseas on trips for our work, we have a duty to do things in a professional way. I should not pre-judge Captain Tashi. But it would not surprise me if he went too far in the wrong direction. This was a weakness I saw in him and that is why, in his own interest, I tried to rid the Trust of him within a year of him joining TASS. As you know, I failed.

If I consider your question from a personal point of view, I never felt I had a close connection with him. I had nothing to do with his upbringing, so I always saw him as one of TASS's staff. Of course, in certain respects he was an irritant – which he is no more. I suppose his time had come.'

The two got up and Duale held the door while Anna walked into the brilliant sunshine.

Although Anna did not talk as they walked the few steps to TASS's building, she was thinking hard. Some years before, Anna had told Duale that there was something strange about him.
Now, she found herself wondering again. Duale, she thought, did not seem to feel strongly attached to anyone. And in basic terms he seemed to be a loner consumed by his own ego. And, she thought, he had never revealed any type of feeling associated with his conscience, that is if he had one.

Once in the office, Duale said, 'If you feel up to it, Anna, I have noted some action for you to take on two or three files. Incidentally, perhaps the first thing to do is to circulate the obituary notice for Captain Tashi. We have the standard text somewhere. Would you try and strengthen the 'deeply regret' part and embellish Captain Tashi's value to TASS; then let me look at the draft. I will check through it, so you can produce the final. Then I think we can say we did our best for the man. Which reminds me, would you be so kind and find out how Captain Tashi's wife and children are faring; my wife gave me the name of the hospital – yes, here it is. The wife and children should travel to Bhutan as soon as they can; ask the travel people to arrange it. Call the wife, I forget her first name, and wish her well. Just explain I am much too busy to personally see them off; but I hope they have a good and safe journey. Thank you, Anna.'

Over the following days, Duale did his best to re-establish his routine. He knew the Inquiry was hard at work and that interviews were in progress. But he refused to permit this to unsettle him. Outwardly, he maintained his air of quiet, accomplished confidence. Inwardly, any nagging thoughts which might have arisen had been suppressed. As always, he was convinced in his righteousness. Of course it was true that it had been his decision to let Tashi perform his visit alone. On the other hand, Tashi had assured Duale and the divisional heads that he would work within his own technical limitations. Duale had accepted Tashi's assurance and the consultancy visit was to be undertaken on that basis – was it not? Duale reassured himself that no decision-maker should be blamed for taking a decision. In this case, Duale was the Chief Executive Officer and he had taken the decision. Was he to be faulted for that? Certainly not!

Like others, Duale played his part in answering the questions of the Inquiry. He cleverly, and convincingly, exploited the image of a group decision; as CEO, his job was to make a decision which reflected a balance of what the meeting's participants had said. He had unquestionably done this. He was relieved to find that the Chairman had accepted his recommendation that Alex Henrikson should be a member of the Inquiry. With Henrikson's ambition to succeed Duale, Duale was confident that Henrikson would tend to give Duale the benefit of any doubt, when others might begin to quietly air reservations concerning Duale's actions; and possibly his motives. Again, Duale was right.

And at some undetermined time Henrikson would seek repayment from Duale; Duale would deal with that aspect in his own way when that time came. In the meantime, the immediate Inquiry had to be faced; and dealt with.

Eventually, in the case of the conclusions and recommendations which resulted from the internal Inquiry, Duale's pre-judgement of the situation exemplified perfection. As an Inquiry document, no one found fault with its form or balance. The substance concentrated on fact and avoided speculation. A reference was included which highlighted the advice which Duale had rejected; it was an established fact that, if Duale had agreed, Tashi could have been accompanied by a navigational aids technician. But it was also pointed out that, pending the accident investigation report, no conclusions should be drawn from this.

It was mid June of 1997. Duale felt well in body and spirit. He had not seen the final version of the Inquiry report; but he reasoned, rightly, that the whole episode of Tashi's death would be 'put to bed' within TASS. He acknowledged that the Styxia aircraft accident report might put things in a different light. He would face that challenge when, and if, it arose.

On his return to the apartment one evening, he found the mail in its usual place on the small mahogany table in the hall. He briefly thought how the cleaning woman was so neat; she always tried to bring order to the apartment. Among the advertizing flyers and bills was a letter from Pema. For some reason, he did not feel that he should rush to open it. Only when he had discarded the advertising material and glanced at the bills did he turn his attention to his wife. Pema's letter was brief and matter of fact. She had had an uneventful journey to Bhutan. Two days after her arrival she had contacted her aunt, who had told her that the UN office had sent a message that Tashi's remains had arrived in Thimphu. Pema thanked Duale for his prompt action. Pema hoped that Patsri and the children would soon arrive. As far as Pema's return was concerned, Duale should expect her to arrive at Chicago's O'Hare airport in mid July; Pema would send the arrival details by fax after she had booked. Duale re-read the letter, hoping to find just a few words of affection, or perhaps that Pema was missing him; his search was in vain.

Within TASS Duale was pre-eminent in his role as CEO. But his personal family relationships were altogether another matter. It was not only that he could not envisage Pema's distress; he did not give it a thought. If he thought about Pema, then it was only to make a mental note of when she should be back. He would be happy to have her in bed; and he liked what she cooked for him. In return he would spoil her materially. And, yes, it was pleasant that she was there for him; and she livened up the apartment.

When Pema had arrived in Thimphu, she had found it impossible to hide her deep distress; she could see only darkness in her tunnel of grief. She had made contact with her aunt and the next day arrangements had been made for Tashi's funeral. Pema had visited the UN and she had asked that Tashi's remains should be brought to her aunt's house as soon as they arrived. Two days later the lama arrived at the aunt's house early in the morning.

Pema knew that the burial ritual was complicated and it would take many days to complete. For the sake of Tashi, she wanted the full ritual to be followed; in this way, Tashi would be re-incarnated at the level he deserved, which Pema hoped would be as a lama. Now they were ready for the first of the three distinct phases of the funeral ritual. Pema recalled the legend which she had once heard of the Earth Mother who had declared, 'At your birth, no sod of earth, stone or the timbers of the house were left untouched. At your death, no sod of earth, stone or timbers of the house will be left untouched.'

As prescribed in Buddhist ritual, the first act of the lama was to separate Tashi's soul from his body. It was essential that the uncleansed soul should be extracted from the body, otherwise family members in general might be endangered. The lama laid a white cloth over Tashi's embalmed body and chanted:

'This is the way for all. What is to be done? Some live longer on earth, some for a shorter period. Today it is your day. Do not be afraid. Now you must go your own way, without your family. Soul! Do not cling to this dead body. Leave the body and transport yourself into the teachings of the Lord Buddha, the teachings of the three jewels!.' The lama continued reading from the Book of Death.

At this stage, only Pema and her aunt were present. Any other members of the family had avoided this part of the ritual for fear of becoming contaminated with any uncleanness which might still be present. When the lama had finished this part of the ritual, he asked Pema to wait until a certain day and time which he would announce; this would be when Tashi's body should be burned. The day would be determined by the lama through astrological calculation.

Two days later, the lama announced his readiness to perform the second phase of the burial ritual, the so-called black burial. The lama and his assistants arrived where Pema was staying and did their best to arrange Tashi's remains in a sitting position; a cord was gently and carefully laced around his limbs to keep them in position. A white cloth was wrapped around his head and then a larger one draped over his entire body. The sitting corpse was slowly lowered into a barrel-like container. The lama read from a holy book, an act he would repeat at the place of the funeral once each day up to the end of the period of 49 days from the death of Tashi.

At this moment four men entered, men who under no circumstances should have a close connection with the family. A white cloth was placed over the threshold and, carried by the four pallbearers, Tashi's body began its short journey to the place where it would be burned. With the lama chanting, Tashi's remains were carried three times around a stake which protruded vertically from the pyre. Then the lama, holding a burning stick himself, walked around the pyre three times; in the name of the Lord Buddha, he implored the pyre to burn.

Now it was time for the ghee lamps to be lit and the *torma*, which were little balls of dough, to be brought so that the Gods, and especially the five wise kings, could participate and bring their good influence to bear on the ceremony.

As the pyre began to burn, one of the assistants took a pole to which a spoon had been tied; the spoon, which carried a little sustenance, was carefully placed near Tashi's mouth. As the corpse burned, the lama chanted in a loud voice to ward off any form of evil. The burning was regarded as an act of well-being. And the fire was seen as the mouth of the gods. When the burning had subsided, the lama chanted once more from a ritualistic text to free the pall bearers from any possible uncleanness.

The lama placed three large stones in a row; from that moment Tashi's soul would recognize the border between harmony and lack of order. The soul would never again trespass into the chaotic and disorderly lives which inhabited this earth; from now on, the soul would eternally maintain its harmony.

The lama stepped forward. He chanted that the name of Tashi had been cleansed; the ashes should be strewn around the pyre. Then the lama spoke in a loud voice:

'From today you have lost your name. Do not disturb the living. Should you speak to us, you will only do us harm. From today your name has been lost; and is nothing. Your name and identity have been burned. Your name has no meaning to us any more. Now you must follow the way to the gods. Do not choose the easy way. The only way to the gods is to follow the difficult path; you must do penance. You must reach the god of hidden treasure if you wish to seek re-incarnation.'

From that day Tashi's name was never again to be uttered within the local community; in time he would be totally forgotten. Now his soul would move into a phase between death and re-incarnation; it would rest for seven weeks, at which point the soul would be finally cleansed. During this period, the close family would stay at home and make little contact with those outside. Only after seven weeks, when prayer flags would be installed at the place of the funeral and ghee-lamps lit in the house, would the wider family become closely involved in the final phase of the ritual, the 'white' part of the funeral.

Pema and her aunt, assisted by the grief-stricken Patsri, were well prepared for the final part of the funeral ritual. There would be a classical tantric Buddhist ceremony to which every member of the family and clan at large would be invited. In addition, several local lamas would receive an invitation to attend. Pema had even made contact with the abbot – the Neten – of the monastery where Tashi had stayed for his retreats when he was young. The Neten, now a sprightly, alert old man of 79, remembered Tashi well; Pema experienced a brief burst of happiness when she received a message that he would definitely be present.

On the appointed day, the large gathering assembled and each guest was deeply conscious that the overriding purpose of the occasion was to support Tashi's soul on its journey to re-incarnation; with the help of the guests, especially the lamas, his way would be eased.

Apart from the readings from religious texts, an important part of the ceremony was the appeasement of the local gods through recitation and singing of songs. As usual, the guests had high expectations of an appropriately sumptuous feast which should fit the great occasion, the funeral of one of the most promising sons of the Kingdom. Pema, her aunt and Patsri were relieved to hear comments of approval. One of those who expressed his appreciation was His Excellency the former Minister of Communications. Now in retirement, although he had gained weight he moved easily and benevolently among the guests. He was attired in his aristocratic clothes; apart from his spotless, deep white cuffs, the orange sash across his broad chest deeply impressed his fellow guests. Patsri's parents were also present and this was a great strength for Patsri.

The ceremony served to ensure that any residual uncleanness of Tashi's spirit would be finally banished. Now it was time for the family to return to their normal social customs. In terms of their religious beliefs and practices, philosophical concepts and the real world would come together in harmony in the overall world order.

Although they would still feel pangs of sadness, at last Pema and Patsri also began to experience moments of happiness and contentment that their Treasure, the dearest and perfect Tashi, had not only been laid to rest. There was a high expectation that in the new life which awaited him, he would aspire to a much higher level of existence. Through their deep-seated faith, each was convinced that through the funeral ritual which had been so meticulously and perfectly followed, the beautiful and harmonious future of Tashi's next life was assured.

When Pema awoke the following morning, she felt better in mind and body than at any time since Tashi's death. As she looked out of the window and took in the magnificent view of the huge mountains lightening in the dawn, it struck her that this was the first time since her return to her beloved country that she had actually noticed her surroundings. Soon she would see the droplets of heavy dew twinkling in the sunlight. Later, when she would walk outside, she would breathe the perfume of the flowers which surrounded the house. An unexpected feeling of homesickness for the Kingdom began to take hold within her. As she continued to gaze in wonderment at the glorious, rose-coloured sky, she heard light footsteps behind her; no, she thought, that cannot be Tashi.

'Good morning, mother Pema,' Patsri said in her gentle voice. 'You know, mother Pema, this is the first morning I have noticed my surroundings; and they are so beautiful. Now things can only get better,' Patsri chuckled, 'I mean, mother Pema, things could not have been much worse! Now we have to face the reality of the future.'

About a week later, in early July, Pema felt she should prepare for her return to Chicago. She sent an email through the UN in Thimphu to Duale, explaining that she would spend two days in Bangkok and help Patsri with the children to settle in with her parents. Then Pema would fly to London, where she would make contact with the Shah family who had looked after Tashi so well during the period that Tashi had attended Dulwich College. Finally, Pema would stop-over in New York for two nights to see friends in the UN. She would arrive in Chicago at 10 o'clock in the morning on 19 July.

'That's a pity,' remarked Duale as he finished reading the email. Anna had just placed some files on his desk.

'Is something wrong, Dr. Duale? May I help in some way?' Anna asked. Duale thought for a moment; then he turned to Anna.

'Thank you, Anna. In fact you could help me. My wife is arriving at O'Hare at 10 o'clock on 19 July; it's a Monday. That is the day the Chairman has asked me to attend a meeting with the Board at 9.30. I am sure it will be about my re-appointment for another term. I don't feel like asking him to change the date of the meeting because I have already accepted the invitation. I wonder, Anna, whether you could meet my wife and explain to her I am involved in an important meeting. If you could see her to my apartment, then I will join her at the end of the day.'

'Certainly, Dr. Duale. Shall I use your office limo?' Anna asked, 'your wife would like that, I am sure.'

'No, I shall need that to go the Board. I know it's only a few blocks, but I think I should arrive in the limo and be properly received. In fact the chauffeur can pick me up at ten past nine at my apartment building.' Duale handed Anna a hundred dollar greenback. 'Take a taxi, Anna. I think that's the best way.'

A week or so later, Duale found himself looking for his charcoal grey, hand-made suit and a lively, but discreet, patterned tie to match. This was the day of the Board meeting. Just before the office limo picked him up, Debbie arrived for the chores. 'Debbie, you are a gift to us!' Duale was smiling at her warmly, 'my wife will return today. I know you will make sure everything is as perfect as usual. May I trouble you to buy some flowers. Here is a hundred dollars; fifty for the flowers and fifty for you. Thank you, Debbie.'

'Thank you, Dr. Duale,' Debbie replied, 'you are such a famous man. Have a good day!'

Duale walked to the elevator. Was he looking forward to Pema's return? Strange, he thought, he was not exactly jumping around with excitement. Probably when he saw her, it would be

325

different. But now he had other things on his mind. He had to deal with the Board.

Duale was received at the Board of Trustees building as he had planned. The door of the CEO's limousine was opened by a uniformed attendant and he was escorted to the Chairman's office. It was 9.28 a.m.

'Good morning, Dr. Duale. I see we are in good time. I hope the meeting can be concluded quite quickly. I won't waste time talking now; let us go in.' The stocky Chairman led the way through the back of his office straight into the meeting room. Duale had attended a meeting there only once before and when he saw the wood-panelled walls they looked familiar.

'Please sit down here, next to me, Dr. Duale.' Duale took his place and looked at the Trustees; there were eight, four on each side of the solid, rectangular walnut table. Their middle-aged, blank, unsmiling faces seemed to confirm something he had already sensed; there was tension in the icily-quiet room. As usual, Duale gave no indication of the message his antenna was transmitting to his sharp brain. Outwardly, he was relaxed; his 'Good morning, gentlemen' cut through the ice effortlessly and, for a moment, it seemed to have a melting effect.

Then the Chairman cleared his throat and spoke. 'Thank you, Dr. Duale, for attending our meeting. We have invited you this morning because we need some help in our deliberations; and we think you might be the best man, given the circumstances. I would like to share with you where we have got to in our consideration of your re-appointment. As you may know, we do not at this stage have another candidate under consideration. This is because up to the recent past the consensus within the Board was that confirmation of your re-appointment should be a formality.

As I mentioned to you, there was a possibility that Captain Tashi might have applied for the CEO post. With deep respect to any member of the Board who might have supported his candidature, I do not believe he would have received much support at this stage; he was too inexperienced. If he had continued to perform well, then he might have become a good candidate in due course, perhaps in a few years' time. That would have probably been an option for the new millennium, even later. In any case, we need not consider that particular possibility further today.

326

Unfortunately, regarding your possible re-appointment, recent events have suddenly changed some of the views expressed by members of the Board. After all, this body has a responsibility to see that everything possible is done to ensure that TASS operates in accordance with the aims and criteria established for the Trust by its founder. Your responsibility is to see that TASS's mission is successfully implemented to technically support, in a hands-on way, the operation of civil aviation, with all that this entails. Are you with me so far, Dr. Duale?'

Duale primed himself for an unknown something that was building up in the Chairman's statement. In spite of straining every nerve, he was at a loss to put his finger on what might be imminent. With a mildly questioning expression, he responded in a quiet, steady voice:

'Certainly, Chairman. No one could disagree with what you have said.'

'Good,' the Chairman went on, 'then let me come to the point. We of course recognized the possibility that there could have been some token competition as to who should fill the post of CEO for the next term; that competition, which we here all agree would not heve been of a very serious nature, would have come from Captain Tashi. Now he is gone. Dr. Duale, misgivings have been voiced by certain members of the Board concerning your judgement in sending Captain Tashi alone to review the organization of what your Heads of Division agreed is the least-safe civil aviation country in the world. In other words, if Captain Tashi had been accompanied by a good technical colleague, that specialist would almost certainly have been a communications or navigational aids man. Without doubt, the second man of the team would have checked the calibration status of the navigational aids; and he would have told Captain Tashi that effectively they were unusably defective. This knowledge might have made a stronger impact on Captain Tashi's decision to flight check the pilots. There was also the factor that two minds would have been better than one. This entire element is one on which I would like to hear your comments. Some members have also expressed reservations about your age and the long period of your tenure as CEO; in other words, perhaps there is a case for considering a new mind, which would usher in new ideas and a different style of leadership.

The question of your re-appointment, or otherwise, has to be dealt with today. As things stand at the moment, four Trustees favour your re-appointment; four are not in favour. In effect, this means that after you leave us today, it is I who will cast the deciding vote.

Incidentally, there have been two developments this morning. I am sure you have seen the mail, Dr. Duale?'

'No, I came here directly from my apartment,' Duale crisply commented.

'In that case, I must inform you, Dr. Duale. First, I have received copies of letters of resignation from four Heads of Divisions; I suppose some might comment that this action speaks for itself. Second, I have received a copy of an email from Mr. Gerald Strong, Head of Communications, who is assisting with the accident in Styxia. I will read it:

'Progress with accident is slow due to difficult site of accident and lack of local infrastructure/expertise. Voice recorders not yet recovered. Check of ILS and local technical enquiries indicate that ILS equipment not calibrated in accordance with norms for at least five years. Alarm system to indicate inaccurate operation of guidance system had been switched off by local technicians, who stated they decided to suppress constant alarm siren because it quote irritated unquote them. If the aircraft was on an instrument approach (not yet verified), then cause of accident (either main or contributory) could have been technically neglected ILS. This is preliminary info. Regards. Strong. TASS/Comm.'

The absolute silence which followed the Chairman's reading seemed to last an eternity. On at least two occasions, Duale looked up. Although he appeared to be the most relaxed man in the room, in fact thoughts of foreboding were flooding into his brain.

Then something welled up in his inner senses which had rarely, if ever, afflicted him before. A feeling of guilt began to take hold. Try as he might, he could not ignore it. His efforts to suppress what for Duale was a rare feeling, failed miserably. If Anna had witnessed that moment, she would have exclaimed that what had been missing during the whole of Duale's career had, stealthily but suddenly, at last made its presence known to its owner. So Duale had a conscience, after all. It was making life unpleasant for him and it had chosen to make itself felt in front of the Board! What

Duale's conscience told him there and then was that Duale had played a part in Tashi's death. And if others were to share this judgement, which would be an accurate judgement, where would it all end?

Up to that moment in his career, Duale had survived through the application of his highly intelligent brain, decisive leadership, hard work, irresistible charm and, above all, an overriding belief in himself. But in his professional adventures, he had never had to cope with his, up to now, suppressed conscience. And he had survived. Now things were different.

Because his conscience had dared to make itself felt, Duale was inwardly literally experiencing discomfort; he suddenly developed a stomach ache. As far as Tashi was concerned, Duale certainly had no feelings, except the now-despatched torment. But as he mused he sensed strong pressure threatening his very own existence. He was beginning to feel frightened. Yes, where would it all end? As for his prospects, Duale did not like what he saw. Depending on the outcome of the accident investigation, the future could be disastrous for his reputation, perhaps personally damaging; certainly, it would be very uncomfortable. True to his nature, he took a decision there and then.

He would resign.

Duale heard the Chairman's voice intruding into his concentration, 'Dr. Duale, I am not in the habit of repeating myself, but again I must ask you for your comments.'

'Oh, excuse me Chairman. I not only pay attention to what I hear; I also have to consider the implications. Certainly, Chairman, I will be pleased to speak to this subject.' Duale's voice was gaining strength. 'First, let me deal with your last point. My age; this is something we have no control over. We are all in the same boat as far as age is concerned. If we were to take a count of the ages around this table, for example, I suppose there would always be those who would say surely it is time for a new, fresh approach. But the Board would probably lecture the upstart for daring to suggest that wisdom gained over time should be thrown out of the window. I put it to you and your Board today, Chairman, that I would certainly agree with the Board's reaction.' Duale's gaze moved from one face to the next around the table. He thought how old the faces looked; some were downright crusty!

Then he said, 'I suggest you apply the same criteria in my case. Do I make myself clear, Chairman?'

The middle-aged Chairman's face flushed. He looked around the table; some of the members also had flushed faces, while others looked uncomfortable.

'Mr. Chairman,' Duale continued. 'You mentioned you are not in the habit of repeating yourself. Nor am I, Mr. Chairman! I have to run TASS and this is the type of job which is outside the experience of most people in the world, unfortunately including those who sit in judgement. I have work, yes, real work to do, Chairman.' Duale looked up and again scanned the faces which were fixed on him. 'Did you hear what I said, Chairman?' Duale repeated.

The Chairman glared at Duale, 'Continue.'

Duale did so in a more moderate tone of voice. 'Since you have failed to answer my question, but you have nevertheless asked me to continue, then I take it that I have made myself clear. Now I will deal with the so-called reservations of certain members of the Board. So far, we have the finished internal Inquiry report, which I am sure everyone in this room has read. As a starting point, may we please hear whether any of the so-called reservations stem from any of the substance of that report? Perhaps I could ask you, Chairman, to seek information now from your members concerning reservations. I will then deal with them, as necessary. Please, Mr. Chairman.' Duale looked at the Chairman expectantly. The Chairman turned to his members,

'Questions, reservations? Who will start?' One or two members moved a little in their chairs. No one spoke. 'Do we have comments?' the Chairman asked. Silence prevailed.

Duale broke the silence. 'Thank you, Chairman. As I understand it you have to deal with reservations, but no one is prepared to articulate them. Is this the case, Chairman?'

'Dr. Duale, I must ask you to moderate your attitude. We are all entitled to our views. If you have anything else to say, let us hear you out.'

'Thank you, Chairman. As I understand it, based on an accident in which Captain Tashi was involved, your Board has reservations. Since no one is, apparently, prepared to substantiate his reservations, you will understand that I am somewhat confused.

The only conclusion I can draw is that either there is something seriously wrong with the way in which the Board functions, or certain members have indulged in an emotional reaction which could not stand up to the examination of the Inquiry.

Before I leave you, sir, I would like to remind the Board that its function is to satisfy itself that the CEO of TASS is performing his duties in accordance with the charter of the Trust; that is all. I have played my part to the best of my ability for the last 20 years. I served under your predecessor with great confidence; in basic terms, I knew that in times of difficulty he would give me a fair hearing and he would support me so long as he was satisfied that the way in which I performed was reasonable. We both acknowledged that, being human, with the luxury of hindsight I would never be perfect. But the fact is that TASS is generally recognized internationally as a wonderful example of an apolitical organization which makes a difference, and a critical one, when it comes to air safety. This is as it should be and I, in all humility, take pride in the fact that I have been associated with this success.

Now I find myself in a different type of situation. I have to deal with a Board which, because I was out of action for one working day, stricken with grief – yes, Mr. Chairman a CEO can also grieve – the Board took it upon itself to take over some of the responsibilities which are exclusively reserved for the CEO. Without reference to me you established the Inquiry and you set in motion TASS's involvement in the accident investigation, a sovereign responsibility of the affected country. Well, after considerable expenditure of time and money, we have all read the Inquiry report. And what is its message? As far as TASS was concerned, everything has been done in accordance with good practice. Even the Board, not to mention the Executive Committee, was sent records of the various meetings. Before the accident, the Board raised no comments, even though it had every opportunity to do so; to this extent the Board was associated with all the actions taken regarding Captain Tashi's consulting visit to Styxia. I regard the money used consequent to your unilateral action as money wasted, Mr. Chairman.

You have told me that four of my Heads have resigned. Perhaps they have been talking to members of the Board; they have never discussed their problems with me. Normally, these men would work out their notice period of three months. Because of the possibility that they will sow seeds of discontent amongst others, I will exercise my responsibility and have them paid the three months salary. And they will leave tomorrow. Their successors will be required to sign an undertaking that their first duty will be loyalty to the Trust, which means loyalty to the CEO.'

The Chairman interjected, 'Dr. Duale, I did not invite you this morning so that you can deliver a lecture. I think you have said enough. You may now leave. I will have to take your comments into account. But I must warn you, I am faced with a dilemma.'

'Mr. Chairman,' continued Duale, his voice rising in firmness, 'you have invited my comments. I am not used to being interrupted; I have not finished. I have a final comment, please.' As Duale's fiery stare rested on the Chairman's face, the Chairman sensed that he was being given an uncomfortable reminder that he was no match for TASS's CEO.

'Good,' the Chairman said, 'please do not labour your point; be as quick as possible.'

'Thank you, Mr. Chairman. Because of my lack of confidence in you and your Board, I am resigning. In this way, I will relieve you of your dilemma! You have stated I have no competition, which I can well understand. With the agreement of the Board, therefore, I will plan to leave at the end of the year. This will give you six months to select my successor. I wish him well. If I can assist in any way with any matter up to the time of my departure, in the interest of TASS which is so close to my heart, please do not hesitate to seek my advice. I am at the height of my proficiency as CEO, which means that you will receive the best possible guidance. What I have said will be confirmed in writing. I will inform TASS's staff of my decision by circular letter, although in their interest I will not inform them of the reasons behind my decision. Good day, gentlemen.'

The only slight noise which penetrated the stunned silence of the room was of Duale pushing his chair back and standing up. He appeared relaxed as he treated the Chairman and the Board to a final smile; some detected scorn, others pity.

As he walked to the door, no one spoke. He closed the door firmly, took the elevator down to the lobby, motioned to the chauffeur and took his seat in the back of the limousine.

A quarter of an hour later, he was dictating his letter of resignation. This was followed by a short circular letter which he instructed Anna to have distributed to every member of TASS's staff. He also sent a note to the Head of Personnel, instructing him that the Heads of Division who had resigned should be seen off TASS's premises as soon as possible. Under no circumstances would Duale receive them; and if they should withdraw their resignations, as a matter of principle this should be refused.

Duale looked at Anna and said, 'I think that's enough for today, thank you Anna.' Then he noticed tears streaming down Anna's cheeks. 'What is it, Anna? You are crying again. What has upset you this time?' Duale asked with concern.

'I am so sorry, Dr. Duale. You are so strong; and I feel so weak! First, we lost Captain Tashi. Now we are going to lose you. Perhaps I am not as tough as I used to be. But I've had enough. You are going at the end of the year. So will I. I couldn't bear to come here again after you leave. I am sorry. Now I must do my work. Everything will be ready for you by 3 o'clock. Should I tell you about your wife, Dr. Duale?'

'I completely forgot about her. Did she arrive, Anna?'

'Yes, Dr. Duale. I took her to your apartment and she's waiting for you. She is not jet-lagged at all; she stopped over in London and New York. She said she is fine; but she doesn't look well. At least I didn't think so. Now, let me get on with the work.'

Anna closed her steno pad and walked towards the door; then she heard Duale laugh. 'Is everything all right, Dr. Duale?' she asked. Duale's eyes were twinkling and he smiled at Anna.

'You know, Anna,' he said, 'I was just thinking. That devil Captain Tashi took me on twice; and on both occasions he won. Now he's dead; but you know, in a way he has just won again. After all these years, I am out of a job. What a record he has; a hundred percent success!'

The tears welled up and moistened Anna's eyes again; as her lips began to tremble, she said, 'That's one way of looking at it, Dr. Duale. But surely the main point is that the wonderful Captain Tashi has lost his life, although you have survived physically – again!'

Duale did not answer. Anna left his office and closed the door. Duale suddenly felt lonely in the spaciousness of his sumptuous office. He got up and looked out over the lake. In contrast to the glorious clarity of the Spring air, now humidity hung heavily, clinging to the buildings; Duale's eyes moved in the direction of the Lake, which was hardly visible. For a brief moment he thought the thick, almost murky air reflected his feelings. He was on the edge of uncertainty; and he could not see very far into his future.

In the afternoon, shortly after Duale had signed the letters, he decided to go home. He felt relaxed. It was true that he had resigned; but he comforted himself that his had been a long and successful innings. He would leave on the crest of his success. As for the future, the main thing now was to strengthen his relationship with Pema. They would lead a pleasant life together. For the first few years of his retirement they could do some travelling and wherever he went there would be a warm welcome from the grateful civil aviation authorities. He would need to exercise his mind; perhaps he could give some guest lectures at civil aviation training establishments, or possibly in the field of air transportation at some universities. Then, of course, there could well be some consultancy work; with his contacts, he could open many doors at the highest level in a number of countries all over the developing world. Yes, he thought, from now on there would be less stress and he should look forward to enjoying his remaining days with Pema. As soon as he saw her, he thought, both would feel happy again.

With his jaunty step, Duale walked the few blocks to his apartment building. The humidity was making itself felt and his pace was just a little slower than usual. He took the elevator and walked to his door. As he took out his keys, the door opened. Pema was standing in front of him. She looked at Duale and did not move. Duale stared back at her. He could hardly believe his eyes. Pema looked at least ten years older than when he had last seen her. He peered incredulously at her face; her high cheekbones were covered with a layer of puffy flesh. He stepped forward and embraced her. As he tried to kiss her, she turned her head downwards; he could see that her cheek barely touched his chest. Instead of the firm, beautiful body of his wife, he felt the soft fat on her limbs. And in place of the vibrant wife he had fallen in love with, he found himself holding a body which was limp and, he thought, almost lifeless.

Duale's arms slipped off Pema's body and he walked past her into the living room. Pema closed the door and slowly followed him. She sat down and said, 'Are you pleased to see me Duale? Or like our son, do you regard me as an obstacle to your survival?'

'I don't understand what has happened, Pema. I can see you are not well. I suppose you are taking medication. I will look after you and we will get you well again. Maybe you need a rest?'

'Probably, Duale, I do need a rest. But before I rest I want you to explain truthfully what part you played in sending Tashi alone to a country which is known for its unsafe aviation. This is the only reason that I have returned to you. To hear the truth. And if you do not tell me the truth, or you refuse to discuss the matter, I will leave you, Duale. If you can satisfy me that you have simply made an honest error of judgement, I may stay; and I hope in time I will recover sufficiently so that we can lead a normal life together.' Raising her voice, Pema said, 'Tell me the truth!'

Duale did not respond immediately. He simply eyed Pema and tried to come to terms with her appearance and, now, her insistent question; he felt as though he was dealing with a foreign intruder who was holding a gun to his head. Eventually, he said, 'Pema, I am distressed that you are not well. At the moment, we do not know why Tashi was involved in an accident. Until the accident investigation is completed, anyone can speculate but no one can speak with real knowledge on the subject. As to my part in this whole tragic business, as CEO of TASS I was the leader of a group of technical and administrative staff who agreed that Tashi should undertake his visit, a visit which he himself, incidentally, had proposed. The records of the meetings which discussed TASS's approach were copied to the Board of TASS's Trustees; to that extent the Board was also involved in the group decision.'

There was a pause. Then Pema said, 'What did you have against Tashi, your son, Duale? Once you called him a devil. Do you think he was a devil? Tell me the truth Duale.'

'Yes, Pema, unfortunately your son was a devil. He tormented me. He took advantage of his birth out of wedlock; in effect, he blackmailed me. And you know, Pema, each time he won. Perhaps it is premature for me to say this, but you have asked for the truth. The truth is that you and I saw Tashi in a completely different light. If we are to live happily together, I personally believe that in our mutual interest we should never mention Tashi's name. Otherwise, he will win again. He will break our marriage, Pema.'

Pema slowly rose from her chair and she stood over Duale. 'Thank you for being truthful, to the extent you know how to tell the truth. I know enough. Now I will go to bed, Duale; I will sleep in the guest room. Last time I slept there I told you that sometimes you should stop thinking about yourself. Now, Duale, you should think of your son. You should think of his lovely wife and their darling children. And you should think of their unhappiness and the tragic dislocation which will affect their lives forever. And when you look at me, Duale, you will think of how I have changed, both in appearance and as a person.

And then, Duale, you must think further. All this ugliness and unhappiness is a reflection of tragedy. Look at me, Duale; take a good, hard, critical look at me! Unfortunately, Duale, you reap what you sow. In the end, you pay for your sins. The more you look at me, the more you should understand what I am talking about. There is only one glimmer of positive, shining light in all this. Tashi is free now; this perfect human being can never again be harmed by the evil which ensnared him in this world.'

Pema turned and walked unsteadily towards the guest room. When she had closed the door behind her, Duale heard her turn the key in the lock. Soon the light which illuminated the slit below the door went out.

Duale poured himself a whisky and meditated on the day's events. When at last he went to bed, he lay awake; what should he do? He slept fitfully that night. After constantly dreaming, at six he found himself waking up yet again; he watched the sun rise. He quietly got up and an hour later he was on his way to his office. The longer Pema slept, the better, he thought. Any onlooker who knew Duale would have noticed Duale's slow progress. He seemed to amble along aimlessly; there was no hint of his usual forthright, jaunty step.

When he walked into the TASS building, the security man said a happy 'Good morning, Dr. Duale.' Then he added, 'It's a pity you have thrown in the towel, sir. You are one of the few people on this planet who is really indispensable, if you don't mind me saying so. Who in the world would come to his office so early in the morning the day after his resignation, or is it retirement?

Anyway, I call that dedication! They will never find anyone like you. But age catches up with us all, I suppose. Have a good day, sir.'

In fact, Duale did not have a good day; he achieved little. Whatever he tried to tackle, he found that his mind was preoccupied with Pema. Always self-possessed and confident, he thought how he had always been able to find a solution to any problem; there must be an answer, he thought. At four o'clock he decided to leave his office; he had to talk to Pema.

'Anna, I am sorry,' he explained, 'my stomach is giving me a hard time again. I think I will go home and rest a little. I must be getting old!.' He chuckled.

'No problem, Dr. Duale, you've earned a rest. See you tomorrow. Try and relax.'

Duale opened the door of his apartment. 'Pema, my darling Pema. Where are you, Pema? I want to talk to you. Pema?' As he walked from one room to another he could not ignore a feeling of weakness which seemed to be overcoming him. Then he saw a note on the living room table; it read:

'I am sorry, Duale, but I think it is better that I return to Bhutan. Perhaps we will meet again one of these days. I feel that you are not the person I married. Or perhaps I am the one who has changed. I really don't know. But the result is the same. In basic terms, we lack harmony. Let me try and recover. If I do, I will contact you. Pema.'

Duale sank into an armchair. He found it impossible to comprehend his new situation. In the last 24 hours or so he had not only given up his job. Now he had lost his wife as well. Then he mused, 'That little devil. He has won again!'

Chapter Eighteen

The Final Curtain

It was mid August 1997. As Duale walked to his office at eight o'clock in the morning, he thought how well most Chicagoans seemed to endure, year in year out, the hot and sometimes humid summers. The people he passed on the sidewalk looked happy. No doubt, many of them had their problems, just as Duale did. But on the whole, the average pedestrian gave no outward sign of the cross which he or she might be carrying. I have always believed in setting a good example, Duale thought; why should I burden others with my cross? He would carry it lightly, like those around him. Of course life had been unfair to him; on the other hand, he mused, in life there are no rules of fairness. He had no intention of sinking into a morass of self-pity. He recognized that from time to time he might lapse in this respect; but he would soon resurrect himself and rise above the jealousy, the pettiness and the spite of others – like those who sat on the Board of Trustees, for example. And if they saw the error of their ways and invited him to withdraw his resignation, he would refuse. He had always demonstrated principle, had he not? His principles would be remembered long after he had left TASS.

Looking happy and self-satisfied, Duale arrived at his office. The view over the lake was becoming clearer each day as the summer showed signs of making way for the fall. As Duale took in the view, he briefly thought of the wonderful weekends he had spent with Pema at the house on Lake Geneva.

'Good morning, Dr. Duale.' It was Anna.

'Morning, Anna,' Duale responded. 'I see there are some files on my desk. Do we have anything special on today?'

'There is an email from a senior vice-president of the US aviation insurers association,' Anna responded.

'I suppose it's the usual chant,' Duale interjected, 'the rising accident rate, the one major accident a week syndrome?'

'Exactly,' Anna confirmed. 'Shall I reply with the standard letter?'

'Yes please, Anna. Doctor it up a little. It's getting a bit tiresome telling these busybodies that TASS is doing everything humanly possible in the field of air safety. As far as I am concerned, now it is up to the Third World countries themselves. You know, Anna, perhaps I should go on a tour and give some speeches? Anna, ask the Head of Flight Safety to come and see me. I will ask him to draft a standard speech. He will know the statistics; you can do anything with statistics. Apart from stressing what we are doing, I will make sure the picture is much more positive than the insurance industry would have people believe. They really are a bunch of Job's Comforters!' Duale smiled; Anna was not smiling.

'Who do you want to see, Dr. Duale? As you know, Captain Tashi was the Head of Flight Safety. When he died, everyone in the Division resigned. There are no staff left in flight safety.'

'What?' Duale questioned. 'That is unbelievable! They are all mad, yes mad!' Although Duale was trying to control himself, he heard his voice rising. He turned his head towards the lake; then he mumbled, 'get the Head of the Public Relations and Information Division up here. He can prepare something for me.' Duale paused.

Anna broke the silence. 'There is one other point, Dr. Duale. The representative of the staff would like to see you. He said it is a confidential matter. May I give him an appointment?'

'Well,' Duale replied, 'I wonder what he is up to. I suppose I had better see him. Let him come in the afternoon, please, Anna.'

'Please go straight in, Mr. Hogg. Dr. Duale is expecting you. It is exactly 4 p.m.' Anna smiled; she thought Godfrey Hogg looked a little nervous. She watched him walk slowly to Duale's door; he knocked gently. 'Mr. Hogg, you don't need to knock,' Anna explained, 'I told you Dr. Duale is ready to see you.'

Godfrey Hogg pushed the door ajar and slipped into Duale's office. Duale stood up and smiled. 'We don't see enough of one another, Mr. Hogg,' he said reassuringly, 'it's always a great pleasure to see you. Let us sit over here. Now what can I do for you?' Duale enquired.

Although Godfrey Hogg had obtained a university degree in the State of Illinois, he was not a member of TASS's professional staff. A statistician by training, he lived and worked in a world of numbers. He was well versed in collating information, as well as in the analytical computer systems used to interpret trends. But his talent for balanced judgement was limited. He would never aspire to manage as such; on the few occasions he had been asked to stand in for his boss, his nervous system had been subjected to enormous stress and he had felt quite unable to take even the smallest decision. He had been elected to represent the lower level staff because he was well regarded as an honest, sincere man; in any case, no one else would take on the job.

Godfrey Hogg took his spectacles off and started to clean the lenses. As he replaced his glasses, he nervously pressed the bridge against his nose. Then he seemed to peer at Duale; he found himself looking at Duale in awe. Although Duale was doing his best to be relaxed and friendly, the mere presence of Duale somehow made Godfrey Hogg feel inadequate. He said nothing. The silence was at last broken by Anna's happy voice; she was following the usual ritual, 'Would you like coffee, tea; or something else, Mr. Hogg?'

'Thank you,' Godfrey Hogg quietly replied, 'tea, please.'

'Yes, Dr. Duale,' Godfrey Hogg tentatively started, 'I am sorry I did not reply immediately. For some reason, my brain feels blocked.' He laughed hesitantly. 'Yes, you see I am here as the staff's representative and I have an unusual message to bring you. In fact, it could be unique, I suppose.' Now his voice was gaining strength as he began to feel more confident. 'Yes, Dr. Duale,' he continued, 'the situation is as follows. Please don't worry, on this occasion we don't want anything from you; I am not going to ask you to do anything for us. Let me say what I want to say; then you can just reply, yes or no.'

Duale felt mystified, but produced an encouraging smile; after all, apparently no issues were to be discussed. Whether he would reply with a yes or a no, that would be the end of it.

Godfrey Hogg continued, 'Dr. Duale, since Captain Tashi was killed three and a half months ago, TASS has passed through difficult times, in more ways than one. No one knows this better than yourself, sir. To us staff at the lower level, we have the impression that one of the casualties of the fall-out has been yourself; for reasons which none of us know, or need to know, you have decided to resign. On behalf of the staff, we want you to know that we have very much appreciated your leadership over the years. Times were not easy; when brief moments of success appeared, they were little luxuries to be cherished. But on the whole, TASS's mission is difficult, very difficult.

You have been our leader. We want you to know that we believed in your leadership. Since Captain Tashi's death, unfortunately there have been those who thought they could be clever with hindsight. A number of the management heads have criticized you; some have even resigned. We staff at the lower end have not been very impressed with this criticism. Even if you might have made an error of judgement, we would not hold that against you; like the rest of us, you are human.

To emphasise the esteem in which we hold you, and as a mark of respect, we would like to commission a life-size bronze statue of you. We know the cost and we are confident that this can be met by staff donations; in addition, we believe there is a prospect of a generous contribution from the city of Chicago. As I stated, Dr. Duale, today we ask nothing of you. All I need is a response, please, sir.'

Duale was almost overcome with emotion. So the staff appreciated him after all. Over the last few weeks he had been the target of criticism and abuse by the Board and some of the Divisional Heads. Now the silent majority had spoken. Yes, they saw him in a proper light. He had dedicated his life to TASS. How appropriate, he thought, that the ordinary staff wanted to honour his memory; and how right they were!

'Mr. Hogg,' Duale responded, 'I could make a speech of appreciation. But that can wait. You have asked for a short answer and you will have it: yes!'

'Thank you, sir. The necessary arrangements will be put in hand. Goodbye, Dr. Duale. I will always remember this conversation with you.' Hogg got up and grasped Duale's extended hand.

'I hope you noticed, Dr. Duale, I did not have to resort to admiring that beautiful view.' Now Godfrey Hogg felt relaxed; as he left Duale's office, he gently laughed.

Towards the end of August, Duale found himself counting the

weeks as they slipped by; eighteen weeks to go, he thought. And at that moment he began to think a little more. What should he do for the remainder of his time? Even if he did nothing, TASS would go on ticking over. But what should he himself do to emphasise that he would be leaving on a wave of success? Why not a victory lap? Yes, he would visit a number of countries. He had already sent them a circular letter to tell them of his resignation. Now, if they wished, they could receive him for one last time; of course, if some of them wished to show their appreciation to him on a personal basis, he would respond with humility and gratitude.

Then he had a brainwave. He would visit Bhutan. He had already written two long letters to Pema; so far, he had received no response. Once in Bhutan, he would see Pema; he would persuade her that he was still the man she married. He hoped the moon would be full; its silvery white light would re-create the magic which had drawn them together. Yes, he would court her again. He would prostrate himself on the floor and beg forgiveness for any error of judgement he might have made; and he would convince her that if there had been a misjudgement, then his error had been an honest mistake. Yes, that was the main thing. He would show her the results of the internal Inquiry which had found his part in sending Tashi on that fateful mission to be of marginal, speculative significance. He would go further; he would retract the negative statements he had made about Tashi. He would promise to love and look after Pema until death would, in time, part them. He would persist until Pema would be persuaded to give their marriage another chance.

Duale looked out over the lake. His eyes followed the slow movement of one or two boats making their way up the coast in the calm, warm water. As he raised his eyes to look at the white clouds floating below the azure backdrop, his imagination began to play tricks with him. In his mind's eye, the top of a large, billowing white cloud became the crest of a huge Himalayan mountain; and the water of the lake stretched into the distance like a carpet of the Bhutanese forest. Then he saw Pema, the Pema he had first met forty years previously. She was wearing her royal blue, silk dress, which followed the contours of her beautiful body. She was slowly walking towards him; she was ready to forgive him. Now he saw her generous lips and he looked into her brown eyes; they were at the same time deep and happy eyes. Soon, he thought, he would smell the roses in her garden.

'Come to me, Pema. I will hold you and I will never again let you go!' Duale raised his arms in anticipation.

'Dr. Duale, you don't seem to hear me!' It was Anna. 'Perhaps you're not well. Should you go home and have a rest?' Anna's voice was anxious. Perhaps all these terrible things are too much for him, she thought; was the man losing his mind?

'Don't be worried, Anna,' Duale responded, 'I feel better than I have for weeks! I have eighteen weeks left. I have now decided how to use them. I will work here in Chicago for the next five weeks; then in the first week of October I will be visiting a number of countries and the visits will extend until early to mid November. If the Board has found the new man, he will have six weeks with me before I leave. There will also be time for me to visit the White House and the UN. In early January I will travel to Bhutan so my wife and I can enjoy my retirement. If we get bored, we can easily come back for a spell during the summer and stay in my country house. I might even give a few lectures, provided they pay me properly of course.' Duale seemed relaxed and happy, Anna thought; and he would be seeing his wife. Thank God!

For Duale, the next six weeks passed in a flash. He had always worked hard; it was a fact that he had spent his working life in productively pursuing thoroughly worthwhile objectives. Now he went further. He was in his office every morning before seven and he regularly stayed there till midnight. Anna concluded that he had become a workaholic. A psychologist might have explained to her that his work had become his refuge. He had lost his job and his wife; now there was little else left to him than the few weeks which preceded his departure. He knew there was no chance of getting his job back; the fact that the Chairman of the Board had made no contact with him was not lost on his intelligent, and sensitive, perception. The only hope of worthwhile continuity which remained to him centred on his wife, Pema. He would do his utmost to win her love and respect back again. But there was another consideration. In a year or two, Duale would be in his seventies. He would need to be looked after. Certainly, it would be much more comfortable if Pema looked after him.

A week before Duale departed on his final victory lap to visit

343

various countries, Anna took a call from Alex Henrikson; yes, he would like to call on Dr. Duale.

'What a very great pleasure to see you again, Mr. Henrikson.' Duale welcomed Alex Henrikson and shook his hand. 'As I mentioned to the Committee I will be travelling to a few countries shortly; so I am pleased we could get together before my departure.' Duale was at his benevolent, polished best.

He knew why Henrikson was standing in front of him; it had taken him a split second to reach the right conclusion. His only hope was that Henrikson would not be too direct; that would be embarrassing because Duale would need to show him that, as far as Duale was concerned, no debt repayment was due. In any case, Duale would not need to mention that he had not the slightest intention of repaying Henrikson with a good turn.

'Shall we sit over here, Mr. Henrikson; you will get the nice view. It's a glorious day; this is what one might describe as perfect Fall weather. The temperature is not actually cold, just crisp. And the atmosphere is wonderfully clear. Good flying weather, I must say.'

As usual, Anna was standing in front of them.

'No,' Henrikson said, 'I won't stay long. No coffee, thank you. Let me sit down, Dr. Duale. What I want to find out from you is important to me.'

'Of course,' Duale rejoined.

As far as Duale was concerned, the point which would be made by the unsmiling Henrikson was entirely predictable. Alex Henrikson started his set piece.

'Dr. Duale, as far as TASS is concerned, since we last met there have been momentous developments in aviation. You have set in motion TASS's involvement in supporting the introduction of satellite technology for aeronautical communications. In addition, TASS will now be helping the developing world with financing for new safety systems. And you have also initiated the airlines' safety checks. These initiatives of yours have been far-reaching. They will be there to remind everyone of your genius in selecting the most important developments for TASS's attention. You have the quality of a world-class collector who has the talent for recognizing the most promising, or indeed the best, pieces. The international community should be highly grateful to you for leading

344

TASS from the front into new technology and into those areas of aviation safety which are most in need of attention. It will not be easy for your successor; no one could dream of following adequately in your footsteps! But of course, we have to face up to the challenge. Provided your successor is made of the right stuff, then TASS could go from strength to strength. But we should never forget that the future rests on the foundation of your successful past.

Of course, it was a tragedy that Captain Tashi lost his life in the pursuit of flight safety. Incidentally, I thought your obituary notice was very good; and you were so generous in your praise for Captain Tashi's contribution to air safety! You will have read the Inquiry report. As you may imagine, there were attempts to raise some criticism of the way you handled Captain Tashi's visit to Styxia. But with my legal training, I made sure the Inquiry concerned itself only with facts. As a result, the adverse comments which had been drafted were taken out.

Now let me come to the point. Of course, I am sorry you have resigned. Personally, I think this was unfortunate; but we should not distract ourselves. You will be leaving. Your natural successor would almost certainly have been Captain Tashi. The fact that he is no longer available, so to say, strengthens my own chances. I have submitted my application to the Board and I have given your name as one of my referees. I am sure, Dr. Duale, you recall our last discussion. In the meantime, I have done everything to support your position, even though this was not always easy.

Now I have a question for you. Have you been in touch with the Chairman on this subject? I think your support for my application would be crucial.' Duale noticed that Alex Henrikson was still unsmiling; he was such a boring man, the ultimate plodder, Duale thought. Why should Duale waste time on him?

'Thank you, Mr. Henrikson. First, I want to thank you for your objective participation in the Inquiry. Yes, it was a pity we lost such a good man in Captain Tashi. As far as your own future is concerned, I wish you all good luck, Mr. Henrikson. You recall I promised to have a word with the Chairman and one or two Trustees at the appropriate time. As you know, I am a man of my word. Of course, I have done this. Do you have other points to discuss?'

Alex Henrikson got up and shook Duale's hand. Duale was not quite sure, but at one point he thought he could see a brief suggestion of a smile. But now the face was again blank.

'Thank you again, Dr. Duale. I will not keep you from your work. I am sure your visits will be a great success. Goodbye; and thank you!'

Once the door closed, the image of Alex Henrikson was instantly erased from Duale's mind. The fact that Duale had never spoken about Henrikson and his qualities to the Chairman, nor to any member of the Board, was not of the slightest concern to him. Without giving the matter further thought, Duale turned his attention to what he saw as more important matters.

'Have you checked your briefing papers, Dr. Duale?' It was Anna. 'Tomorrow will be the fourth of October. You are leaving on the Saturday evening flight to Honolulu.'

'Yes, thank you, Anna. Everything is perfect. I have done so much work in the last few weeks and I have had so many meetings with the Divisions; the new initiatives we discussed should keep everyone going for at least a year! So even if my successor is not as good as he needs to be, at least his first year will be a success.' Duale laughed for a moment.

'If you have a moment, Dr. Duale, I would like to say something.' Although he was busy, Duale always had time for Anna. 'Of course, Anna. One thing about you and me is that we always found time for one another. And I think it paid off. Please, go ahead.'

'Thank you. You remember I mentioned to you that once you resigned, I would leave too? Well, I gave my notice and my last day was yesterday, the thirtieth of September; I have given TASS three days free of charge. But of course I came in for you. I think it is better that I leave you today. I don't know why, but I have a strange feeling we will never meet again. In any case, I want to say goodbye now. I hope I am wrong about not seeing you again. And I also hope you reach your wife and that the future will be all that you both want. We have been together, one way and another, for a long time. Most of the time we were going up; in the last few months we came down, I am afraid. But that is life, isn't it? Ups and downs. I have the feeling that if Captain Tashi had lived, we would still have been going up.' Duale was looking at Anna's face and he watched a tear making its way over her cheek.

'Goodbye, Anna. We have been together, off and on, for 42 years. There is nothing I could say to express my gratitude to you. You have given me so much of your life. Now your husband should feel happy he has you all to himself. Why don't you go now and let me get used to the idea of life without you. I won't say anything else. But I will do one thing. On my trip I am going to buy you a very expensive present. When I come back, I will call you. Then perhaps we can have lunch together and I can give you your present; and whenever you look at that present you can think of my gratitude. You are the one who did not desert me in the last few months; I am so grateful to you for that, Anna. Go now.'

Duale smiled a little and looked at Anna, a woman with whom he had shared not only work, but physical love. To his surprise, this good-looking woman did not turn and walk to his door. Anna walked around Duale's desk. She embraced him; and kissed him on his lips. She smiled gently. Just before she disappeared through the door of his office, she turned and said, 'Au revoir, Duale.'

Later that evening Duale boarded his intercontinental jet. As he settled into his first-class seat, he was offered a wide choice of newspapers. Duale took the New York Herald Tribune together with a European newspaper. In both, there were articles about the worrying air safety situation, especially in developing countries. The well-trained flight attendant offered him a drink, 'Dr. Duale, we feel so honoured to have you on board. Some champagne, sir?'

'Certainly, yes please,' Duale crisply responded.

Duale's visits were, as he had expected, an unqualified success. At each of his destinations, he said his farewells to ministers and senior civil aviation executives; in three countries he was accorded a reception by the heads of state. The countries which he visited expressed their gratitude through decorations, citations and plaques. They all seemed to be conversant with the bronze statue project; and they all wanted him to know that they had sent a donation to TASS's headquarters in Chicago to help pay for it. Duale was left in no doubt that his leadership of TASS had been appreciated. And he was relieved to be able to state that, at last, TASS was establishing a financing facility. In the past, this had been a stumbling block. Instead of telling the developing countries to arrange their own financing, now he could advise them to contact TASS in the confidence that TASS would organize some studies, followed by investment finance for much-needed equipment and the all-important development of the human infrastructure. Yes, Duale thought, this was exactly as things should be; he would make his exit from the civil aviation scene on the crest of a wave!

His feeling of well-being was almost complete. Once he had made his peace with Pema, then he could feel rewarded and happy for the rest of his life. Towards the end of his long trip, before leaving for Thimphu, he visited Bangladesh. In spite of its poverty-stricken state, the civil aviation authority put on their best face. As he was escorted to the VIP lounge, the security guards snapped to attention and saluted him. He found a new minister had been installed; and several of the officials had been replaced. Nevertheless, he was accorded a warm welcome and he was the guest of honour at a special reception. As he had progressed from one country to the next, he had grown accustomed to expressions of respect and gratitude; but he found the Bangladeshi experience the most poetic, and touching, of all. When he left for Calcutta, all of the civil aviation staff assembled on the apron and waved him farewell.

As Duale was seen off from Calcutta late in the afternoon by the director of civil aviation, his thoughts turned to Pema. He was shown into his seat by a good-looking flight attendant. The captain of the aircraft came aft and shook Duale's hand. 'It's an honour for us to have you on board, Dr. Duale. I just wanted to mention that this is not an aircraft of Himalaya Airways; it has been leased complete with crew. It's not every day we have the privilege of having the Chief Executive Officer of TASS with us. Please feel free to sit anywhere you wish. We have heard of your retirement. As a mark of our respect for you, on this flight you are the only passenger. If you are ready, we can depart. We expect to arrive shortly before dusk.'

Duale sat near the wing. He looked outside as the aircraft began to taxi; the director was waving and Duale waved back with a smile. Now all his thoughts centred on Pema. He had been writing to her every two or three weeks. He had given his arrival details. Should he dare to think that she might be waiting for him at the airport? After all, they had fallen in love; they were still man and wife. Surely, even with the tragic loss of Tashi, feelings within Pema would soften.

Pema had received Duale's letters. She was beginning to feel better and her appearance reflected the improvement. The puffiness had left her face and she had regained her poise. But she still could not quite bring herself to come to terms with her husband. She enjoyed his letters; but she had no wish to meet him. Her feelings towards him were softening; but she did not yet feel ready to meet him again face to face. Perhaps it would be different in a year.

When his last letter had come announcing his visit to Bhutan, she had become alarmed. Duale had enormous powers of persuasion, she thought; and his charm was irresistible! Once he would begin talking to her, she was afraid it would only be a matter of time before he would persuade her that the past was passed. It would be time for a new start. He would beg forgiveness; and how could she refuse? She knew that if she met Duale, she would forgive him. But she did not want this to happen, at least not at this stage. Pema decided, there and then, to leave Thimphu for a week's holiday. That way, she would avoid meeting Duale; and she would be spared the anguish of yet again reconstructing the circumstances which had led to Tashi's death.

Three days before Duale was due to begin his visit to Bhutan, Pema wrote a note to Duale to say she was sorry that she would be out of the country; she thanked him for his letters and promised to reply to the next one. She hoped this would be a first step in the coming to terms with her husband. Pema left the note with the UN, who promised to pass it to Duale. Then she took the flight to Bangkok. There she would stay with Patsri and enjoy the family for a few days.

As Duale sat in the small regional aircraft, he felt relaxed and secure. Looking down, he could see the vast tea plantations of Assam stretching over the gently undulating hills. The pilot would soon be flying over the southern border of the Kingdom, he thought. Duale thought how pleasant it would be to breathe the fresh, crisp mountain air of Bhutan. He had just spent three weeks in countries which only seemed to have one thing in common – heat and humidity. And if Pema would be waiting at the airport? He would run and embrace her. Then his life would be whole again!

Duale felt the aircraft climbing into the gathering dusk. Surely it would soon be time for them to be on that unique, crooked approach which passed through the cleavages of the high mountains, he thought. Then the captain appeared. 'Dr. Duale,' he said, 'I thought I should mention we have a minor problem. There is nothing to worry about, but I wanted to keep you informed.

You may have noticed that it is prematurely dark outside; this is because we are approaching a storm, an electrical storm, and it is a big one. We can't avoid it. If it is very strong, I may have to climb to a higher flight level to try to get out of it. There could be severe turbulence ahead, so please keep your seat belt well fastened. We are trying to pick up a navigational aid, an omnirange – you know a VOR. It was installed last year near the top of a mountain ahead of us. We think it is strange that we haven't had a signal from it so far. It could be that we have a problem with our receiver; or perhaps the omnirange has been struck by lightning. It was definitely working last week when we flew to Calcutta.'

The Captain smiled before going on. 'It would certainly be ironic, Dr. Duale, if the omnirange is not working when we have the top man of TASS on board. After all, TASS helped us install it.' The Captain felt embarrassed for a moment; then he said, 'Excuse me, I should not have said that. In fact, now I remember; we did hear that there had been a delay in checking the fuel supply for the generator which the VOR needs to keep the electronics functional. I hope they are not out of fuel – again. That's the problem with a lot of developing countries, isn't it? I mean today we absolutely must be able to use the VOR. But we can't be sure it is serviceable – we certainly need it! If the omnirange is not working, the air traffic controllers should have heard the alarm. We have to use that VOR to confirm our position; there are some pretty big mountains around here. I'd better get back to the flight deck. It might be a bit rough; don't worry, we'll manage one way or another.'

As the Captain was passing through the bulkhead door, Duale felt the aircraft sink as though it was in a vacuum. Duale watched the captain struggling towards the flight deck. He felt the aircraft climb and concluded that the captain had decided to try and fly out of the storm. Whether the captain would still try and reach Paro, or if he would return to Calcutta, seemed to be of secondary importance at the moment. The immediate challenge was to gain altitude as quickly as possible and escape from the violent turbulence of the storm. Duale was briefly distracted by the sound of huge ice pellets which were ferociously hitting the windows; perhaps they were hail stones, he thought. Then, above the din, he heard the captain shout, 'First officer, look ahead! That blackness! It's not only the storm. That is a mountain! Turn right. Quickly! We have to get out of this!'

Then the captain cried out, 'Om Mani Padme Hum!' words of desperation reserved for impending disaster.

Whether the gods heard the captain's desperate plea is a matter of conjecture. If the gods had been able at that moment to talk to the captain, they would have explained that the aircraft in distress was only one part, albeit an important part, of a much bigger picture; unfortunately for the aircraft's illustrious VIP passenger, a decision had been reached that the whole expansive canvas should be taken into consideration. Instead of concentrating on the aircraft's immediate, hopeless situation, as they took in the entire scene the attention of the gods was directed toward another part of the picture. Their favours would rest on Pema; surely it was Pema who deserved peace and harmony.

As someone who epitomized ambivalence, depending on the view which anyone might have had of Duale some would be happy for him that his end was instant; others might have wished that he should have survived and suffered for a period from his injuries, before finally expiring. In any case, as Duale would have said, fate is fate; his number was up. When the aircraft hit a windswept, barren rock face at 23,000 feet above sea level, no one in the aircraft felt anything. On this particular occasion, not even the Survivor could survive. A year earlier, in his meeting with Duale, it had been Tashi who had highlighted the main category of accidents: Controlled Flight Into Terrain (CFIT). Now, yet another CFIT accident had taken its toll.

The following morning, in Bangkok Pema turned on the radio at eight o'clock. Routinely, she liked to hear the BBC's news on the overseas service before her breakfast. That morning the announcer read one item which was of particular interest to her:

'A report has just been received from a news source in the Kingdom of Bhutan that an aircraft has crashed in a severe storm in the Himalayan mountains. It is understood that there were no survivors. A passenger on the aircraft was the Chief Executive Officer of the Trust For Air Safety Support, who was visiting a number of countries to hold discussions on ways to improve air safety.'

Pema heard Patsri's voice, 'Mother Pema, please come to breakfast.' Pema joined Patsri on the verandah.

'How are you, mother Pema; I hope you have slept well?'

'Yes, thank you, Patsri. Now I will eat a big breakfast. You know, Patsri, I think it is time for me to return to Bhutan. It's difficult to explain, my dear Patsri, but I suddenly feel so much better; somehow, a dreadful burden has been lifted from my shoulders. I have the feeling that a mystical force has been at work. Now I am ready to re-build my life in harmony with those around me; as the emancipated women in the West would say, Patsri, I feel liberated. Now I am at peace with the world. And I am sure you too will soon be happy again – yes, Patsri I am sure!'

Epilogue

The Truth Will Out

The Styxia aircraft accident investigation report was completed about eight months after Duale's death. After a study of the flight plan which had been filed on that fateful day a year previously, and having listened to the aircraft's voice recorders, the accident investigation team was able to reconstruct, in detail, the various elements which had led to the accident; the team also looked into the procedures and practices used to assure the airworthiness of aircraft, as well as the maintenance arrangements for ground navigational aids. They also reviewed pilot training practices. Some of the main findings of the accident investigation included the following:

- The Chief Pilot had agreed that he should be checked out by Captain Tashi under visual conditions. In basic terms, the Chief Pilot disregarded this agreement and, in his capacity as commander of the aircraft, he contradicted and ignored the instructions issued by Captain Tashi. If he had followed Captain Tashi's guidance and instructions, the accident would almost certainly not have occurred. The primary cause of the accident was pilot error;
- The orientation of the runway did not represent the optimum in terms of safe operation of aircraft. Specifically, because of the proximity of hills, in the event of an emergency the hills could cause danger to aircraft, as had happened in this case;
- The flight on which Captain Tashi was checking the Chief Pilot of Styxia Airlines was quite definitely to be conducted under visual flight rules, but the Chief Pilot (unsuccessfully) attempted an instrument approach;
- Although the meteorological officer told the Chief Pilot and Captain Tashi that the weather forecast was for a perfectly

clear day, his weather charts indicated the probability of cloud. When questioned on the subject, the man agreed and said he 'forgot' to give the Chief Pilot the true weather picture;

- The instrument landing system, which the Chief Pilot insisted on using (contrary to the visual approach requirement), had not been calibrated for accuracy for at least five years. The normal period between calibration checks is four to six months. Furthermore, the alarm system which automatically sounds in the control tower to indicate a fault in the ILS, had been disconnected. Engineering technician staff stated they were 'irritated and tired of the noise.' The Chief Pilot's statement to the effect that the ILS had been recently calibrated and successfully used did not correspond with the truth. The reason given by the civil aviation adminstration for the lack of calibration of ground navigational aids was that to bring in a specialist calibration unit from western Europe would mean payment in foreign exchange. The civil aviation administration had requested the central Treasury to allocate the required foreign exchange, but this request had been rejected;

- The engineers who certified airworthiness checks on the airline's aircraft were far below the required experience level; this meant that, routinely, work was being certified as having been properly carried out when the supervising engineer did not have the technical knowledge and experience to verify that this was, in fact, the case;

- The pilots' mandatory simulator training included approaches on only one airport, instead of the wide selection usually used. The explanation given was that the only way to avoid repetitive failures by pilots undergoing simulator checks, and consequent loss of 'face,' was to use the one airport scenario;

- The mandatory airport crash, fire and rescue facilities were non existent.

As a result of the accident investigation and its findings, the airline suspended operations. After re-organization, advice and training under an agreement with TASS, the airline resumed operations two years later. Since that date, it has not suffered any accidents; nor has it been involved in a single incident.

No reference was included in the accident investigation report regarding Duale's wisdom, or otherwise, in sending Tashi on his own to check Styxia Airlines, one of the least-safe airlines in the world. Without wasting a word, the report was clinically sterile; it only dealt with facts, not speculation. The team had the facts and stayed with them. No one, except Duale, knew his motive in sending Tashi on what might, and did, develop into a dangerous assignment. Within his technical limitations, Tashi had conducted himself perfectly; unfortunately, his judgement of the reliability and credibility of the Chief Pilot was too positive.

As for Duale's anxiety that he might be incriminated by the findings either of the TASS Inquiry or the accident investigation, his deep concern turned out to be groundless. Duale had resigned when his conscience told him that he was almost certainly guilty of having played a part in Tashi's death; he had actually begun to feel frightened of the possible consequences of his actions. Although he consistently denied his evil intent in his dialogue with Pema, Duale was the only person in the world who really knew the truth.

The Board of Trustees selected Duale's successor in March 1998. Alex Henrikson, who desperately wished to be selected for the job of TASS's Chief Executive Officer, and who had left no influential stone unturned in his quest, was included in the final short list of candidates, not because of his suitability but simply as a courtesy. At the final meeting of the Board to select the new CEO, Henrikson's name was the first to be discarded.

The new man, who was in many ways quite different to Duale, proved to be effective. If Duale had lived, he might have felt a little irritated to find that the new CEO did not regard himself, as so many at the top would prefer the world to believe, as indispensable. In fact, in this particular case the different and new approaches embraced by the CEO were positively refreshing. He took over the Trust which in certain respects had been for too long almost headless. With the departure of some of the Divisional Heads and consultants, not to mention Anna who always had seemed to know everything, some of the limbs had been lost as well. The new CEO strictly followed the guiding principles of the Trust under which TASS had been established. He ensured that TASS functioned apolitically. And he saw no reason to visit the authorities in Washington, nor the UN in New York. It was only a matter of time before the overall efficiency and purposeful approach of TASS improved by leaps and bounds. Was it a coincidence that from the time of Duale's death the airlines' accident rate significantly improved?

On a hot summer's day in July 1998, the unveiling ceremony of Duale's life-size statue was held in front of the TASS building. The reticent and nervous Godfrey Hogg, who represented the lower echelon of TASS's staff, had done an excellent job in organizing the occasion. He had written a courteous letter to the Chairman of the Board of Trustees, inviting the Chairman to speak and unveil the statue. He received a curt response explaining that the Chairman would not be available; however, the Chairman would be prepared to release his deputy to perform the function, provided the deputy agreed. Godfrey Hogg and his colleagues felt that the attitude of the Chairman was unfortunate. And they politely said so; the Chairman's office was informed that alternative arrangements would be made.

For the appointed day, the Chairman made sure he would not be available to attend the ceremony by taking a short vacation in Florida. In fact, TASS's travel office made arrangements for him to stay at the same hotel in which Duale and Tashi had stayed in 1991. The Chairman later realised he had badly misjudged the situation; neither he, nor any of the Trustees who sat on the Board, received an invitation to attend the ceremony.

The Mayor of Chicago performed the unveiling ceremony, which was attended by about one thousand guests; the President of the United States sent his special representative. Anna was also one of the guests. When she saw the bronze at the moment it was unveiled, she caught her breath. As she looked at Duale's face through the tears which were welling up and blurring her vision, she thought how she had kept a special place in her heart for him for just about the whole of her working life. Yes, she had her loving husband and her children; but there was always a little love hidden in her being which was reserved for Duale. And no one else. Sometimes she questioned her good sense and logic in holding him in such high esteem. However, the fact was that in her early days with TASS she had felt that she belonged to him. And as the years would pass, more and more she would tend to remember only the good things about Duale, a process which had already begun.

The Mayor's office had shown thoroughness in preparing the Mayor's speech. Ideas to be incorporated in the speech had been invited from many sources, including TASS; apart from the contribution of TASS's public relations office, Godfrey Hogg and his colleagues had submitted some background material. At the ceremony, in addition to the usual platitudes, the Mayor said: 'Perhaps the most memorable of all of Dr. Duale's achievements was his dedication to the latest aviation technology and his critical perception in putting forward ideas which would enable others to reach the highest standards of aviation safety. In this context, I would in particular like to single out the recognition he gave to the need for TASS to support aviation administrations, especially in the Third World, in the introduction of satellite technology; in addition, Dr. Duale was the brainchild of the establishment within TASS of an international financing facility, which is primarily for the use of countries in the developing world. His initiatives in both of these fields have been extremely rewarding and the support of the Trust has directly led to much safer skies, especially in the Third World. These initiatives were born of him; next time we travel by air, Ladies and Gentlemen, as the aircraft safely touches down at our destination I suggest we give a thought to the genius of Dr. Duale and his inestimable contribution to supporting, through the Trust For Air Safety Support, the safe development of the aviation industry!'

It was natural that at that memorable ceremony, there would be no hint of a mention of the accident rate, which had received so much publicity over the previous few years. But many of the invited guests were anxiously conscious of a safety situation which had so often been highlighted in their newspapers. Insurers were on the offensive, like a pack of howling dogs. According to the insurers, as aviation growth continued the number of accidents would increase; this was a simple and obvious deduction, at least to them.

Looking beyond the millennium, it would only be a question of time before there would be an average of at least one major accident every week or so! The situation which was unfortunately developing would have repercussions; the insurers would have to review their options, otherwise one day they might have to go out of business. In fact, now that TASS had lost its incredibly clever and effective CEO, the outlook was suddenly more dismal than ever. Actuaries know their business. When the insurers were asked whether anything could be done to save the situation, their response was negative. It would only be a question of time before the cost of insurance would rise yet again; and some airlines would be grounded because they were judged to be unsafe. There would be no alternative.

For a period at the end of the last century, the insurance industry expressed its deep concern by either refusing aviation insurance altogether, or demanding what many felt were astronomically high premiums; it was only through Herculean efforts by the aviation industry that the situation was stabilised and partially resolved.

With their extrapolations, logic, computer models and other studies, how right have been the dire predictions of the aviation insurance industry? Fortunately, the actual safety situation has not proved to be so frighteningly dangerous as forecast. Certainly, it was true that during Duale's tenure of office the accident rate was rising; sometimes the degree of the rise would cause concern, especially if extrapolations had been based on past data. However, in the years after Duale lost his life although aviation continued its growth, with the exception of the years 2001–2003, the accident rate tended to drop.

It was also of the utmost importance that the area of acts of unlawful interference should be vigilantly kept under surveillance. Especially with the proliferation of terrorist networks, the risk of seizure of aircraft as well as acts of sabotage, were likely to increase. This possibility was not lost on the new CEO and he immediately added a new division to TASS whose job it would be, using a hands-on approach, to help and support civil aviation bodies in their efforts to counteract terrorism.

The horrific terrorist acts which were perpetrated against the United States in 2001 caused a colossal degree of dislocation in the air transport industry. After two to three years of attempted adjustment in the face of chaos, the airline industry slowly recovered its growth pattern. In spite of this, the current trend consistently indicates low accident rates.

With this possible dawn of improved aviation safety, many became concerned that this might lead to safety taking second place to profits; in other words, if from the psychological aspect safety were taken for granted, then a new priority could take its place – profits. Unquestionably, this concern was valid. However, rather than concentrating almost solely on profits, there were also those within the industry who were uncomfortably and nervously conscious of the fact that there were still many areas where a strong and dedicated safety culture was patently lacking. In addition, the gaps and flaws in the overall aviation infrastructure in various parts of the Third World had not dramatically improved; in some countries, if anything it had become worse as the workload became heavier due to increased air traffic volume. It was one thing to develop improved technology; and all praise for positive steps in that direction. But it was quite another to establish the necessary human infrastructure to support the new technology.

With the continuing infrastructural and administrative drawbacks in many countries of the Third World, it is incredible that over the years the global statistics show that the operation of civil aviation has proved to be remarkably safe – safer by far than other forms of mass transport. And if, for example, we look at the most recent statistics, in terms of global scheduled air services the number of accidents involving passenger fatalities for the year 2003 was the lowest for almost sixty years, even though in the intervening period the annual volume of passengers who were carried had increased by one hundred and fifty times; the safety statistics for 2004 also reflect the high level of safety.

In this context, we can never underestimate the dedicated professionalism of those who practice the art and science of aeronautics, linked as they are to the genius of so many branches of engineering. It is the extraordinary performance of these superb workers which leads to the hope that the consistently good air safety trend will continue. It is also heartening that the occurrences of hijacking appears to be on the decline (although in 2004 there were ugly exceptions). However, the overall declining trend is a reflection of measures that have been put into place by many countries to improve aviation security.

In the first quarter of the new century satellite technology should be brought into use globally; this will lead to an enhancement of air safety and the more efficient management of air traffic. If the introduction of this new technology can be successfully accomplished on a large scale, then the outlook for the new millennium is good as far as aviation safety is concerned. In particular, developing countries will benefit from satellite systems, especially the automation on the ground and in the air which goes with the new technology.

So the race has begun. If the finishing line is not crossed on schedule, then within ten years the world should probably prepare itself for unpleasant news as far as air safety is concerned. If, however, the race can be won, there is little doubt that air travel will remain by far the safest form of transportation during the twenty first century. Until the race is won it is inevitable that there will be a period of continued vulnerability, in the sense that the technology which had been in use for so many years will continue in use until it is superseded by the latest technology. During this interim period a much greater degree of support, relatively speaking, will be needed by many countries of the Third World, especially with respect to equipment, its proper maintenance and development of the specialized human infrastructure.

One of those who had not attended the unveiling ceremony of the bronze statue of Duale was Gerald Strong, the Head of TASS's Aeronautical Communications. Gerald Strong had intended resigning when he had learned that Tashi had lost his life in the Styxia Airlines accident. Because the Chairman of the Board of Trustees had asked Gerald Strong to participate in the accident investigation, he had stayed on with TASS. And by the time the investigation had been completed, Duale had lost his life.

In early 2005, a few days after celebrating the fourth year of the new millennium, as Gerald Strong entered the TASS building one day he looked up at the shining statue of Duale. For reasons which he could not explain, he had been musing on the events of Duale's leadership of TASS; he had been thinking how the seven years which had passed since Duale's and Tashi's deaths had passed in a flash. As he admired the bronze in the brilliant winter sunshine, he walked around Duale's figure; now he was standing behind the statue of Duale. He heard a gentle voice, which was Anna's.

'Yes, Mr. Strong, I also come here every so often and look at the statue; it's so lifelike, don't you think? I love the way Dr. Duale is looking into the distance; I am sure he is gazing at the lake. You know, Mr. Strong, he loved to watch the lake.'

'Yes,' answered Gerald Strong, 'it is a good bronze. I walked behind because I found myself looking for someone else, but he's not here, unfortunately.'

'Oh, really,' replied Anna. 'So – who were you looking for?'

'I was looking for Captain Tashi. Dr. Duale owed his ideas to Captain Tashi, you know. Without Captain Tashi's good advice, Dr. Duale would have been just another CEO. It was certainly ironic that, for too long perhaps, Dr. Duale tried to resist and ignore what Captain Tashi wanted TASS, led by Dr. Duale, to do. Thank goodness Captain Tashi persisted. And it was only when against his will, and I must say for the wrong reasons, Dr. Duale accepted what Captain Tashi knew had to be done, that TASS became known for its up-to-date technical approach. I only hope the time lost by Dr. Duale before he got the message will not prove too damaging in the long run as far as aviation safety is concerned, if you see what I mean, Anna. In any case, the fact is that it was Captain Tashi who made him famous; no one else.

And if you looked at their characters, Dr. Duale loved the idea of a statue; as for Captain Tashi, this would have been the last thing he would have wanted. But in fact, Anna, this statue should have been of Captain Tashi, whether he liked it or not.

You know, the world is full of Captain Tashis. With very few exceptions, they are unknown. They are the ones who are truly professional. They give the best advice; and in an honest way they constantly try to do the right things in this world. They are the unsung heroes. It's a pity, Anna, don't you think, that they are somehow rarely recognized?'

Anna was not quite sure what was expected of her, so she said, 'Yes, you are quite right. It is a pity, Mr. Strong.'

Then Gerald Strong turned to Anna, 'You know, Anna, I think we learned something today. Behind most great men or women, there is usually a Captain Tashi who persuaded them to do something good, often against their will, at some particular juncture; and with hindsight, it was what these famous people were forced into doing which often made them great. To put it in simple terms, Anna, from now on, if ever we look at the statue of a great man or woman, perhaps we should also meditate a little and think of the Captain Tashi who was often behind the greatness. It was a tragedy that Captain Tashi lost his life; but, you know, the more I think of what he forced Dr. Duale to do, the more I feel that it was Captain Tashi's destiny to give his life, so that others would benefit from safer aviation.

Yes, Anna, his contribution was his life. Fortunately, not all those Captain Tashis who acted on their convictions through history needed to make the ultimate sacrifice; and thank God for that! But when I think of what Captain Tashi actually did, I realise that although their deeds and qualities are hardly ever given the slightest attention, the Captain Tashis are the truly heroic characters of this world!'

Then Gerald Strong disappeared into the TASS building to get on with his work.